# That Summer in Cornwall

## CIJI WARE

# Praise for Ciji Ware's
## Contemporary and Historical Fiction

"A fascinating portrayal...with characters convincingly drawn...Ware again proves she can intertwine fact and fiction to create an entertaining and harmonious whole."
– *PUBLISHERS WEEKLY*

"...Fiction at its finest...beautifully written."
– *LIBBY'S LIBRARY NEWS*

"A mesmerizing blend of sizzling romance...love and honor...Ciji Ware has written an unforgettable tale."
– *THE BURTON REVIEW*

"...Intriguing characters, exciting dialogue, and a highly interesting woman at the center of it all...a must read."
– *NIGHT OWL ROMANCE REVIEWER TOP PICK*

"A great fiction author...Ciji Ware certainly knows how to touch hearts."
– *READING EXTRAVAGANZA*

"Ciji Ware is a master storyteller."
– *LIBBY'S LIBRARY NEWS*

"A stirring, sensually tantalizing read...phenomenal storytelling by Ciji Ware."
– *BLOG CRITICS*

"Ciji Ware has created a gorgeous tapestry...This is a glorious book."
– *BOOKSIE'S BLOG*

"A masterpiece read...an epic on its own."
– *ENCHANTED BY JOSEPHINE*

"A novel so lively and intriguing, you don't realize you've learned anything till after you close the book. Exciting, entertaining, and enlightening."
– *LITERARY TIMES*

"A well-researched and entertaining novel...excellent."
– *LIBRARY JOURNAL*

32858 5832

Cover design 2012 by The Killion Group, Inc.
Cover and colophon design by Kim Killion.
Formatting by AThirstyMind.com

ISBN: 978-0-9889408-1-9

Additional Library of Congress Cataloging-in-Publication Data available upon request.

1. Women's fiction 2. Search and Rescue dogs and organizations—U.S.A.—Cornwall U.K. 3. Pet Therapy—U.S.A.—U.K. 4. Modern Estate Management—U.K. 5. Psychological impact of war on returning soldiers—U.S.A.—U.K. 6. Registered Nurses—U.S.A. —21st century—Fiction.

EPub Edition © January, 2013
Print Edition © March, 2013

Published by Lion's Paw Publishing, a division of Life Events Media LLC, 1001 Bridgeway, Ste. 224, Sausalito, CA 94965.

Life Events Library and the Lion's Paw Publishing colophon are registered trademarks of Life Events Media LLC. All rights reserved. No part of this book may be reproduced in any form or by any electronic or mechanical means including information storage and retrieval systems—except in the case of brief quotations embodied in critical articles or reviews—without express permission in writing from its publisher, Lion's Paw Publishing / Life Events Library / Life Events Media LLC.

For information contact: www.cijiware.com

# DEDICATION

Dedicated to novelist CYNTHIA WRIGHT, lover of Cornwall and stalwart friend who has *twice* conquered Hall Walk with me and has often been a companion during our other research adventures as novelists…

And to ALISON THAYER HARRIS, registered nurse with a specialty in pediatric oncology, backyard organic food gardens consultant, and an extraordinary parent who could be the inspiration for any number of heroines.

In tribute to search and rescue organizations worldwide, but especially to the SEARCH AND RESCUE FOUNDATION'S TRAINING CENTER for Canine Disaster Search Teams in Ojai, California; to the Cornwall Search and Rescue Team based in St. Dennis; and to Anthony Jordan, Dog Unit Manager, Devon and Cornwall Police, whose love of dogs and expertise in his field were invaluable.

With gratitude for the extraordinary SEARCH DOGS and their HANDLERS who responded to the cataclysmic events at Oklahoma City, Ground Zero, Hurricane Katrina, Haiti, Japan, Hurricane Sandy—and every day are dispatched to the cliffs, moors, and abandoned mineshafts of the British Isles.

With appreciation to the owners and staff of CAERHAYS CASTLE near Gorran Haven, Cornwall, for preserving this landmark and allowing annual public visits to its magnificent gardens.

And in memory of the late EDD NORTH who discovered "Barton Hall," and with his wife GAY—my treasured cousin—showed me their beloved Cornish countryside.

# SEARCHER FOR THE MISSING

*"He is your friend, your partner,*
*your defender,*
*your dog.*
*You are his life, his love, his leader*
*to the last beat of his heart."*

Anonymous

# PROLOGUE

## LAST WILL AND TESTAMENT
## OF
## ELEANOR BARTON STOWE

I, Eleanor Barton Stowe, of Beverly Hills, California, revoke my former Wills and Codicils and declare this to be my Last Will and Testament.

## ARTICLE 1

### IDENTIFICATION OF FAMILY

I am married to **Christopher Stowe**, of Beverly Hills, California, and London, England, and all references in this Will to "my spouse" are references to Christopher Stowe.

The name of my only child is **Janet Barton Stowe**. All references in this Will to "my child" are references to the above-mentioned Janet Barton Stowe.

## ARTICLE II

## NOMINATION OF EXECUTOR

Upon my death, I nominate my spouse, **Christopher Stowe**, of Beverly Hills, California, and London, England, and my attorneys, **Jerald Polter**, of Beverly Hills, California, and **Sir Anthony Jennens QC**, of London England, to serve as my executors, to execute my Will as set forth below.

## ARTICLE III

## DISPOSITION OF PROPERTY

I direct that my entire estate, including all monies, property, and real estate, be distributed equally to **my spouse** and to **my only child**, my child's portion to be held in Trust for her until the age of twenty-one (21).

## ARTICLE IV

## NOMINATION OF GUARDIANS

Should it become necessary to appoint guardians of my minor child, I nominate my first cousin, **Meredith Champlin** of Jackson Hole, Wyoming, to serve as co-guardian, with my spouse, of my surviving child, Janet, at the time of my death...

# CHAPTER 1

"Meredith, if you make me stay in stupid Cornwall all summer, I'll run away!" announced Janet Barton Stowe as she stared morosely at sheets of rain pelting the Land Rover's windows.

The fifth grader, late of Beverly Hills, California, was hunched in a backseat corner of the large, vintage vehicle that her aunt, Lady Blythe Barton-Teague, had sent to Heathrow Airport to fetch her two American relatives—Janet, her pre-teen niece, and Meredith Champlin of Jackson Hole, Wyoming, a first cousin in her early thirties. The visitors' journey down to England's West Country and the venerable Barton Hall had been accompanied by one, long litany of complaints and accusations from the youngest passenger.

"I'm gonna call my father!" Janet whined to no one in particular. "I'm gonna tell him how I've been *kidnapped.*"

In the roomy front passenger seat, Meredith, Janet's newly appointed guardian, was doing her level best to tamp down her annoyance while ignoring her young ward's unrelenting protests about everything from the food on board their transatlantic flight, to the fact they had a four-hour drive from Heathrow to Barton Hall, on the south coast of Cornwall, an hour beyond Plymouth.

Meredith affected an unruffled response to Janet's latest threats to go A.W.O.L., replying, "Your father's secretary said that he was fine with visiting your Aunt Blythe in Cornwall until your school starts in September."

"Well, I'm not gonna go to that stupid school in Wyoming, that's for sure!" Janet exclaimed. "I hate your dumb ranch. I don't want to live with *you!* I don't want to visit horrible Aunt Blythe! I want you to call my father right *now!*"

There was no arguing with a child whose mother had died in a private plane crash five weeks earlier, and whose film director father had coolly deposited his only child in the middle of Wyoming with a cousin she'd never met. Poor Janet had been virtually off-loaded on her mother's side of her family at the Crooked C Ranch with a copy of the dead woman's unorthodox will packed at the bottom of her suitcase.

Meredith inhaled deeply and tried to keep her voice even and conversational.

"We'll place a call to your father when we arrive at your Aunt Blythe's," she promised, "though, as you know, he can be hard to reach in Alaska."

"Well, duh!" was Janet's rude reply. "He's shooting a film, stupid. Try his cell phone again!"

By this time, Meredith was fast approaching the limit of her patience. "I've already told you, Janet, while we're in the UK our American cell phones have to stay in airplane mode until we get to a Wi-Fi connection to avoid ridiculous phone bills. We can use free texting once we get to Aunt Blythe's."

Before they'd left Wyoming for England, Meredith had made successive attempts to contact Janet's father Christopher Stowe, "the cinematic genius," by phone, email, and text to Los Angeles and his film location in Alaska about plans for Janet's summer, until he'd finally sent word through his underlings that three months in

Cornwall was an agreeable proposal, given Mr. Stowe's "extremely busy schedule" and sent a check to purchase their business-class plane tickets.

Meanwhile, Meredith's calm, reasoned tone with Janet was not having the desired effect.

"I bet you're lying about the cell phones!" Janet declared suddenly. "Let's see. Gimme yours!"

Incensed, Meredith turned around in her seat. "I'm *not* lying. Our phones need to stay in airplane mode, and that's *it*! Just cool your jets, Janet, until we get to Barton Hall."

"My dad will pay for it, so *call* him!" she ordered with the vehemence of a child accustomed to getting her own way.

"No, I won't. Just drop it, Janet, will you please?"

"I *hate* you, I *hate* Aunt Blythe, and I want to go *home*!" came the cry from the back seat.

Struggling to maintain her sympathy for a child in Janet's unhappy circumstances, Meredith glanced across the passenger seat at their volunteer chauffeur, eighteen-year-old Richard Teague, Cornish native and grown son of Cousin Blythe's second husband, Sir Lucas Teague, Life Peer, thanks to being nominated for the Queen's Birthday Honors List the previous year. Blythe's stepson politely kept his eyes on the road as he piloted the lumbering vehicle down the A30 motorway. When he finally looked in Meredith's direction, she cast him an apologetic lift of her eyebrows, which he returned with a slight shrug, a signal that he didn't take the histrionics of their backseat traveler very seriously.

Softening her tone, Janet's new guardian tried a different approach.

"Look, sweetheart, you can't really dislike an aunt that hasn't seen you since you were three months old."

"I'm not your 'sweetheart,' and my mother *hated* her

sister!" She pointed an accusing finger at Meredith and cried, "You just want to get rid of me, and you're dumping me with the person Mom said I was never to speak to— *ever!*"

"I am not 'dumping' you, Janet" Meredith replied, her ire rising despite her best efforts. "As a matter of fact, I'm taking a leave of absence from my *job* so that I can go with you and spend some time here as well. We're doing this for everyone's benefit. Your Aunt Blythe is a lovely person. She wants to get to know you and—"

"She's a bitch!"

Meredith whirled in her seat. "Janet, you stop that kind of language this *instant!*"

"That's what Mom always said she was—a bitch!" Janet retorted. "Dad loved Mom and *me* and hated Aunt Blythe! You're horrible to make me come here. I'll run away…I swear I will!"

Meredith knew any ongoing discussion was pointless. For the weeks that the precocious eleven-year-old had officially been consigned to her care, Meredith had done everything she could think of to offer the child compassion and understanding. Even so, the pudgy youngster who had been indulged with a steady diet of junk food, too much television, and unlimited access to the Internet by her Beverly Hills housekeeper had rejected all expressions of empathy and kindness. Ironically, she apparently had been deprived of the very basics of parental care and guidance as a child of the Hollywood elite. Up to now, Janet was the least likable young person Meredith had ever encountered, which was saying something, given her employment as a nurse in the pediatric ward at St. John's Medical Center in Jackson Hole where she dealt with ailing children of all temperaments.

Meredith peered down at her feet wedged next to the

dog carrier resting on the floor in front of the passenger seat. The back compartment was piled high with suitcases, most of which belonged to the eleven-year-old. In contrast to Janet, Meredith's two-year-old Welsh Corgi had behaved angelically during the entire trip, having been granted the privilege of riding in the plane's cabin, thanks to Holly's status as a service dog certified through the pet therapy program at St. John's.

Meredith gazed through the windshield of the dented Land Rover and wondered if the persistent rain were some sort of dire omen about the months she'd committed to staying in Cornwall. She still could hardly believe the call from Christopher Stowe's lawyer in Beverly Hills confirming that her cousin Ellie was *dead,* and that her will contained quite a surprise in Article IV.

Fortunately, Janet's Aunt Blythe had responded to Meredith's frantic, transatlantic plea for help and guidance by calling from Barton Hall the very same day Meredith had sent her an email with the harrowing news that she, a mere first cousin—once-removed—and not Blythe, Janet's blood aunt had been unexpectedly named legal guardian of the late Ellie Barton Stowe's young daughter.

"But, Blythe," Meredith had demanded over the phone, "what kind of father just abandons his child like that, right after her mother *dies?*"

"A bloody bastard," Blythe had answered matter-of-factly. "When it comes to Christopher Stowe, I speak with authority, remember? I used to be *married* to the man."

It was impossible for either cousin to ignore the past. A decade earlier, the Academy-award-winning director had had a well-publicized affair with Blythe's younger sister Eleanor Barton that resulted in the birth of Janet, now a pre-teen. Christopher had swiftly divorced his first wife-and-partner in Stowe and Stowe Productions to marry the woman who had once been his own sister-in-law.

In the years that followed, the original Mrs. Barton Stowe—who had fled to Cornwall to escape from the relentless paparazzi chasing one of Tinseltown's juicier scandals—remained in the land of her Cornish ancestors and eventually married a local laird and widower, the celebrated Sir Lucas Teague of Barton Hall, who had gallantly co-mingled his name with his adored second wife.

Without any further discussion during that fateful call, Stowe's ex-wife Blythe, now the mother of two young children herself, had generously urged Meredith to take a leave from the hospital, bring Janet with her, and spend the summer with the Barton-Teagues in Cornwall on their eight-hundred-acre working estate.

And thus it was that Janet and Meredith were now headed for a corner of Britain where the ancestors of half of Wyoming's mining and ranching families, including their own, had once called home. Blythe's returning to live there permanently had a mysterious symmetry to it, thought Meredith, watching the bucolic scenery fly by her car window.

*Who knows? Maybe the same thing applies to me?*

Blythe's stepson, Richard, interrupted her meandering thoughts, pointing to a wide swath of water and a bridge that the car was about to cross.

"Look up ahead," he said. "That's the River Tamar. Crossing it means we're finally in Cornwall proper, Janet," he announced over his shoulder for the benefit of the youngster continuing to sulk in the backseat. "In fact, we should make it to Barton Hall in time to snag a few scones from the tea shop before it closes."

"Who drinks tea? I *hate* tea!" Janet proclaimed. "I want a coke."

"No Coca-Cola, I'm afraid," Richard replied, "but lots

of sweet raspberries and blackberries growing on the estate's Home Farm."

"Fruit? Yuck!"

Richard appeared to suppress a smile indicating he wasn't in the least offended, personally, by the child's bad manners. He flicked his left turn signal, wheeling the big car down an impossibly narrow lane. Within minutes of making the turn toward the coast, Meredith caught a glimpse of a stretch of slate-blue water on the horizon.

"Ah…the English Channel, am I right?" she murmured excitedly.

She studied the map in her lap, reckoning that they were now heading due south over a green quilt of rolling hills and fields.

"We'll be at the gates to Barton Hall in just a tick," Richard announced, and Meredith felt a little thrill of anticipation.

As the road narrowed even more, the vine and flower-strewn stone hedgerows on both sides of the Land Rover stood six feet high, crisscrossing the property that Cousin Blythe and her second husband had fought so fiercely to keep in his family.

"This is just amazing," Meredith murmured, as she took in the sight of mid-May's remaining spring colors dazzling her in all directions. Meanwhile, the rain let up and visibility improved, minute-by-minute. The undulating hills, slick with moisture, looked like smooth, green velvet and were neatly intersected with stone walls and blanketed by hedges in varying shades of emerald and jade. The spectacular views that were unfolding with each twist and turn of the road took her breath away. A wave of unexplained happiness swept over her.

*I love it already! How can that be? No wonder Blythe never came home…*

"Barton Hall Estates is situated near the village of Mevagissey to the East and the River Luney, toward the West," Richard announced. "It's just a brisk walk to the even smaller village of Gorran Haven."

"Good heavens!" exclaimed Meredith. "Look over there, Janet. The sun has broken through!" But there was only silence from the back seat.

Richard chuckled. "The old saying in Cornwall is that 'if you don't like the weather here, wait five minutes.'"

"That's what we say in Wyoming, too," Meredith exclaimed, feeling her spirits rise even higher as she and Richard exchanged smiles. She pointed out the front windshield. "Wow! It's totally clear over there. The cliffs overlooking the Channel are amazing."

"And *dangerous*," Richard replied. Looking back briefly in Janet's direction, his tone became serious. "If either of you ever go on the walking paths up there or on Bodmin Moor while you're here, you must truly mind your footing. The winds can be fierce and weather can blow in suddenly. We keep the Cornish Search and Rescue Team busy year 'round, but especially in summertime when a lot of careless tourists find themselves in trouble and have to be plucked off the precipice by land and by sea."

"Whatever," was Janet's response.

"They rescued *me* once," Richard continued conversationally. "Or rather they and Her Majesty's Coast Guard did. Saved me when I was about your age, Janet, from drowning in a cave I had no business being in as the tide rolled in."

"Wow," Janet replied in a sarcastic tone, adding "*Boring!*"

Meredith whirled in her seat. "Janet, I've had enough! You just cut that out right now, do you hear me!" she ordered, her patience utterly exhausted.

"Cut *what* out?" Janet asked with feigned innocence.

"You *know* what!" Meredith countered, eyes flashing. "I won't stand for any more rudeness. Since the day I met you, Miss Janet Barton Stowe, you've behaved like a total brat, and, believe me, young lady, *that* is really *boring!* You are on a time-out until we get to your aunt's house, do you understand? Do not say a *word!*"

"You're not the boss of me!" Janet shouted, her round face red with fury.

"Oh, yes I *am*, and so is Richard, here, and so is Aunt Blythe, Sir Lucas, and every single adult you are going to be with this summer. I mean it, Janet! Not another sound out of you until we get to Barton Hall and after that, see that you mind your manners, young lady!"

*Oh my God! I sound just like every parent alive!*

Meredith turned back in her seat, amazed at how good it felt to tell her unruly charge exactly what a pain it was to be in the presence of such ill mannered, insolent behavior. She picked up her conversation with Richard as if nothing had happened, sensing a stunned silence pulsating from the back seat. Little Miss Janet obviously had seldom been severely admonished.

"Richard, tell me how your dad and stepmom are doing these days with their nursery business," she asked in as calm a tone of voice as she could muster while she waited for her blood pressure to lower a couple of notches. "And what about running the tea room and gift shop and taking paying guests, now, at Barton Hall? Is all that helping to keep the coffers filled?"

"Well, with such a small staff, it's been a challenge, to say the least," he replied, and described the rigors of turning his ancestral home into a paying concern. Waving hello to a car coming toward them on the narrowing lane, he said, "But then, you know how hard it's been to maintain a big enterprise since the worldwide recession. Blythe told me a bit about the big ranch you live on…in the Rocky Mountains, isn't it? What's running that like?"

Meredith, in turn, portrayed the trials of a life raising sheep and her seventy-five year old father's dogged determination to keep the ranch going.

"It's so strange," she said, breaking into her own narrative about the daily chores on a modern-day ranch. "All the cousins of my generation in this family lost our mothers at young ages. I was fourteen when my mom died. Blythe and Ellie's mother died, too, when they were still kids. And now Ellie, herself…"

She could sense that Janet had straightened up from her slouching position in the corner of the car and was all ears.

"And I as well," Richard disclosed quietly. "I was just five when Mum died. Breast cancer."

"*Five*? Oh, that is so sad, Richard."

"It was Blythe who persuaded Father that he should rescue me from boarding school that first summer she was here as Father's tenant. She had to campaign very hard to allow me to go to the village school. I think *I* fell in love with her before Father did."

"You were in boarding school at age *five*?" she repeated, horrified.

"To be fair, I was nearly six. But it's a British tradition in some circles," he added lightly. "Especially when there's only one parent."

"You know, the last time I saw Blythe was at my mother's funeral…years ago. I am so looking forward to really getting to know her better."

"She a very wonderful person," Richard said quietly. "And I think you'll like Father, too."

"I'm sure I will.

Richard made a sharp left turn into a shaded drive,

providing Meredith with her first view of Barton Hall's turreted gatekeeper's cottage. Marking the entrance, a solid stone crenelated tower on the left also incorporated a wide granite arch branching off its top section, anchored by a similar stone tower on the right side of the driveway. Posted near the open, forest-green wooden gate was a discreet sign in gold leaf letters that announced "Barton Hall Estates - Guest Entrance."

Their hulking vehicle continued down the gravel driveway that stretched nearly half a mile, framed by a leafy green tunnel created by sixty-foot larches whose top branches mingled overhead. Through the Land Rover's windshield, Blythe caught a glimpse of a massive stone dwelling and another crenelated roofline up ahead.

"Why, it really *is* an honest-to-goodness castle!" Meredith exclaimed as the full magnificence of Barton Hall hove into view. A huge expanse of gray stone in the shape of a squared-off U featured matching round towers at each corner in keeping with the style of architecture that Meredith had noticed at the gatekeeper's cottage when they'd turned into the drive. Perched on a wide knoll of close-cut green grass, the castle was surrounded by a velvety incline that ended in a large pond edged with tall reeds and dotted with waterfowl, including a gaggle of ducks and two swans.

Suddenly, up ahead in the gravel circle that fronted the impressive castle entrance, she saw a cluster of official-looking vehicles, including an ambulance and a police car.

"Oh dear. Look, Richard! What do you suppose is going on?"

Her heart speeded up at the sight of a yellow and white van even larger than the Land Rover with "Cornwall Search and Rescue" emblazoned on its front hood. Nearby, the ambulance was branded in similar fashion among the collection of other officially marked vehicles.

Under the stone portico, a uniformed officer conferred with several people wearing matching red-and-black parkas whose markings announced that they, too, were part of the local search and rescue team. A few others were clad in bright yellow foul-weather gear stamped in bold, black lettering: H.M. COAST GUARD.

"Oh, Lord, Richard!" she exclaimed, a knot of fear in her stomach. "What's happened? Who's *hurt?*"

Her nurse's training led her to wonder aloud that perhaps the forty-something Lucas Teague had had a heart attack, or Blythe or one of their children had been seriously injured.

By this time, Richard had halted the Land Rover because of the jumble of emergency vehicles blocking their forward progress.

"No, No...they're all right, " Richard assured her, pointing. "See? There's Blythe and Father and the two children."

"Oh, thank God!" Meredith exclaimed, sinking back into the passenger seat with relief.

Richard gestured in the direction of a smartly-dressed middle-aged couple standing near the ambulance and engaged in earnest conversation with a tall, broad-shouldered man who looked to be in his middle thirties, also wearing a red and black parka with an embroidered patch that declared he was with the Search and Rescue Dog Association. The K9 handler loosely held the leash attached to the collar of a black and white Border Collie wearing an electrifyingly orange vest studded with embroidered patches proclaiming it, too, was a certified member of the rescue squad.

Meredith now recognized the Barton-Teague group from family photos: her first cousin, Blythe Barton, and her

husband, Lucas Teague, along with their four-year-old
daughter, Lucinda, and their eight-year-old son, Matthew
Barton-Teague, whom Meredith surmised had been named
after Blythe's brother Matt who'd died in a Wyoming rodeo
accident at seventeen

Breathing much easier, now, Meredith couldn't help but
notice that the arrestingly attractive dog handler her hosts
had been talking to was tanned, with dark hair, a day's
stubble, and the brooding good looks of a model in a Ralph
Lauren clothing ad. Embarrassed to be caught staring out
the car window at the handsome stranger, she swiftly
shifted her gaze to his right where the copper-headed
Lucinda threw her arms around the neck of his black and
white Border Collie and covered its fur with a shower of
kisses.

"Let's go see what's happened," Richard said, opening
the driver's side door.

"There's someone in the ambulance," Meredith noted,
climbing out of her side of the Land Rover and gingerly
hopping onto the gravel. Both she and Richard peered
more closely at the parked vehicle whose service door was
open, and inside, a medic was tending to an elderly man
lying prone on a stretcher, waving his arms.

"Oh...that's old man Quiller," Richard said, sounding
relieved, "our retired head gardener. He must have
wandered off again. Early Alzheimer's, we think."

In the midst of this activity, Meredith saw that her
cousin Blythe had shifted her attention to the ancient Land
Rover and immediately broke away from the group to greet
their arrival.

"Oh, dear, isn't this classic?" the lady of the manor said,
swiftly walking toward them. Clad in a pair of pressed jeans
topped by an azure cashmere turtleneck, Lady Barton-
Teague cut a svelte figure with caramel-colored hair like

Meredith's own, though Blythe's was curly and fell to her shoulders.

"Blythe!" Meredith called. "Thank goodness you're okay!"

"Welcome, welcome, Meredith! This scene must have given you quite a turn."

"No kidding," she replied, stepping into Blythe's outstretched arms for a hug.

Blythe held her tight for a long moment, and then stepped back. "It is *so* good to see you after all this time." Then, she pointed to the ambulance with a rueful expression.

"Our retired gardener, John Quiller, strayed a bit too far from his cottage on the property early this morning in the pouring rain, and we had to call out Search and Rescue. Fortunately," she continued, "by the time the sun came out, Sebastian Pryce, over there," she said, pointing to the canine specialist that Meredith had noted as the Land Rover rolled to a stop, "found him fast asleep under a tree along the walking trail. Quiller apparently grew tired and a bit confused as he was heading for Dodman Point, poor dear."

Meredith turned toward the striking male figure in the red and black parka whose dog was docilely allowing Blythe's four-year-old—known by family and friends alike as "Little Lucy"—to smother the canine with kisses.

Blythe paused and took a deep breath. "Sebastian and his search dog, T-Rex—that Border Collie my daughter Lucy's strangling—found John not much worse for wear, can you believe? But it gave everyone quite a good scare." She smiled broadly at Meredith. "Well, once again…*welcome* to Barton Hall!" she exclaimed and gave Meredith another warm hug. Looking over her guest's shoulder, she said, "Thank you so much, Richard. I know you've all had a long drive. Let's go in the house. Tea's ready. We all need a

cup—or something stronger, I expect. Where's my niece?"
she added, smiling and in a voice loud enough for Janet to
hear.

As for the eleven-year-old, she sat sullenly in the
backseat, making no move to get out of the vehicle.
Meredith retraced her steps and opened the Land Rover's
door as Blythe stepped forward and greeted her with a
friendly grin.

"The last time I saw you, Miss Janet Barton Stowe,"
Blythe said, pointing toward the English Channel glinting in
the distance, "you were barely three months old and you
slept soundly for hours at Painter's Cottage, at the bottom
of our Hall Walk, overlooking the sea." Holding out her
two hands, Blythe formally introduced herself. "I'm your
Aunt Blythe, and everyone at Barton Hall is so *very* happy
you've come to stay with us."

"Yeah, right," Janet said, crossing her arms and refusing
to look at her aunt.

"Shall we go in? I want you to meet your cousins,
Matthew and Lucy."

"I don't want to," Janet announced, not moving an
inch.

Blythe paused and leaned closer to the door, both
hands on her jeans-clad knees to be able to look at Janet at
eye level.

"Janet, darling, I know you've had a long, tiring journey,
and many unhappy things have happened to you," Blythe
said quietly, "but you're part of *our* family this summer, so
you'll just have to pull your socks up and join in the fun.
Come meet T-Rex, at least, our doggie hero of the hour.
Come on, come on!"

To Meredith's complete amazement, Janet got out of
the car and walked beside Blythe in the direction of the tall,
utterly dashing man and his orange-vested dog. Then a

thought struck Meredith with a jolt.

"Oh my God! Holly! *My* poor dog!" she exclaimed to Richard.

Reacting immediately, Richard walked to the car's front passenger door and eased the animal carrier out of the Land Rover and onto the gravel drive. Meredith fumbled with the lock and finally got it open while Holly wiggled and squealed with excitement. Before Meredith could stop her, the Corgi pushed open the gate like the little tank she was—her bright yellow "Therapy Pet" vest in plain view—and took off, running as fast as her stubby legs would carry her, over to a tree to relieve herself in a low squat.

Just as quickly, the Border Collie leapt from little Lucy's arms and ran to investigate the newcomer, his leash trailing in his wake. The larger dog immediately stuck his nose in Holly's rump, prompting the Corgi to bolt toward the castle.

The man from the search and rescue team that Blythe had called Sebastian Pryce swiveled his head and took in the scene of two supposedly well-trained dogs running circles around each other and barking furiously.

"Rex! Come!" he commanded sharply, obviously embarrassed that his dog should behave so poorly. But both canines had already taken off at a dead run and disappeared around the corner of Barton Hall. He sprinted after them, shouting, "Come, Rex! Come right here!" Before he, too, vanished around the edge of the castle wall, he turned toward Meredith and called out in his clipped British accent, "Can you *please* control your dog?"

Meredith bristled and began to run after both man and dogs. "She was quite under control before *your* dog accosted her," she shouted at the man's back, trotting faster in an attempt to catch up with him.

*A dishy-looking guy, but what an ass!*

The two of them came upon a scene both wished they could have avoided: Rex was rapidly shunting his hindquarters and doing his best to get a purchase on Holly's backside, but without the cooperation of his potential ladylove.

"No! Rex! Get away from her! Bloody hell!"

By this time, Sebastian had his large hands around his dog's flanks and literally yanked Rex into his arms before penetration took place.

"Oh, Christ!" he said between his teeth. He shot a look of disdain at Meredith's dog. "Rex has never done this sort of thing before. You should thank God they didn't tie, or I'd never have been able to pull them apart!"

Meredith had caught up with them and grabbed Holly's collar, attempting to catch her breath.

"Well!" she exclaimed between gulps for air. "Don't you reckon Mister T-Rex needs a *tad* more training to behave properly in mixed company?" she declared, thinking the K9 Adonis could stand a dose of the same medicine. She managed to secure Holly's leash to her dog collar and heaved the over-excited twenty-eight-pound furry bundle into her arms. "You might have noticed from my dog's vest, she's a service-qualified animal. She was merely having a pee after nearly five hours shut up in her crate."

*Men! Always thinking they know who's screwed up.*

With Holly weighing heavily in Meredith's arms, she quickly turned and marched to the front of Barton Hall where Richard greeted her return with a faint grin.

"No harm done?" he asked, having followed the dog owners far enough to witness the short but animated exchange between Meredith and Sebastian.

"Saved by inches," she replied grimly. "But a very close call."

# CHAPTER 2

Meredith set Holly down on the gravel drive, doing her best to regain a semblance of calm after her heated run-in with Sebastian Pryce. Richard still had a questioning but amused expression, so she elaborated, "We got there pretty quickly, and his dog hadn't quite hit the bulls eye, so, yes…no harm done."

"How about we don't worry about the luggage just now?" Richard proposed. "I think you are in grave need of a cup of tea and a scone."

"Good idea," she replied. "Frankly, I could also use a bathroom break myself."

Pryce now had Rex firmly in hand, the dog quivering in disgrace by his side. During this fracas, Blythe had been preoccupied with instructing the ambulance driver to take the unharmed patient back to his cottage where she assured the medics that Quiller's wife would be there to look after him. Their hostess appeared oblivious to the drama that had just transpired between the two dog owners. The mistress of the manor officially introduced Meredith to her tall, distinguished-looking husband, Sir Lucas Barton-Teague, and her children, and then turned to the search and rescue officer.

"Sebastian…please *do* join us for a nice cup of tea and one of Mrs. Quiller's famous scones, won't you? Have you met Meredith Champlin, my cousin who's just arrived from

America? She'll be staying with us all summer." She turned
to Meredith, completing her introductions. "Meredith, this
is Sebastian Pryce—*Lieutenant* Sebastian Pryce—who's
returned to Cornwall from Afghanistan safe and sound,
thank heavens." She bent down and gave Holly's head a
friendly pat. "And this, Sebastian, is Meredith's Corgi who
has won all sorts of awards in sheep herding contests in
Wyoming. Not only that," Blythe enthused, "Holly does
double duty at the hospital where Meredith takes care of
very sick children and runs the Pet Therapy program." She
smiled warmly at her cousin, adding, "In fact, it's Nurse
*Matron*, isn't it, now, Meredith?"

"We call it Nurse Manager, my ex-pat Cuz," she replied
with a laugh, ignoring Pryce.

"Right." Blythe cheerfully pointed to the chastised T-
Rex. "And, as you must realize by now, Sebastian, dogs are
always welcome at Barton Hall—especially Rex, who
certainly earned his title as ' rescuer' today."

*Not to mention the moniker 'Canine Romeo,'* Meredith
thought sourly.

"Thank you, Lady Barton-Teague," he replied and
nodded briskly at Meredith in acknowledgement of Blythe's
compliment-laden introduction. "How do you do?"

Meredith bestowed upon him a faint, disinterested
smile, enjoying the slight flush that she noted had spread to
cheekbones tanned by exposure to sun and wind. In
response, the K9 specialist paused as if deliberating about
Blythe's invitation to tea, and then shook his head.

"I'm so sorry," he said, addressing them both, and
Meredith wondered vaguely if his apology included any
regret for his sharp-tongued rebuke about her handling of
Holly. "That's really kind of you, but I'm due back at the
incident debriefing, so I'm afraid I must be off with the
others."

"Ah, yes, of course," Blythe replied with a nod. "Well, another time. And please don't wait to be asked. You know the estate's tea shop is open seven days a week," she added with a wry smile that indicated she'd most likely be the one on duty, "so just come around one afternoon when you have a free hour or two and let them know to tell me you're here. We'll all have a proper cup together soon, I hope," she urged warmly. "You and the team were absolutely wonderful, as always, and we're very grateful to you all."

Sebastian gravely accepted the thanks of his would-be hostess, and angled his dark, slightly shaggy mane in Meredith's direction.

"Welcome to Cornwall, Ms. Champlin," he said, his friendlier tone indicating an attempt to make amends for his hasty words earlier. "I hope you'll enjoy your time here."

She merely nodded thanks, thinking absently that his longer hairstyle certainly suited his dark good looks, as did the vibrant red jacket issued to the members of the search team

*Whoa there, gal...what do you care? The guy may be bordering on hunk status, but he made a pretty snap judgment about Holly.*

She turned her back in a show of dismissal and started to walk toward the castle's arched entrance where its enormous oak door stood ajar.

Suddenly she was struck by an unhappy thought: Holly was due to come into season any day now. Poor Rex, with his well-trained nose, probably got an irresistible whiff of her Corgi's come-hither hormones and did what any self-respecting male dog would do, highly trained or not. He'd surrendered to his DNA.

*Maybe I've been too tough on the guy...*

Meredith turned around to voice her theory about why Rex might have ignored proper canine protocol only to find dog and master were already heading for the vehicle in which they'd arrived. With a mental shrug, she glanced at Holly on the ground where her dog immediately began sniffing the new territory at the end of her leash.

"Holly, come! Heel," she ordered, pointing to the gravel near her feet. Without hesitation, the Corgi trotted to her side and looked up expectantly. "Good girl!"

Then she heard Sebastian Pryce bid Blythe and Lucas a final farewell. She saw out of the corner of her eye that he had turned in her direction just in time to see Holly instantly obey her commands. For her part, she ignored his stare, but she could feel his eyes follow her as she and her dog mounted the stone steps and disappeared into Barton Hall's cool, dark vestibule with its raft of Barton and Teague family portraits staring down from the richly paneled walls.

There would be all summer to tell T-Rex's handler that, perhaps, the Border Collie's shortcomings could be forgiven. That is when—or if—dog and master ever came to Barton Hall for afternoon tea.

❦

A few hours later, Sebastian and Rex were winding up the incident debriefing at the Cornwall Search and Rescue Team's headquarters in St Dennis.

Colonel Graham Wainwright, H.M Royal Army, Ret. and the volunteers' team leader, glanced down at the reports on the John Quiller rescue submitted by each of the members that had participated, and then looked up at Sebastian.

"By the way, good work, you and Rex."

"Thanks," Sebastian replied. "It must be about the fourth or fifth time we've been out on that call, the poor fellow. I headed for Dodman Point, just like last time, but it took a while to get to the spot where Quiller had fallen asleep, and meanwhile, the Coast Guard had been called out. Then, as we drew near the little glade directly off the cliff path, Rex picked up the scent and found him quickly."

Graham consulted his notes. "The fourth incident. You know the family, don't you?" he asked. "Maybe you could have a word with his wife to keep the old boy on a shorter leash now that his dementia seems to be getting worse."

"Mrs. Quiller still works as head housekeeper at Barton Hall, so I suppose it's hard for her to be in two places at once," Sebastian replied, "but I'll speak to Lady Barton-Teague about it next time I'm in the neighborhood."

"Yes, do," agreed Graham. "Remind her that we've got limited resources and—"

Just then, Beven Glynn, an equipment driver with the search and rescue team, broke into their conversation.

"I doubt Sebo, here, will be welcomed back at Barton Hall anytime soon," he said with a short laugh, filing his *Vehicle Use Report* into a nearby cabinet. "Not after the way Rex went after their houseguest's Corgi. Right randy fellow, our aptly-named T-Rex!"

Graham frowned. "Did Rex misbehave?" He glanced down at his sheaf of papers detailing today's incident. "It wasn't in your report, I see."

"A rather minor event," Sebastian replied with an annoyed glance in Beven's direction. "It happened after the rescue."

The little toad was always looking to gain points by taking to task his fellow volunteers for even the slightest variation to the rulebook in order, Sebastian could only surmise, to enhance the bugger's own standing with their team leader.

*I'd have loved to see Beven on patrol with the Counter-IED squad in Afghanistan,* he thought. *Not knowing how to improvise occasionally could get a bloke killed.*

But rather than challenging Beven, Sebastian ignored him and turned to answer Graham, "A guest from America arrived at Barton Hall just as we were winding things up with Mr. Quiller. She took her dog out of a carrier crate after five hours traveling and…well…Rex went to investigate."

"Investigate?" Beven scoffed. "So that's what you call full-body sex."

"Maybe two seconds of rutting in the air is the definition of sex in *your* world, Beven—"

"All right, you two," Graham interrupted. "Next time, Pryce, put such incidents in your canine behavior log, will you please?" he ordered. "Rex is young, yet, and still a novice. We need to know whether he's going to really make the grade. I must say, though, from all accounts to date, he certainly performs well during the rescues. Keep him in hand at all times when you're out, though, will you? After all the training you've put in with him, I'd hate for him to be a washout."

"Yes, sir," Sebastian said. He looked straight at Beven. "And don't worry, sir. He's no washout." Then to Graham he added, "See you on the next call. I'm due back at the farm."

❦

Sebastian climbed into his Mini Cooper All Wheel Drive and lowered the windows a couple of more inches so Rex could enjoy the cool breeze, fresh from the rain earlier in the day.

*Beven Glynn's such a pathetic sod…*

He inhaled deeply and tried to put the entire afternoon

out of his mind. The air-scenting dog's white paws and black, shaggy forelegs were covered in mud from tramping along the fields and ultimately the paths that led to Dodman Point. Despite Beven Glynn's deliberate dig just now, Rex had definitely proved his mettle once again. Still, the dog had a lot to learn, Sebastian acknowledged to himself, and *first* on the list was to come when called—no matter *how* enticing the distraction.

After five minutes of driving along the A3058 toward St. Austell, he headed the car down Burngullow Lane. The rolling fields of William and Susanna Jenner's Cow Hollow Farm unfolded gently outside his window, and suddenly he found himself grinning. Poor old Rex! There were some times in life when pure instinct took over, and the desire for mating with such a saucy female was likely one of them.

Without warning, his thoughts turned to the leggy young lady, recently arrived from the States. He wagered that even the Queen would judge Meredith Champlin's Pembroke Welsh Corgi a fine example of the breed—and her mistress wasn't bad looking, either. Both had caramel-colored hair, but where Holly was short and built as solidly as sheep-herding dogs must be, the young woman he'd met today was appealingly slender and barely came up to his shoulder. With her sleekly cut, chin-length mane and tight-fitting jeans topped by her cream-colored cable knit sweater, she appeared surprisingly well suited for life in the country. Large, penetrating brown eyes—and a bit starchy, like several army nurses of his acquaintance—she clearly was not about to take any nonsense.

Especially not from him.

His tone to her had been preemptory, bordering on rude. No wonder she had dismissed him without a backward glance when she entered Barton Hall, he reflected glumly.

As he wheeled the Mini into the drive leading to the milking barns and his own retrofitted living quarters above the stone livery stable, he thought about his utterly lame remark scolding her to control her dog. *He* was the one who hadn't kept his dog under control. In Afghanistan, that could have gotten them both killed.

He mused about Lady Barton-Teague's disclosure that her attractive cousin not only nursed extremely ill children, but also ran a pet therapy project at the hospital where she worked. Surely, she couldn't hold that position unless she knew a considerable amount about dog behavior. In hindsight, he'd made a perfect fool of himself.

Feeling almost as burdened as if he still had his search and rescue backpack weighing him down, he shut the door to his car, it's British racing green color coated, as usual, with streaks of mud. Glancing down, he saw that the same sticky substance covered his boots as well. With Rex trotting obediently beside him, he trudged toward the back of the farmhouse and swiftly hosed down Rex's paws and his own encrusted Wellington boots, stamping his feet a few times to shed the water before heading into the farmhouse kitchen.

"Hello there, Sebo," called his employer's wife—and a friend of nearly a decade. Rex had already settled down on the slate step outside the door by the time he entered through the back pantry.

A tall, willowy blond Londoner whose nails no longer wore polish and whose hair was pulled back in a serviceable ponytail, Susanna Jenner eyed his boots, shining from the water he'd sluiced on them before walking onto her kitchen's slate floor. She moved a teapot from the hob to the nearest counter and cast him an appreciative, welcoming smile.

Thanks for cleaning off your Wellies, love" she said,

adding, "So, you've been out on a rescue call, have you?"

"That I have," Sebastian replied, pointing to the refrigerator in a gesture that asked for permission to see what he might find there for a five o'clock snack.

Susanna nodded. "There's some Stilton on the second shelf. Biscuits are in the pantry. Help yourself. William'll be in soon from the milking. He said to tell you he wanted to discuss something with you when you got in."

"I'll go find him once I get something to eat. I'm famished."

"Oh and before I forget, your mother called again. Mentioned she hadn't seen or heard from you in donkey's years."

"Hmmm…"

"Are you ever going to call the poor woman?" Susanna demanded. And then, as so often happened with the thirty-five-year-old, another thought grabbed her attention before he was required to come up with some flimsy excuse as to why he probably *wouldn't* ring up Elizabeth Pryce. "Did you find the missing person?"

"Ah yes…it was just old man Quiller again." Sebastian related the story of how Rex had found him eventually, up on the cliff path to Dodman Point. "I imagine Mrs. Quiller is finding that keeping an eye on her husband has become a full time job. Maybe that's why an American cousin of Lady Barton-Teague's arrived today."

"What do you mean?" asked Susanna, her interest obviously piqued as in recent years, Blythe Barton-Teague had become a good friend. "Who arrived?"

"A woman of about our age named Meredith Champlin, and she had a young child with her as well. Perhaps she's come over to help with running all the different aspects of the estate?" he speculated.

"The American cousin arrived with a child?" Susanna

asked, all curiosity.

"I don't think the little girl is hers. I believe she's just another member of the Wyoming branch of the Barton clan. The child is Lady Barton-Teague's sister's youngster I think I heard someone say. Which would make the girl her niece, wouldn't it?"

"You are *joking*!" Susanna exclaimed. "That would be the child of *Ellie Barton*, the sister who stole Blythe's first husband, that famous movie director." She related to Sebastian the scandal that had rocked Hollywood a decade earlier. "The woman who's visiting must be Blythe's relative who was made the child's guardian after the mother died in that awful plane crash a few weeks ago. It was all over the news."

"So Blythe's cousin, Meredith Champlin, was made the girl's legal guardian? Why not the aunt?"

Susanna nodded. "The two sisters never spoke after the huge family uproar. Quite a right bollocks it was, from all accounts."

"It certainly sounds like it." Sebastian shrugged and popped a piece of cheese into his mouth as Susanna poured him a cup of freshly brewed tea. "The cousin's very fine Corgi came with her, which certainly added to the excitement caused by the search for Mr. Quiller," he added dryly, speculating about what further questions his inquisitor was going to ask him.

"Now this *is* getting juicy!" chortled Susanna. "What's Blythe's cousin like? Is she as good-looking as Lady Barton-Teague, herself?" she inquired mischievously.

"Susanna, you are a wicked woman," Sebastian commented mildly. "I know where this is going."

"Well, *is* she?"

"As a matter of fact, she's quite lovely looking," replied Sebastian, recalling his view of Meredith Champlin's very pleasing derriere as she marched toward the entrance to Barton Hall in an obvious display of annoyance at him. "She's also Nurse Matron at some hospital in America."

"If *you* say she's attractive, she must be an absolute stunner!" Susanna enthused. "It's about time some halfway interesting female who's single, attractive, well-educated, and *eligible* arrived on our shores. In *your* case, especially, O confirmed bachelor," she teased. "I've warned you that one of these days you'll turn up lovesick—despite your best efforts since getting out of the Army—and have to give up that flat above the stables, which, by the way, might inspire me to get back to my weaving." Susanna paused for breath and reflected, "Now, where *did* I store that loom, I wonder? Well, never mind. Anyway, it's time you found someone to live with, moved to new quarters that's more than just a loft, and got yourself a *real* life instead of constantly playing Rescue Ranger!"

"Susanna," he said firmly, "I'm ready to find new quarters whenever you need me to vacate, but I doubt Miss Meredith Champlin will quite be the one to offer me shelter in a storm."

Susanna cocked her head and allowed her eyes to rove from his head to his booted toes. "Ah, such false modesty, my friend." She put a hand on his sleeve, adding with a fond smile and an affection for him she'd held since their university days together, "You are a smashing, handsome fellow with a kind and good heart, Sebastian Pryce, though, for some daft reason, you do your best to hide it when in the company of the opposite gender. Except with *me*, of course," she added, flashing him a grin. "All my women friends are dying for me to arrange dinner parties and picnics so they can cozy up to you. *Of course*, this Meredith person would want to get to know you! And you obviously have canines in common." Her eyes narrowed suddenly.

"Uh oh…all right," she continued, frowning now. "Tell me. What did you do? You can be *the* biggest buffoon, sometimes, when it comes to women."

Sebastian stared into the smooth surface of his mug of tea. "I reprimanded Ms. Champlin within about ten seconds of her arrival at Barton Hall."

"You did *what?*"

"As I mentioned, she arrived with a dog. A female Corgi. It pushed out of its traveling crate and Rex did what aroused male dogs do…he went for the bitch."

"You mean the dog, right?"

"Yes, I mean the *dog*! I'm not *that* rude, am I?"

"No, Sebastian, you're not," she replied patiently, "but shouldn't *you* have been the one to be reprimanded, to say nothing of Mr. T-Rex? Did you eventually apologize to the poor woman?"

"I was too occupied pulling Rex away from the Corgi in the knick of time to apologize, or even make the lady's acquaintance, really."

Susanna covered her mouth as she started to laugh. Sebastian was surprised to find himself smiling as well.

"Well, I grant you, it was a pretty comical scene."

"I'll just bet it was. What did you actually *say* to this Miss Champlin?"

"I asked if she could please control her dog."

Susanna began to laugh hysterically while shaking her blond head from side to side in disbelief.

"Sebastian, you really should sign up for the long course at Charm School, my friend." She crossed to the pantry door and allowed Rex to bound into the kitchen. "Oh, T-Rex…come in, you poor, poor baby," she cooed, giving him a friendly pat on the head. "It's perfectly obvious to me that your handler needs training in the art of wooing ladies far more than you do!"

The dog immediately ran to Sebastian's side and sat down obediently next to his boots as if trying to make amends for his previous transgressions at Barton Hall.

"Rex, my boy," Sebastian addressed his canine companion who was looking at him with melting eyes that pleaded to be returned to his master's good graces. "According to Susanna, here, you and I *both* owe those visitors from America a *mea culpa.*"

"You certainly do! And when will that happen, may I ask?" Susanna queried, her lips twitching with a suppressed smile.

"When it happens," Sebastian replied evasively. He might well owe Meredith Champlin an apology, but he certainly didn't look forward to delivering it.

Just then, the back door banged once again and William Jenner strode into his wife's domain, his Wellington boots also slick with water from the hose-down they'd received outside the entrance to the kitchen. The men at Cow Hollow were well trained.

"Who owes whom an apology?" inquired the barrel-chested man who had been Sebastian's friend for many years and, along with Susanna, his savior for the last two since he'd returned to Cornwall. William gave his wife a buss on the cheek, swiftly sliced a wedge of the Stilton cheese from the brick that Sebastian had been eating, and popped it into his mouth. "Tea ready, darling?" he asked her. Then to his third-in- command he said, "Well, now, Sebo. Whom have you insulted *this* week?"

"A gorgeous young visitor to Barton Hall from America!" Susanna offered enthusiastically as she put a fresh kettle of water to heat on the smooth surface of her Aga cooker.

"I wouldn't say 'gorgeous,'" Sebastian interjected. "'Very pretty' about describes her...in a Wild West sort of way," he added, as a sudden vision of Meredith's sleek, golden tresses and her long legs clad in their thigh-hugging jeans freshly assaulted his senses.

"Other than my wife, no one fits the description 'gorgeous' around here. Not even our prize milking cows."

"Oh, you silver-tongued devil!" Susanna said, standing on tiptoes to kiss William firmly on his mouth. Then, she put her arm around her husband's waist and explained to him T-Rex's recent transgression and Sebastian's hair-trigger response.

"You can't be serious, Sebo?" William chuckled. "I'd have liked to have seen *that.*"

"Rex's attempts to hump the Corgi, or my telling its owner to rein in *her* dog?"

"Both, I think!" William swiftly looked down at his watch. "But enough frivolity at our friend's expense, Susanna." He turned to regard Sebastian. "I want to talk to you about going over to the Moorland Creamery tomorrow to negotiate a better rate for the milk, and Gordon agrees we definitely should," he said, referring to Dr. Gordon Dobell, senior on-site livestock veterinarian and head of animal management for Cow Hollow Farm. "And don't worry, Sebo," William added as an apparent afterthought, "I don't think there's much chance of our running into the dreaded Claire Gillis."

Sebastian arched an eyebrow at the mention of Claire's name, but made no comment. In addition to volunteering for the Search and Rescue Team out of St. Dennis, he had been earning his veterinarian's license certification hours these past two years as a kind of apprentice to Dobell, a large animal specialist whom Sebastian considered a far better teacher than even the professors he'd had at the Royal College of Veterinary Medicine in London. Moorland's, the largest maker of Cornwall's famous clotted cream, bought milk from Cow Hollow Farm, along with some 150 other dairies in England's West Country, and their products were among the best, thanks to Dobell's meticulous animal management practices. William had inherited the farm upon his father's death four years earlier and, along with Dobell and Sebastian, oversaw its 250 acres and the production of the high quality milk for which the region was justly noted.

"For the price Moorland's paying, it's too demanding on everyone, including the livestock, don't you think?"

"No discussion required," Sebastian replied. "I agree completely."

"Good!" William gave a slap to the kitchen table. "Then, you and I will don our armor and do battle on the morn."

Sebastian paused before replying. For more than two years, he had successfully been able to avoid any visits to Moorland's Creamery and could easily list a number of reasons why it was prudent to give the place a wide berth. Then he chastised himself for wanting to duck this visit as well.

*If you could patrol Helmand province looking for IEDs, surely you can endure a trip to Moorland's Creamery, you sorry bloke!*

Meanwhile, William confided, "I think Gordon is finally starting to slow down, Sebo. Just a few minutes ago, he actually admitted that he doesn't have the stomach for these battles with the Big Guns any longer." He clapped his friend on the shoulder. "*You*, mate, may lack certain social graces with the ladies, but I must say—given the dilemma before us—I am very grateful you got out of the business of defusing bombs, went to veterinary school on that government grant, and can direct your residual pugnacity in the direction of Moorland's Chief of Operations."

# CHAPTER 3

At the bottom of the stone stairs leading to his flat on the Cow Hollow property, Sebastian wearily pulled off his boots while Rex waited patiently near the half-opened Dutch door that had once been part of a horse stall until Susanna had so cleverly renovated the top floor of the livery stable. He leaned one shoulder against the ancient slabs of granite, quarried back in the mists of time from nearby Bodmin Moor, and contemplated the entrance to his cozy retreat.

What a relief it was to have this refuge, he thought with a familiar rush of gratitude. Upstairs was a sanctuary where he could turn off his mobile phone, eat a tin of soup for supper if he pleased, and answer to no one.

Susanna had called him a professional "Rescue Ranger" earlier, and the label had given him pause. For a dangerous moment, he allowed himself to think about his two-year stint as a member of the Royal Army's Military Working Dog Regiment, 104th Squadron. For most of his tour of duty, he had been a handler in its Arms and Explosives Search Dog Unit assigned to Afghanistan's Helmand Province to ensure the safety of the troops working there.

*And the only reason I found myself in that God-forsaken hole was because of a blasted* female!

How pathetically stupid had *that* been? He'd escaped from the disaster with Claire by volunteering for dangerous duty in a desert and among a people who treated women far worse than he ever had. He'd hated what he saw there, so one would think by this time he could just put the events involving Claire Gillis behind him. The colossal irony was, for all that far-away misery, he hadn't been able to let bygones be bygones with total success, so he simply accepted that he might always feel this ambivalence toward certain members of the fairer sex.

Sebastian heaved his CSRT backpack over his shoulder and headed up the stairs in his stocking feet with Rex following in his wake.

Thank God, he could at least still feel a flutter of physical arousal when he encountered an attractive female, he reflected, as witnessed by the day's bizarre encounter with the tasty-looking American visitor to Barton Hall. But when he considered all the wretchedness that various relationships with the opposite gender had created in his thirty-five years of life, his brain overruled his heart and other regions of his anatomy and said, "No thank you, m'lady."

Tiredly, he mounted the top stair to his flat and tossed the backpack onto the floor near his galley kitchen. He then opened the half-sized refrigerator wedged below the counter and stared at several take-away cartons that were at least a week gone. Closing the door, he leaned against the small kitchen island, still deep in thought.

For a long while, his chronic chilliness toward females of his acquaintance had served him rather well. Since leaving the Army and finishing veterinary school, he'd continued to play the role of rescuer as a volunteer with the local SAR team that specialized in finding lost pensioners like John Quiller, holiday makers stranded on the moor or down an abandoned mine shaft or clay pit, or prevented a steady stream of "despondents" from throwing themselves off a cliff. Given this work and his full-time job at Cow Hollow Farm, he'd nicely compartmentalized his life, thereby avoiding a number of dicey entanglements with the opposite sex. And thankfully, there'd been no repeat of the debacle with Claire.

And as for the mental health of Lieutenant Sebastian Pryce—now *Doctor* Sebastian Pryce, with his BVetMed degree and further study at the Farm Animal Hospital at the Hawkshead Campus in the Lake District? Oh, yes, he had the occasional nightmare about time spent in Afghanistan half a decade ago, but he wasn't one of those chaps who ducked for cover whenever a milk lorry backfired. Now that he was almost a full-fledged large animal veterinarian, the principal aftereffect of his military service as part of the canine corps was that he trusted and liked animals such as his new dog T-Rex far more than people.

*No coddling for* you, *Sebo, my boy, just because you've witnessed a big dose of man's inhumanity to man in that desert hellhole.*

As Susanna had noted so astutely, he'd cleverly managed to recreate life as a Rescue Ranger here in Cornwall, just as he had in the army.

*It's the perfect cover. Everybody thinks you're a hero.*

Since his return to Great Britain, he'd discovered to his utter frustration that merely *knowing* the probable cause of why, under stress, he tended to behave as he did toward perfectly nice females provided little in the way of fixing the problem.

Too much introspection, however, never helped anything, he thought, searching for his one wooden spoon to give the pureed bean concoction a stir. Better to simply "Keep Calm and Carry On" and acknowledge that he had a bizarre sort of ancient wound predating his military service that most likely would quietly fester forever, with no known cure. It was time simply to get on with his life despite his personal handicaps—the way the military men who had *really* suffered injury were so gallantly doing when they returned to England.

Sebastian motioned to Rex to sit near the small table where he ate his meals. He stared moodily down the steep, stone stairs he'd just ascended. The treads had been hollowed by centuries of horse grooms that had made the stable their home. He gazed about his cheerful, one-room living quarters with a double bed under one dormer, and the minuscule but efficient kitchen under another, and told himself for the hundredth time that he was bloody lucky to be as content as he was—most of the time.

*Mother can call me as often as she pleases. I'm not biting.*

Let his two brothers deal with her push-them-away-hold-them-close approach to her offspring, he thought, swiftly finishing the soup and flopping down on the bed, suddenly exhausted. He watched Rex circle once and then slump onto the carpet nearby. The two of them must have walked eight to ten miles on some fairly rough terrain today, and they'd both earned their rest.

Sebastian put his hands behind his head and stared at the rough-hewn beams supporting the ceiling overhead, carved by some anonymous carpenter a few centuries earlier.

*Life goes on, regardless of who currently inhabits the planet, or what their troubles might be*, he thought, though his mind continued to drift into areas he usually kept buttoned up tight. Fortunately, he had not laid eyes on Claire Gillis since he'd stormed out of their shared flat in St. Austell more than half a decade ago. And, for a couple of months now, he'd managed not to let Elizabeth Pryce get under his skin.

*Mission accomplished, old boy.*

A flash of memory sprang to mind: Max, the Springer

Spaniel assigned to him in the bomb squad. Sebastian could almost feel the dog's muzzle, moist despite the scorching temperatures, nestled in his hand when they slept in their tent at night and it sent a stab of loneliness right through him.

The unvarnished truth was, he'd been scared witless most of the time he was in the Middle East, wondering in that insufferable heat if either he or his dog would return alive and intact from their daily missions ferreting out improvised explosive devices—the IEDs that had blown so many of his fellow British soldiers and the American troops to bits. So how dangerous could a trip to a Cornwall creamery be, for bloody sake?

Of course, tomorrow's visit to Moorland's might wipe out his admirable record of avoiding Claire these last years. He'd heard a while back that she'd gotten a job as a recipe developer in the test kitchen there and thus he had never set foot in the establishment. As former Lieutenant Sebastian Pryce had learned so well when serving on the bomb squad: when it came to things that could blow up in one's face, it was always best to remain at a safe distance.

Or was it?

❦

Meredith heard a faint knock on her door and paused in unpacking the suitcase that she'd carefully laid on the damask-covered *chaise longue* in a bedroom she assumed was called "The Red Room." It was located halfway down the paneled hallway in the mammoth north wing of Barton Hall, and not only was the *chaise* covered in red silk, but also the fourteen-foot draperies that pooled on the floor, the fabric on the massive four-poster canopy, and the coverlet and large, square pillows gracing the mattress. Burgundy and royal blue Persian carpets—a little threadbare given that they were probably a century-and-a-half old—covered the floor from under the tall, casement windows overlooking the enormous front lawn to the edge of the marble hearth and ornate fireplace.

"Come in," Meredith called, and immediately the door opened revealing Blythe carrying a tray with two tea cups and a pot covered in a thick, quilted tea cozy. Meredith pointed to the rug beside her bed and ordered Holly to lie down. "Over there, girl. That's right. Good girl!" She greeted Blythe with a grin. "Wow, what a pile of rocks you live in, Cousin mine! This place is spectacular!"

"The roof leaks in places, and the plumbing's quite eccentric, but it's pretty gorgeous, isn't it?" Blythe agreed, advancing into the room.

Behind her hostess framed by her bedroom door, Meredith caught a glimpse of one of the many statues dotting the corridor outside her room, busts celebrating a number of obscure scientists and botanists that previous Bartons and Teagues admired in their pursuit of bringing exotic rhododendrons and camellias back from India and China in the eighteenth and nineteenth centuries. The gardens had flourished since their original plantings and currently provided a substantial income stream to the Hall's owners when they opened the estate to show off the forty-foot-tall rhododendrons to paying visitors during the spring and summer months.

"Not crashed from jet lag, yet?" Blythe asked, gently kicking the door shut with her heel and putting the tea tray on a mahogany table near the *chaise*.

Meredith laughed. "I'm fighting it with all my strength, trying to stay awake at least until nine o'clock tonight."

"That's what I figured," Blythe said, chuckling. "Maybe some good strong tea will get you over the finish line."

"You are the best!" she exclaimed, then sobered. "Did Janet go to sleep?"

"Instantly. Almost finished unpacking?"

"Just about," Meredith said, "and thank you for assigning me this stunning room. I hope you didn't evict Richard or someone…"

"Oh, heavens no!" Blythe replied. "We've got a dozen more guest rooms where these came from. I've put Janet next door to Lucy, with Matthew's room on the other side and ours next to that, mid-way down the hall. I thought it might be nice to give you a little breather," she added, pouring steaming tea into two exquisite bone china cups. "Milk? Sugar?"

"Just milk, please," Meredith said.

"See? You're getting the hang of being British already. Milk, only, is what we all take here at Barton Hall," Blythe teased. "Shall we sit over here in front of the fire? Can you believe we still need one to stay warm at night, given it'll soon be June?"

Meredith sank into one of two red and cream striped slipper chairs positioned in front of the glowing hearth and felt as if a load of hay had just been taken off her shoulders.

"Oh, Lordy, it's good to be here at last," she murmured, taking her first sip of the bracing liquid. "You are some kind of saint, Lady Barton-Teague, do you know that?"

"Not at all," Blythe demurred. "We're just happy you're here."

Meredith almost laughed when she saw Blythe kick off her shoes and tuck her feet under her on the chair, just as her visitor had already done. She pointed at Blythe's abandoned flats.

"Do you think this is a family trait?" she asked with a laugh.

Blythe laughed, too, and then a somber expression took the place of her smile. "I've been thinking ever since I got your call…what a shock it must have been to wake up one morning and discover a child you'd never met was about to land on your doorstep!"

"Shock doesn't even begin to describe how Dad and I felt," Meredith replied, taking another sip of tea. "Chris should have ignored Ellie's will and made *you* a legal guardian instead of me. I mean, this is crazy! Dad and I had never even laid eyes on Janet, nor had we even met her father before Ellie died!'"

"I didn't realize that…" Blythe murmured.

"And two days after your sister's funeral, Chris flew into Jackson in his spanking new jet, left Janet with us, and off he went! I suppose it's not surprising to say that this kid—born and raised in Beverly Hills—absolutely *despised* it at the Crooked C and has threatened to run away umpteen times already."

"Actually, she was born in Africa when Chris filmed *In Kenya*," Blythe corrected her about a movie on which Blythe had served as production designer in its earliest stages and won several awards after the couple had split up. "But yes, you're right. I imagine Janet's spending eleven years in La-La Land in the Stowe household hasn't been particularly beneficial to her character."

"To put it mildly," Meredith responded. "That kid has been over-indulged and deprived simultaneously, which isn't that easy to do," she added. "Dad got so mad at her rudeness and bad behavior one day that he called her the 'Beverly Hills Brat' to her face. That's the morning I called you, begging for advice."

"Look, Meredith, with my two and all their little friends, there are so many youngsters running around our place, Janet's bound to find her footing in Cornwall after a few weeks here."

"I'm not so sure about that," she countered, giving Blythe a more detailed description of the youngster's difficult behavior that started the moment her father had dropped her off at the Jackson airport.

"But think what a terrible time the poor child's been through!" Blythe insisted.

"So you knew that Ellie died in the private plane crash after a visit to Christopher's film location near Mount Everest?" Meredith asked cautiously. "Frankly, I had no idea what information you had about the situation when I placed that call to you."

Blythe fell silent for a few moments as she contemplated the rim of her teacup. Then she said quietly, "Oh, I knew, all right. The news was all over CNN."

"Janet was in Beverly Hills with their housekeeper," Meredith elaborated. "Apparently, Christopher was behind on his shooting schedule, so Ellie left without him after visiting him in Nepal. Sheer fate, I guess, that Janet wasn't completely orphaned in that crash. The cinematographer's wife was also onboard...and the pilots, of course. Everybody died."

Blythe nodded gravely. "I immediately called Christopher, and left a message with his secretary to offer Lucas's and my condolences and ask what we could do to help, but I never heard back."

"Dad and I did the same thing," Meredith said, "never dreaming, obviously, I had been named in Ellie's will as a legal co-guardian. When the lawyer called me later with the news, I nearly keeled over." The younger woman heaved a sigh. "Oh, Lord, Blythe. What an unholy mess."

"It's pretty gothic, all right," Blythe agreed, "but we'll figure this out together. And I want you to know how much I appreciated your letting me learn what had befallen my niece," she added, her voice tight. "I've wondered about her for years. And besides, I love the idea that I also get to spend time with *you*, my little cousin from Wyoming! What are you now, twenty-eight or something?"

"Thirty-three." Meredith laughed. "But thank you for shaving off a few years!" Then, her smile faded. "Oh, Blythe, I feel just terrible that we've landed on your doorstep when you've got so much else on your plate right now, but I was completely baffled about how to handle all this, given Janet's unrelentingly atrocious behavior. I do appreciate how awful it's been for her...but I'm also totally aware of the stress that's going on in *your* life...the strain of keeping Barton Hall going in this lousy economy. The problems with the Quillers, and—"

"What really matters is that I am *so* glad you're here," Blythe interrupted. "I adore Lucas and I love my life with him. I'm so blessed to have had Matthew and Lucy, but I've missed not having any Wyoming family part of it. *Trust* me, having you in Cornwall this summer will be a joy, to say nothing of being a huge help. Somehow, we'll sort out the problems with Janet."

"Just the way we all dealt with Ellie all those years?" Meredith replied, shaking her head doubtfully. "I swear...there's some scalawag Barton gene that keeps punching through the family DNA."

Blythe laughed. "Well, Janet's only eleven, so that gives us a head start."

Meredith shook her head and then asked suddenly, "May I be so bold as to inquire: why are you willing to take this on?"

Before Blythe replied, she got up and poured them each another cup of tea. Settling back in the chair, she stared at the orange glow of the low-burning wood logs framed by the ornate marble fireplace.

"Because I feel so terribly sympathetic toward a little girl who lost her mother like that. Especially a mother like Ellie whose innate selfishness, I'm willing to bet, provided little warmth for an innocent child growing up."

"Believe me, Blythe, Janet's no innocent *now*."

"From what I've seen and heard in the short time she's been here, I can understand why you'd say that." Worry lines radiated softly from the corners of Blythe's eyes, as her features grew even more contemplative. "I held Janet in my arms when she was barely three months old. She was adorable, and *totally* innocent that day. I can't bear to think about all the things that must have happened to her in the meantime to make her so unhappy now."

Meredith felt a pang of guilt. "Losing a mother is awful," she agreed. "Both you and I know exactly what that's like. But I'm telling you Blythe, if you can figure out how to reach this kid, I'll bow down before you, believe me."

Blythe looked across the carpeted space separating the two cousins, grinned in a very unladylike fashion, and announced, "Oh no you don't! Not just *me*, white woman. We're going to do the rehab of Janet Barton Stowe *together*, cousin mine."

"You sounded *so* Wyoming, just now."

"Well, you can't completely take the Rockies outta a gal, now can you?" Blythe joked, affecting a deliberate western twang. Still with a mischievous glint in her eye she asked suddenly, "What did you think of our handsome friend from the local search and rescue team?" Before Meredith could summon a properly disinterested reply, Blythe added slyly, "I saw him watching your every move as you headed for the front entrance this afternoon." She pursed her lips to keep from smiling. "I really must invite the chap to a proper tea."

Blythe soon bid Meredith goodnight, removing the tea tray as she left.

"Try to stay up one more half hour and maybe you'll make it through the night," she urged. "Sleep well, Cuz."

Meredith brushed her teeth in the enormous, marble-tiled bathroom and padded over to the bed, using the small, needlepointed step stool that was probably a hundred years old to practically vault onto the mattress. The linen on the bed was shiny with age, but starched and pressed, and felt luxurious when she slipped between the sheets and laid her head on the down-filled pillow. She switched off the bedside lamp and saw with surprise how light it still was at nearly nine o'clock.

*A different latitude…a completely different world…*

Her thoughts were a whirl with the sights and sounds of the last twenty-four hours. With the window cracked, she could hear the low clucking of waterfowl nestled among the reeds skirting the pond below the sloping lawn. Closing her eyes, she felt mildly disoriented by the castle's grand surroundings, and yet excited to be a part of a family she'd only known from the yawning distance of four thousand miles and a universe away. She heard Holly shift her weight on the rug beside her bed and suddenly thought of the black and white Border Collie that had wished to "befriend" her dog that afternoon—and almost burst out laughing. A vision rose beneath her closed lids of a dark-haired man with somber brown eyes whose gaze had followed her from the gravel drive, all the way through the front entrance to Barton Hall. So different from Shep O'Brien's blond mane, bleached by years riding bulls in the hot sun on the rodeo circuit.

"Hmmmm," she murmured, snuggling deeper beneath the feather duvet.

She wondered as she drifted off to sleep what the

summer would bring?

The next morning, after a breakfast served the family in the big kitchen while the paying guests enjoyed kippers and scrambled eggs in the formal dining room, Lucas and Richard prepared to head off in various directions to start the day's chores.

"Bye, my love," Lucas said and bent down to kiss Blythe on the lips. "I'll be back from our beloved bankers by teatime."

Blythe reached up and put her arms around his neck, kissing him back, and Meredith felt a kind of referred glow to note how affectionate the two were after a decade of marriage.

"Drive safely, darling. The Men In Gray are bound to be impressed by the progress we've made this spring."

"I sincerely hope you're right," he said, and Meredith noted that Lucas gave his wife's *derrière* a discreet squeeze.

The Lord of the Manor headed for the kitchen's rear door and the inner courtyard where the family and staff vehicles parked. Blythe turned to her American visitors.

"Ready for a little sight-seeing, you two?" she asked and scanned down her list of To Do's that she hoped to accomplish while they were out.

"I *don't* want to go!" Janet pronounced. Her small lips puffed away from her teeth in a combination of a sneer and a pout.

Blythe and Meredith exchanged looks of mild exasperation, but before either could remonstrate the girl, Blythe's son Matthew chimed in cheerfully.

"That's all right, Janet. Want to see the hidey-hole in Father's library? We can play smugglers, like in Great,

Great, Grandfather's time, and—"

"*Bor*-ing!" declared Janet, her chubby arms folded across her chest.

Undaunted, Matthew suggested, "Well, if you want, we can help Richard plant his new lettuces later, or play hide-and-seek in the barn."

"What*ever*," she intoned without enthusiasm. "Anything's better than riding around in a car all day with *them.*"

"All right, then," Blythe said evenly. "Matthew, you run to tell Richard that's the plan...that you, Lucy, and Janet are staying here while Meredith and I run some errands and see something of the countryside. Mrs. Quiller will see that you get the lunch I've left in the cooler for you all."

"Yes, Mummy," Matthew replied. He turned eagerly toward Janet whose features remained composed in a scowl. "Let's go find Richard!"

"What*ever*," the eleven-year-old repeated, her voice a reflection of the boredom she wanted her audience to know she was enduring at their hands.

Meredith longed to take Janet to task once again for her obnoxious behavior, but Blythe put a restraining hand on her sleeve. "Right, then," her older cousin said swiftly. "We're off."

Blythe gave Meredith a quick tour of the estate lands and the seven-hundred-year old stone parish church of St. Michael's Caerhays, and then set out along the coast route to show her the picturesque village of Gorran Haven, the sweeping views that arched toward Dodman point, and then continued on to the town of Mevagissey, where they stopped for lunch. A half an hour later, the Land Rover arrived in the market town of Redruth and Blythe drove past a large sign that announced Moorland's Creamery and turned immediately into the car park.

"Well," she said with a determined look in her eye, "shall we see if we can get them to give us a price break on the masses of clotted cream that we buy for the tea room each week?"

The two women set out across the car park past a dark green, mud-splattered Mini Cooper with its windows partially rolled down. Meredith glanced over to see a very familiar face peering at them, tail wagging.

"Oh boy. Isn't that—?" Meredith began.

"Rex!" Blythe exclaimed. "Hello, lovely boy! Has your handler abandoned you today?"

"Not really," replied a deep voice. The two women whirled in place. "Hello, Lady Barton-Teague. Good morning, Ms. Champlin."

Sebastian Pryce and another tall figure that looked to be about his same age were striding toward them.

For some reason, Meredith felt her breath catch and she barely nodded a greeting to the two men.

Her cousin, however, was all smiles.

"After all those searches you've done for Mr. Quiller, Sebastian, please call me Blythe. And hello, William! I've been meaning to call you and Susanna for the longest while!" Blythe lowered her voice a notch. "I've been wanting to speak to you about possibly buying some of the milk we use at the tea room from you directly. Would that be a conversation we could have sometime soon?" She turned to Meredith. "Oh, please forgive me! Meredith Champlin, do meet William Jenner, one of the finest dairy farmers in our county."

Meredith shook hands with the sandy-haired, robust fellow who was smiling at her broadly.

"Ah, my wife Susanna and Sebastian, here, have already told me a bit about your American visitor. Welcome, Meredith." He turned to address Blythe once more.

"Absolutely, we can discuss your acquiring our milk, if you and Lucas would be willing to supply us with a sheep or two in exchange. Barter, don't you know?" He flashed a conspiratorial grin. "Keep Moorland's and the Inland Revenue's noses out of it, eh what?"

Blythe explained for Meredith's benefit, "The Inland Revenue is the UK's version of America's Internal Revenue Service...the IRS."

William nodded and then said, "Susanna's of a mind to start a rug weaving business and she'll need an economical source of wool, so she tells me. You know, crafty items to sell on the roadside to the holiday makers." He glanced toward the door to the creamery offices. "We'll do a trade, shall we?" he asked softly, "and supply, say...half of your milk requirements over the summer months...with the big boys at Moorland's none the wiser, yes?"

"Exactly!" Blythe agreed. She had already described to Meredith what a stranglehold the big dairy processing businesses had both on the farmers who produced the milk, and enterprises like the Barton Hall Tea Room, that bought their dairy products. "And what a great idea of Susanna's to weave rugs. She is such a talented artist. If she does some for the bath and boudoir, tell her we can sell them in our gift shop."

While this exchange was going on, Meredith watched Sebastian shift uncomfortably in his Wellington boots and studiously stare at the scenery to his left.

"Lieutenant Pryce," she ventured. "Could I speak to you for a sec?"

With a look of surprise to hear Meredith address him directly, he nodded and then the pair stepped aside from William and Blythe's on-going conversation.

"I'm not a lieutenant any longer. Just call me Sebastian," he said.

"Sebastian, then," Meredith began. "This is a little bit embarrassing." She glanced at Rex whose nose was pressed eagerly through the open section of the Mini's backseat window. "I can see Rex, there, is a very sweet dog, and well-trained, of course."

Sebastian merely continued to lock glances with her, but remained silent.

"And...well...I-I think you should know that my Corgi came into season this morning. I'd lost track of when that was due to happen, given our trip here, and all...and so your dog's reaction to Holly...um...well, it wasn't really *his* fault. The scent she was giving off was near irresistible to a boy with a trained nose like Rex's, don't you imagine? Therefore, I felt I should apologize to you for my...my...overreaction to your telling me to control my dog."

"So you're saying that one can't really blame Rex for—"

"For trying to get friendly? No. If I'd remembered Holly was coming into season, I'd have never let her off the lead with another dog around. The incident at Barton Hall was really *my* fault. I'm so sorry, especially as Rex is still in training. It wasn't a fair test, at all."

Sebastian had a look of mild amazement etching his handsome features, but all he said was, "Good to know that. Thanks."

Meredith waited, wondering if he would also apologize for *his* sharp remarks, but when he remained silent, she shrugged. "I guess you can't fight Mother Nature in these things."

Sebastian cocked his head, the faintest smile beginning to crease his lips.

"Let's just say yesterday's events provided my dog and me with an interesting learning exercise." There was another pause and then he added, "Do forgive me if I was a bit…preemptory in what I said to you yesterday."

"You were kinda *mean*," Meredith corrected him, softening her words with a broad grin, "at least your tone of voice was, but I understand. Rex's pretty young, isn't he, and still being exposed to new situations, and you probably have high hopes for him? I suppose you'd have to call what happened 'a slip?'"

"Yes. Not good. Even for a novice. He's two. Just certified, but still on probation." He laughed shortly. "Rather like me with you, am I right?"

Meredith could feel warmth invade her cheeks but she couldn't resist flashing him another grin.

"Hey, you apologized…sort of…which makes you what we'd call in Wyoming a straight-shooter."

"A what?" Sebastian asked with a puzzled expression.

"A straight-shooter? Someone who tells it like it is. I think the expression comes from the idea of a gun shooting accurately…from the barrel to the target. You know, like a cowboy who can shoot a can off a fence post? He shoots *straight*. Oh…I give up!" she said, exasperated with her attempt to translate American slang.

"You mean someone who just says what's on his mind, without prevarication?"

"Ah…yes. I think you've described it exactly."

She laughed suddenly. "Hey, I have an idea! Why don't we just start over, do you want to?" She stuck out her hand in an offer to shake his and suddenly wondered if she were actually batting her eyelashes.

Sebastian hesitated, and then reached out and grasped hers.

"Hello," he said with mock formality. "I'm Sebastian Pryce. As I said, no longer a lieutenant in the Royal Army, but nearly qualified as a large animal vet—that is, when I'm not volunteering for search and rescue. I work for William, here, as assistant animal manager at his dairy a few miles up the road."

"Ah, a Cornwall cattle wrangler!" Meredith found the warmth of his hand somehow comforting. "And a large animal doctor, no less."

"And you, miss?" he said, with a slight bow.

"I'm Meredith Champlin..." she replied, adopting his teasing, formal tone while giving his hand another shake. "A cowgirl-sheep herder from Wyoming. I used to be a nurse and—"

"Have you given that up?" he interrupted with genuine surprise.

"For the summer I have," she replied, withdrawing her hand and adding, "and maybe forever. At least the branch of nursing I was in."

"Ah, yes. Blythe said you've taken care of very ill children."

"I have a specialty in pediatric intensive care, so they're *very* sick kids, for sure."

"And your pet therapy work? I remember her mentioning you ran a service like that at your hospital?"

"That's the part of my job I loved the most. Spending this time in Cornwall over the summer will give me a chance to think about a lot of things and consider all my options, now that I'm the official guardian of an eleven-year-old." She glanced at her cousin and lowered her voice a notch. "I'll also be giving Blythe a hand at Barton Hall. And we'll see if we can...cheer up her niece, my ward. She lost her mother a few weeks ago and—" She looked down with embarrassment and mumbled, "That's probably way too much information, isn't it?"

"Sounds like an excellent way to spend the next few months," he said with a sincerity that startled her, given their initial angry exchanges. "Lovely to meet you, Ms.

Champlin."

"Meredith," she insisted. "Out West, where I come from, you get introduced and you call each other by first names, right off the bat."

"Meredith and Sebastian, it is, then," he countered. He turned toward the car, gesturing at Rex. "And may I *re*introduce our Cornish Romeo."

Meredith extended her hand, and with her palm down, leaned toward the Mini's open window, allowing his dog to sniff the backs of her fingers.

"Delighted to meet you *officially*, T-Rex," she offered. "And believe me, *so* was Holly!"

Sebastian hesitated and then asked, "May I inquire why Holly hasn't been spayed? I thought most pet therapy dogs are, in order to avoid…problems in the field."

Meredith knew that the look she gave him was a bit sheepish. "I was going to have that done before she turned two, but friends in Wyoming wanted Corgi puppies and I was going to breed Holly once, before having her altered." She gave a little shrug indicating how her life spun out of control recently. "Then my cousin—Blythe's sister—died in that plane crash, and the next thing I knew, I had her fifth grade daughter in my keeping. My 'To Do' list kind of fell by the wayside."

Sebastian nodded. "I could certainly understand how that could happen."

Just then, Blythe tapped Meredith on the shoulder.

"Well, Cuz, shall we go pick up our milk order?" She and William Jenner had wound up their conversation, agreeing to work out the details of trading two sheep for a bi-monthly supply of milk and cream.

Nodding agreement, Meredith leaned toward the Mini's open window and said, "Goodbye, Rex. Be a good boy, now."

"He'll *try*," Sebastian replied, both hands in his pockets as he smiled first at her and then at his dog. The effect was dazzling, Meredith thought, completely transforming his solemn, chiseled features.

William regarded the trio and cocked a sandy eyebrow as if to say, "Well! What do we have here?"

Just then, Blythe's mobile phone rang. Fishing it out of her handbag, she frowned to see who was calling.

"Yes, Richard? What?" she asked, with a worried frown. "No, Lucas has gone to Plymouth for the day to see his bankers. Well, what does Matthew *say*? Janet *what?*"

"Oh, blast!" Meredith muttered. "What's that kid done *now?*"

# CHAPTER 4

Meredith searched Blythe's expression for a clue as to what was transpiring at the other end of her cousin's mobile phone.

"Okay, okay, Richard. You've done exactly right," Blythe said, nodding. "Keep looking along the cliffs near Painter's Cottage. And be sure you have your mobile with you." She paused, and then added, "Yes, but the signal's a bit spotty down near the cliffs, I've found, so you may have to walk halfway back up toward the Hall to call or text us if you find anything. We'll just collect our milk order at Moorland's and come right home. Yes, have Mrs. Quiller look after Lucy and Matthew till we get there. No, no, tell Matthew it's *not* his fault...not at all. We'll find her. No, I'm glad you called. All right. See you in a bit. Bye."

To the men she said, "Apparently, my niece and son Matthew and daughter Lucy had played together in the house all morning and everything seemed to be going along swimmingly." She turned to Meredith. "Then, after their lunch, Janet proposed a game of hide-and-seek outdoors, so Matthew took her to the big field skirted by the coast woods near Painter's Cottage at the bottom of Barton Hall Walk...and now, no one can find her. She's simply disappeared."

"She can be such a little wretch," Meredith exclaimed. "She could just be trying to upset everyone."

"But you told me that she's threatened to run away before," Blythe reminded her. "Do you think she'd actually do it?"

"She's completely capable of it, but she doesn't know the estate grounds or much of anything about where she is, so I doubt she'd really—" Meredith fell silent, and then added fearfully, "But there are those cliffs and caves that Richard was telling us about..."

Her sentence drifted off as a sense of dread and worry took hold. Here she was, Janet's legal guardian, and already the girl—

"Shall I follow you in my car?" Sebastian proposed without preamble. "We've got Rex, here, who might be of some help."

"Oh, Sebastian, that is so kind of you," Blythe said gratefully. "Maybe we can locate her without calling out the Search and Rescue Team, *again*."

"Well, let's see what we find when we get back to Barton Hall and assess the situation. We may have no choice but to call them in, I'm afraid. I'll just come now as a...a friend, if that suits."

Meredith sensed he was in a professional quandary. "Yes," she chimed, "I was about to ask you to come have that cup of tea and a scone that Blythe had promised you. You'll be our guest and then, if we need to, we'll call in the police and your team if it's deemed that Janet has truly gone off on her own somewhere."

"Right. That makes good sense," Sebastian replied, sounding relieved. "William, are you all right if I drop you back at the farm and then follow them?"

"You go ahead directly. I'll ring Susanna to come collect me here. We did what we had to do here at Moorlands," William nodded, and then added with a sly wink, "with nary a glimpse of you-know-who, thank the good Lord."

Meredith saw an annoyed scowl cross Sebastian's face, but all he said to the women was, "So, Meredith and I will head to Barton Hall straightaway to see what's what, shall we?" To William he added a gruff, "I'll ring you later."

"Fine," agreed William, seemingly oblivious that he had somehow gored Sebastian's ox. "And call us, too, if you need more help looking for the little scamp."

"Hope not, but thanks," Meredith replied.

Sebastian volunteered, "Let me help you load your car with your milk order."

Blythe replied, "I'll get William, here, and Moorland's people to do that. Why don't you and Meredith head out to Barton Hall right away and get a proper search started? I'll come along as quickly as I can, all right?"

"Right," Sebastian and Meredith said in unison, both striding toward the Mini.

"Sebastian, what's your mobile number?" called Blythe. "I'll ring you if they find Janet in the meantime."

Sebastian called out the number while Meredith quickly jumped into the front seat and fastened her seatbelt. Rex barked excitedly when Sebastian got into the car.

"Steady on, boy!" he said sternly, turning on the ignition and wheeling the car out of the parking lot. Within seconds, the three of them were speeding down the road toward Barton Hall. During the half hour drive back to the estate, Meredith gave a more circumspect recital of the information about Janet that she'd earlier given to Blythe.

"She's probably the youngest "Ugly American" you're likely to encounter," she warned with a rueful glance across the short distance that separated them in the Mini's front seat, "but I'm keeping the faith that an eleven-year-old can change her negative attitude with some love and attention, which both Blythe and I are trying to give her. So far, I'm sorry to report, neither empathy nor understanding, nor even a good dose of Wyoming tough love has done a thing to improve the situation. And now—"

Meredith felt her throat catch and fought the wave of emotion that filled her chest.

"We'll find her," he said with conviction. Sebastian didn't take his hands off the wheel, but his sympathetic glance in her direction soothed her ragged nerves to a surprising degree. "She hasn't been gone long and her little legs can't have carried her very far." He cast a glance through his windshield at clear skies overhead. "Thankfully, the weather's holding."

"But the cliffs…and those caves that fill with water at high tide!"

"We don't even know if that's the direction she headed."

"Oh, God, Sebastian, if anything happens to her, I don't know what I'll do. She's been a royal pain since the moment her damn father committed her to my care, but I want to help her! Blythe wants to help her…it's just we don't know *how!*"

By this time, Sebastian's small car was speeding up the long drive toward the gravel turnaround in front of the looming castle walls.

"We'll find her," he assured her once again. He glanced over his shoulder to the back seat. "Won't we, Rex?"

Sebastian's Mini came to a halt under the portico just as Richard bolted out the front door.

"I saw the car turn into the drive," he said, panting from exertion. "Hello, Sebastian…did you get a call from Blythe about this youngster going missing? What luck you were nearby!"

"William Jenner and I just happened to meet at Moorland's. No sign of young Janet?" Sebastian asked.

"Nothing since earlier this morning. I've asked Mrs. Quiller to stay with Matthew, who's quite upset."

"I'll go speak to him and Lucy," Meredith said quickly. "He needs to know from me that this is absolutely not his fault!"

Sebastian nodded and looked at her strangely. "That's really kind of you," he said, as if she had bestowed some sort of absolution on him as well. Then he turned to Richard. "Tell me where you've looked already while Meredith gets me a piece of Janet's clothing. Rex isn't trained to look for any specific human, but it can't hurt."

Meredith immediately sprinted for the front door, calling over her shoulder, "Too bad I can't have Holly looking, too. She knows Janet's scent so well by now."

"We don't want Rex distracted, do we now?" Sebastian called back.

Smiling in spite of the seriousness of the situation, Meredith paused by the door. "Oh, for sure not. I'll lock her up in the library so she doesn't drive your boy wild."

"Very good of you," Sebastian replied. They both recognized that a female dog in season was the last thing they needed.

Meredith entered the front door and sped down the hallway and into the big kitchen at the rear of the castle. Mrs. Quiller sat at the large oak table with Matthew on one side and a wide-eyed Lucy on the other. Lucy had Holly next to her on the bench and was caressing the Corgi's velvety, pointed ears. Meredith swiftly announced that help had arrived and that they were sure to find Janet in short order.

She put her arms around Matthew and said, "Janet can be very naughty sometimes, so I want to be sure you understand that you have done nothing wrong, Matthew. You've been a very good cousin and a friend."

"But Janet is lost," Lucy wailed.

"She'll soon be found," Mrs. Quiller reassured the child, but she raised her worried gaze questioningly at Meredith.

"You're not to worry, any of you," Meredith assured everyone, but despite her words, a hollow feeling was growing in the pit of her stomach. Matthew, too, looked as if he was about to cry, but before he started she said, "You'll see. Everything will be all right. And you were a dear boy to be willing to play with her all morning. You're a good friend," she repeated urgently. "I'll be back soon, so you wait here with Mrs. Q."

Holly jumped off the bench and followed along as Meredith ran up the servants' stairs to the raft of bedrooms along the upper, wood-paneled hallway. She swiftly found a blue cardigan that Janet had tossed thoughtlessly on the floor in a corner of her room and noted that none of the child's other possessions, including the rest of her clothing and a small, bright pink, wheeled suitcase, appeared to be missing.

In less than three minutes, she returned down stairs, swiftly shooed Holly into the library and closed the door, and returned to the drive, waving the sweater like a flag. Richard had just finished filling in Sebastian with details of the search thus far.

"We scoured the sheds bordering Home Farm...looked down by the old Limekiln Cottage...and searched all through the barns. I've had my helper scout around Painter's Cottage, which was the last place Matthew saw Janet, but so far, nothing there, either."

"How about Hemmick Beach?" Sebastian asked Richard, opening the car door so Rex could jump onto the ground. He fastened the dog's leash. "It's less than a mile to there from Painter's Cottage by the Coastal Path. Let's head down Barton Hall Walk and allow Rex to check around the fields again where the children were playing hide-and-seek. From there we can search Portluney Beach near the gate at Bottom Lodge, and then go along the cliffs toward Hemmick if we have to."

The trio soon plunged into a leafy tunnel, thick with English oak and dense underbrush, where dappled sunlight filtered through the trees and arched overhead. Meredith felt herself enveloped by the cool, green, shadowed habitat. On the right, some fifty yards down the path, she spied the gnarled roots of an enormous oak that had pushed up thick, bark-covered tentacles from the moist ground, forming small caves that a child could hide in.

"Janet! Janet!" She called insistently. "If you are here, you *must* come out. We've got everyone looking for you. We're all worried. *Janet!*"

Other than the rustle of the wind through the trees and a scurrying of animal life somewhere off in the thickets, silence was the only answer.

Eventually they emerged into an open public pathway with an iron sign enameled white with the black letters "Coastal Path" marking the entrance to a network of trails that skirted the cliffs for miles. The three of them, plus Rex, climbed over a wooden stile that consisted of four spiraling steps, cleverly designed to allow humans access to a broad field while keeping the sheep from getting out on the road that bisected the land near the cliffs from the rest of the estate's higher ground. The air was redolent with the scent of freshly mowed hay in the adjoining fields and Meredith could faintly hear surf crashing on the other side of a pasture dotted with woolly creatures raised on the estate. Gulls circled overhead, and near the cliff, she spotted a chimney rising from a stone dwelling that could only be Painter's Cottage.

When they entered through another wooden gate to the field skirted by a wood, Richard pointed to the area where Matthew had told him that he and Janet had played hide-and-seek near the cottage and the surrounding trees and hedges. Sebastian asked Meredith to hand him the sweater.

"Here, boy...here boy," he said, allowing the dog to bury his nose in Janet's clothing. To Meredith he added, "Rex is trained to bark as an indicator he's either picked up the scent of a human, or actually found someone...but I'm curious to see if this jumper will help."

"Jumper?" she asked. "Oh...you mean sweater, don't you? A cardigan, yes?"

The corners of Sebastian's mouth twitched slightly as she translated for herself.

"That's right," he confirmed.

Meredith's breath caught at the brutal reality that a search and rescue dog was now the means by which they might find her eleven-year-old ward.

Sebastian unfastened the leash from Rex's collar, patted him on the head, and commanded, "Find... *find*, Rex!

Sebastian, Meredith, and Richard had to move swiftly to keep up with the Border Collie racing across a field full of sheep that inhabited the same land as Painter's Cottage, a dwelling perched near the cliff overlooking the English Channel. Rex worked his way down field in a pattern of elongated figure eights. Eventually they arrived at a dirt track that led to the door of the small stone building, lichen clinging to its slate roof, and a many-paned floor-to-ceiling artist's window built into the front wall, looking forlornly out to sea. The cottage, so named because a long-dead member of the family had once painted seascapes there in the eighteenth century, sat a mere thirty feet from a sheer cliff with a view of Dodman Point to the east, and a good mile or so from Barton Hall itself. The door was firmly locked, so there was no need to look inside.

"If they were playing hide-and-seek near the cottage, I can't imagine where she could have gone without Matthew seeing her!" Meredith exclaimed as the wind off the Channel whipped her hair into her face and stung her eyes.

"Let's have a look in the wood and then go down to the big beach," Sebastian said. "Rex doesn't seem to be catching any scent here at all."

The dog ran back and forth around the small thicket of trees, but didn't probe deeply and didn't bark.

"He's not getting anything," Sebastian said, shaking his head.

The trio peered down fifty feet, over the cliff directly in front of the cottage, to what Richard explained was normally a narrow strip of sand and pebbles edged with larger boulders. The tide was in, crashing against the rocks below, erasing any sight of a beach. Sebastian stood, with Rex by his side, gazing down at the churning water with a strange, thousand-yard stare.

"The high tide is about at its fullest, now, and lasts an hour or more," Richard said. "I can't see her attempting to go down there to hide when there's no sand, now, can you, Sebastian?"

As if waking from a deep sleep, Sebastian pulled his gaze away from the pounding surf. "I pray not, but if we don't find her soon," he said grimly, "we'd better put in a call to the police who will make the decision as to whether my volunteer group should get involved, or initiate the Coast Guard or the Air Force. It's best for them to operate in the daylight, should they think it necessary to launch a boat or helicopter."

"What if she fell?" Meredith said softly, her voice barely audible above the incessant wind. "What if she were running as part of the game, and she *fell* down there?"

"It's always a possibility," Sebastian said. He pulled out a set of binoculars from his backpack and spent several minutes scanning the rocks and steep sloping cliffs to his right and left. Then he reached for his mobile phone, glanced at the number of bars, and cursed. "Damn! No signal."

"You didn't spot anything at all?" Meredith asked anxiously.

"No," he replied shortly, and then added reassuringly, "That's a good sign, actually."

Once again, he raised the binoculars and swept them back and forth along the wider strip of sand known as Portluney Beach that lay two hundred yards beyond the cliffs where they stood braced against the wind. It was utterly deserted, with only seagulls flying overhead.

"I think we'd better go back to the main house," Sebastian declared, lowering the field glasses. "Maybe she's turned up by now." He glanced down at Rex who sat motionless by his handler's side, neither sniffing the wind nor looking agitated in the slightest. "Our search team or the Coast Guard can scour Hemmick Beach."

By the time the trio and Rex retraced their steps to the castle, Blythe's car was parked in the inner courtyard at the rear of the mansion. Meredith called out as soon as they approached the kitchen door, and then spotted Blythe taking off her coat in the mudroom. Sebastian commanded his dog to lie down on the back step as they all trooped into the large kitchen with ancient copper pots hanging in a cluster above their heads. Mrs. Quiller still sat with the children at a long wooden table, reading them a story.

"No luck?" Blythe asked *sotto voce*, with a worried glance in young Matthew's direction.

"Not yet," Sebastian said.

"And you?" Meredith asked Blythe. "So you didn't see

anything on the road as you came in?"

Blythe merely shook her head.

Sebastian spoke under his breath. "May I speak to you both for a moment? I think we need to make some calls."

Meredith asked, "Do you think it's all right if I put Holly on a leash and go out the front door to let her do her business? She's been in the house for hours."

"I'll secure Rex back here," Sebastian said, "and it should be fine." He handed her the blue cardigan. "Would you hold on to this for me for a bit?" He turned to Richard. "Can you get us a map of the entire estate?"

"Certainly," he replied, "there's one in the library." With Meredith striding on ahead down the hall carrying Holly's leash, she and Richard walked toward the castle's magnificent book-lined room whose windows faced the north lawn that sloped down to the small, placid lake. As soon as Meredith opened the library door, Holly greeted her excitedly, running in circles, and then racing over to the floor-to-ceiling bookshelves on the south wall.

"Come on, girl," she chided. "Let's get your leash on you while the going is good. Come on, Holly...potty break."

While Richard rifled through a desk drawer looking for the estate map, the Corgi continued to run in circles and repeatedly crossed to same bookcases while whining loudly.

Blythe, Sebastian, Matthew and Lucy suddenly appeared at the library door.

"Blythe agrees...we're calling the police in St. Austell first," Sebastian announced. "They'll assign a missing person officer called the Lead Search Advisor who takes charge of the situation and summons personnel from the various organizations, as needed." Then he noticed Holly's frantic movements. "Something wrong?"

"I don't know what's going on with her," Meredith

said. "She's acting very wiggy."

Holly started barking and pawing at the bookcase as if she were digging for a bone.

"She's barking at the hidey hole!" Matthew exclaimed, pointing. "Holly wanted to play hide-and-seek with us in there, but Janet said 'no fair' and so we—"

"You played hide-and-seek in the smugglers passageway?" Blythe asked quickly.

"Yes," Matthew said with a worried look in his mother's direction, "but just for a little while 'cause Janet said she was bored and wanted to go outside. That was all right, Mummy, wasn't it? You've let us before. I told her about the hidey-hole but said she didn't believe it was there, so—"

Blythe said quickly, "It's all right, sweetheart. As long as you told Mrs. Q where you were."

"She knew we were in the house playing hide-and-seek, but not in the hidey-hole," Matthew replied with a guilty look. "We weren't in there long…"

Blythe turned to Meredith and Sebastian explaining as she strode toward the bookcase, "There's a tunnel behind here that used to lead all the way to Portluney Cove. The Teague and Trevelyan ancestors would sneak port and fine lace into the country to avoid the King's tax collectors. It's sealed off now about a hundred yards from the house, but the children love to—"

"You don't think—?" Meredith interjected.

Without answering, Blythe extended her fingers beneath the middle shelf on the right side. A soft "click" resounded in the room and the entire bookcase swung inward. Holly dashed past Blythe's feet and disappeared into a dark hole. Her continued barking grew fainter as the dog ran further away from them.

"Where's a flashlight?" Meredith asked hurriedly.

"You mean a torch?" Sebastian asked.

"I'll go fetch one," Richard volunteered.

"No, no! I've got one right here," Sebastian announced. He'd brought in the CSRT backpack he'd carried to the cliffs and it was now at his feet. Digging into a side pocket, he easily found what he was looking for and immediately strode through the open space beside the bookcase, his light casting a strong beam to illuminate the way. Meredith, Blythe, Richard, and Matthew—holding Lucy's hand—quickly followed suit, entering a tunnel that sloped slightly downward. Less than fifty feet beyond the open bookcase, there was a small, shadowy form curled up on the dirt floor, arms flailing above her head to ward off Holly, who was happily licking Janet's face.

Meredith ran to her side. "Oh my God, Janet! We were so worried! Are you all right? How did you get *in* here?" To her dog Meredith said sharply, "Holly, *sit-stay!*" and the dog immediately complied with her commands.

The pudgy, eleven-year-old girl looked up at the adults and two children that had formed a circle around her and thrust out her lower lip.

"I got tired of the wind and cold down by the cottage, so while Matthew covered his eyes and counted to one hundred, I went into the woods and just came back here to hide."

"In the hidey-hole?" Matthew said admiringly. "You found the secret button on your own?"

"Easy-peasy," she replied with a smug smile. "I came in the front door, tip-toed real fast into here, and pushed the button under the shelf. Once I got into the tunnel and shut the door, I waited and waited for you," she said accusingly to Matthew. "When you never came, I tried to get back into the library, but I couldn't find the stupid button on *this* side of the bookcase that would let me back in." She pulled herself to a standing position, brushed off some dirt that had collected on the front of her blue jeans, and added in a defensive tone, "I got real bored, Matthew. You don't play the game very well."

Meredith was incensed. "He thought you would play by the *rules*, Janet! Why in heaven's name didn't you pound on the back of the bookcase to let someone know where you were? " she demanded. "You must have heard Holly barking after I put her in the library before we left to search the cliffs!"

"I'm jet-lagged, okay?" she retorted crossly. "I got tired of waiting for Matthew and I fell asleep. I didn't hear your old dog barking until she started licking my face. It was yucky."

Meredith leaned weakly against the tunnel carved so many centuries earlier by smugglers in league with Lucas Teague's Barton ancestors who wished to avoid the taxing of their smuggled wares. She covered her face with both hands and felt tears of relief and frustration wash over her. Then an arm encircled her shoulders and she was aware that Sebastian was pulling her against his chest while Holly had decided to snuggle against her feet.

"She's unharmed, and that's the main thing, isn't it?" he said in a low voice.

"Yes, but—" Meredith murmured.

"Young lady," Blythe said firmly, leaning forward and cupping Janet's face between her slender fingers. "You...Cousin Meredith...and I are going to have a long conversation later and go over the rules that prevail at Barton Hall—and she and I *both* expect you to obey them."

"You can't tell me what to do," Janet replied sullenly.

"Mummy makes *us* obey the rules," piped in Lucy.

Before Janet could protest any further, Meredith stepped away from the circle of Sebastian's arms and spoke up.

"We *are* telling you what to do!" she added sternly to Janet. "Aunt Blythe and I *are* the 'boss of you,' do you understand? And Rule Number One around here is: *always* let people know where you are. We were so scared something bad had happened to you."

"Yeah," Janet retorted, "like you really care."

"We *do* care!" chimed in Matthew. "I thought you might have fallen off the cliff and it would have been all my fault. I felt terrible, didn't I, Mummy?"

"I know you did, sweetheart," Blythe said soothingly. "We all felt terrible when we'd lost our cousin Janet. We love you, sweetheart!"

"Well, I don't love *you*, and neither did my mommy!" she snapped at Blythe.

"Oh, Janet," Meredith said with a sigh, "don't you understand? We didn't want anything terrible to happen to you. We were scared to death. *All* of us!" she added with a meaningful look at Blythe.

For the first time, Janet looked slightly chastened, but mumbled, "Yeah...sure."

Blythe clapped her hands, unfazed, apparently, by Janet's invective. "How about we celebrate Janet's being found, safe and sound, with cocoa for all in the kitchen?"

"And biscuits for Rex and Holly!" Matthew said excitedly, reaching down to pet the Corgi still sitting patiently beside Meredith's feet. "She and Rex worked *so* hard to find you," he confided to his young cousin. "C'mon, Janet, I'll race you to the kitchen."

Ignoring the adults, Janet scrambled to her feet and the three youngsters ran down the smugglers' tunnel with the rest of them silently following, single file, toward the lights shining in the library. When they emerged into the room, standing in the opposite doorway was Lucas Teague.

"Well!" he said. "I wondered where everyone was. I walked in the pantry door, and the only one I saw before three children streaked past me was a well-behaved Border Collie, condemned to the back step." He paused, recognizing Sebastian Pryce among the family group. "Oh no…not Quiller again!"

Meredith laughed and patted Sebastian's arm. "Don't worry, Lucas. Mr. Quiller is safe in his cottage. We'll tell you what happened later, but Sebastian's here to finally collect his cup of tea." She turned to flash her comforter a watery smile. "Or do you prefer cocoa?" she teased.

"A brandy's more like it," pronounced Blythe, pointing to a console table against the library wall with a silver tray laden with a raft of liquor bottles.

"But first let me take poor Holly out for a bit," Meredith proposed, leaning down to finally attach the Corgi's leash to her collar. "She's earned it!"

"Lucas, darling," Blythe said to her husband, "you cannot imagine everything that's happened here today. While you gents have a drink, we'll get the children fed their dinner. The paying guests are all checked in, so I let Mrs. Quiller head home and we'll have a nice bit of cold chicken later—and whatever else we have in the 'fridge." She turned to Sebastian. "Please do stay to supper. We'd love your company, and besides, offering you a meal is the least we can do."

Sebastian appeared to hesitate and then nodded. "Let me just ring up William and Susanna and let them know all's well."

# CHAPTER 5

A few minutes later, Meredith tied one of Mrs. Quiller ample aprons around her slender waist and began to slice thin pieces of roasted chicken from a half-consumed bird and line them up on a platter surrounded by boiled potatoes garnished with herbs from Richard's Home Farm plot.

"I'll slice some tomatoes, shall I?" Richard asked. "We had our first from the greenhouse today. That glass building is about to fall down, it's so ancient, but the plants are growing very well this year, even so."

"Perfect," replied Meredith, adding for Sebastian's benefit, "this will be a supper based on 'what hast thou in the house?' as my mother used to say."

Richard soon had a plateful of fresh tomatoes that he garnished with basil leaves chopped to a fine *chiffonade*, along with sprinklings of fresh pepper, olive oil, and red wine vinegar.

"What can I do to help?" asked Sebastian. He leaned against the wall near the ancient stone hearth that was no longer used for cooking in the castle, and sipped a glass of red wine Lucas had given him instead of Blythe's recommended brandy.

"Feed my dog?" Meredith asked, her hands coated with chicken grease. "And how about Rex? Can he eat a foreigner's food? "

"And be quite grateful for it too," Sebastian replied cheerfully. "But I've got an emergency tin in my car if it's a bother."

"No bother. Poor guy, he's been languishing out back forever." She directed the guest to fill a bowl with water and another with dog food stored in the back pantry. "Let's feed him first on the back step, and then I'll refill these for Holly," she added, nodding in the direction of the Corgi snoozing near the Aga cooker on the far side of the kitchen.

Blythe appeared at the bottom of the old servants' staircase, having put the children to bed with a light supper.

"Ah, you are angels!" exclaimed the lady of the household to those assembled, noting that their meal consisting of leftovers was nearly ready to be served. "And you've already set the table!" She turned to Sebastian, who had just come in via the pantry from feeding Rex on the back doorstep. "I hope you don't mind eating ranch house style in the kitchen? We save the formal dining room for our visitors. Less to keep clean."

Lucas, despite being Lord of the Manor, gladly set plates and glassware beside the flatware and napkins already placed on the long, wooden table. Soon the group was seated, each passing the food from person to person in a manner Meredith assumed Blythe had instituted that was reminiscent of family dinners in Wyoming.

"So darling, how did things go in Plymouth with the little Men in Gray?" Blythe asked her husband as she took her first bite of cold chicken.

"Ah...our Almighty Bankers? Well, at least they didn't cancel our line of credit. However, they urged us to find even more ways to economize around here, and declared no more renovations for the next while."

"And I've *so* been dreaming of new curtains for the tea

room and a new greenhouse for the garden." Blythe sighed.

"The Men in Gray believe we've sunk quite enough of your capital left over from your Hollywood days into this pile of stones, my darling. And I quite agree with them."

"Oh well, Lucas. Never mind," she said with a resigned shrug, giving his hand an affection squeeze. "It could have been worse."

"I'm afraid our most pressing problems are closer at hand," Richard said, spearing a potato from the platter as it was passed. "Mrs. Q. confided in me today that she can't find anyone she trusts to look after John and thinks she's going to have to cut back even further on her hours here."

"Oh Lord," Blythe moaned. "Now that *is* a problem. We *have* to have a cook other than yours truly."

"I can help with that," Meredith interjected. "I'm no great chef, but I could learn to make scones, I imagine. And certainly, I could hostess or serve during afternoon tea at the shop."

"Absolutely not," Lucas replied. "You're a guest in our home."

"I'm a *cousin*...and considered family, I hope," Meredith protested. "I want to pull my weight while I'm here. In fact, I've been racking my brains trying to think how I could contribute to the overall Barton Hall enterprises."

"Well, *I* have an idea."

All eyes shifted to Sebastian who, to this point, hadn't yet participated in what had essentially turned into a family meeting.

What idea?" Blythe asked curiously.

"It's probably not my place, but given that Meredith coordinated the pet therapy service at her hospital and is so good with dogs, what if she taught obedience and dog agility classes here? From what I've seen since I moved back to Cornwall, half the county's canines could use instruction."

"Truly?" Meredith asked, surprised by Sebastian's complimentary evaluation of her dog handling skills. She felt her excitement mount at the notion of having a project that might help ease her hosts' strained financial circumstances.

Blythe clapped her hands. "What a brilliant idea, Sebastian! Meredith, this would suit your talents *so* well, don't you think? What's your view, Lucas?"

The laird of Barton Hall paused in thought and then nodded. "I think it's rather scandalous to put our guest in harness so soon after her arrival, but, actually, I think it's a splendid idea and I don't think it would cost that much to launch. We've certainly plenty of fields for it...and plenty of sheep to serve as distractions."

"And she could explore the need to train service dogs for the various pet therapy programs at hospitals and nursing homes around here," Sebastian added. "We get people wanting to volunteer with their dogs quite often for search and rescue work, but usually the animals would be better suited for less vigorous service, yet they still need training."

Blythe turned toward Meredith. "The business would be yours, of course, Mer, but having a Cornwall canine obedience school on the property would be one more reason for the public to visit Barton Hall, the tea room and shops, and the nursery!"

"I wouldn't think of keeping all the money," Meredith countered firmly. "Not as long as I'm sleeping under your roof and eating your food. Any earnings go into our joint coffers, okay?"

"Well, let's not let that debate stop such a grand idea," Lucas said, his eyes alight with interest. "We'll sort out all those details, but in the meantime, it wouldn't take much to fence off a section of that broad field down near Painter's Cottage, where people can park in that broad section by the side of the road."

"Do you think there'd be any interest if I taught local dogs sheep herding as well?" Meredith wondered aloud. "I haven't done it for years, but I gave classes in that when I was in 4H."

"What's 4H?" Richard asked curiously.

Blythe put her hand over her heart. "Why, you Cornish are in the presence of two sterling former members of a youth organization dedicated to teaching the art of ranching, farming, and animal husbandry!"

In unison, she and Meredith said in a sing-song, "The 4H credo: I pledge my *head* to clearer thinking...my *heart* to greater loyalty...my *hands* to larger service...and my *health* to better living for my 4H club, my community, my country, and my *world!*"

"My God!" Lucas said, laughing, and the others clapped enthusiastically in response to Meredith and Blythe's performance. "We've been married all this time, Blythe, and you never told me about this secret coven you both belonged to in Wyoming."

"Well, I quit 4H at about thirteen when I got into rodeo riding," Blythe explained with a grin, "but Meredith, here, was a total star. Didn't you win some state award or something?"

Meredith darted a glance in Sebastian's direction and revealed hesitantly, "Well...I won a blue ribbon for a program that taught high school kids my age how to train smaller dogs to do sheep herding. That's how I fell in love with Corgis...long before I learned they were so fashionable over here, thanks to your Queen!"

"Well, that's settled, then," Lucas said. "The part of the lower field near the cottage shall be yours."

"But what about helping out Blythe?" Meredith objected. "What if Mrs. Quiller completely retires or something..."

"I've known this was coming for some time now," Blythe interjected somberly. "For the moment, what if we divide your time until we can find someone to help out in the kitchen and the tea room itself? That will give you a chance to make a business plan and get organized about your dog training classes, and still fill in when Mrs. Q can't tend the tea room or cook in the kitchen. Meanwhile, I'll be on the lookout around Gorran Haven and elsewhere to hire and train someone who can gradually take over her duties. It's inevitable, I'm afraid."

"But how will we get customers for the dog training classes?" Meredith fretted. "At home, getting people involved in pet therapy training and small dog sheep herding was all by word of mouth. Except for you folks sitting around this table, I don't know a single soul in Cornwall, and certainly no one knows me—or my credentials."

"But *I* know nearly every dog owner in the entire county," Sebastian declared. "And the good news is, there's not one person in these parts that can train in obedience, agility, sheep herding, *and* preparation for training service dogs. Maybe you and I could even develop a kind of preparatory search and rescue dog training unit together. As I said, I get calls all the time from people wanting to volunteer for the Cornwall Search and Rescue Team, but qualifying their dogs is always an issue. It takes time to judge if a dog is going to make the grade or not. Believe me, around here, there are a limited number of people with the multiple skills that *you* have, Meredith."

"Wow..." she said on a long breath. Then she frowned. "Do you think I could get something like this up and running before too much of the summer had passed? And what about a work permit, and red tape and things like that?"

Lucas rose from his chair and started gathering the dinner plates nearest him to deposit in the sink behind him. "You forget," he said with mock solemnity, "I am 'Sir' Lucas Barton-Teague, Life Peer, and a county magistrate, to boot. I'm sure I can have a word with the proper officials and work something out. Maybe Sebastian, here, can serve as your 'sponsor' or something? He's a respected man in the community…associated with dogs, search and rescue, dairy cattle—and he's also a vet! What do you say, Sebastian? Can you help us with this, though, frankly, it's rather unorthodox for an English chap like me to admit Barton Hall needs all the revenue sources it can get." He paused and then added, "In fact, I'd appreciate it if you'd keep all of this under your cap, if you will."

"Certainly. Everything you've said here is strictly confidential," Sebastian replied as everyone at the table shifted their glances to their guest. "Although I'm not sure if…"

For a moment, Meredith thought Sebastian's apparent hesitation meant he might bolt their company right then and there. She jumped into the conversation with her best Wyoming drawl.

"Look, I don't want to put the poor man on the spot to serve as my sponsor. He's a busy guy, with a lot of other responsibilities. Let's wait until—"

"I'd be glad to help Meredith get this started," Sebastian interjected. And for the second time that day, he offered to shake her hand, sealing the proposition. "After all, it was *my* idea. I can juggle my commitments and let's just see where it takes us."

Instead of shaking, she balled her right hand like a

prizefighter, feinted to one side, and bumped his knuckles in a mock salute.

"Fantastic! And once my sweet girl can rejoin mixed company in a week or so, why don't we make Rex and Holly—wearing their official service vests—our poster children?" she suggested, trying to contain her excitement. She felt relieved that she might have found a way to help Blythe and Lucas cope with the financial pinch they were in. "We can put pictures of the two dogs on the public notices announcing the class schedule!" Then she sobered and seized his hand in earnest. "Thanks, Sebastian. You've certainly done a lot for us today in about a million ways…"

"You're welcome," he replied, his gaze steady. After a long pause, he pushed away from the table, and prepared to take his leave. "And thank you, Bartons and Teagues," he added, glancing around at his dinner companions, "for the good company and delicious supper. Definitely an improvement over my normal fare."

Sebastian was well on his way to his car before Meredith spotted the flashlight he'd left on the kitchen sideboard. She grabbed it and bolted for the pantry door. She dashed across the inner courtyard, rounding the castle's corner just as her quarry had reversed direction and was heading back to the kitchen.

"Ooooff!" she exclaimed as they ran into each other. His arms went around her shoulders to steady them both and save her from falling down. Rex barked excitedly at their feet.

"You forgot—"

"I realized I'd left my—" they said in unison.

"My torch—" he said.

"Your flashlight—" she corrected him with a grin. "You left it on the kitchen counter."

Both laughing, Meredith stepped out of the circle of his

arms, handed him the lost object that he swiftly stowed in his backpack. "You know what Churchill said?"

"No, what?"

One of Sebastian's rare grins emphasized his high cheekbones and the slight shadow of stubble that now grazed his chin. "We Brits and you Yanks are separated by a common language, you know."

"Ah…" she replied, pointing to Rex, "but here's the good thing. You and I both speak 'Dog.' That should help a lot."

"That should," he said, taking a step closer. Eyes riveted on each other, the moment was framed like a snapshot on her iPhone, crisp and colorful—a memory she would keep filed somewhere so that she could gaze at it again.

Finally, she said, "Thank you especially, Sebastian, for all you did to help us find Janet."

"Holly found her."

"Yes, but you were ready to go into commando mode, and that was enormously comforting to me." Meredith impulsively hooked her arm in his and said, "Let me walk you to your car."

They strolled down the gravel path in the direction of the dark green Mini Cooper that Sebastian had left parked in the gloom beneath the castle's stone portico. The tall, silent walls of the stone castle and towers loomed above them and she felt his gaze slanting over to her side of the path.

"Becoming young Janet's legal guardian must have been a huge upheaval in your life."

"Huge," she agreed. "I was astounded, actually, that Ellie put me, specifically, in her will, but given her estrangement from everyone in her family, I was the only female relative left, I guess. Nobody ever thinks they're going to die at age thirty-seven."

"You left your work at the hospital to come here, and you left your home…"

"I pretty much left everything," she admitted.

"And a lonesome cowboy somewhere as well?"

Meredith was ludicrously pleased to realize he wanted to know if there was someone back home. For the first time in months, the thought of Shep O'Brien didn't make her feel so hollow inside.

"An *ex* boyfriend. It ultimately turned out that my cowboy drank more than was good for him, never paid his debts, and had a big problem telling the truth. I'd ended it a few months before I left, so there was nothing, really, to…"

"To prevent your coming over here for a while?" he finished the sentence for her.

"Exactly. Given everything that was going on in my life, I also needed a break from my job taking care of all those sick kids. It's a tremendously rewarding profession, mind you, because I really felt I was helping the children and their parents deal with some awfully tough stuff, but it's pretty heavy-duty, as I'm sure you, especially, can appreciate. So yes," she finished, "I was definitely up for a change of scene. Strange to say, the only thing I really miss at home right now is my Dad."

"Back in Wyoming?"

"He's there on his own, running the Crooked C."

"What's that?"

"Our sheep ranch."

"A rancher's daughter, like Blythe."

"The family business, I guess you could say."

"No wonder you fit in so well around here. And your mum?"

"Died when I was fourteen," Meredith replied, "which is probably why—as you witnessed today—I've been a total bust as a substitute mom. That's the reason I sought Blythe's help, even though she and Janet's mother were estranged for a decade before Ellie was killed in the crash. I just felt Blythe was the only person I *could* turn to."

"I've heard a bit about that history between the sisters from the very nice people I work for. You met William Jenner at Moorland's Creamery today. His wife Susanna is now quite a close friend of Blythe's. I'm sure you'll meet her eventually.

"Asking my cousin Blythe for help was my only option, really. She's got kids and tremendously good sense, as you've seen."

"So do you," he countered. "Have good sense, I mean."

"It hasn't gotten me very far with the eleven-year-old set."

"Don't worry…Janet knows you care and that's probably the key to all this."

"I don't think she thinks I care in the slightest. You heard what she said when we found her in the hidey-hole."

"She saw you cry with relief when we figured out where she was."

For a moment she flushed with embarrassment at the memory of Sebastian seeing her become so emotional when they first found Janet.

"But does *she* care?" Meredith exclaimed. "Care about anything, I mean? She just seems so…"

"Self-centered? Unpleasant? Disconnected?" he asked rhetorically. "Definitely all of the above. But behind all that—"

"Behind all that is a world of hurt. I understand that, but—"

"Exactly," he agreed. "Just knowing what started the problem doesn't always guarantee a solution, does it?"

"You are so right," she agreed glumly.

"You'll figure it all out eventually, I'm sure of it."

"Well...I have the summer to try," Meredith responded, not sounding convinced.

In a move she wasn't anticipating at all, Sebastian gently seized her chin between the fingers of his right hand.

"Only the summer, Nurse Meredith? Then I'd better not waste any time before I say goodnight," he murmured.

He leaned forward and ever so gently brushed his lips against hers. It was a light kiss, a kiss that could easily be misinterpreted, but his lips were soft and delicious and his breath laced with red wine, mildly intoxicating, she thought. Warily, Meredith observed him as he pulled back and held her glance. She read in it that he, too, was a bit wary, but for some strange reason, was willing to make a move in her direction. She inhaled the cooling night air and then exhaled, very slowly.

"We-ell-ll..." she breathed. "*That* was nice."

Sebastian tilted his head back and laughed in a way she'd never heard him do, deeply and with genuine mirth.

"It was *very* nice," he agreed. He put a hand on each shoulder and she felt the same peculiar warmth as before, only this time the liquid heat flowed down her arms as far as her fingertips. "And after today, what I can see most clearly, Meredith, is that you're a...what did you call me earlier?"

"Straight-shooter?"

"Yes! You're a straight shooter as well. I like that. And since I'm to be your official sponsor, shall I ring you tomorrow and we can plan when and where we should post the notices around the county announcing the launch of the 'Barton Hall Canine Obedience Academy?'"

She laughed at the stentorian tones he'd used to pronounce their new endeavor. Then she stood on tiptoe and bussed him lightly on the cheek. He looked at her questioningly, as if he never expected her to offer a sign of affection in return.

"That was just a token of my thanks for thinking I could teach dog obedience as a way to contribute to my keep around here," she explained, " and...for being a generous enough person to suggest it, given the rocky start we had."

"Well, let's just say our introduction was...memorable. Is there a good hour to ring you tomorrow to set up a time to post our adverts?"

"Adverts? Oh! You mean our flyers about the classes?" she asked, grinning as she "decoded" his English. "Call any time. I'll be in the kitchen all day, learning how to make Mrs. Quiller's scones." She patted Sebastian's dog on his furry head. "Goodnight, Mister T-Rex. Be a good boy." Then she raised her index finger and lightly touched Sebastian's lips. "Goodnight, Doctor Dog. Sweet dreams."

oᕱ

Sebastian's dreams that night weren't sweet in the slightest—they were positively prurient. He awoke near dawn the following morning with an erection that could have rendered him a champion pole-vaulter at the London Olympics. He stumbled over to his claw-and-ball bathtub behind the wooden screen, turned on the recently installed chrome shower apparatus arching above it full blast, and allowed cool water to cascade down his six-foot frame. His dreams, still vividly recalled, had placed Meredith Champlin and him on a picnic blanket near the cliff overlooking the Channel where they enjoyed *the* most amazing sexual encounter of recent memory.

*The mind can tell a man one thing, but the body doesn't lie.*

Meredith was the first woman in years to elicit this kind

of a response, he thought, running his hand through his wet hair.

*But near Hemmick Beach—of* all *places? Not bloody likely!*

What had prompted this extreme reaction to a single kiss on the lips, he wondered, besides her obvious charms, good looks, and a genuine *niceness* he found almost erotic— to say nothing of her passion for dogs? Answering his own question, he swiftly reminded himself that Meredith was only in Cornwall for the summer, according to what she'd said. Could it be that the veteran escape artist in *him* found that particular fact highly arousing and an irresistible challenge—and yet offered no danger of a long-term commitment?

No, by God, he genuinely *liked* the woman! On the drive home last night, he'd found himself wanting to know every little thing about her. Was the Wyoming cowboy ex-boyfriend still pining for her somewhere out West? Did her hospital give her a genuine leave-of-absence, or had she cut her ties completely? How long did one suppose it might take for young Janet to become a decent human being? Could the lovely Meredith make a go of it establishing a dog obedience school as a newcomer in the tight knit Cornish community in which they lived? Might success in that endeavor induce her to stay longer, or would the pull of her father, the Crooked C ranch, and America itself ultimately send her back to the States?

He was astounded to acknowledge he wouldn't like *that* to be the way the summer ended, would he now? On the other hand, he certainly didn't need to be dropped from a dizzy height by a woman for a second time.

He reached for the big bar of soap on the stone ledge and forced his mind away from these disturbing alternatives. Instead, he attempted to think about milk production quotas and unusual bovine diseases, along with speculation about diplomatic ways to assume more of Doctor Dobell's duties, since inevitable changes at Cow Hollow Farm were clearly in the wind. When those trains of thought didn't manage to banish the libidinous visions of Meredith on a tartan picnic blanket with a surprisingly placid English Channel in the background, he debated whether he should report to Graham Wainwright at Cornwall Search and Rescue the incident concerning his unofficial participation in the short-lived search for young Janet. Beven Glynn was bound to hear of it from someone, and—

"Oh *bugger* all," he said aloud. "What do *I* care about Beven Glynn?"

He toweled off in a more subdued state than when he'd awoken and decided to make some coffee and check in at the milking—even though it was only four-thirty a.m.

After all his mental gymnastics, one thing was clear to him, however: Meredith Champlin was the first woman in five years who'd invaded his consciousness both awake— and asleep.

# CHAPTER 6

"Why, look! Those scones are ever so nice," Mrs. Quiller complimented Meredith as the younger woman pulled out a large baking tray full of golden biscuits studded with plump, black currants. "You be makin' the next batch on your own in perfect order," she added in the soft, elongated manner of native Cornish speech.

"Oh, Mrs. Q, I don't know about that," Meredith replied, gingerly placing the hot tray on the wooden kitchen table where they'd had their meal of leftovers the night before. She stood back with her hands on hips protected by her calf-length, white apron and admired their joint handiwork. "I've been taught by a master chef, for sure."

Mrs. Quiller chuckled just as the door to the back pantry banged shut and Richard and the three children trooped in with baskets filled to the brim with ripe, early tomatoes that had been grown in a rickety greenhouse that had been constructed in the early twentieth century by another generation of Teague garden enthusiasts.

"Can you believe these early ones?" Richard said excitedly, adding them to the bounty on the kitchen table. "Matthew, Janet, and Lucy helped me pick the first substantial crop by searching under the plants to find those that were about to fall off the vine, didn't you children?"

Meredith was pleased to note that even Janet nodded her head proudly.

"In the main garden, we're going to have cucumbers, and pole beans," Matthew announced with obvious pride.

"There's going to be tons of lettuce, too," Janet said enthusiastically, and then added for Meredith's benefit, "but too bad I *hate* salad."

"Ooh, but our payin' guests will *love* all those fresh greens," chortled Mrs. Quiller. "If this is just the first crop of tomatoes, I imagine we'll be cannin' an awful lot of produce over the next few weeks," she added, a frown suddenly creasing the forehead below her snow-white hair.

"Oh, I'm sure our neighbors will help us eat the extras," reassured Blythe who had just walked into the kitchen, her arms filled with supplies she'd bought in St. Austell.

"Here, let me help you with that," Richard said, easing the cardboard box to add to the items now crowding the table.

Meredith pursed her lips in thought and then asked, "Given all the vegetables our Home Farm is going to produce this summer, have you ever thought about hosting one of those Farm-to-Table outdoor dinners, open to the public?" she asked. "They've become hugely popular in the States, especially out West."

"That's probably because they have summer weather that's more reliable than it is in Cornwall," Blythe said, smiling wryly.

"Yes, but you know, if rain threatened the Home Farm fields, you could always hold it in the stone barn at the last minute, couldn't you?"

Richard cocked his head and surveyed the piles of glowing, red tomatoes he and the children had just picked.

"Wouldn't it be smashing to hold a series of evening meals that spotlighted some of the wonderful things we're growing at Home Farm and in the region?"

"Ummmm..." Meredith murmured, taking in the sight

of Richard's beautiful tomatoes, "grilled leg of lamb, vegetable ratatouille...yum, yum!"

"And Mrs. Quiller's blackberry pie!" squealed Lucy, clapping her hands.

"And strawberry shortcake!" chimed in Matthew. He turned to Janet, "Even people who hate fruit like you do *love* blackberry pie and strawberry shortcake...with fresh cream and brown sugar sprinkled on top!"

For once, Janet looked intrigued, but remained silent.

Richard nodded. "I mean, I can just see a bunch of tables put end-to-end between the rows of vegetables we've planted. We could cover them with bed sheets or something, and set up a buffet line where guests in anoraks and Wellies—local people as well as visitors—could file by and get their supper on a fine summer night!"

Richard then looked over at Mrs. Quiller who had acquired a pained expression clouding her features. "You don't like the sound of this, do you Mrs. Q? You've got more than enough on your plate as it is, am I right?"

"I would have to say...it would be hard on me, you know, what with John being so poorly."

"Well, hold on!" Blythe interjected with excitement. "What if we hired someone just to cook these Farm-to-Table dinners? There's a woman in the test kitchen over at Moorland's Creamery I was talking to today. I could tell she's perishing to use her skills on more dishes than those featuring only clotted cream!"

"You wouldn't be offended, Mrs. Q?" Richard asked. "If we had someone in your kitchen who only did the occasional outdoor dinner?"

"Oh, noo-oo," Mrs. Quiller responded, looking as if the weight of the world had been lifted from her shoulders. "That would suit me ever so well, I'm sure. And I'd help out when I could."

"How many of these evenings do you think we should do—and make a profit for our time and trouble?" Blythe asked Richard and Meredith.

Meredith looked thoughtful for a long moment while she made some mental calculations. "Well, in order to end up in the black, I heard that the chuck wagon dinners at the dude ranches outside Jackson Hole during the summer months are held a couple of times a week in order to amortize advertising costs, buying food in bulk, and so on."

"Well, given the amount of produce we expect from the Home Farm, and our lamb—which saves on costs since we won't have to buy it—maybe we could start out doing these once a week, and then increase the number if we get customers," Richard suggested. "And, by the way, I'd love to help with the cooking. In fact, I've been thinking about enrolling in a culinary course this winter between my classes at University."

"Can *we* help?" piped up Matthew, gesturing toward Janet and his little sister.

"Not *me!*" announced Janet, her arms crossed in protest.

Richard and Meredith exchanged glances, but Lucy was jumping up and down excitedly, ignoring them all.

"I'll help, I'll help! Please, Richard, can I help too?" Lucy pleaded with her half-brother.

"*May* I help, sweetheart, " her mother corrected. "I'm sure you can."

"Of course, Lucy, and thank you," Richard said, adding, "We'll need you children to help set the tables." He turned to address his stepmother. "So, what do you think, Blythe? Should we add one more project to bolster our bottom line, as they say in America?"

Blythe smiled broadly. "I think that ever since Meredith and Janet, here, arrived, Barton Hall is cookin' with gas!"

Meredith had noted that her cousin's Wyoming drawl kept surfacing more and more frequently, which made her smile.

Blythe told Richard, "We'll have a family meeting with Lucas tonight and crunch the numbers to see if our budget will stretch to underwrite your outdoor dinners as well as Meredith's dog obedience school." She paused and then raised an index finger in the air, indicating another brainstorm. "What if we call our venture 'Heirloom Edibles: Home Farm-to-Table Summer Suppers at Barton Hall Estates?'"

"Smashing!" replied Richard enthusiastically. "And I like calling them 'suppers,' not formal 'dinners'—so people will understand this is a fairly casual enterprise."

"You know," Meredith mused, looking pensive, "we could save on time, money, and effort if we created a Barton Hall poster with ads that promoted *both* the 'Farm Supper' dates, and the schedule for the dog obedience classes."

"Now that is another brilliant idea!" Blythe exclaimed. "We'll make an advertisement on the order of 'Look what's new at Barton Hall!'" Blythe paused and gazed at Meredith with a sly smile, fishing in her pocket and pulling out a grocery receipt with a number scrawled on the back. "I almost forgot. Your dog academy sponsor, the excellent Sebastian Pryce, called my mobile while I was in Redruth. He said please ring him right away on *his* mobile to set up a planning meeting about the dog obedience project—*and*—also to tell you that he had some other good news to impart, but that you had to act fast. Sounds most intriguing," she added with a wink.

Meredith swiftly retreated to the library and carefully dialed the number written on the sales receipt Blythe had handed her, listening to the sound of distinctive pips ringing Sebastian's phone while doing her best not to think about his unexpected kiss the previous night. A deep voice answered, sounding harried.

"Doctor Pryce, here." And then, Sebastian said in a muffled voice as if he'd put his hand over the telephone, "Yes, Beven, I'll be right there."

"Sebastian? This is Meredith. Look, I can call back later if you're busy."

"No, no, not at all. You've reached me on my mobile. I'm at Search and Rescue in St. Dennis. Just winding up here."

"You had to respond to another call this morning? Poor you."

"By the time I got to the location, they'd already found the chap."

"Oh, that's a relief."

"He was dead."

"Oh, my gosh...that's horrible. An accident?"

"A despondent, we call them. Took pills and went up on the moor."

"I am so sorry. Look, why don't we speak later?"

"I'll be finished here in an hour and then I have to check things at the farm. Could I come by the Hall at the end of the afternoon? I'll need a good, strong cup of tea right about then—and we can talk over our plans about dog obedience training." Sebastian sounded as if he were anxious to speak to her in person.

"Sure," she answered. "That would be fine. What time works for you?" She heard a door shut and the ambient noise from before disappeared. "Where *are* you? In a closet?"

"How did you guess? A supply closet, to be exact at our search and rescue headquarters. A little privacy, don't you know?"

Only he said "prev-e-cey" and Meredith giggled. "That language thing again."

"What if I come over around half past four?" he suggested. "I want to sample one of those scones that Blythe said you were learning to make today. And I also want to tell you about some interesting developments regarding what kind of dog obedience training might go over most successfully around here."

"And I've got some news for you, so that would be fine for you to come by later."

"You're still keen to do this, aren't you?" Sebastian's tone changed suddenly and he sounded wary and rather clipped, as if he expected her to back out of the idea. "Haven't had remorse in the morning?"

"No, no, I'm totally on board with the idea," she assured him. "In fact, we've thought of another scheme to enhance the coffers at Barton Hall. It's all *good*," she said emphatically. "I'll fill you in when you get here." She paused and then added, "I'm really so sorry you didn't find the man in time. When we lost a child at our hospital because we'd run out of treatment options, I was…affected for quite a while myself. Sometimes it's not easy to do what you do, is it, Sebastian?"

"No…it's not," he said quietly. "I can see you understand that very well."

"Yes, I do. Bye for now." And then to lighten the mood that had bloomed between them, she added quickly, "I'll have the scones warming when you get here and you be the judge of how they came out."

She heard a soft chuckle. "Excellent plan," he replied.

"Meet me at Painter's Cottage, though, will you? That way we can save time and pace out the field to see if it will work for what we're planning? We can have our tea and scones there…I'm told it's got a sweet little kitchen and a spectacular view through those artist's windows we saw from the outside the other day."

Meredith was aware of a long silence on the other end of the phone.

She asked quickly, "If that doesn't work for you—"

"No, no. Never mind," he interrupted. "Painter's Cottage it is. At half past four, today. Cheerio, Nurse Meredith."

She laughed. "*Chef* Meredith to you, Doc. Bye now."

She replaced the receiver, feeling the same, peculiar glow run up her arm and fill her chest that she'd noticed yesterday. She looked at her feet and saw that Holly was furiously wagging her stubby tail.

"Okay, okay, girl…I get it. Let's go outside."

❦

Late in the afternoon, Mrs. Quiller handed Meredith a wicker basket with a half dozen scones, butter, jam, and the requisite items for brewing tea.

"Down at the cottage, you'll be finding the brown tea pot and the creamer under the kitchen counter," she advised, "but I fear you'll only have fat mugs to drink from." Clearly, Mrs. Quiller was a devotee of fine bone china, but she smiled as she also gave the younger woman the large, iron key that would gain entry to the dwelling built for Lucas Teague's ancestor, seascape artist, Ennis Trevelyan, in the 1790s.

Meredith and Holly departed from the pantry door and soon were enveloped by the cool, green tunnel of Barton Hall Walk and its renowned "thousand shades of green"— foliage bursting on both sides of a shaded path clad in every emerald hue. The dirt track sloped down to a narrow road, and across it, to the field full of sheep. The wide expanse of verdant grass ended at the steep cliffs that stood sentry above the shoreline winding its way East toward Hemmick Beach, and eventually Dodman Point, a promontory that thrust an arm deep into the English Channel.

Once she emerged from the leafy enclosure's mile long walk, she kept the basket on an even keel as she carefully navigated the wooden stile and waited for Holly to heave her sausage frame up and over the steps. The pair crossed the road, entered through the second wooden gate and into the pasture nearest the English Channel, the thick grasses moist from a recent rain shower.

"Heel, Holly!" she cautioned as the Corgi's ears perked to attention and the dog sniffed a wind embedded with the scent of some fifty white-faced Devon and Cornwall Longwool sheep that dotted the large field surrounding Painter's Cottage. The stone dwelling, sunk far into the Cornish soil, had a slate roof, and deep-set windows, with walls two feet thick.

Meredith shivered to recall how afraid she'd felt the day when she and Sebastian and Rex had searched the cliffs for the missing Janet. True, her young cousin wasn't much chastened by that momentous event and had, thus far, failed to drop her unpleasant, pre-teen, precocious manner, but Meredith, herself, felt as if she had somehow slipped into a place and lifestyle that felt comfortable and oddly familiar, despite the grandeur of living in a mammoth castle.

She glanced around at the spectacular surroundings of wide, blue sky, velvety green fields, and the expanse of water that stretched some hundred miles toward France. The stretch of jade green and sapphire blue colors close into the shore were dappled with small, boisterous white caps—more evidence of the early morning rain.

In fact, once the rain and clouds had cleared off to the

southwest, the broad fields and English Channel on the horizon were as vibrantly hued as colored crayons. Meredith and Holly trod across the pasture just as a subset of the flock of sheep that were peacefully munching the grass nearby looked up, skittish and alarmed. This swiftly became a challenge to Holly, who quivered with desire to herd them back to the larger group.

"Steady, Holly!" Meredith said firmly. "Heel! That's a good girl."

After a few moments, the sheep ducked their heads and returned to their grazing as Meredith and Holly continued to walk toward the stone cottage. Her eyes scanned the bucolic scene when a thought suddenly struck her, full-force.

*This is where my people* came *from! These fields, these stones...*

Her Champlin and Blythe's Barton forebears had come to America nearly a hundred and seventy years earlier, but Meredith began to wonder if there wasn't such a thing as a memory gene that twanged when a person came back to their ancestral beginnings? No wonder Blythe had made such a life-changing decision a decade ago to remain in Cornwall and start anew. In a way, she'd come home. And in the strangest sense, that was what Meredith was feeling...and it took her completely by surprise.

By this time, she and her dog had reached the front of the cottage.

"Good girl, Holly!" Meredith declared encouragingly. "Sit...*stay*!" She set the basket on the stone step and inserted the heavy iron key in the metal lock that pierced the thick oak door with its matching metal hinges.

She entered the dim, shadowed interior and easily found the solitary electric switch. As light flooded the cottage, she was arrested by the sight of a spectacular series of paintings that hung on all four walls. As she drew closer, she saw that the images depicted the very same coastline that lay directly outside her windows.

"Oh, wow…" she said on a long breath, taking in the series of stunning seascapes that captured the distinctive jade-green light and pristine white foam that she could see in the rolling surf outside the big artist's windows that faced, from roofline to floor, onto the broad expanse of the Channel.

*Ennis Trevelyan may be considered an amateur artist on Lucas Teague's family tree, but this guy was good!*

Meredith slowly circled the room, examining each painting in turn, until she found herself back near the kitchen counter that was built into the stone wall.

She set her basket on the counter and quickly spied the electric kettle and the brown ceramic pot in which to make the tea—and began to heat water. A massive fireplace made of the same stone as the cottage stared at her blankly, wood piled neatly on the hearth. Turning to survey the rest of the one-room dwelling, she noted the sleeping loft overhead and then, shifting her gaze back to the main room, caught sight of an old-fashioned bath tub sitting on the floor next to another window that also provided a spectacular view toward Dodman Point.

She began to imagine what a sybaritic pleasure it would be to soak in a long, hot bath and simply stare out the window at the amazing view.

Meredith recalled that Blythe had leased this place for half a year when she first came to Cornwall. And who wouldn't have, given a chance? Now it was used for an overflow of guests—although that was rarely, of late, given the down turn in their business these last few years.

Meredith noted a large desk against one wall that Blythe told her she'd used when designing the interiors of the tea room and plant nursery layouts. If the dog obedience school became a reality, perhaps Lucas and Blythe would allow her to use the place as a kind of office when she held her classes in the adjacent field?

Just then she heard a knock on the door she'd left half open.

"Tea ready?" asked a deep voice. "I certainly could use a cup."

She turned around and felt a little *frisson* of anticipation ripple in her chest. Sebastian stood silhouetted like a giant in the doorway.

"Come in, come in! Just heating the pot."

# CHAPTER 7

Sebastian was clad in his red search and rescue anorak with a black turtleneck underneath, along with dark moleskin trousers and mud-spattered boots—all of which indicated that he'd recently been in rough terrain. His dark, shaggy mane was windblown and his cheeks were ruddy for having been outdoors most of the day.

"Well, hello there," she greeted him a second time, doing her best to keep an idiotic smile under control. She leaned to one side to peer through the open front door. "Where's Rex?"

Sebastian pulled off his boots before coming into the cottage.

"He's asleep in the back seat of my car." Meredith arched an eyebrow and Sebastian hastened to add, "Windows down for air, of course."

"Of course," she said, busying herself with her tea making.

"I figured we'd better keep him away from Holly for a little while longer."

"Good thinking," Meredith said with a chuckle, pointing to her dog curled up on the rag rug near the hearth. "She should be receiving guests by the time we have to photograph the two dogs for our poster advertising our obedience classes."

Sebastian shed his parka and looked around the room.

He stepped closer to one wall and examined the oil painting of the rolling surf on Hemmick Beach below the cliffs, the same picture that had held Meredith's attention longer than any other of the works.

"Nice, isn't it?" she said. "I had no idea Lucas had such artistic ancestors."

"Ah...the eighteenth century Trevelyan seascapes. I've heard about them."

"I know very little about art—or Ennis Trevelyan," she admitted cheerfully, "but I just love these."

Sebastian glanced around the room at the other paintings decorating the four walls. His gaze had suddenly grown somber as he stared at Trevelyan's depictions of land and sea, with nary a human in sight.

"He's captured the desolation, all right...the beauty of this place, and the sense that something sinister is just around the corner."

Meredith turned her attention to the first painting. "Really? That just shows you how much *I* know about art. I thought it showed the magnificence of this coast. Nothing sinister came to my mind at all."

Still focused on the painting, he said, "That's because you haven't lived your entire life along this coast. It's beautiful—and treacherous."

"Probably a lot like the Grand Tetons, where I live. They're gorgeous, snow-capped mountains, but if you set a foot wrong, they can kill you."

Sebastian turned to meet her gaze, but his eyes were strangely shuttered. An uncomfortable silence grew between them for reasons Meredith was at a loss to understand. He'd seemed so glad to see her, and she him, but suddenly she had the strong sense that he wished he were anywhere but in Painter's Cottage.

Finally she assumed the role of hostess and said, "Let's

have that tea and get to measuring the layout in the field, shall we?"

Sebastian politely praised the quality of the scones and listened without comment as Meredith described the Barton-Teague family's latest idea to hold farm-to-table casual suppers over the summer as another income stream for the estate, advertising both the dinners and their dog training classes on the same poster to be distributed around the county. As her final sentence trailed off, she sensed an unexplained tension permeating the room. Finally, unable to stand it another moment, she reached across the small table where they sat having their tea and lightly touched his hand.

"What's wrong, Sebastian? Something switched off with you as soon as you came in here."

Startled by her directness, he looked down at his half-empty cup. "You are quite observant, aren't you?"

"What is it? Did I say something—?"

"No! No, of course not. It was the painting...of the cliffs...and Hemmick Beach."

He ducked his head to avoid her gaze and linked his large hands around the thick ceramic mug in a kind of a death grip.

"Did these paintings make you think about all the rescues you've made along this coast?" she asked quietly. "Some which were successful, and some not, right?"

"Ah...right you are."

"And today, you were looking for a man, but found him dead? That can make a person blue, for sure. I've come into a patient's room at the hospital and a child had died in the bed when no one was there. I felt terrible. Those moments haunt me still..."

He raised his eyes to meet her glance. "It's the same for us, especially when it's a suicide."

"One time, we lost three kids in a single week," she confided. "I thought *I* might die of the sadness." She filled her mug and his with more tea and poured milk into both. "Now mind you, we were able to cure, or at least send most of our patients home from the hospital in better shape than they arrived, but when we couldn't save them...it was awful. It takes its toll on the doctors, of course, but more so the nurses, I think. *We* are the ones who are hands-on throughout the process, if you get my meaning."

"Losing children is the absolute worst," he murmured, and Meredith was struck by the bleakness of his demeanor.

"I guess I'll never really get over that particular week," she said, watching him closely.

"It never leaves one, does it?"

Meredith studied the melancholy expression that had invaded Sebastian's handsome features and wondered, suddenly, if he were speaking about more than merely his work this day on the search and rescue team.

But she merely said, "No, I don't think those memories ever completely fade away. Those kids and their parents are always lurking somewhere in the back of my thoughts and then, something else might happen as a kind of trigger, and they pop up every so often and I feel sad all over again." She heaved a sigh and shrugged. "Fortunately, the feeling eventually recedes, but I totally get what you're saying about what happened today."

Sebastian nodded, and reached across the small table separating them to put his hand over hers. "Do you realize that you are a pretty amazing woman?"

She wrinkled her nose. "Not really. Look at how I'm doing with Janet. She mostly refuses to take part in anything up at the house, although I sometimes see her sneaking off to play with Holly. If I could only make her see what an incredibly lucky little girl she is. She's healthy, with a family here in Cornwall that wants to take care of her…and in such a beautiful place this summer." She sat up straighter, pulled her hand from beneath his, and put both her palms decisively on the table. "Speaking of which," she declared, attempting to shake off her own melancholy that had taken hold when she described the heartbreak she'd witnessed in her job at the hospital, "we'd better pace out the field before it starts to get dark." She stood up and rested her hand on top of the almost empty teapot. "Unless you want another cup?"

"No, thank you. Yes, let's get cracking," he agreed, also rising and carrying their two cups to the sink as Meredith followed with the other tea things, setting them on the counter.

"And what was the news you told Blythe about?" Meredith asked, turning around and leaning against the kitchen counter. "I've talked so much, you haven't gotten a word in edgewise."

"I was telling my supervisor, Graham Wainwright at the Cornwall Search and Rescue Team, about your plan to start teaching small dog sheep herding and obedience as well as service dog training here on the estate. Believe it or not, he was quite enthusiastic."

"Really? Well, that's a good sign."

"In fact, Wainwright proposed that since I was involved as your 'official' sponsor as far as Lucas' paperwork is concerned, it would be a good idea if I also held a beginning class for volunteers interested in enrolling their dogs to become part of our CSRT. The team never has enough volunteers—either dogs or people—but Wainwright hasn't been able to figure out quite what to do about it. This would be a sort of introductory course that could be a way of determining which dogs and handlers were likeliest to succeed with further training—and our potential volunteers would be paying for the privilege, which would save the CSRT some preliminary funds."

Meredith clapped her hands excitedly. "I think that's a fabulous idea! And it will add to the heft of what we're trying to do here."

"You don't feel it's stealing any of your thunder?"

Meredith reared back and shook her head vigorously in denial. "Absolutely not! In fact, it's a terrific addition!"

"I won't charge for my services," he hastened to add. "Barton Hall will make the profit."

"That's not fair," Meredith responded. "We're partners with Barton Hall in this. We'll share, fifty-fifty of our fifty percent, and Lucas and Blythe will get the other fifty percent. I insist that you get paid for teaching your classes, just as I will. Deal?"

"Then I'll give my portion as a donation to our search and rescue team toward new equipment," he insisted. "Graham said that any teaching I did would count toward my volunteer hours, which is fine with me. Barton Hall is closer to Cow Hollow Farm than the St. Dennis headquarters, and I have a limited amount of time I can devote to the Cornwall Search and Rescue Team these days, given my increasing duties as an animal manager for the Jenners. Teaching here would actually lighten my load, but I want to be sure it sits well with you, Nurse Meredith."

"*Instructor* Meredith," she reminded him, smiling at their running joke. She raised her right hand in a 'high-five' that Sebastian attempted to match. "This is super...with your teaching search and rescue to novice dogs, and my giving regular obedience, agility, pet therapy training classes, and sheep herding courses, we'll be offering a pretty broad range of 'canine education' in these parts, don't you think?"

It was amazing to see the way that both Sebastian's and her moods had gone from gloom to gusto.

"Cornwall will never have seen the like," he replied, poker-faced.

"Our empire will be huge!" she laughed, stretching her arms wide. She flashed a smile and looked up at him in a deliberately flirtatious manner. "Don't you think it's time we shook hands on our newly *expanded* project?"

"No," he replied abruptly.

"No?" echoed Meredith, taken aback.

"No."

Before she realized what was happening, Sebastian took her in his arms and kissed her more thoroughly, even, than under the castle's portico.

For her part, Meredith was so surprised by his actions that she bumped her derriere against the edge of the kitchen counter, and then leaned on it for stability as warmth deliciously flooded her limbs. Soon, she became conscious of one broad hand on her back and the other cupping the side of her face. She felt herself meld against his tall frame, eager, now, to return his embrace. It had been a very long time since she had kissed a man this deeply and her lips seemed to seek his of their own volition. In fact, the kiss was long and shared—and intensely un-businesslike.

Finally, she murmured, "Haven't you ever heard the warning: 'Don't dip your quill in office ink?'"

"No, never," he mumbled, his lips moving to a tender spot at the base of her neck. "You Americans have a language all your own," he whispered, nibbling her ear in a move clearly intended to distract her from further conversation.

Despite the incredible sensations radiating in her solar plexus, she couldn't suppress a laugh.

"Oh, Lord, Sebastian. We haven't yet hung up a single poster advertising our wares, and look what we're doing!"

she protested, pushing playfully against his chest. "Really, show a little discipline, Doctor Dog!"

Reluctantly, he pulled away and chucked her under the chin. "I don't know what it is about you, lady from Wyoming, but you've gotten me into quite a state. I even dreamt about you."

"You did? That's so un-British of you to admit it. What happened in the dream?"

Sebastian shook his head and remained mum.

"Oh, come on! *Tell* me!"

One of his rare grins creased his lips and he took another step away from her, gesturing toward the door. "I am not at liberty to divulge that information. And I think we'd better go measure the field—or at least pace it off."

"Talk about not fair!"

"I'll tell you sometime," he replied, and she thought he might kiss her again.

When he didn't, she said, regret tingeing her voice, "You're probably right, we'd better get busy." She picked up her notepad and pen, and then called to Holly who'd been curled up, asleep, during their tea. "Come, girl!" she beckoned. "I seriously need you as a chaperone."

◦℮ᘐᕽ᠙

Once Holly was out of season, the photograph of the two dogs completed, and Sebastian was able to grab a few hours free, the new "partners" drove all over central Cornwall in his green Mini distributing what they considered to be very handsome posters.

At the top of each was an image of Rex and Holly in their brightly-colored service dogs vests, posed in the field to the left of Painter's Cottage with sheep dotting the landscape and the blue-green English Channel serving as a dramatic backdrop. Below was the contact information for signing up for the schedule of the various classes in dog obedience, along with an opportunity to take part in an orientation class for anyone interested in becoming, along with their dog, a volunteer with the Cornwall Search and Rescue canine corps. A second image in the lower half of the poster featured Barton Hall Home Farm's lush tomatoes piled high in a bowl that was set on a long table, visible outside the greenhouse door, and laden with linens and chinaware awaiting a gaggle of guests.

Surprisingly, there had been little response to either proposed new enterprise.

"It seemed like such a natural," Meredith complained to Sebastian when he'd offered to take her for fish and chips one evening at a little shop in St. Austell.

"Hold steady, now, Meredith," he replied, pouring half his beer into an extra glass and handing it to her over the newspapers that had wrapped their dinner. "We've only just tacked up those posters. Give it some time."

"Time isn't in much supply," she countered glumly. "Please don't repeat this, but I overheard Lucas saying the bankers called and they weren't happy with last week's financials. 'Not enough progress,' they said. I'm really anxious that Richard's Farm-to-Table suppers, as well as our canine obedience effort get off the ground as quickly as possible and add to Barton Hall's profit margin."

Sebastian raised the remnants of his glass of beer in a toast.

"Well, here's to the eventual success of the Barton Hall enterprises—each and every one."

Meredith raised her nearly empty glass as well and said, "Amen and ditto, ditto!"

After their supper, Sebastian and Meredith ambled through St. Austell's White River Place, a redeveloped section of the town known for its shops and "pedestrian only" strolls.

Suddenly, a voice called out from across one courtyard.

"Yoo-hoo! Sebastian!"

Meredith felt her walking companion stiffen and cast a brief glance at a tall woman in a shapeless housedress layered with a three-quartered camel haired coat and a knitted cap partially covering her gray hair, untidy wisps flying in all directions. A good fifty feet behind them, she was carrying a string basket plump with items she'd obviously been buying in town.

Sebastian seized Meredith's arm and swiftly guided her to their left down a narrow lane and turned a corner into a street full of traffic that would take them in the direction of their parked car. They traveled at a fast pace along the sidewalk in silence until they reached the Mini and Sebastian pulled out his keys to unlock the passenger side door.

Meredith leaned an elbow on the car's roof and said, "And *that* was?"

"My mother."

Startled, Meredith could only ask, "And we didn't say 'hello' because?"

"It's a long, rather tedious story," Sebastian replied, his eyes focused on the key in the lock. Finally, he looked up to meet her gaze. "Forgive me for being so abrupt and hustling you down the street as I did."

Startled by his apology, Meredith felt a wave of compassion for this six-foot former warrior who appeared deeply shaken by the encounter. It was almost as if he'd sensed danger and ducked for cover. Meredith placed a hand on his sleeve.

"Sebastian, what's wrong? Why did you want to avoid her like that?"

"I just couldn't...I just didn't want to..." Sebastian's words trailed off.

"Was it because I was with you?"

Sebastian shook his head emphatically. "No! Although I certainly didn't want to subject you to a conversation with the woman, or myself, either." He opened the car door for her and she slipped into the passenger seat while he went around the front of the vehicle and got in behind the wheel.

"You and your mother are obviously...estranged?" she asked hesitantly when he'd shut his door.

"Yes...and for a complicated set of reasons I don't want to bore you with."

He was staring out the front windshield, a play of emotions she didn't understand flickering across his features.

"Learning to understand more about you, Sebastian, isn't boring in the slightest," she said softly. "It's what I'd really like to do." She reached for his hand. "I like you. Very much."

Without the slightest warning, he turned toward her and fiercely pulled her into his arms, kissing her as if it were the end of the world and she, the last female on earth. In a part of her brain not overwhelmed by the sheer force of his desire to touch and hold her, Meredith was shocked by the intensity of his heated embrace as her body yielded to the urgency of his lips and the longing for warmth and closeness she sensed was behind this sensuous assault.

When, at length, he pulled back, he cupped her face in his hands and showered gentle kisses on each cheek, her nose, and both eyelids.

"Thank you for being who you are," he said softly.

Meredith smiled faintly and replied, "You're welcome. And as far as I'm concerned, if you'll kiss me like that again, I'm happy to run into your mother anytime."

Sebastian's expression shifted from an almost haunted look to one of pure mirth.

"I never, *ever*, thought anyone could make me laugh about an encounter with Elizabeth Pryce!" he said, still smiling.

Meredith pointed to the windows that had steamed up with their heavy breathing.

"Hey! No worries. She'll never find us here," she replied, and leaned forward to kiss him back just as ferociously as he had her.

After several delicious minutes, Meredith leaned back and said, "This is ridiculous! We're acting like teenagers."

"Yes," Sebastian replied. "Yes, we are. " He kissed her nose once more. "But I think I'd better take this fair damsel back to her castle. I have to be up at five."

Meredith nodded regretfully, her thoughts filled with a replay of the strange, almost-meeting with Mrs. Pryce. Whatever had happened between Sebastian and his mother, surely he would tell her about it sometime?

$\sim$

In the days that followed, Richard, Blythe and Mrs. Quiller spent whatever free moments they could steal from running the estate's main business enterprises to develop menus and plan the details for the series of suppers scheduled for the next fortnight—that is, if anyone made reservations.

Then, unexpectedly, the local television station got wind of Barton Hall's newest schemes and asked the "American cowgirl, who is also a nurse with a sheep-herding Corgi" to show viewers how Holly could perform in both a field of woolly creatures and at the local nursing home, offering comfort to residents with long-term illnesses.

Part of the story featured Richard picking produce at Home Farm and Mrs. Quiller instructing him and the children how to make delicious ratatouille in a big pot on the Aga in the castle's kitchen. In the shots featuring the children, Janet took on the role of film director, urging Matthew and Lucy not to chatter when it wasn't their turn to speak. After the film crew departed, Meredith gave her a hug.

"I could certainly tell you know a lot about making movies," she congratulated her. "You and your cousins were terrific today, and I'm very proud of you!"

Janet appeared on the verge of making some retort and then hesitated, shrugged, and merely said "Thanks. Daddy always said he had to be a general in the army."

Meredith felt as if she'd won a major victory and found herself whistling as she walked down the hall to the library to leave Sebastian a voice message about when the TV spot would be aired. A few days later, she had reason to call him again.

"Good heavens, Sebastian, the phone's been ringing off the hook!" she reported, again speaking from the library. "My four classes and your search-and-rescue one are nearly full, and will be *totally* by Friday, if this keeps up!"

It was late afternoon, and she thought merely to leave a message of her good news on his voice mail, but Sebastian disclosed that he'd just gone upstairs to take a shower after a long day dealing with an ailing calf in the Jenners' herd.

"And Richard's suppers?" he asked. "Any sign-ups?"

"The first two dates are totally sold out, as of today, and the others for the rest of the summer season are selling at an amazing clip! The woman reporter said she'd seen our poster at the local post office and thought our new schemes had 'brilliant visuals.' She also put our contact information on the station website! Isn't that amazing?"

"Not really, considering there isn't exactly a lot of *new* news or entertainment around here," he replied dryly. "What do you say we head into Gorran Haven in about an hour and have supper together to celebrate?"

A delicious little zing fluttered somewhere in her diaphragm.

"In the words of that reporter, sounds like a brilliant idea—except why don't we save you some driving and I'll make a picnic the two of us can take down to Portluney Cove, or even Hemmick Beach, if you feel like a brisk walk? It's glorious here right now. Nice and warm and no wind. I imagine it will stay light until nearly ten o'clock tonight." Meredith couldn't get over how long the summer evenings were in Britain.

A long pause ensued and then Sebastian said, "You know, Meredith…on second thought, I think I'd better not. William's worried about the Hereford. I think I rather need to stay close by tonight. Sorry to extend an invitation and then rescind it. I should have thought it through."

"Well, what about Doctor Dobell?" she asked, unable to keep the disappointment from creeping into her voice. She found it unsettling that Sebastian's enthusiasm to celebrate their first success should suddenly do such an about-face in response at her suggestion of a cozy beach supper. "Couldn't Dobell stand watch?"

After all, they were talking about a *cow*.

There was another long pause and Meredith could almost hear the wheels turning in his head while he searched for a more plausible excuse to bow out of an intimate dinner for two on a secluded beach. Perhaps she was being a pushy American? Maybe his kisses had meant a lot more to her than to him and that taking their relationship up a notch was not at all what he had in mind.

"Doctor Dobell is—well, I mean, he's not—" Sebastian was clearly fumbling for words.

Meredith interrupted before he could come up with some lame excuse.

"Look, Sebastian, this isn't a command performance, or anything...and come to think of it, I just realized that tonight isn't really good for me either. I'm going to help Richard do an inventory of—of what he's going to need to have on hand for those suppers. I'll keep you posted about our class sign-ups, okay? Take care, now. Bye."

It was all she could do not to slam down the phone in frustration. Something just now had bothered him enough to short circuit their evening's plans, but he wouldn't come clean about what it was.

*I know that feeling of push-back all too well...*

What was it with her, she wondered bleakly. Did she give off some sort of signal that spelled danger, "This woman is starting to get too serious for comfort?" Shep O'Brien would run hot and cold like Sebastian just had, even after he'd begged her to move in with him in Jackson Hole. She honestly felt she was the kind of person who never "assumed" something unless the evidence was in front of her. Yet, once she put her toe in the water, the men in her life seemed to remove theirs!

The memory of Sebastian's recent, heated embraces in the car after the near encounter with his mother made her even more upset about this last exchange.

*I just can't sign up again for this kind of on again-off again relationship...*

It's too painful, she thought, feeling the first, real stab of homesickness since she'd arrived in Cornwall. She missed her Dad's reliable expressions of care and concern for her welfare that had been her rock since her mother had died.

*Oh...Dad...I wish you were here to explain Sebastian Pryce to me...*

Her father had ultimately been the one who helped her understand about Shep's particular brand of alcoholism.

"That cowboy is basically a nice fella," he'd said once when Meredith had fled back to the ranch in tears, "but this binge drinking of his is kinda like he's got diabetes or asthma or something. He's got a disease that comes and goes, but unless he gets some help and does what the docs tell him to, he'll never be a healthy man. The bad thing is, though, Meredith, the sickness he's got could kill *you*, too...that is, if you stick close by."

Did Sebastian have some other kind of malady she didn't understand, but one that could break her heart, nonetheless?

Meredith slowly walked out of the library and headed down the carpeted hallway in the direction of the kitchen. To shake off her depressed mood, she proposed to Richard and Blythe that after dinner they actually should *do* a rundown of the supplies they'd need for the first Farm-To-Table suppers.

"Other than the vegetables grown in the castle's gardens, and the lamb we raise, why don't we make a list of items we'll have to budget for in order to seat fifty guests each week?"

Blythe agreed whole-heartedly to the project of doing an inventory of what Barton Hall had on hand in the big pantry, and what they'd need to buy. "Then we can run it by Mrs. Quiller to see if she'd add anything. The next step is to calculate how much outlay this would require, and we'll see where we stand."

It was easy to see that her cousin was greatly worried about costs.

"The good news is, these meals are well on their way to

being sell-outs," Richard said. "That means we'll have the funds, up front, to buy what we need as we go along. And if we're careful of every pence, at least we won't *lose* money on them."

"Well, that's a half-way blessing, isn't it? " Blythe nodded, plainly relieved.

"But the trick will be turning a profit, won't it?" Meredith commented.

"That's always the trick," Blythe responded with a wan smile. She looked tired and mildly depressed, which was exactly how Meredith felt. "And if we hire a new cook..."

"Hey, Blythe...what do you say I trade you working with Richard on the inventory and crunching some numbers tonight, if you'll take on getting Janet to go to bed on time like Matthew and Lucy. You're so much better at it than I am."

"Deal! I'm sick of looking at figures all day today. I'd much rather immerse myself in the world of *Babar* or *Curious George* tonight."

Blythe pushed away from the kitchen table where they'd been having their discussion after doing the "washing up," as Mrs. Quiller called their after-dinner chores. The serving staff and the housekeeper-cook had long departed so the older woman could make her ailing husband's evening meal.

Blythe put her hand on Meredith's shoulder and said, "Actually, Janet's made far fewer protests about our enforced bedtime the last day or two since I said she could read her *Nancy Drew* mysteries as late as she liked."

"*Nancy Drew!* Where'd she find those?" Meredith exclaimed. "I loved those books."

"Dad sent a huge trunk full of my childhood stuff over here when he sold the Double Bar B. I put a couple of volumes on Janet's beside table, and lo and behold, she likes them."

"No wonder she's finally stopped complaining about not being allowed to get on that blasted Webkinz game site. She's actually reading a book!"

"Books," Blythe corrected, and then bid them both good night.

# CHAPTER 8

Meredith and Richard spent the next hour surveying the large pantry off the castle's kitchen and estimating what they would need to purchase additionally in order to produce the menus that had been worked out.

At one point, Richard asked her how her own project was going.

"Well, our classes are nearly filled, too," she replied, "but I'm a little worried about my partner in this enterprise."

"Sebastian Pryce?" Richard asked. "Why? He seems a very reliable sort."

She hesitated and then recounted to Richard the odd exchange they'd had earlier on the telephone. "In one breath he was inviting me out for dinner in the village, and in the next, he was *un*inviting me—or at least, he was totally not interested in having the picnic supper I proposed we take to Hemmick Beach. It was weird!"

"Sounds like he wanted to have dinner with you, just not on a beach."

"C'mon, Richard! The way he handled it *was* weird," she insisted.

"Not if you knew that his sister drowned...on Hemmick Beach, to be precise."

"*What?*"

"Remember I told you once that I nearly got washed

out by the tides down there? I was eight years old and hid in the back of a cave playing 'smugglers', not aware the water was coming in."

Meredith nodded, mystified how Richard's near catastrophe years ago related to Sebastian's about-face earlier that evening.

"Well, Father wanted to underscore back then how dangerous it was for children to go down there alone. He illustrated his point by telling me that, when Sebastian Pryce was a boy, he and his two younger brothers and sister were picnicking with their mother when a big wave knocked the little girl off a rock and swept her out in the current before anyone could save her."

"How horrible! And how awful for his mother not to be able to do anything."

"That was Father's point. Even with an adult *present*, the beach is still treacherous if the tide's coming in."

"Sebastian's father wasn't there when it happened, I take it."

"He worked for the railroad and I gathered wasn't home a lot. It was just Mrs. Pryce and her four children down on the beach on a blustery day."

"It's probably no accident Sebastian volunteers for the Cornwall Search and Rescue Team after witnessing that," she mused. "But why didn't he just *tell* me about it...and say that he'd rather not go down to that beach?" she wondered aloud.

"He's British, and besides, he doesn't know you that well...yet," Richard replied with a twinkle.

*Sebastian Pryce knows me better than you think, Richard...*

Meredith realized that Blythe's stepson was teasing her about her obvious interest in the handsome former lieutenant, but it disturbed her that—given Sebastian's having kissed her to within an inch of her life—he didn't feel he could confide in her, or at least try to persuade her to meet him in Mevagissey or Gorran Haven instead of host a picnic on the Hemmick or Portluney beaches. He simply withdrew with no explanation and no regard for how such an abrupt change-of-heart must make *her* feel.

*Why just go cold and push me away?*

She suddenly recalled how Sebastian had stared, mutely, at the seascape by Ennis Trevelyan hanging in Painter's Cottage that depicted a desolate Hemmick Beach. He'd had *two* opportunities to tell her about an important part of his past—the way she'd told him about her relationship with Shep turning out to be such a disaster and of losing three children on her watch in a single week at the hospital. But the facts were, he'd declined to confide in her both times.

And she hadn't pressed him to explain the reasons that he was at such odds with his mother when he had them duck down an alley to avoid her. Obviously, he had some "family issues," but why wouldn't he confide in her something of what they *were*?

*Men!* she thought with exasperation, followed by a wave of disappointment. Why was there always a hidden whammy?

It was probably a good thing to discover Sebastian's confounding come-hither-go-away style sooner, rather than later, and avoid getting her heart handed to her—given that she became increasingly beguiled every time he kissed her senseless. In a strange way, she understood completely that he was not doing anything *to* her, but the mixed signals he sent because of his own personal problems were beginning to make her very unhappy.

*Elusive males are not my specialty anymore...*

Even so, there was no denying the good doctor was one sexy guy and certainly great with dogs. She attempted to cheer herself up with her conviction that if she could simply scale down what had been her rising expectations and think of him as a friend—and nothing more—he'd be a good partner in their obedience school.

*Safer for all concerned to just leave it at that…and keep your quill out of office ink!*

*Pity*, echoed a voice in her head.

෴

Ten days later, Meredith peeked into the book-lined room where young Janet had locked herself into the secret smuggler's passage earlier in the summer. On this late afternoon, Blythe sat behind the desk framed by a large family genealogy chart that hung on the back wall and traced the Teague, Barton, and Trevelyan antecedents for some ten generations.

The lady of the house was staring at her laptop's screen with grim concentration. Beside her was a calculator on which she was tapping in some numbers. Meredith waited until Blythe punched in a final sequence and leaned back in her chair, grimacing at the result.

"Sorry to interrupt," Meredith said, announcing herself from the open oaken door. "Okay to come in?"

"What? Oh, hi," Blythe said. "Sure. Come in. Sit down. Glad for the distraction."

Meredith pointed to the computer. "How are we doing?"

"You mean our Profit and Loss? Well, you and Sebastian launching the obedience school have really helped to swell our coffers quite a bit this month with all the pre-payments of fees you've brought in…"

"But?"

"But, I don't know what to do about Richard's new venture."

"The Farm-to-Table suppers? The first ones were tremendously well received, I thought. He said reservations have poured in like crazy. I think he'll make a great success of them, long term."

"Not if we don't have someone to cook them."

"Oh, dear."

"Mrs. Q. and I had a heart-to-heart chat this morning. With all the extra work that first dinner required—even though we hired on extra help—the poor woman reached her limit. She wants us to hire someone to replace her, right away. Apparently, John's dementia just keeps getting worse and worse, but she's just not ready to put him in a facility, so she feels a tremendous pull to stay home with him. Meanwhile, she's tired and worn out as his caregiver as well as our cook, and besides, she's a woman in her late seventies! Basically, she wants to retire from her work here—and I don't blame her for that one bit."

"Oh boy," Meredith said, only too aware of the disturbing implications of Mrs. Quiller's retirement on the entire running of Barton Hall. She pointed to the calculator. "You were trying to figure out how much we could pay a cook-slash-housekeeper on the open market, right?"

"Exactly," Blythe agreed. "And it ain't going to be cheap. I'm wracking my brains how to find someone, fast, that we can afford and make a smooth transition without having to cancel any of Richard's suppers."

Meredith sat down on the chair facing Blythe's desk. "That's trouble, for sure," she sympathized. "Sadly, I've never advanced beyond scone making, I'm afraid, so I'm not very much help. What about Richard taking on more of a role in the culinary department? He says it's something he wants to do and I can certainly help with the housekeeping chores."

"That is so sweet of you," Blythe replied, "but you and

Sebastian would help us the most by staying on track with the dog stuff. And Richard can definitely do more of the cooking, but he's got a lot to do looking after Home Farm. And besides, he isn't ready to run what is basically a full-time restaurant here, what with the daily tea service, our breakfasts for the paying guests, and these labor-intensive evening meals that require a lot of fetching and carrying to get them on that long table in half-way decent style." Blythe shook her head. "No, we need to *hire* someone else, full-time, and a professional, but given our balance sheet, we simply cannot pay an arm and a leg to do it."

"Well, what about that person you mentioned a while ago that works in Moorland's test kitchen?" Meredith asked hopefully. "Did you ever talk price?"

Blythe cocked her head and said with a sly smile, "I was just about to find you to ask you to come with me to the Creamery on a stealth mission."

"Ah ha!" Meredith chortled. "You want *me* to act as a decoy for her bosses so that you can lure her to come to work for you, right? Oooh, you are a wicked woman!"

"That I can be," Blythe agreed. "Are you game, little Cuz? I don't want to get Moorlands so cross with me that they refuse to sell us those buckets of clotted cream we still need. Cow Hollow Farm can supply us just so much in exchange for those two lambs. But I have one trick up my sleeve that I'll tell you about in the car."

"Really? Well, then…to Moorlands we a-hunting go!"

⟳

Blythe and Meredith sat in the estate's battered Land Rover in a far corner of the car park of Moorland's Creamery and lay in wait for Claire Gillis to finish her day's work. They'd come in the late afternoon on the pretense of picking up their order, and now they were keeping their eyes peeled on the door at the far end of the building.

"What's she like?" Meredith asked curiously.

"Claire? I've only chatted with her a few times in the test kitchen. She seems very knowledgeable about food, of course, and always asked me a bunch of questions about how we run our tea room and the breakfast service for the Hall's B&B, and so forth. I just got the sense she has more ambition than to spend the rest of her life testing recipes that only utilized local dairy products."

"Has she also had any restaurant experience?"

"I think I remember her telling me she worked in some café in St. Austell for a time," Blythe replied. "She later studied cookery at the branch of the Cordon Bleu in London a few years back and appears to know her stuff."

"How can we afford to hire such a paragon?" Meredith asked doubtfully.

"That's why I want a chance to speak to her face-to-face and sell her on what we're doing as sort of an upwardly mobile career move. There aren't many places in an area as rural as this is to find someone who is competent enough to fill Mrs. Q's shoes. *And*, I'm going to offer her one of the cottages on the estate, rent free, in addition to a modest salary, in hopes that might entice her to give us a try."

"Not Painter's, I hope," Meredith said quickly, and then immediately felt that she had over-stepped her bounds. "I mean, I've sort of taken it over as an office for the dog obedience project, but if you think—"

"Oh, heavens no! Painter's Cottage, now, is set aside strictly for the family," Blythe replied with a reassuring smile. "I have too many fond memories of my first summer in Cornwall renting the place from Lucas to ever give it over to strangers, long-term. No, there's a converted limekiln that few guests ever request because it's rather near the road. It's completely renovated, though—"done up" as they say around here—and an easy walk to the Hall."

"Surely she'd be interested in a new challenge like our farm suppers, don't you think?" Meredith said encouragingly. "She'd certainly get the credit for putting her personal stamp on something new in the area."

"Well, the tricky thing is, she'd have to leave her steady job here at the creamery, yet I can't guarantee that things will work out so—we can't offer her a permanent position. *If* the suppers succeed, and *if* our tea room continues to do a decent business, and *if* our numbers of paying guests at least hold steady, we can perhaps start to serve evening meals year round for the B&B guests and also be open to the locals. Sadly, I can't promise her a chef's toque, though, until I see how she is in our kitchen, and if she fits into the lifestyle we have at the estate where everyone pulls his oar."

"Yeah," joked Meredith. "She may have some mistaken notion that Barton Hall is some cushy job where we all lie around the castle expecting the staff to wait on us, not realizing we *are* the staff."

"Exactly. I have to persuade her to take a chance on us, the same way we'd be taking a chance on her."

Blythe glanced at her watch.

"It's just five o'clock. She should be coming out any minute now."

"Well, while we're waiting," Meredith said, "give me your assessment as to how you think Janet is doing? Some days she almost acts like a normal little girl, and others she behaves like the brat she was at the beginning of the summer. Is there something I should be doing…or saying?" she asked. "At least she's not being as rude to *you* anymore."

Blythe paused in thought for a long moment. "Just imagine the years that Ellie filled her head with all that negative stuff about me…and about her family in Wyoming, which includes you, of course. Janet's distrust of us isn't going to disappear overnight. But there's one thing I *have* noticed."

"What?" Meredith asked curiously.

"When she's outdoors, running all over the fields, or playing with your dog, or learning about the sheep, or just lying on the front lawn with my children, staring up at the clouds, it's almost as if she's learning from scratch how to be a normal kid."

"That's true…" murmured Meredith. "Animals, the natural beauty around here, and your very nicely brought up children have done much more than I ever could to change her behavior, that's for sure."

"Well, thank you!" Blythe said with a pleased smile. "That's quite a compliment. But you know, I'm beginning to think you and I don't have to do too much, actually, other than make sure she's safe and sheltered and fed healthy food. Just learning to be part of our crazy family may eventually do the trick."

"Dear heaven, I hope so!" Meredith said fervently, thinking to herself that the summer seemed to be flying by.

*But how much of a miracle can be wrought in only three and a half months?*

Before Meredith could speculate what was going to happen, come September, Blythe pointed through the windshield, gesturing in the direction of an attractive and very buxom redhead exiting the back door of the creamery.

"Oh, goodness! There she is! You go back inside and chat up the manager about his favorite scone recipe, or something, while I hail Ms. Gillis!"

⁂

An hour later, Blythe and Meredith were on their way back to Barton Hall in triumph.

"Blythe Barton-Teague, you are one sweet-talkin' gal!" Meredith declared as the Land Rover left the parking lot of a small café a few blocks from Moorland's and headed toward Gorran Haven and home. "By the time I arrived at your secret rendezvous, I could tell right away Claire was thrilled at the prospect of taking on these farm suppers and also supervising the rest of our food service!"

"It was Limekiln Cottage that clinched it, I think," Blythe mused.

"That, and your glowing endorsement of your good-looking stepson whom she's apparently already met a few times at The Ship Inn Pub in Mevagissey."

"Yes, wasn't that something?" Blythe said with a laugh. "Oh dear. Do you think that was it? Do you think she's a fortune hunter?" she asked with a grin. "Listen, Claire's at least ten years older than her ostensible boss, but I probably should have let Richard vet her as well as us before I offered her the job."

"Well, you were perfectly clear to her that she is going to work this summer on a trial basis," Meredith pointed out. "If Richard can't stand her, you can give her the boot."

Much to Meredith's surprise, not only did Richard Teague *like* Claire Gillis, he immediately offered to help her move her meager possessions into her newly requisitioned cottage. The next day at dinner, the subject came up concerning the arrival of Ms. Gillis on the estate.

"Quite a tasty new hire, don't you think, Richard?" Lucas teased after he'd met their new cook, a woman in her late twenties who wore tight-fitting T shirts under her chef's apron and sported a Cornish accent like Mrs. Quiller's, although muted to some degree by her three years in London studying the culinary arts.

Richard's fair skin suddenly stained pink and he stared at his dinner plate, mumbling, "Yes, I should say...she *is* rather pretty."

"Well, so far, she's a very hard worker," Meredith chimed in, hoping to save him further embarrassment.

"She's got great big boobs, that's for sure," Janet commented, sending Matthew and Lucy into paroxysms of laughter.

"Janet!" Meredith exclaimed.

"That's quite rude, you know," Blythe admonished.

"Well, she *does*," replied Janet truculently, and Matthew and Lucy burst into another round of merriment.

"Richard's already quite sweet on her, don't you know!" Matthew said, sending his compatriots into even more giggles.

"That will be quite enough from all of you!" Lucas said sternly. He looked over at Richard whose entire face and neck had, by then, turned beet red. "Sorry I mentioned it in front of this lot, son," he apologized, nodding in the direction of the children sitting around the table. "She seems to want to do a good job." To the three youngsters he added, "Miss Gillis has got a decade on Richard, here, so I don't know why you children are making such a silly fuss."

In the next days, Meredith noted that Claire Gillis, from all indications, was a model employee. She immediately fell to work refining the menus, reorganizing the kitchen with more efficiency in mind, and helping Richard to harvest Home Farm's many rows of vegetables—produce that had already become a central feature of the outdoor meals.

Within the week, she had also taken on her younger "partner" as a kind of apprentice *sous chef* during the day-and-a-half of food preparation that led up to each event. By any measure, they appeared to work well together and produced meals worthy of a favorable write up in the local newspaper. And given the nine years difference in their ages, Meredith decided that if Richard was a bit smitten with the woman's arresting figure and flaming red hair, it would be a mere summer's flirtation, and end when the heir to Barton Hall returned to Oxford in the autumn.

Sebastian, meanwhile, had left several messages and invitations to dine, but ever since their aborted dinner date, Meredith had made up her mind to keep their relationship strictly a business one. Consequently, she phoned or texted her regrets at times when she knew he'd be working and unable to respond.

On the day he was due to teach his class of would-be search and rescue volunteers and their dogs, she scribbled a note left at Painter's Cottage that she had errands to run.

The following afternoon, a half hour before she was to greet a new group of pet owners interested in qualifying their canines as nursing home service dogs, Sebastian appeared without warning at the door to Painter's Cottage.

"You've been avoiding me."

Meredith looked up from her desk where she'd been stuffing bills into envelopes to give to her clients after class. She surprised even herself with her candid reply.

"I have, actually. Been avoiding you, that is."

"And may I ask why?"

"Because I didn't like it when you uninvited me to dinner and didn't give me the true reason. After that, it just seemed best to keep everything on a professional level. You teach your dog classes and I'll teach mine."

"The reason I...preferred not to meet for a seaside supper that night had nothing to do with you."

"I know that, now. Richard told me that your sister drowned at Hemmick Beach when you were a little boy."

Sebastian's startled reaction and the look of pain that

invaded his features felt like little stabs to her own heart. She sought his gaze and said, "Oh, Sebastian, I was so sad to hear of it, and so very sorry to learn such an awful thing happened to your family."

He was too far away for her to touch his sleeve, but she wanted to.

"But the way you just went cold with me and didn't tell me the real reason upset me," she said softly. "Especially since I'd told you about the children at the hospital who died on my watch, and then you just...well...*made up* a reason why you didn't want to have a beach picnic with me." She paused, and then added, "That exchange with you on the phone last week just pointed up several other times you declined to share with me what was actually going on with you, and I just figured that I...I was reading more into things than was there."

She waited for a response, but Sebastian merely stared at the floor.

Exasperated by his silence she blurted, "Look, Sebastian, I've already had a relationship where the guy made me guess about everything and it didn't end well. I'd rather not do it again. We can still be friends, and—"

"My behaving like that on the phone had nothing to do with you," he insisted, "it was *me*."

"Fine. But the way you handled it all fried my bacon, big time!" she said, a Wyoming colloquialism bursting forth. "Why not just deal with whatever was bothering you?" she demanded. "Why not tell the lady who you were willing to kiss senseless that the beach reminded you of a horrendous family tragedy and tell me what it was! *That's* genuine intimacy, in my book. I would have understood if you'd explained your aversion to going down to a particular stretch of sand, and I would have respected your wishes to avoid the place. But you ducked the entire issue—and you avoided *me,* and that, precisely, is what hurt my feelings. You weren't straight with me and I didn't like it."

Sebastian remained standing in the door as if absorbing her words. Then, at length, he replied, "I'm not ducking anything, now. I came to see you."

Meredith shifted in her chair and shook her head.

"You didn't come here today with the intent of telling me why you didn't want to have a picnic on the beach. You came to try to smooth things over *without* disclosing a thing about yourself, am I right?" she insisted. "All I'm getting is Doctor Pryce, ace veterinarian and dog handler—buttoned up tight. Okay. That's your right to be that way, and it's your choice. You want to keep a wall up? Then so do I— for my own protection, do you understand?"

"Meredith, I am so sorry—"

To her dismay, she felt tears welling in her eyes. "Listen, Sebastian, why prolong something that probably shouldn't happen and is mighty complicated, anyway, given our working together, so—"

"Well, what if I *want* it to happen?" he challenged her, stepping inside the cottage and shutting the door. The room suddenly dimmed and Sebastian seemed much larger than his six-foot frame. "What if I came to apologize for the way I...*avoided* things?"

By this time, Sebastian stood close enough to her chair to place his hands on her shoulders, but Meredith didn't look up from the surface of her desk.

His fingertips began to lightly massage the stiff muscles at the base of her neck in a manner she found thoroughly distracting and rather distressing, given her former determination to keep things purely businesslike between them.

"Look, Meredith...you're a very perceptive woman...almost uncanny, in fact, in the way you fathom things about my character. I *do* avoid what makes me uneasy, but this time I want it to be different. I apologize for…putting up the wall, as you so aptly describe it. I did do that with you the other night on the telephone, and I regret it a lot. And I realize full well that it hurt your feelings."

"I appreciate your acknowledging that, Sebastian, but—"

She felt the sudden warmth of both his palms that had ceased their feathery strokes and now rested quietly, possessively on her shoulders.

"And to prove it, I came to ask you to join *me* on a picnic. After your class today. At Cow Hollow Farm. I'm cooking…with a little help from Susanna Jenner."

"I don't know…" she replied, giving another small shake of her head.

"Please, Meredith," he said, threading the fingers of one hand through her hair at the base of her scalp, and sending little bolts of electricity down her spine. "I behaved like a complete blighter."

"You sure did…whatever that means," she agreed, darting a look at him over her shoulder.

"I think you'd call me a 'jerk,'" he said with a faint grin. "You have to remember, though, that I used to live in a desert where all the women wore burqas, can you imagine? And the only living creature I ever trusted or touched for years was a Springer Spaniel named Max. I'm just getting used to being around females as…friends. Perhaps I'm a little like Rex on the first day he met Holly. I am very drawn to you, but I had a slip."

She turned in her straight-backed chair and tried to avoid losing herself in his steady gaze.

"Well, I admit I'm drawn to you too, in a big way" she disclosed, "but *my* heart's pretty sore from my last serious encounter with a man I liked a lot who refused to tell me what was really going on with him—including that he had a serious problem with alcohol."

"Well, that's *one* malady that needn't concern you about me," he teased.

She rose from the desk and mirrored his previous actions, placing her hands on both his shoulders and daring to look directly into his eyes

"I'm not a mind reader, Sebastian. Either you trust me and I trust you to say how we feel about the personal stuff that's important to us, in real time, or we've got to stay just business partners. Period. No half measures. And believe it or not, as of this moment, at least, I'm fine with that, either way."

"Well, what an easy choice," he said, and in one fluid movement, he gently pulled her against his chest, swiftly kissing her as if she might turn and run away. "I vote for the trusting option," he said, a smile that spelled triumph creasing his mouth as he bent forward to seize her lips again.

Despite feeling herself surrender to the delicious warmth of his mouth probing hers and the strength of his arms around her, a part of her brain fought off his heated advances. She struggled to think clearly. Elusive men were akin to the Phantom of the Opera. Sometimes they were center stage, full of charisma, and other times they locked themselves in the attic—or even lashed out. She couldn't handle that again.

"Oh, Miss Meredith…" he whispered into her hair, "I hated hearing your cool tone when you left messages about class schedules on my voice mail…"

"I was mad at you," she whispered back, "and I hated feeling like that because I *like* you." She paused and then added, "A lot."

She was aware that she was slowly losing the battle to remain rational, what with Sebastian's arousal clearly making itself felt against her thigh.

"Oh, and I like *you* so much that I'd like to roll up with you in a tartan picnic blanket..." he murmured against her throat, and then blew little hurricanes softly against her ear. "That way, you could never stay angry for long..."

Meanwhile, a cacophony of approaching canines, their excited yelps wafting across the field outside Painter's Cottage, brought her out of her haze. With a great act of will, she gently untangled herself from his heated embrace.

"Uh oh, " she said breathlessly. "Saved by the bark."

"Now who's avoiding something?" he said, still holding on to one of her hands.

"Let's just say it's a simple act of self-preservation on my part."

Sebastian gently pressed the hand he still gripped against his chest.

"*Feel* that?" he demanded. Meredith could only stare at her hand locked in his and nod her acknowledgement that she could, indeed, feel the agitated beating of his heart.

"Yes...yes I do."

"Everything's going to be all right," he said softly. "But, please...may I wait for you here? Will you come home with me to Cow Hollow after you teach your class?"

With her free hand, she wagged one finger at him and said, "You are a very dangerous and persuasive fellow, Sebastian Pryce. But I'm only agreeing to a picnic lunch. That's *it*. No funny business on any blankets, understood?"

"Understood," he agreed promptly. "And anyway, aren't you curious to see where I live—and meet my landlady?"

"I liked her husband," was all she was willing to admit.

"You'll like Susanna, too."

"We have to stop off at the Hall so I can grab another jacket. The one I've got on smells of sheep."

Sebastian flashed a grin. "I hardly noticed."

She had to laugh. "You are...such a rogue."

He raised the hand he still held in his own and brushed his lips against the backside of her fingers. "Listen, my Lady of Wyoming...would you mind wearing that cable knit sweater you had on the day you arrived?"

Meredith couldn't help but smile.

"May...*be*. That is, if you play your cards right."

# CHAPTER 9

Meredith taught her pet therapy class until one-thirty, during which time Sebastian put Rex through his paces among the training obstacles on another part of the field. Janet, along with Blythe's two children turned up in time to watch admiringly as Rex ran the agility training course equipment.

When Sebastian summoned Rex back a final time and Meredith walked over after her last students had left, Janet ran out into the field, offering to collect the metal water bowls that Meredith routinely put out at the beginning of every class.

"Thanks very much," Sebastian said as Janet handed him a stack. "That was very kind of you, indeed."

Janet smiled up at him. "You're welcome." Then she added, "Can I come watch you teach your search and rescue class?"

"May *I?*" chimed in Matthew.

"Oh, please, Sebastian, may I, may I, too?" begged Lucy.

Sebastian glanced at Meredith questioningly, who nodded her permission, adding, "but you know you three must be absolutely quiet on the sidelines. If you distract the dogs, even once, Sebastian will have to ask you to leave. Can you all do that?"

Janet appeared about to protest, and then shifted her

scowling face toward Sebastian just in time to see he was nodding in agreement with Meredith. Meekly she said, "Okay then. We'll be good, won't we?" she asked her cousins.

"Yes, yes!" they chorused.

"Excellent," Sebastian said. "Everybody into the back of the Mini with Rex and I'll give you all a lift to the Hall."

Five humans and two dogs squeezed into Sebastian's car parked on the road running between Painter's Cottage and the major tracks of land that comprised the bulk of the Barton Hall Estates. Soon they arrived at the back entrance to the castle and found a space next to a battered gray Vauxhall parked in the inner courtyard. Meredith got out and pushed back her seat so the children and Holly could scamper across the paving stones and into the kitchen to have their lunch and Holly a dog biscuit.

"Whose car is that?" Sebastian asked sharply.

Meredith bent down to speak to him through the open passenger door.

"Our new cook's."

"When did she come on the scene?"

"Claire Gillis? A week ago, it is now. Do you know her? We hired her when Mrs. Quiller suddenly decided to retire. Blythe wooed her away from Moorland's Creamery to manage the tea room and work with Richard on the Home Farm suppers. Quite a sexy miss, it turns out, and a little too keen, in my view, toward our son-and-heir who's nine years her junior, but—" Meredith tilted her head in a gesture of trying to render a fair opinion, "she's a very hard worker and quite a good chef. Want to come in and say hello?"

Sebastian shook his head. "Listen, you run in and get your jacket, why don't you, and I'll wait here."

"Okay. I'll just tell them where I'm going and be back

in a sec."

Meredith made a dash for the back door. Sebastian watched her go and then banged the back of his head a few times against the cushioned headrest.

"Damn and blast! I cannot *believe* this!"

He sank more deeply into the driver's seat and waited, his stomach clenched, for the welcome sound of Meredith returning to the car. Instead, he saw the door to the mudroom open and a redhead walk in his direction clad in black slacks and a tight T-shirt, her ample bosom subdued somewhat by a white chef's apron. With a silent groan, he opened his car door and stood to his full height.

"Well, fancy this," Claire said. "The decorated warrior returns."

"I've been back in Britain for five years, Claire, and I didn't get in touch. That should tell you something."

"I *heard* you managed not to get yourself blown up, but that's about the extent of what your mother knew."

"And why in heaven's name would you expect to hear from me again?"

He felt some satisfaction when she avoided meeting his gaze and clasped and unclasped her hands that she held tightly at her waist.

"Actually, I didn't expect any communication from you after you left for Afghanistan. I—well…the restaurant failed during the financial crisis and Charles and I split up soon afterward. Eventually, I went up to London on my own to earn my culinary certificate, all nice and proper like. Your mother knew you'd enrolled in the Veterinary College, but I realized our paths would never cross up there."

"Did you, now? Fortunately, that turned out to be true—until today." He paused. "And so here you are at Barton Hall, of all places. Becoming good chums with the heir to the estate, I understand."

Claire flicked a thick strand of her luxuriant red hair over her shoulders and then, once more, clasped her hands tightly at the waist.

"I'm here for the summer, at least. I hope it will turn out to be longer."

"I'm sure you do."

She shifted her glance from her entwined fingers and searched his face. "What's that supposed to mean? And what do you care anyway? Richard tells me you and Meredith have quite the little dog academy launched here. So you've also put your stake in the ground at Barton Hall, I see."

"As you've pointed out yourself. Life moves on. Let's keep it that way, shall we? I'll keep clear—with my mouth shut—if you will."

"Are those your terms for a Peace Treaty?" she asked sharply.

Over Claire's shoulder, he saw the castle's back door open halfway. Meredith appeared to be speaking to someone just inside the mudroom. Holly ran ahead of her and then, at her mistress's command, skittered to a stop halfway to the car and sat on her haunches until Meredith caught up with her.

"Here she comes, dog and all," Claire said with a mocking edge to her voice.

"You'd better go," Sebastian replied. "*Now.*"

Meredith was wearing the cream colored cable-knit sweater she'd had on the day she arrived at Barton Hall and hailed them both as she and Holly trotted toward the two parked cars.

She slowed to a walk and said, "You two know each other, I see."

"From another life," Sebastian said shortly. "We'd

better get going, or Susanna will have given up on us."

Claire arched a henna eyebrow. "Ah, Susanna and William. They're still together?"

Sebastian didn't answer and the three stood in a tight little circle, staring at each other. Finally Meredith broke the silence.

"Right. Well...is it okay if we bring Holly, Sebastian? She and Rex get along fine, now, and—"

"Absolutely. Hop in."

Meredith opened the door to the Mini, allowing her dog to jump into the back next to Rex, and then climbed into the front passenger seat. She waved through the window.

"Bye, Claire. Richard said you two had a mountain of potatoes to peel, poor you. I can give you a hand later slicing the apples, if you like."

"No worries. We'll make fast work of all of it and stash everything in the freezer," she replied, and then bent even with the open car window to address them both. "After that," she added, darting a glance at Sebastian and smiling brightly, "I expect, we'll have our own picnic down at Hemmick Beach. Richard says the tide will be out all afternoon. Should be nice. So, ta for now."

Sebastian sat staring out the windshield for a few seconds and then started the engine and put his car in gear. He swiftly maneuvered the vehicle out of the courtyard and accelerated down the long gravel drive, away from Barton Hall.

They rode in silence for a few miles with Holly and Rex curled up companionably in the back seat. Once the female dog had gone out of season, the two canines got along famously, with Rex behaving like a perfect gentleman.

"Okay," Meredith said, finally. "What gives?"

"You're asking how do I know Claire Gillis, yes? "

"Her crack just now about having a 'nice picnic at

Hemmick Beach' was obviously intended to stick a knife in your ribs. Call me crazy, but I think you know her pretty darn well."

"Knew her. Well. But not as well as I thought. I haven't laid eyes on her in more than five years."

"And?"

"And, it's a longer conversation than the time it takes to drive these last three miles from here to Cow Hollow Farm."

"*Sebastian...*" Meredith said in a warning tone.

At that same moment, his mobile phone emitted a series of insistent beeps.

"Oh, bugger all!" he cursed. "That's CSRT."

He pulled over to the side of the road and pushed the talk button, greeted the caller, and then listened gravely for a few minutes.

"Right, Colonel Wainwright. Yes, sir...all right. Up beyond St. Austell? The area west of Bodmin Moor? Yes, the Holbush mine. Copper? Ah...tin. *Right.* I know the one." He reached for a pad and pencil in the car's glove box and jotted down some notes.

Meredith whispered, "Somebody's missing?"

Sebastian nodded and said into his phone, "Colonel, I've got Meredith Champlin with me...that's right, from Barton Hall. Where I teach the potential CSRT volunteers and their dogs. She's got her herding dog with her, a highly trained Corgi, as I've mentioned. Yes, certified. She's also a pediatric nurse in the States. I'd like to—That's all right with you? Good. Yes, Rex is with us. Better to come straight to the site, yes? Excellent, sir. Meet you there."

He clicked off his phone, punched in another number, handed her his mobile and swiftly put the car in gear. "Here, can you speak to Susanna and tell her that, hopefully, we'll be back in time to eat our picnic lunch for supper? The number is queued up."

"Sure," she agreed, pressing the call button as Sebastian quickly reversed the car's direction, heading at top speed for the road that led to the hills beyond St. Austell.

Before Susanna Jenner answered the phone, Sebastian asked Meredith, "Do you think you're up to being an unofficial member of the Cornwall Search and Rescue Team for a few hours? A little boy is missing. He may have fallen down a mine shaft...or off a cliff."

⁰⟲⟳⁹

It was a good ten degrees cooler up on the moor and Meredith was grateful for her cable knit sweater and an extra CSRT jacket that Sebastian requisitioned out of one of the team's vans. She made a quick call on Sebastian's mobile to Blythe to let her know their picnic plans had altered drastically.

"Don't expect me for supper," she warned. "There's no telling how long this will last."

"You stay safe, you hear?" Blythe cautioned.

"Holly and I will be protected by the entire Cornwall Search and Rescue Team," Meredith replied, hoping to reassure her cousin that she'd be fine, despite the challenging mission ahead. "I'm really just tagging along, trying to stay out from under foot. It was quicker to have me come with Sebastian than for him to have to drive me all the way back to the Hall. Don't worry...I'll be fine, but I may be out of mobile range at times, so I didn't want you to worry."

"Thanks for the call," Blythe replied. "We'll see you later, or tomorrow, if the search runs really late."

Meredith handed the phone back to Sebastian as Colonel Wainwright began to describe to the assembled volunteers the array of abandoned deep shafts and smelting towers dotted the craggy area behind the town of St. Austell where the mining industry was long a thing of the past.

A base camp had already been established by the CSR Team at the direction of the Lead Police Search Advisor from the St. Austell constabulary that had been the first to arrive. The family of the missing twelve-year old, Rodney Bain, was huddled near their small car packed to overflowing with camping gear, his young mother clutching the shoulders of her daughter and trying not to cry. The police officer in charge was on his car phone, presumably talking to headquarters, while Rodney Bain's father dug into a canvas bag for various items of clothing that had the child's scent. The boy had gone missing right after breakfast when the parents were busy packing up their gear after their morning meal.

"We'd done the big moor trail yesterday," Mr. Bain was telling Graham Wainwright, the volunteer search and rescue team leader she'd heard Sebastian talking to earlier. Wainwright was a man of middle stature with thick, steel-gray hair and the erect posture of a former career army colonel, which he had been until his retirement and return to his native Cornwall. The boy's father continued, "Then we came down here on the lower moor to have our lunch. Young Rod was fascinated, he was, by the old mines we passed on the walk. He wanted to 'explore' for a bit, as he put it."

Rod's mother said tearfully, "We *told* him not to go far while we packed up and I definitely warned him not to go near the mine shafts…" and then she stifled a sob.

"But you know boys that age…" said Mr. Bain, his sentence drifting off, remorse for their having allowed their son to wander off clearly etched on his brow.

"He can't have gone far," assured Wainwright, clad as the entire team was, in their red and black CSRT anoraks. The lead police officer assigned to the case had called them out within fifteen minutes of receiving the request to help with the search. "We'll check all of the shafts in the region, Mr. Bain, but we'd best get started."

Wainwright then turned to greet Meredith cordially when Sebastian introduced them, and soon set to giving the various team members their directives. They were to fan out in a systematic way to search the territory surrounding a number of old, abandoned mineshafts in the area that were marked on maps he distributed to each group.

"Pryce, you and Ms. Champlin give a good search up at the Holbush mine engine house area and everything within a half-mile radius of it, if you will. It's a two-story stone building above the ground floor, abandoned, of course, and with numerous hazards, I'd expect, so do watch your footing as you tramp around. Here's the lad's jumper," he said, handing Sebastian a brown cardigan.

Meredith noted the stricken expression on Mrs. Bain's face, and her heart went out to the poor woman. She recalled how frightened she had been when Sebastian had allowed Rex to sniff Janet's blue sweater. Wainwright passed other items of the child's clothing to the other members of the K9 team, and gave instructions to some additional volunteer searchers.

Wainwright addressed his search troops. "If you find something, or a situation that calls for an air evacuation, call here at once." Everyone in the SART group nodded assent.

"All right, searchers," said the Lead Police Search Advisor to the assembled, "Do check in here by mobile, if you can get a signal, every half hour, and come back to this post before dusk if you haven't found anything. All right, chaps, ladies…let's go! Good luck! "

Colonel Wainwright then instructed a man he addressed as Beven Glynn to take the Bains into the van out of the wind and wait for word. It was decided that Holly should remain behind in the car, as she might be a distraction to the other dogs that hadn't trained with her.

"You're all right with that, are you, Meredith?" Sebastian asked as they prepared to set out on foot for their assigned search area.

"Yes fine," she nodded. Then she had a thought and turned to address the SAR leader.

"Colonel Wainwright, as you know, Holly is a certified therapy dog. What if we allowed the Bain family's little girl to keep Holly company while we're out searching? It might serve as a distraction for a while. If they have to leave, just have someone give the dog a bit of water and then put her in Sebastian's car with the windows cracked. It's a cool day. She'll be fine with all you around her until we get back."

"Excellent suggestion, and very kind, I must say," Wainwright replied. "I'll just have a word with the Bains."

Meredith quickly introduced little Charlotte Bain to the Corgi and left them both in the back seat of the van. As Holly had been taught, she soon rolled on her back, allowing the child to stroke her tummy. Mrs. Bain looked up at Meredith, her eyes brimming with gratitude.

"Thank you *so* much," she said, again close to tears.

"You're welcome," Meredith replied, giving the distraught woman's arm a gentle squeeze. "Stay, Holly." And to the Bains, "We'll be back as soon as we can."

Meredith hurried to catch up with Sebastian who was fifty yards beyond the base camp, holding a child's pullover in his hand. He urged Rex to bury his nose in the knitted material belonging to the missing child.

"As I said when we were looking for Janet, our SAR dogs are trained to locate any human being in the region and bark before running back to us as an indication they've made a 'find,'" he explained, "but I think allowing them sniff a piece of clothing from the missing person, if it's available, can't hurt and it might help."

"Bloodhounds are trained differently, aren't they? Scent-specific, or something like that?"

"Not only trained differently, their noses *are* different, with two hundred and thirty *million* scent receptors that can distinguish various smells and keep track of them." Sebastian looked down at his dog, "Rex and other smaller dogs can remember a general scent—human—but I always wonder if we gave him more 'information,' so to speak, whether, over time, that wouldn't give his olfactory memory a boost. Okay boy…" he commanded. "Find, Rex! *Find!*"

The Border Collie scampered ahead, his orange vest a bright beacon as Sebastian and Meredith immediately set off in the direction marked on their map. After a half hour of searching, Sebastian made his first call to Wainwright, reporting no sightings.

Five minutes later, a large, abandoned building hove into view, perched on a rugged slope where mining operations had been halted nearly a century earlier.

The Holbush engine house was constructed of pale stones, now smothered in a cloak of green vines that covered several windows of the narrow building that had once housed a huge metal apparatus used in the extraction of tin ore buried deep in the rolling hills beneath the stonework foundations.

Without speaking, Sebastian pointed at Rex who had lifted his head, sniffing the air. The collie paused a few seconds longer before setting off on a course that would take him to the left of the building. In the distance stood a tall stone chimney with the top of its stack broken off in jagged pieces. Behind it was another structure, some thirty feet high, also made of stone, that was shaped like a bottle with a wide base and narrow throat. Unlike the smoother stone surfaces of the two other structures, this smelting stack's exterior had jagged pieces of rock sticking out of its perimeter in a curious pattern that that allowed admittedly precarious footholds for a climber to access the top portions.

"Would you have a look in the engine house, over there," said Sebastian, pointing at the vine-covered building, "but mind you, don't step on any wooden covers that might have been put there to protect the shafts," he warned Meredith. "They're usually rotted, and if you see any broken ones, or if you see any evidence that the boy has crawled above the first floor, just give a shout, but don't go up higher on your own, agreed?"

"Right," Meredith confirmed, heading off in the direction Sebastian had indicated.

"I'll have a closer look at those smelting stacks and that huge section of brambles over there that Rex seems so interested in," Sebastian called back to her, hurrying to catch up with his dog.

Meredith entered through the stone arch that gave access to the abandoned engine house, calling Rodney's name, and hearing it echo back to her from the barreled ceiling overhead. She had barely worked her way gingerly across the floor, avoiding the wooden covers that Sebastian had warned her about, when she heard Rex's insistent barking fifty yards away.

She carefully retraced her steps, emerging into the sunlight and shading her eyes against the glare. Suddenly, she caught a quick glimpse of Sebastian's red anorak among an enormous growth of bright green vegetation near the tall chimneystack in the shape of an old-fashioned milk bottle that she'd noted earlier.

"Found him!" Sebastian shouted. "Over here!"

"I hear you!" Meredith responded excitedly, and took off at a dead run toward the mass of brambles up ahead.

"Is he conscious?" Meredith called as she drew closer.

"Yes, but he's hurt. I've called in for a medevac."

Meredith sprinted the rest of the distance separating her from Sebastian and the boy. The twelve-year-old was a few feet from the base of the second chimney stack, lying on his back with one leg bent at the knee and pinioned at an alarming angle behind his prone body. She quickly knelt by his side and removed her jacket and gently placed it over him to keep him warm.

"I've got a thermal blanket in my pack," Sebastian said under his breath. "It should be on top of the hand-held video computer in there."

"The what?" she asked quietly as she put the thermal over the child, careful not to move him in any way in case he had suffered more injuries than the leg that she was certain was severely broken.

"Is it possible little Cornwall is ahead of the States? This contraption will link us to a high-tech health facility where we'll feed them information and they can do an assessment of how he's doing."

"Wow..." she murmured, peering at the device. Meanwhile, her own medical training kicking in, she smiled and said, "Hello, Rodney." She gently pressed her fingers on his pulse and smiled. "My name is Meredith and I'm a nurse. You're going to be all right, sweetheart. Sebastian and I are here to take care of you and get you to doctors who will fix your leg."

His pulse was within the normal range, given the trauma he'd experienced, and she was relieved to see the boy seemed alert, but to test his responses, she asked him his full name, what day it was, and if it hurt anywhere else beyond his leg. She was concerned that he might also have suffered internal injury, a spinal fracture, or a possible concussion. For his part, Rodney had easily answered all her questions and performed well when she asked him to wiggle the fingers on both hands. "How about the toes on your good foot? That's excellent!" she said, as Sebastian entered the information she gave him into his device and followed any additional prompts from the telehealth center.

"My other leg hurts awfully," the boy whispered.

"I know, sweetheart. I'm sure it does." She smiled encouragingly. "But the doctors will take care of you and you'll be back with your parents very soon. They will be *so* happy to see you."

"They'll be angry," he murmured, his freckled face pale with a degree of shock that had already set in and his cheeks stained with tears he must have shed before Sebastian found him in a heap near the smoke stack that he'd obviously attempted to scale.

"Oh, I wouldn't worry too much about that. They'll be so happy to know you're all right, you may only get a stern lecture," she said, smiling reassuringly.

"I didn't go near the shafts, like they told me not to," he said, anxious to explain how he'd ended up on the ground. "But I...I tried to see how high I could go on those footholds on the chimneystack and one of those stones broke off when I stepped on it. It really wasn't my fault, Nurse. The stone just...broke. Will you tell Mum and Dad that?"

Meredith tried not to smile and said soothingly, "We'll explain how it all happened, but let's not worry about any of that right now." To Sebastian she said in a low voice, "We shouldn't move his head or neck, but perhaps you can give him a few sips of water from your canteen."

Within twenty minutes, the bright yellow Royal Air Force helicopter set down in a clearing a hundred yards from the mine engine house. The emergency crew had already received the information sent via the telehealth device, but asked Sebastian and Meredith to give their own summation of the child's condition. She swiftly concluded by advising that she and Sebastian had been careful not to move the child's leg, head, or neck.

"Excellent," said the chief medevac officer. "We'll get him on the stretcher, now, as carefully as we can."

The medics eased on a brace to stabilize Rodney's neck and back, and then gently placed him on the stretcher they'd brought to the site. Within minutes, he was in the chopper and the team was ready to take off.

"Thanks, both of you," shouted the officer over the drone of the revolving blades. He smiled at Meredith. "Nice to have a real, live nurse in these situations, I can tell you. See you next time, Sebastian. Good work, both of you, and that includes *you*, Rex!" he added, ruffling the fur on the dog's head.

The helicopter crew lifted off, and soon, the large, yellow Westland Sea King was a mere speck in the sky and heading for the nearest hospital. In less than half an hour, Sebastian and Meredith returned to base operations with the triumphant Rex trotting along beside them.

"Good job!" Graham Wainwright said as they approached the CSRT vehicles. "As soon as we heard you'd found the lad, I sent Beven to lead the Bain family in their car to the hospital where they'll meet up with the youngster." He smiled broadly at Meredith. "Your Holly is curled up in Sebastian's Mini, sound asleep, but she was a grand companion to the little girl while they waited for word."

Meredith crossed quickly to the car and let the Corgi

hop out and run directly toward Rex, who gave a welcoming bark. Meredith was glad that Holly had served as a distraction during the search, and could only imagine the relief the family must be feeling as they sped toward their rescued son.

"The co-pilot radioed us how smoothly the retrieval went," Wainwright continued. "He mentioned specifically that it made a big difference to have a qualified nurse on the ground," he addressed Meredith with a pleased expression.

She hastened to assure him, "I only did what any volunteer with first aid training would do." She was only too aware that it probably wouldn't be sanctioned in Britain for someone without local certification to be functioning in the official capacity of a nurse. "We didn't move the child but merely did the basic checks to make sure there was nothing more serious than a broken leg. Fortunately, young Rodney seemed otherwise okay, but I'm sure they'll assess him thoroughly at the hospital."

"He was a lucky lad," Sebastian agreed, giving Meredith's shoulders an appreciative squeeze. He glanced down at Rex who was waiting close by. "And Rex, here, did his job perfectly and took me right to him."

By this time, the team's search and rescue van had pulled parallel to Sebastian's Mini. Its driver, Beven Glynn, returned from the local hospital where he'd dropped off the Bains, entered their circle, listening intently to the last of their conversation.

"So, I take it that no unexpected events occurred between these two this time?" he said, gesturing to the two dogs. He thrust out his hand toward Meredith. "Hello, I'm a colleague of Sebastian's. We weren't formerly introduced at Barton Hall that day you arrived in Cornwall. Beven Glynn's the name."

Meredith briefly took his hand, regarding him coolly. Why in the world did he have to bring up the incident between Rex and Holly in front of Sebastian's supervisor?

"Yes, I'm happy to report, all went perfectly today. Rex found the boy as soon as he got within the zone of scent, and Holly, as I'm sure you noticed, remained here keeping the Bain daughter company during the search for her brother. I guess you could say we were two-for-two," she added with a smile in Graham Wainwright's direction.

"Sebastian," said Graham, "why don't you file your report via email first thing, tomorrow? You two are probably knackered by now, and the medevac team gave me most of the information I need. I'll email you my draft and you can fill in any details I've missed, and send it back." He returned Meredith's smile. "And thank you again so much—may I call you Meredith? It was certainly a bonus to have you with us today. How long will you be visiting Cornwall?"

"My plan has been to stay the summer."

"Pity. I thought if you decided to continue with your dog obedience school, I might persuade you to sign on with us. We could certainly use someone with your unique combination of skills."

Meredith felt her fatigue melt in the warmth of Wainwright's praise.

"Well, thank you, Colonel Wainwright! It was a pleasure to have been of whatever help I could render in the situation. I'm just glad young Rodney is going to be okay."

"Ready?" Sebastian asked. "Shall we go?"

Meredith nodded affirmatively, then thought, *Ready for what, I wonder?*

# CHAPTER 10

Famished after being denied their lunchtime picnic, Sebastian and Meredith decided to head directly for Cow Hollow Farm, just a few miles to the other side of St. Austell.

"Shall we make a late supper out of the fare Susanna has undoubtedly left in her refrigerator?" he suggested.

"Sounds great," Meredith answered. "What's with that Beven character?" she asked as they sped toward Sebastian's farm. "He sure seems to want to put you in a bad light with the Colonel."

"It's just a game he plays," Sebastian replied with a shrug. "He's the only man on the rescue team who hasn't seen some sort of military service and I think he attempts to bolster his image with his superiors by looking for chinks in our armor."

"What a drag," she commented.

"He's just a pesky gnat. I must say, though, that he does a good job with the vehicles. Virtually never has a breakdown. Ah...here we are!" he said, wheeling the Mini to a stop outside the Jenner's farmhouse. "Come meet Susanna and say 'hello' to William again." He pointed to the kitchen windows aglow in the dusk. "I think they've sat down to dinner."

"Oh, I don't want to barge in," she said hastily.

"There's a picnic basket waiting for us," he reminded

her. "We won't be disturbing them. But first, we'll feed the dogs, yes?"

Susanna and William Jenner were, indeed, at the kitchen table enjoying the last of their evening meal. Susanna jumped to her feet to bid them welcome.

"So this is Meredith!" she said, smiling warmly. "So lovely to meet you. I've got your picnic all ready, stored in the 'fridge, though where you want to eat it, now that the sun's nearly gone down, I'll leave to Sebastian."

Meredith shook hands with both Jenners, while Sebastian set about quickly filling two bowls with food for the dogs.

William said, "Actually, we've just finished our supper, but Meredith, would you mind awfully if Sebo had a look at an ailing animal we've been nursing all day? She's still got some problems, Sebo, and Gordon appears as puzzled as I am. Maybe you have some notion of what we should try next. I really think another sort of antibiotic cream for that skin infection is called for. Can you come see what you think?"

Sebastian looked at Meredith questioningly.

"Oh, absolutely, you go...go on. What I need at the moment is a good face wash and a cup of coffee to revive me, if you have one, Susanna?"

"Just brewed a new pot on the hob," she replied cheerfully. "And that will also give us women a chance to exchange information about dear Sebo, here," she added with a wicked smile.

Sebastian wagged a finger at his landlady. "I'm asking you not to disclose any military secrets to this woman, Susanna," he said, and though smiling, Meredith wondered if he didn't have a few secrets that she'd like very much to know?

*Like what's the deal with Claire Gillis?*

And she still wondered why he hadn't told her before Richard did what had happened at Hemmick Beach.

*And then there's the story with his mother…*

After Meredith used the washroom, Susanna poured them both cups of coffee and put out some cheese at the table where the dinner plates had been cleared. They settled down to wait for the men to return.

"So what happened on the search and rescue call?" Susanna wanted to know.

When Meredith recounted their afternoon, her hostess gazed across the table and said, "Well! Sebo has never, *ever* taken a woman with him on an incident call. That must mean he's quite taken with you, Miss Meredith Champlin."

"Oh, I just happened to be in the car on our way to our aborted picnic when the team leader called."

"Trust me, under normal circumstances, you would have found yourself dropped at the nearest bus kiosk," Susanna said, laughing. She pointed to the two dogs that she'd given special dispensation to remain indoors. "Look how your pups are curled up together in front of the Aga. They already look like an old married couple."

"Susanna!" Meredith protested, joining in with her hostess' laughter.

"I think it's a sign," Susanna pronounced solemnly.

"Of *what*, I have no idea," Meredith shot back. "Sebastian and I have only known each other since mid-May, may I remind you." She paused, and then plunged ahead with the question uppermost on her mind. "But, as a matter of fact, Susanna…can you tell me who the heck Claire Gillis is—or was—regarding Sebastian?"

"Uh oh. Has Sebastian *seen* her? If so, it'll be the first time in five years."

"She's been hired to take over the cooking chores from Mrs. Quiller, the cook and housekeeper, who's retiring from service at Barton Hall. Claire and Sebastian virtually ran into each other at the estate this afternoon. The two of them were having what looked to me like a rather heated discussion when I came out of the Hall and headed for the car. Afterward, all Sebastian would say is that 'it's a long story.' Frankly, I could tell right away that he wanted to avoid talking about it, but he was saved by the call from his search and rescue leader and then off we went to the site."

Susanna set her coffee mug down with a bang. "Oh, Sebo!" she said in frustration as if he were in the kitchen with them. She rose from the table and reached for the coffee pot, pouring herself a refill, and then topping off Meredith's cup. "The pair were an item right after he was at University with William and me," Susanna said, wrinkling her forehead in thought. "In fact, they shared a flat in St. Austell at one time. Claire worked at some restaurant when he was working for his uncle. Then they suddenly split up and he never would say *why*, even to William and me, and we're his best friends! Claims he's too much of a gentleman, and rubbish like that, but she's definitely a sore spot with him. I haven't seen her in donkeys' years, though I'd heard she was working at Moorland's. All I know is that after their breakup, he immediately signed on for the most hazardous duty imaginable and went off to Afghanistan with the canine bomb squad—can you imagine? We were in a state of total anxiety the entire two years he was in service."

"I *can* imagine," Meredith murmured, thinking of Shep O'Brien's mother who said she never drew a peaceful breath while her son was in Iraq. "Thank God Sebastian came back in one piece. No wonder he loves dogs. They probably saved his life any number of times."

"Absolutely…though whether he came back in one piece is a matter for debate."

"What do you mean?" Meredith asked, alarmed by Susanna's ominous tone. She mentally scrolled through a list of maladies that Shep had brought home with him following two deployments to Iraq. "Do you think he suffers from Post Traumatic Stress Disorder?"

"Oh, no...at least I've asked him that, point blank, and he said that he's had very little sign of PTSD. I think part of whatever Sebo suffered from after he broke up with Claire—and until now—predates his military service."

"Really? Well, here's another wrinkle," Meredith said, wondering at the intimacy of a conversation with a woman she'd only just met. Even so, she felt instinctively she could trust Susanna only to have Sebastian's best interests at heart. "Claire Gillis is nearly a decade older than Richard Teague, with whom she's doing our Farm-To-Table supper series this summer. But already, you can cut the sexual tension between them with a kitchen knife—or at least plainly see how attracted to Claire that *Richard* is. Claire looks like potentially big trouble, no matter how I view this."

"Oh, now *that* little development certainly makes life interesting, doesn't it, given that Richard is the heir to Barton Hall, and all?" Susanna paused, mulling something over. Then she said, "Well, if I were you, I'd just flat out ask Sebo what he feels about Claire. It's time he dealt with whatever it is."

"No, I've already asked him about it in the car earlier today," she countered. "It's his decision whether he wants to tell me about it or not. But you said something earlier...that you think there's something in Sebastian's past that predates his problems with Claire. Any idea of what it is?"

"Not really, except my guess is that it involves his mother somehow," Susanna replied thoughtfully. "One thing is for certain...I can tell he's quite smitten with you, and you with him, am I correct?" Susanna didn't wait for Meredith's reply, but continued, "So I'll give you my—albeit amateur—observations. Whatever happened with Claire Gillis was just another nail in the coffin and certainly plays a part in his having been, to date, gun-shy about seriously having a woman in his life. Still and all, from what I've seen during the decade I've known Sebo, it's his rather sketchy relationship with his mum—and his brothers, too—that holds the key, but don't ask me what that is, because I simply don't know."

"Have you asked?"

Susanna nodded. "Directly, indirectly, and skirting the edges, but nothing."

"I saw his mother from across a street in St. Austell, but Sebastian hurried us away."

"Elizabeth Pryce? Well, she lives in St. Austell in the old family home. It's just a cottage, really...and she's still making life miserable for her three surviving sons, from all I've been able to gather. Sebo simply refuses to return her calls."

"I do know that his little sister drowned at Hemmick Beach. I wonder if it had something to do with that?"

"He *told* you that?"

"No," Meredith admitted. "Richard Teague mentioned it and then I asked Sebastian about it, but he sort of clammed up on that, too, as a matter of fact. It's a bit complicated to relate here, but I think his not wanting to talk about his sister's death, either, is why he asked you to help him prepare a picnic we could eat *here*, instead of on Hemmick Beach." Meredith stared somberly across the table at Susanna, who was gazing at her with an expression of both warmth and sympathy. "He definitely is a man of mystery who keeps his troubles to himself."

"Give him some time," Susanna urged. "I think his meeting you this summer has helped him turn a corner. For example, he's never once asked a woman to come here to meet us, before now." Then she emitted a loud chuckle. "That's probably because he knows I'd be all over him, as I intend to be, now that you're on the scene." She sobered. "You should know by now, we're very, very fond of Sebastian, Meredith. He's one of the best friends I've ever had and has helped us keep this place afloat during some pretty harrowing financial times these last few years. He's a wonderful man, and both William and I think that from everything we've seen and heard so far, you're very good news yourself."

Meredith wondered if the blush she felt had reached her cheeks. She smiled at Susanna, hoping she'd become a friend.

"That is so sweet of you to say. I'll admit that I'm very drawn to the guy, but there are some things that make *me* gun-shy...such as this hangover he appears to be suffering regarding Claire Gillis."

"I know, I know," Susanna interrupted, shaking her head in agreement, "but as I said...give him time to get used to being with someone who won't sting him where it hurts." She laughed again and added, "As you can see, I'm the Queen of making snap judgments about people, and as William will tell you, I'm almost always right!"

Meredith herself laughed aloud. "You know, Susanna, I think this is the start of a beautiful friendship."

"Well, if you're anything like your cousin Blythe, whom I *adore*...I think so too!"

Just then, the sound of stomping of feet could be heard on the stone slab outside the kitchen door and both women heard water hosing off the barnyard debris from men's rubber boots.

"Well, here they come!" Susanna chortled with a Cheshire cat smile. "I have no idea where Sebastian plans to have this supper I made you, but I hope you two have a lovely time tonight!"

Her words of benediction were barely out of her mouth when Sebastian and William entered the kitchen. Susanna immediately pulled food items out of her refrigerator, packed them in the waiting basket, and handed her tenant the bulging picnic hamper and a bottle of French burgundy.

"You two and the dogs are most welcome to eat right here in the kitchen, but you'll have to excuse us. We're both totally knackered, aren't we, William, and we're usually in our beds by nine."

And, within moments, Meredith and Sebastian found themselves alone.

"Well, that was a quick exit," Meredith observed dryly.

"Susanna obviously likes you, but sometimes she's as subtle as a lorry loaded with a million liters of milk," Sebastian replied, his hand resting on the heavy basket. "She clearly wanted us to eat alone."

"I'm fine with wherever we eat," Meredith said and pointed to the picnic hamper, "but it's getting late and I'm starving. Feed me, Doctor Dog, will you please?"

"I've got an idea!" Sebastian proposed suddenly. "I promised you a picnic, and a picnic you shall have." He walked swiftly to the pantry door and opened it. "Come, Rex, Holly…everyone follow me."

He turned off the lights in the kitchen and led the way out through the mudroom and across the fifty yards between the farmhouse and a large stone building.

"This is the old livery stable," he explained over his shoulder. "Susanna's done up the loft where I'm living, and she's in the process of turning the old horse stalls down here into two apartments, but that's on hold right now. It's cleaned up, though. We could spread a blanket down here and—"

"A picnic on a horse blanket?" she asked with a grin. "I've done *that* before…"

"I was going to fetch a proper blanket off my bed upstairs."

"And then you'll sleep under it after it's been on the ground in a livery stable? You are a rugged sort, Sebastian Pryce, but then, of course, you probably endured worse in Afghanistan, so it wouldn't faze you."

Sebastian raised a questioning eyebrow, "Of course," he suggested with a sly expression, "we *could* simply spread out our picnic on the floor upstairs…or top of my bed, which would be a softer surface?"

"Hmmm…" she responded, "Would that be the tartan blanket you mentioned you'd like to roll us up in?" She meant her tone to be light and joking, but Sebastian paused and appeared rather sheepish.

"Yes it is. I forgot. Well, perhaps we could—"

"I think a picnic in your loft sounds wonderful. But you've just gotta feed me—and fast," she said, teasing. "I can get a little snarly when my blood sugar runs too low."

Meredith followed Sebastian up a set of well-worn stone steps—the dogs trailing behind—and waited at the top as he flipped the switch that instantly illuminated his one room living quarters.

"Oh…this is wonderful," she breathed, running her hand along the stone wall nearest her, her gaze taking in the ancient, hand-chiseled beams overhead, along with the dormers where a bed sporting a garnet and forest green tartan blanket stood under one window, and a small efficiency kitchen was tucked under the other. As with Painter's Cottage, she caught a glimpse of a claw-and-ball footed bathtub positioned behind a large wooden screen.

"This place could be in a cottage magazine or something," she exclaimed, noting how squared-away everything looked and thinking this must have been how Sebastian learned to live in the military.

"Susanna's an artist at heart," he agreed. "She can paint, weave, and even do interior decoration on a non-existent budget. I love this place, though in the winter, these stone walls can get pretty cold and dank."

He deposited the picnic basket at the foot of his bed and set to opening the bottle of wine. He handed her a glass of a strong, red burgundy and clinked the edge of his goblet to hers.

"Here's to one of the best field partners I ever worked with." He gestured toward the bed. "Have a seat."

Stunned by the compliment, she managed to smile her thanks and sank, crossed legged, onto the tartan blanket near the bed's wooden headboard. Then, she took a long draught from her glass, feeling in serious need of the stimulating liquid. Rex settled himself on a rug on the floor at the side of the bed, leaving room for Holly, who lay down next to him and the two dogs immediately closed their eyes.

"They're both exhausted," Meredith said, gazing over the lip of her wine glass at Sebastian who remained standing by the side of the bed. His dark brown eyes held hers for a long moment and everything in her universe seemed to freeze within a frame.

"I bet you're tired too," he said after a long pause, breaking the moment as he set his wine glass on his bedside table. "So, *food...*food is next, m'lady."

*And for dessert?*

Meredith watched expectantly as Sebastian swiftly brought two china plates from a shelf in his galley kitchen and placed the picnic hamper between them on the side of the mattress. He took his place, also cross-legged, at the foot of the bed while she unpacked a delicious meal of Cornish meat pasties, potato salad, and sliced tomatoes and mozzarella, drizzled in olive oil and balsamic vinegar. To top off their meal, Susanna had tucked in a slice, each, of chocolate cake.

"Oh, Lordy, did anything ever taste so good?" she said with her mouth full.

Sebastian refilled her wine glass and his own as well. Fully sated, Meredith leaned against the carved wooden headboard of what she surmised was an ancient farmhouse bed that had been in William's family for generations. She folded her hands contentedly around her wine glass that was balanced in her lap.

"What a day we had," she said with a glance at a large, round, railroad clock face that hung on the opposite wall. "I should probably ask you to drive me home pretty soon before we both doze off."

"Aren't you interested to learn about how I know Claire Gillis?"

His surprising words instantly roused her from the soporific effect their meal had been having on her and she couldn't help but allow her astonishment to show. Taking another sip of wine to give herself time to think, she finally said, "I believe I could keep awake for that saga...yes."

"Even Susanna doesn't know the whole story."

"So I gathered. I swear I didn't ask her much, but she volunteered that you and Claire were once an item and all Susanna knew was that you broke it off abruptly and you never revealed why." She cast him a direct look. "So, why *did* you break up?"

"The *why* isn't relevant to what I want you to know now, Meredith," he said, and set his glass on the bedside table once again.

Next, he reached across the small space separating their seated positions on the bed and retrieved her glass, stowing it next to his. Taking her hands, he encased them both in his own.

"Hear this," he said, gazing at her intently. "I have absolutely no interest in Claire Gillis. It's been five years and a lifetime since I've seen her—until today, as a matter of fact. There's no unrequited love on my part. No pangs of regret that I broke it off. No desire—ever—to rekindle my former relationship with her. It's finished, period. I want you to know that, since I expect you're going to see the woman often, now that she's employed at Barton Hall."

Meredith flushed and stared at their joined hands. "She's been given a cottage on the property rent-free as part of her compensation, so I'd be lying if I didn't say I'm really glad to hear what you just told me." She paused, and then added in a low voice. "Since we're trading need-to-know memos tonight, in anticipation of who-knows-what—"

Sebastian's loud laugh cut her off, mid-sentence.

"You are a complete original, Meredith Champlin!"

"Thank you for the compliment...I guess," she replied, "but I want you to hear something from me about Shep...Shepard O'Brien, the boyfriend I told you about before," she continued. "I'm glad our relationship is over, but, unlike what you've just said to me, I still feel some regret and sadness it didn't work out and that he's in such a bad way. I guess you've had more time and distance than I..."

"Didn't you tell me that Shep served in Iraq?" he asked, retrieving their wine glasses and handing her hers.

"Three deployments," she confirmed. "He saw some terrible things, Sebastian, like you probably did. He came back a different guy, and, as we say in my trade, he began to 'self-medicate' with drugs and booze.'"

"Couldn't he get the help he needed?"

"In the wilds of Wyoming? Kids who have *cancer* in our state have to go miles beyond our borders to get treatment. So in a word: no, except for Alcoholics Anonymous, which he said 'wasn't quite his style.'" Meredith focused her gaze on one of the blanket's intricate tartan squares. "Shepard O'Brien had a killer grin and a sweet-talkin' western drawl, and could be lovable as a newborn lamb when sober—and mean as a rattlesnake when he hit the bottle, which he did in binges separated by a few months of good behavior."

"What finally…well, prompted you to end it?"

Meredith looked up and shrugged.

"Paying ten thousand dollars of my own money to send him to a private rehab facility and then seeing him—the same day he was released—totally wasted at the Cowboy Bar in Jackson, sitting on a stool, feeling up a girl he'd met during his stay at the addiction treatment center."

Sebastian gave a low whistle. "That would tend to disillusion one, I suspect."

Meredith shot him a look. "No kidding! Volunteering for the U.S. Army and taking part in that war were the worst things that could have happened to that Wyoming cowboy. Now that I've gotten over being so furious at him, it just makes me sad. But as happens so often in these situations, I finally figured out that I didn't cause what was wrong with him and, at long last, I've accepted the fact I sure can't cure it." She raised her eyes to meet his gaze. "Being with that charmer nearly killed me, Sebastian. I blame the U.S. Congress for sending our troops over there—and I blame whatever horrors he witnessed for turning him into not much more than cannon fodder."

Sebastian gave her a look of such tender sympathy, her heart turned over, and she steadied herself by reaching for her wine glass and taking another sip.

"Oddly enough, for me," Sebastian mused, tracing an index finger along a line in the blanket's tartan pattern, "the military probably saved my sanity. I had lived on my uncle's small dairy farm since I was eleven—"

"Eleven?" she interrupted. "You didn't live with your parents?"

"My father worked for the railroad and was gone most of the time, and my mother apparently couldn't cope with three boys after...well, after my sister died. Actually, it was good that I went to live on the farm. I learned about animals, took care of stray dogs, that sort of thing. When I applied to join the K9 IED Abatement Squad—"

"That's the Improvised Explosive Devices unit, right? In other words, bombs? Shep told me about you guys. You *chose* to join the bomb squad?" she asked, incredulous.

"Well, mostly we were checking everything on wheels that came in and out of the base. When we went outside the perimeter on patrol, we worked with a lot of medics, which I found rather inspiring, and of course, the dogs were absolutely amazing out there, and especially Max, the Springer Spaniel assigned to me. When I got back, the Royal Veterinarian College seemed a good choice for me, and I could get a government grant to pay for it, thanks to recommendations from my superior officers."

"So you enrolled in large breed care," she murmured. "Why didn't you go back and work for your uncle after you graduated?"

"My uncle had a small operation, an antiquated approach to things, and a son that will inherit the place," Sebastian replied with a shrug. "William offered me the job, here, to earn my certification hours, and it gave me a chance to learn from Dr. Dobell, who's head of animal management on this sizeable farm. He's an amazing man...sort of a mentor, I guess you could say, to both William and me—though I think he's going to retire before too long. The signs are all there."

"And your father? You've never mentioned him until today."

Sebastian paused and Meredith could see he was marshaling his thoughts.

"He and my mother split up while I was in Afghanistan," he said finally. "Didn't surprise me, actually. He's retired from the railway service to a cottage somewhere in Scotland. He even has a woman friend—or so one of my brothers told me."

"So you don't see him much?"

"I don't see him—ever. It's not that we have huge animosity or anything...rather we just never knew each other very well to begin with. He was always gone when he worked as a conductor on the railway, and now he lives up north in a new home with a new life."

"And what about your brothers?" Meredith was surprised that Sebastian had been so forthcoming about his family and decided to push her luck to ask him about an upbringing that sounded diametrically opposite to the type she'd had with her mother and dad. "Susanna mentioned you have two?"

"My middle brother sells insurance in Plymouth. Has two kids. A nice fellow, although I can't say we have much in common. And my youngest brother...well, he's not doing too well, from what I hear. Has his own version of the same problem as your Shep. Hangs out in the pub a great deal more than is good for him."

"Shep O'Brien is not 'my' Shep now, remember?" Meredith said, with a steady gaze. She was touched by how much this usually reticent man had revealed to her this night. Perhaps it was the wine...

As if he'd read her thoughts, Sebastian said suddenly, "Well, enough of these mildly depressing sagas. Set your wine glass on the table there and come here, will you please?" She did as he'd instructed and then he pulled her toward him across the bed, shifting her weight to position her between his crossed legs with her back pressed firmly against his chest. He whispered in her ear, "You were amazing out there, today."

Sebastian's hands clasped each of her shoulders as he nuzzled her neck, his lips grazing her hairline—an act that sent highly charged shivers down her back.

"I loved the way you went into commando mode when we found the boy," he said between gentle nips of her earlobe. "You know your job and I found it marvelous to watch you do it."

Meredith barely nodded her thanks for all his compliments, as her mind was awash with the sensation of mini bolts of lightning coursing down her spine. Sebastian folded his arms around her entire torso, his kisses nibbling the side of her jaw, and then down to her collarbone, all with the clear intension of wearing down any resistance.

"Sebastian…is this a good idea?" she asked turning her head to look at him.

"Oh, Meredith," he responded, laying his cheek against her sweater-clad shoulder, "I think this is a *very* good idea."

# CHAPTER 11

"Office ink, remember?" Meredith warned over her shoulder, and barely above a whisper, as Sebastian raised his head and his caresses began grazing the nape of her neck. "We're *sitting* on your tartan blanket, so we're already in the danger zone."

"No danger whatsoever," he said, gently pulling at the neckline of her sweater so he could kiss the exposed flesh. "Such a sweet woman you are. So soft…"

"It's probably just that very good red wine talking…"

"It is absolutely *not* the wine. It's you."

Encasing her in the circle of his arms, his chest continuing to press against her back, he cupped a hand tenderly around each breast and Meredith could only abandon all the 'should nots' careening in her brain and give way to the incoming signals surging from his body to hers.

"Meredith…Meredith…you have no idea how much I love you in this…sweater, I think you call it…but would you allow me to—?"

He began to lift the hem, but Meredith stilled his hand.

"If this is going where I think it may be going—" she began, her body responding to the amazing heat radiating from his touch.

"It is, definitely, headed in that direction, don't you imagine…?"

She wrapped her own arms around his and slumped against him, admitting defeat.

"How can I not agree where this is going?" she mumbled over her shoulder. "Look where I am? In your arms, in your bed, and barely able to hold my head up when you touch me like this."

She heard him chuckle and then saw that he had reached one hand into the drawer of his bedside table and was withdrawing a small, square, silver package. She shifted her weight and rose to her knees, facing him across the blanket.

"You are not to worry about anything tonight," he said, arching an eyebrow in the direction of the condom he held between his fingers.

"You had a plan all along to lure me onto this plaid blanket, didn't you?" she accused him playfully. "First, a lovely picnic, followed by—"

"A bloke can hope, can't he?" he said with a sheepish grin as he put the silver foil next to his abandoned wine glass.

"Beneath all that do-good persona, you are a rogue, Sebastian Pryce."

He rose to his knees so they touched thigh-to-thigh. Looking down at her he said, "I want you to know I have never made love to another woman on this bed, and—"

"What a lovely admission to make," she blurted, touched that he should want to reassure her in this way.

"Oh, there's more," he said, a wry smile playing at his lips. "I haven't bought a box of these contraptions since I moved back to Cornwall two years ago."

"Poor you," she teased, adding, "...then I take it back."

"Take what back?" he asked in mild alarm, sinking on his haunches.

"You are not a rogue after all," she said, leaning

forward to cup his face between her hands, the faint stubble on his cheeks grazing her palms. "You are a drop-dead gorgeous, dog-loving, condom-buying man—which I consider a tremendous turn-on."

He kissed her on the nose.

"And you are so wonderfully direct," he said. "Bless you for that, you dog-loving woman. What more can a man desire?"

"You want direct?" she asked, leaning forward to kiss him fully on the lips. In reply, he slipped one hand past the back waistband of her jeans and pressed her firmly against his pelvis.

"Actually," he mumbled, "I can't wait for this…"

By this time, she was rivetingly aware of his arousal nudging her midsection.

"I can't wait, either," she murmured. She fumbled to locate the top button on his jeans.

"All in due time, lovely lady. All in due time." He pushed her gently onto her back and held her against the length of him for a long moment. Then, moving swiftly, he rolled away from the center of the bed and sat up. "Hold that thought, will you? Close your eyes and wait right here."

She followed his directive and felt him stand on the floor beside her, leaving her with a distinct sensation of bereavement. Before she could wonder what in the world was happening, she heard the water running in the bathtub on the other side of the room and the faint scent of lavender tickling her nostrils. A delicious relaxation washed over her. Replete from the food and wine they'd consumed, and warmed by Sebastian's touch and his reassuring words, she kept her eyes closed as instructed and nearly drifted to sleep.

"Oh, no you don't," she heard him say and felt his fingers working the fastenings on her jeans. "Wake up, my lovely Meredith. You—and especially I—have the scent of the moor about us—which I immediately plan to remedy."

While she continued to keep her eyes shut, reveling in the startling sensations swirling around her, Sebastian glided her clothing down her legs. In the next instant, he gently lifted her to a sitting position and skimmed her knit sweater and T-shirt over her head as the cooler air of the room caressed her bare skin. With her arms dangling off the side of the bed like a rag doll, he made quick work of the rest of her underclothing.

"Come, Nurse Meredith...the water's ready."

She opened her eyes and felt her lips part. Sebastian was completely naked, and before she could absorb the sight of his muscular chest and the arresting view of his midsection, he pulled her to her feet and pressed their bodies together from head to toe.

"Hel-lo...hel-*lo*," she said, her smaller form melting into his. "You sure do know how to surprise a gal."

Without answering, he released his hold and led her toward the bathtub brimming with bubbles. Gesturing to a bottle of bath gel on the deep-set stone windowsill, he said, "You should have seen the look on the chemist's face when I purchased that, along with the box of condoms this morning in Mevagissey. It must be the talk of the village by now. The envy on the man's face was a thing of beauty to behold."

"If *I* saw you buying a box of condoms and lavender bubble bath, I would probably have jumped on your bones, right then and there," she said, feeling any tension melt away as she drank in the heat of his gaze leisurely surveying her naked form.

Sebastian leaned over the faucets positioned in the middle of the tub's edge nearest the stone wall and shut off the water. For a moment, they stood in their bare feet on the slate floor, arms around each other's bare shoulders, listening to the soft hiss of the bubbles.

"You are just as beautiful a woman without your clothes as you are in them, but then I knew that," he said almost as if to himself. He grinned suddenly. "There's a serious draft in here. Come, let's get in…let me hold your arm."

The water was the perfect temperature and Meredith sank below the line of bubbles in a state of complete bliss.

"Oh, lordy, lordy, Sebastian Pryce," she moaned happily as he eased into the other slanted end of the tub, making an effort not to slosh water over the edge and onto the floor. "I honestly think this is better than sex."

He carefully moved one of his feet between her legs and gently stroked the apex of her thighs with his big toe.

"Really?" he said with a wicked smile. "Better than sex, you say?"

"Oh…my…goodness," she responded in a small voice.

"Given how good this feels from where I am, I'm quite sure I don't agree…"

"Neither do I," she mumbled, nearly slipping beneath the water in ecstasy.

Sebastian regarded her reactions to his gentle message with a faint smile.

"Two can play this game, you know," she said, amazed at how husky her voice sounded. She fumbled for the large sea sponge that rested on a wire soap dish hooked to the rolled lip of the old fashioned tub and sat upright. Leaning forward, she splayed one hand on Sebastian's broad chest and the dark hair curling in a small cluster and allowed the sponge she held in her other hand to graze his nether regions in a deliberately provocative fashion

"Oh…my…you are a saucy wench," Sebastian groaned as she released the sponge and her hand's feathery ministrations took effect. "Is this some Wild West technique you've brought to our shores?"

"I just thought of it," she murmured. He reached across the water and cupped both breasts, circling her nipples with his thumbs. "Oh...*my*...yourself," she gasped.

Slowly, deliberately, and with an increasing sense of delight, they explored each other's bodies as the water cooled against their overheated skin.

At length, Sebastian said, "May I invite you back to bed, my Lady of Wyoming?" He hoisted himself to a standing position as water cascaded off his six-foot frame and splashed back into the tub. He stepped gingerly onto the floor and reached for one of two fluffy bath towels stacked nearby on a straight-backed chair. "All right, up with you, now. Here, take my hand."

Once outside the bathtub, he wrapped her in the towel's thick absorbency and hugged her entire body tightly against his.

"Oh, Sebastian," she said leaning into his chest, "this is so lovely. I feel as if I'm on another planet."

He took a smaller towel and fashioned a turban around her damp hair and then kissed her forehead. "So do I."

She tucked the edges of the terry cloth around her bosom to secure it, and when he turned to retrieve his own bath sheet, she caught one end, took it from him entirely, and began to towel him dry.

"There," she announced softly, looking up at him and marveling how he towered over her in her bare feet. "Fair's fair," she said, handing him back his towel that he then wrapped around his waist.

In silence, he took her by the hand and they padded across the floor, leaving wet footprints that led straight to the wide expanse of his bed.

"Will you stay with me tonight, my mermaid

Meredith?" he said, wrapping both arms around her waist and leaning back so he could gaze directly into her eyes. For her part, she found it challenging not to allow her gaze to drift down to his broad, bare chest.

"I will stay with you till just before dawn if you will then whisk me back to the castle so I can sneak inside like some guilty teenager before the household wakes up," she answered, suddenly feeling almost teary with happiness that this man for whom her feelings had grown stronger each day, had plotted and planned this night for their pleasure. "I want to keep this just *ours* for a while. Just us. Our perfect night."

He seized a corner of the towel wrapped around her chest and pulled at the edge. The fabric fell away and landed on the floor between them in a puddle of terry cloth.

"Ta da!" she declared softly.

"I was dying to do that…"

"You were, were you?" she said, laughing. "Well, I'm dying to do this…"

She knelt on the fallen towel and caressed Sebastian intimately through the fabric wound tightly around his waist. Then she pulled its folds away from his torso and touched him gently, reverently, looking up with a gaze she knew reflected her naked yearning. She was aware, suddenly, that his expression revealed a vague state of consternation, and he caught her hand, stilling her movements.

"You don't like me to—?" she asked, suddenly embarrassed.

"No, no. It's all right. Just come with me, you sweet, generous woman."

"But Sebastian, I want to—"

He bent towards her, and with a single, swift

movement, pulled her to her feet. With one hand, he swept
back the tartan blanket and the bed's top sheet. Then,
scooping her into his arms, he carefully laid her on her
back, removing the towel wrapped to dry her hair. Sitting
on the edge of the bed beside her, he threaded his fingers
through her damp locks, smoothing away any stray strands
and then bent down to kiss her forehead once again in a
touching act of benediction.

Meredith stretched her arms overhead like a cat,
luxuriating in the smooth nap of the sheets. Then, holding
her arms wide in welcome, a part of her wondered why he
only seemed to want to be the one giving—not receiving—
in the sensuous dance they had begun.

He hovered above her, one bare knee on the bed, his
brown eyes intense with the same longing that she also felt,
along with a slight wariness reflected in his gaze.

Looking down at her he said, "Good Christ, you are
lovely. I don't think you have any idea how much I've
wanted you here."

Her heart turned over at his sweet words. She reached
up and ran the back of her fingers along one side of his
face, a gesture she'd thought of making since the day he'd
apologized in the car park at Moorland's Creamery. She
held out her arms for a second time.

"Come here, Doctor Dog. I need a little search and
rescue."

Sebastian slid into the bed beside her. He skimmed the
flat of his palm from her knee to thigh to torso, along the
side of one breast, and then buried his hand in her hair.
Resting the side of his head in his other hand, his elbow on
the pillow, he paused. "I am giving you fair warning, my
mermaid, I may be pathetically out of practice—"

"No, no..." she scolded gently, "no worries in that
department that *I* can see. And besides, everyone says it's

exactly the same as riding a bicycle or a horse. It all comes back to you. Just come and get me, pardner, will you please?"

"Who could resist such a wanton invitation?"

Sebastian, whose demeanor— except for some notable exceptions—had thus far been controlled and contained, proved to be a wildly affectionate, selfless lover. He smothered her with kisses over nearly every inch of her body, bringing her to such a state of tingling desire that she heard herself begging for release. She felt him pull away from her briefly and realized he was sheathing himself with the condom.

When he entered her, they both sighed, as if they'd finally reached some precious zone of safety, a place where no harm would come, no threats loomed, no perils lurked in unseen corners…only a piercing, pulsing, intense pleasure that continued to build between them, enveloping them in a cocoon of utter contentment. Yet, somewhere in the reaches of her fevered consciousness, she imagined him sleeping in a desert tent with a dog his only companion, his only warmth in a lonely, dangerous world, and her one aim became the urge to offer him aid and comfort, as well as slake her own driving desire.

When she opened her eyes, he was holding himself above her again with hands on either side of her shoulders. His eyes were moist as his movements increased and she instinctively responded, willing him to feel the safety and security offered by their linking of body and heart.

She could love this man, she thought with both clarity and apprehension. She could be his safe oasis, and he, hers. She could offer a place of refuge from whatever had wounded him in the past. If he had grown to manhood with only the affection of the animals he cared for, without the certainty of truly being loved by another human

182        Ciji Ware

being—that could be ended now. She already knew what it felt to be loved, even if it had ended badly with Shep, even if sometimes certain wounds were too deep to be healed.

But Sebastian was a loving man, she thought, moving in concert with him as if they'd been together forever. He loved animals and he loved his friends and maybe he could love her.

"I'm here," she heard herself crying, almost in a sob as his form completely smothered hers "I'm here, Sebastian. I want you so much. I—"

Sebastian, too, cried out, and then stopped her words with a raft of passionate kisses. In the next instant, she felt them both shudder and then slowly relax against each other's bodies in a haze of delicious lassitude that melted into sleep.

Wrapped in Sebastian's arms, Meredith drifted into five dreamless hours of the deepest rest she had enjoyed in years.

"Mermaid..." a voice whispered from afar. "I promised I'd return you to the castle before dawn...come on, Meredith, wake up, darling."

"No...no...let's sleep," she mumbled into her pillow that now nearly covered her head. "Or at least let's rest a while..."

"I wish we could, but you made me promise to—"

"I didn't mean it..." she sighed, turning on her side to face him.

A hand that she realized with surprise was her own had slipped between Sebastian's thighs seeking that warm, vulnerable part of him.

"Meredith! Now, none of that," he scolded, seizing her

wrist. "I have to get you home, or you'll have more than you bargained for in terms of explaining to your relatives where you've been."

"I'm a free woman...way older than twenty-one," she said, still half asleep. "I can come home when I want." However, the part of her brain that was waking up and recalling the amazing evening that has just transpired wondered why Sebastian had deflected nearly all her attempts to pleasure him as much as he had her. She forced her eyes completely open and cradled the side of her head in her hand.

"Ready to face the day?" he asked, smiling.

She was far from ready, but she nodded her assent. "And I thank you for trying to save my reputation, and for the shattering loveliness of last night...but may I ask you something?"

"Yes, of course," he replied, a look of wariness she was learning to recognize flickering in his eyes.

"I loved how we were together," she began.

"But?" he asked, and she could feel a wall rising up between them.

She stretched out her hand and once again gently stroked the side of his face with the back of her fingers. "But...I love giving as much as receiving...and I get the sense that whenever I reach for you, it makes you...uncomfortable."

Confirming her supposition, he didn't answer as she continued to gaze at him with an overwhelming sense of compassion. She waited for him to speak, and when he remained silent, she leaned forward and brushed his lips gently with her own.

"I've had the most delightful fifteen hours imaginable, but you're right," she said, signaling that she wouldn't press the issue. Not now, at any rate. "I suppose we should proceed to slink back to Barton Hall. Any idea of where you left my clothes?"

She swung her legs to the side of the bed, but before she could stand up, two arms wrapped themselves around her waist and pulled her against a deliciously warm body, spoon-style.

"Meredith...Meredith, how did you land in my life from far-away Wyoming?" he mumbled into the nape of her neck.

And then she felt Sebastian's hands firmly span her waist. He began undulating movements with his midsection against her derriere, actions calculated to melt every ounce of resolve she'd had for heading back to Barton Hall before dawn.

"Oh...oh, goodness me," she murmured as he swiftly commenced to make heart-stopping love to her. When at length, she rose from his bed a second time, morning sun had begun to filter through the windows. They slowly, silently dressed each other, item by item of clothing, until they could face the chill of a foggy morn.

Quietly descending the stone stairs, they piled the dogs and themselves into the Mini, and within twenty minutes, two of the four passengers in the car were deposited a hundred yards from Barton Hall's inner courtyard at the back of the castle, just as the sun's beams began to slant through the tall larch trees that lined the drive.

"See you at Painter's Cottage at four?" Sebastian asked when Meredith came around to give him one, last, lingering kiss through the car window.

"Can you meet me at the Hall, instead, after your obedience class?" she asked. "I promised Richard I'd help him pick blackberries this afternoon and pitch in making the berry crumbles for tonight's farm dinner. We've got fifty guests signed up."

Sebastian's disappointment was obvious. "Do you also have to help serve?"

Meredith grimaced. "I should at least offer. Do you know anything about tending a bar? Lucas could probably use an assistant. We'll all get paid with a fabulous meal afterward," she added as enticement.

"Cooked by Claire Gillis."

Brought up short, she paused and then nodded. "That's right. Are you sure you're ready for that?" She felt certain he'd beg off.

"Are *you?*"

Meredith laughed, pleased by his reply.

"I can take it if *you* can!"

"All right, then. I'll be a junior barista."

"See you around four-thirty or five?" Meredith said, shivering slightly in the early morning air.

"You're getting chilled. Get yourself inside your castle, m'lady, and see you tonight." And within a minute, the Mini Cooper was a speck at the end of the drive.

# CHAPTER 12

That night during the Farm-to-Table supper, and in the days that followed, Sebastian Pryce and Claire Gillis were perfectly civil toward each other, but each gave the other a wide berth, which suited Meredith perfectly.

Not long after Sebastian had served as a volunteer assistant bartender under Lucas Teague's tutelage, the Sunday supplement in the Plymouth paper did a highly laudatory write-up that stimulated even more advance reservations than before. This resulted in Claire and Richard working longer hours in each other's company, not only doing the preparatory work in the kitchen, but also toiling in the garden and scouring neighboring farms for the additional supplies they needed.

One morning when the duo had set off to source pork loins at a neighboring pig farm, Meredith and Blythe sat chatting in the kitchen before their workday began.

"Are we starting to show a profit on the farm-to-table project?" Meredith asked when the conversation rolled around to the upcoming event.

"A small one, but it's improving every week, especially now that we've added an extra dinner once a fortnight."

"Well, that's good news," she said, adding cautiously, "and Richard and Claire seem to be getting along all right."

"More than all right, I'd say," Blythe replied, amusement tingeing her voice. "Rather flattering state of affairs for us 'older women,' wouldn't you say?"

"You don't think we should be at all worried about Richard?" Meredith ventured. "You know...the son-and-heir being side-tracked from finishing Oxford, and all that?"

"He's being side-tracked, all right," Blythe admitted. "But I think, come September, he'll see it was just a fling that probably is doing them both some good. I understand that Claire hasn't had a man in her life for quite a while."

For Meredith's part, she was sorely tempted to tell Blythe that the last man in Claire's life was Sebastian Pryce, but decided not to stir the pot.

"Well," she said, her mind searching for the proper way to couch her next words, "This...flirtation...is probably a welcome shot in the arm, I'm sure, but what if—"

"It's nothing more, I don't imagine," Blythe overrode her with a shrug. "At least, Lucas assures me he doesn't think it is. He wagers it'll probably burn out by summer's end."

*I'm not so sure either Richard or Claire sees it that way...*

But once again, Meredith kept her opinions to herself and changed the subject.

⚬⚬⚬

A week after this conversation, Meredith, along with Sebastian, who'd stayed for supper after teaching his class, were taking Holly and Rex out for their last stroll of the evening before Sebastian returned to Cow Hollow Farm. Along the gravel drive that wound from the back of the castle toward the east gate, they saw Claire's battered Vauxhall pull up to Limekiln Cottage a hundred yards from where they stood. Claire and Richard got out of the car—oblivious to anything but each other—raced to meet on the front stoop and flung their arms around each other's waists, swiftly disappearing through her front door.

Meredith glanced sideways to see if Sebastian had noticed, which—from the scowl on his face—he clearly had.

"You know," she said cautiously, "I mentioned to Blythe that Richard and Claire seemed to be...well...pretty damned cozy these days, but for some reason, she didn't seem particularly bothered."

"Really?" he replied noncommittally, glancing at his watch as if preparing to leave.

"They're together a *lot*, Sebastian, and—"

"Well, they work together."

Surprised by the curtness of his reply, she said, "Obviously that's the case but...you don't think Claire might be angling...well, you know...?"

"What?" demanded Sebastian, irritation tingeing his voice.

"To trap Richard. Entangle him so—"

"You mean, take him to bed?" he asked, his jaw solid granite. "I imagine that's already happened."

"No, not just that! How...how should I put it? Okay, here goes: intentionally get herself pregnant as a leg up around here."

Again, Sebastian glanced at his watch, only this time he turned on the path, as if to retrace his steps back to the castle.

"I'm *worried!*" Meredith exclaimed to his back. "He's so young...so totally trusting—"

Sebastian looked at her over his shoulder.

"And I can do...*what*...about this?"

Meredith could tell Sebastian was getting angry at the direction their conversation had taken. She circled around to face him.

"I'm not asking you to do anything. I just want your opinion about her...her character. If you think she'd deliberately—"

"I haven't been with the woman in more than half a decade, Meredith," he replied, biting off each word.

"Well, you *lived* with her," she said defensively. "Who else can I ask about this? And let's face it, it'd be one way for her to feather her nest as the future Lady of the Manor, which is certainly a nice advancement from a test kitchen in Redruth."

The instant the sentence escaped from her lips she could tell her words had infuriated him. But rather than explain why, she was met with stony silence.

"Sebastian, come on!" she said, exasperated. "I'm only asking if you think she'd be that mercenary? I don't really know the woman!"

For a third time, he glanced at his watch and said in a clipped tone of voice, "You know, it's getting late. I need to get back to the farm."

Without replying, Meredith swiftly walked past him heading in the direction of castle. She recited to herself Sebastian's words the night they'd first made love: that Claire meant nothing to him now. But if his reaction tonight was any indication, the suggestion that Claire might have designs on a young man a decade younger clearly riled him. Meredith couldn't help but surmise that, despite his words to the contrary, there might, in fact, be plenty of unfinished business between Claire Gillis and him. He'd certainly avoided telling her why they'd split up.

An old, familiar feeling of powerlessness took hold, the same sense she'd gotten whenever Shep clammed up, refusing to talk about past devils that might be bothering him, and then eventually falling off the wagon—again. She speeded up her pace, calling Holly to follow her.

"Wait," Sebastian called after her. "Come here...why so fast?" he said, taking a few long strides to catch up.

"You said it was getting late. I'm heading back to the Hall."

"You seem upset about something."

Meredith halted abruptly and turned to look him directly in the eye. "No, *you* seem upset...about seeing Claire and Richard together and about my voicing my concerns about that because Richard still has two years of college left."

Sebastian turned and stared at the tall larches lining the long drive. "What I find *upsetting*," he said in a low voice, continuing to keep his gaze on the trees in the distance, "is your thinking I have any special knowledge that would explain Claire's behavior toward Richard. When all's said and done, I never understood what motivated that woman and now—years later—whatever is happening in her life is really none of my business."

"End of story, then?" Meredith said more sharply than she intended. "Given what we've just witnessed, it's your view that I shouldn't voice my concerns to Blythe and Lucas at all...is that what you're saying?"

Sebastian affected a shrug and appeared to want to de-escalate the tension that threatened to explode between them. "No. I'm just saying I hope, like you do, it's merely a summer's crush on Richard's part—and God knows, I hope he uses condoms—but it's really nothing to do with me."

"Richard is *eighteen*-years-old!" she exclaimed, "and in some ways, a rather vulnerable young man, to say nothing that he's nine years younger than your former girlfriend! And those two," she declared, gesturing over her shoulder in the direction of Limekiln Cottage, "are definitely generating some serious steam between them. I don't think

Blythe or Lucas have any idea how hot and heavy this is getting to be, or if our *chef de cuisine* is about to throw a bomb into our midst!"

"Well, let's hope they notice before she does create an explosion. *If* she does," he added quickly.

"Let's hope they do notice, since they're not likely to get a 'heads-up' from the one person who knows her best," she retorted, and starting walking at a fast pace toward the castle's front entrance.

"Meredith, please," he called after her. "Can't you just drop all this?"

She whirled in place and they nearly collided.

"Look, Sebastian," she said, no longer able to keep her cool, "I'll try not to mention my concerns about this to you again, but let me just say this: if you're so 'over' Claire, as you claim, why do you go cold and affect an attitude that I'm exaggerating a dicey situation between Richard and Claire—a possible train wreck that we can both see with our own *eyes*—unless it bothered you *a lot* just now when you saw those two go into her cottage?"

Sebastian shot her a look she couldn't define but that nevertheless sent an arrow straight into her heart.

"I meant what I said that night," he said, steely-voiced. "It's finished between Claire and me, and it bothers *me* very much if you don't believe me. Good night, Meredith."

"I *do* believe you, but I just want to know what you think your former lover is capable of!"

Sebastian, his mouth a grim slash across his face, turned his back without another word, walked to his car, and in less than a minute, was swiftly speeding down the drive into the gloom.

❧

Meredith didn't hear from Sebastian the following three days during which she was kicking herself each night while she tried to go to sleep, constantly rehashing their last conversation. Was *she* the one who was unsettled about Claire's being at Barton Hall? Was it her fault that things between Sebastian and her had suddenly gone awry?

The following Tuesday, he appeared on the field beside Painter's Cottage in plenty of time to teach his search and rescue class, but didn't come inside to speak to her until all the dogs and their companions had departed. He knocked on the door and much to her amazement, she found him standing on the stone step flanked by Matthew and Lucy on one side and Janet on the other.

"Look who was in the audience today," he said cheerfully, as if nothing had been amiss between them.

Blythe's two children occasionally came down from Barton Hall to watch the puppy obedience classes, but Janet's consistent observation of the search and rescue training was a first.

"Well, what did you three think of Sebastian's class today?" Meredith asked the children, avoiding his glance.

"Really fun!" declared Lucy. "I love all the doggies."

"Me too," agreed Matthew. "Sebastian is teaching them to be really *smart!*"

"Awesome!" Janet said, with a worshipful gaze in Sebastian's direction. "I think Holly should become a search and rescue dog. I don't think she likes having to visit all those *old* people anymore!"

The other two children covered their mouths, giggling.

"That's not very kind," Sebastian said. 'Holly gives very sick people comfort when she comes to see them and she's helping Meredith teach other dogs to be equally friendly to people who are really ill."

Janet ducked her head and said to Sebastian, "Sorry."

Then she looked up at him with a bright smile, pleading, "Don't you think I could take your class and see if Holly can learn all the stuff you're teaching?"

Meredith didn't know whether to be more flabbergasted that Janet apparently wanted to learn to train a dog, or that she had actually made an apology to Sebastian for her rude remark.

"You would first need to take a beginning obedience course from Meredith," Sebastian said firmly, "and if that seemed to suit you, you could eventually take more advanced courses, like the one I'm giving."

"But Holly already knows all that obedience stuff!" Janet complained, looking at Meredith resentfully.

"Yes," Meredith said, "but *you* don't. You've never trained a dog."

"Well then, I'd need a puppy to train," Janet said, a familiar, petulant tone creeping into her voice. "I want a puppy, Meredith, so I can take the beginning course, like Sebastian says I should do. Dad gives you an allowance for me, doesn't he? It's *my* money. I want you to buy me a dog!"

Meredith inhaled and attempted to keep the irritation out of her voice.

"You're welcome to observe the puppy obedience classes for a while longer, and if you're still interested, we could certainly talk about getting you a puppy...that is if you're willing to feed and take care of it."

"We'd help you take care of it," chimed in Matthew, "won't we, Lucy?"

"Yes, yes!" Lucy said, jumping up and down excitedly. "Let's go ask Mummy what she thinks. "

"Maybe Lucy and I could get a puppy, too," Matthew proposed. "Our old dog died last winter," he explained to the adults. "Mummy said we had to feel sad for a while longer before we got a new one. C'mon!" he exclaimed to the two girls, "let's go tell her our plan!"

Janet cast a triumphant smile in Meredith's direction and then turned and scampered away with the Barton-Teague children across the field and into the leafy tunnel that led to Hall Walk.

Still standing by her desk with Sebastian remaining silhouetted in the door, Meredith folded her arms across her chest and fell silent, not sure of what to say next.

"May I come in?" he asked politely.

"Yes, of course." He took one step and stood in the doorway. "Want a cup of coffee?" she asked, equally politely. "Or I can make some tea."

"No...no, I have to get back to the farm. I just wanted to ask..."

"What?"

She sounded defensive, even to her own ears.

"If we could be friends again?" he said with a crooked grin. "I'm sorry I went off in a huff the other night."

"It was nearly a week ago."

"Yes, I know. It seemed like *more* than a week."

"To tell you the truth, Sebastian, I'm still not even sure what the huff was all about," she admitted, feeling suddenly tired and drained, "but if I contributed to it, I'm sorry, too."

"If I remember correctly, it all started when we saw Richard entering Claire's cottage rather late at night."

"Well, here's a news flash: now that Mrs. Quiller has officially retired from running the kitchen, the two are together more than ever," Meredith disclosed, watching Sebastian's reaction closely, but all he did was nod once. "Blythe has offered Claire a permanent, full time job running the tea room as well as cooking for the farm suppers, along with breakfast for the B and B guests.

They're even talking of eventually opening a restaurant that would serve gourmet dinners to the public as well as guests at the castle. It would seem she's here to stay—at least for the foreseeable future."

"Has Blythe or Lucas shown any concern about...well..."

"How totally smitten Richard is with his fellow foodie?"

"His what?"

Meredith laughed. "It's that language thing again. Where I come from, a foodie is someone who is knowledgeable about, and crazy for...food."

"Ah...a culinary enthusiast."

"Exactly. And to answer your question, Blythe continues to treat this as only a summer's fling. Lucas and she have finally started to notice how enamored Richard is, but apparently they both see as a fleeting thing. I don't think that either of them are as finely attuned as you and I are to the...uh...sense of sap rising, as they say in Wyoming."

Sebastian shut the door behind him.

"Well, I also wanted to tell you that I've had time to think about what you said, and I honestly have no idea if Claire is angling to be the eventual mistress of Barton Hall without really caring deeply about Richard. But..."

"But what?"

Sebastian shrugged. "It's always a possibility. And I certainly understand why this could become a...problem for the owners of Barton Hall."

"It's a problem if she's doing a con job," Meredith agreed, gratified that Sebastian had apologized for stomping off. "If she's revving up his engines without really caring about him and only to move up to a better station in life, that could really end up hurting the poor guy and mess life up a lot for Blythe and Lucas. Frankly, for me, it's not so much the age thing between our lovebirds, but whether she truly has Richard's best interests at heart—and not merely her own."

Sebastian was slow to reply. Finally he said, "I honestly can't help you with that. I truly have no idea."

Meredith took a moment to absorb what he'd just said. "You know, Sebastian," she ventured, "you've still never told me why you and Claire split up...and it would seem that it's relevant to all this."

Sebastian grew pensive and shook his head.

"Let me just put it this way: speaking only for myself, I found, to my sorrow, the lady doesn't always tell the truth. Can we leave it at that?"

"Well, that's a pretty serious charge and—"

"Let's not talk about Claire anymore," he interrupted, advancing further into the cottage. "Let's talk about you and me."

With a flash of insight, Meredith judged that getting to know Sebastian's inner thoughts was like peeling one of the onions grown in Home Farm; he revealed what was at his core, layer by layer. Eventually, he would tell her what had really happened between Claire and him five years ago, but it would be at a time of his choosing, and she knew, suddenly, she'd be wise to merely let matters unfold.

She placed a hand on each of Sebastian's shoulders.

"Here's another suggestion: let's not talk at all," she replied, and lifted her face to be kissed.

⊰℀⊱

During July, Meredith's young ward faithfully observed every single beginning obedience class and some of the agility and puppy sessions as well. One afternoon, Meredith handed Holly's leash to Janet and pointed to the series of obstacle poles.

"Here...want to give it a try? Just put Holly on your right and walk her in figure eights around the posts."

Janet obediently seized the lead as instructed and said, "Heel, Holly," and trotted in and out of the obstacles in perfect order.

"Terrific!" Meredith exclaimed as Janet returned to the beginning of the course. "You did that absolutely perfectly! Good girls—both of you!" Then she added, "Now give Holly a nice pat on her head," and when she had, Meredith patted Janet's head as well and was rewarded with a broad grin.

Janet also never missed an opportunity to watch Sebastian work with clients who hoped, one day, to join the volunteer Cornwall Search and Rescue Team. On the days of Sebastian's class, Janet tended to follow him around like a puppy herself, and willingly gathered up the equipment used during the training sessions and stowed it properly— to say nothing of filling the various water bowls positioned at strategic spots around the training field.

"Blythe said she'd consider allowing us to have a puppy if we kept up our chores," Janet said proudly, adding, "so be sure to tell her, Meredith, how good I'm being!"

"Absolutely...will do," Meredith said with the ghost of a smile.

One evening after Meredith had a long day teaching and doing paperwork, Sebastian arrived at the edge of the field just as she was bidding the last dog and its owner adieu. The air was balmy off the Channel after a delicious day of warm weather due to the Gulf Stream warming the waters off shore.

"Susanna sent this, and *me* to deliver it," he shouted from across the pasture, hoisting a familiar picnic hamper over his head. As he drew closer, he added, "And I've supplied a few other items for a mermaid's pleasure."

"Hmmmm...sounds delicious!" she said with a laugh, waving for him to come into the cottage. "What a lovely surprise!"

Without even shutting the door, Sebastian deposited the picnic basket on the small kitchen table and then pulled a vial of lavender bath oil from his pants pocket.

"This will be for pudding," he announced smugly, taking her in his arms and kissing her soundly. "I think in America you call it 'dessert.'"

"Pudding. Dessert. What*ever*!" she replied in a fair imitation of Janet's Valley Girl intonation. "Bring it on!"

As if she'd heard her named called, Janet was barreling across the field calling to Rex, who had obediently lain down on the stone step outside the cottage door.

"Oh, blast!" exclaimed Meredith, disentangling herself from Sebastian's embrace. "Here comes your *other* faithful shadow."

Janet slowed to a trot in order to bestow a series of pats on Rex's head as she came to the open door.

"I saw the Mini coming up the road," she said panting. "Remember, Sebastian, you promised you'd take me to see all the cows at your farm this week. I've been waiting and waiting!"

Sebastian grimaced faintly at Meredith before turning to address Janet who, by this time, was standing on the cottage's front step, attempting to catch her breath after her exertions.

"That's right...I did. You wouldn't consider visiting the farm tomorrow, would you, Janet?"

"But you *promised*..."

"I did promise, but things ran late all day, and..."

"You *promised* I could come for a visit by Friday, at the

latest," she said, her voice rising shrilly, "and it's *Friday*!"

He looked from Janet to Meredith and said, "I hate to put the cooking on your shoulders, but Susanna said the lamb needed forty minutes in the oven. I can show Janet the farm and return here in an hour. I'll help you peel the potatoes when I get back. Would that work?" he asked apologetically.

"The potatoes will take thirty minutes to cook. I'll peel them myself while you're gone."

Stifling her disappointment that the cozy, impromptu evening Sebastian had planned was to be interrupted by her hero-worshipping ward, Meredith heaved an inward sigh and pulled out a kitchen drawer, searching for the potato peeler.

True to his word, Sebastian fulfilled his promise to Janet and afterward, dropped her off at the Hall and sped back down to Painter's Cottage—but it was two hours later, not one.

By the time he finally arrived, Meredith was at her desk finishing up her daily paperwork.

"Blood sugar attack," she said, over her shoulder, not looking up. "I got hungry and ate. I left a plate for you staying warm in the oven."

"I'm really very sorry," he said, hesitating at the door. "You know what Janet can be like. She even insisted that Susanna show her how a weaving loom works. That's what made us so late. At least she's interested in something other than the Internet these days," he offered tentatively, sensing the tension in the room.

"Well, I was interested in us having dinner together," Meredith said, and then was embarrassed at how petulant that sounded.

"So was I," he said, walking over to stand behind her and began to kneed the knots in her shoulders. "I was the one who brought the picnic, remember?"

Meredith gave a slight shake of her head. "I guess this is what it's like having kids," she said. "I'm sorry for being so...well...you know—"

"Put out?" he supplied.

Meredith swiveled in her chair. "Look, I'm glad Janet is showing an interest in animals, Sebastian, really I am, but she's a little manipulator, you know, always wanting what she wants *when* she wants it with no consideration for anyone else."

"She's definitely like that," Sebastian agreed mildly, "and part of her being attracted to me and Cow Hollow Farm these days is that she knows exactly how to make you a bit jealous."

Meredith looked indignant. "I'm not jeal—" She stopped mid-sentence and shook her head once more. "Yes I *am*. Jealous, I mean. Jealous she whisked you away when I was thrilled you'd just arrived." She made a face. "I'm sorry...it's just that I loved that you surprised me with bringing dinner, and I was tired and hungry and *so* looking forward to having some time together...alone."

"That's what I love about you," Sebastian said, pulling her to her feet and enfolding her entire frame in an embrace. "You are so astonishingly honest, especially with yourself. Do you have any idea how rare that is?"

Meredith ignored the compliment and raised her face within inches of his to be kissed. Sebastian obligingly brushed his lips against hers, and then began a journey from her mouth to her earlobe, probing its shell with his tongue.

"Uh oh."

"Something the matter?" he asked, pulling away.

"Not with your technique," she teased, "but since your trip to your farm, you've gone from Doctor Dog to Doctor

Cow, I fear. I'm picking up a distinct scent of your barn and my sheep field. I think we should first use that lovely lavender bath oil you gave me earlier this evening and then serve you your dinner. What do you say?"

Sebastian quickly began to unbutton his shirt. "Lovely idea, Mermaid," he murmured. "And it's your turn to draw the bath..."

# CHAPTER 13

After Sebastian and Meredith indulged in a leisurely soak in the tub, they wrapped themselves in bath towels and sat together at the small table while Sebastian ate his warmed up supper. Later, upstairs, he rolled onto his side in the bed that was tucked under the ancient eaves in Painter's Cottage's loft and described how well behaved and polite Janet had been earlier when he escorted her to Cow Hollow Farm and introduced her to the Jenners.

"I think that just her living here in Cornwall these months, with normal children involved in normal, childhood pastimes, is starting to make a difference in her behavior," he mused. "Plus, she loved meeting Susanna, and begged her to let her weave a few rows in a rug she had working on the loom."

"There is something so grounding about living close to the earth where we're conscious of the tides and the weather and notice the animals around us and grow the food we eat," she mused. "I feel it myself." She paused in thought, and then added, "And as far as Janet's concerned, it's almost as if her being with, as you say, normal, nice kids like Matthew and Lucy and having the freedom to play and roam these beautiful fields have begun to heal her in some way. She's far from a totally happy child, but she's sure come a long way from when we first got to Cornwall, don't you think?"

"You've taken the brunt of Janet's misbehavior, and you've been so patient and kind," he said, leaning forward to kiss her gently on the lips.

Meredith reached over and brushed a lock of Sebastian's hair off his forehead. "*You* are the one who's kind, do you know that? To take the time to show Janet the farm and the world you have there. I doubt her father even *once* took her on one of his movie sets without a nanny to keep her at bay."

Sebastian's brow furrowed and he shook his head. "Sounds like *my* father, without the nanny. I longed to ride on the railroad with him, but he said there were three of us boys, and his supervisor would never allow it. He always said he couldn't do it for one son without doing it for all, and he didn't have time to arrange it, and so on and so on. I think it was just an excuse, actually. We wouldn't lay eyes on him for weeks at a time."

"Why do people *have* children if they don't want to spend time with them?" Meredith asked rhetorically. "It makes me so mad!"

"Then I don't think you would enjoy knowing my mother, much."

Meredith was brought up short. How could she forget that brief glimpse of Elizabeth Pryce, nor the way Sebastian wanted to escape from even exchanging a hello?

"She didn't want to spend time with her own children?" she asked cautiously, sensing immediately she was wading into quicksand.

However, for some reason, Sebastian appeared willing to talk about her, as if the time he'd spent with Janet that day had prompted him to think about his own childhood.

"I believe I'm rather sympathetic to young Janet's plight with her family because it reminds me a lot of how I reacted as a young boy when my sister died."

"It must have been horrific for your whole family."

Sebastian stared past her shoulder toward the small, square window embedded in the opposite stonewall.

"I remember when the Coast Guard rescue boat came around Dodman Point with my sister's body wrapped in a bright, red blanket," he said, as if telling the story to himself. "By the time they found her, the tide had gone out again on Hemmick Beach, so after they plucked her floating in deep water, they ran the craft up on the sandy part of the shore. I could just glimpse the top of a patch of red fabric where they'd put her on the bottom of the boat."

"Oh, Sebastian..." she murmured, gently laying her hand on his.

"We other children and my mum also had the same red blankets wrapped around us that the Coast Guard had given us as we waited for word in the cold wind. My mother threw hers aside as she ran toward the boat. One of the officers tried to restrain her, but she threw herself on top of Gemma, keening like a mother wolf on the moor. She just lay there, cradling my little sister in her arms, making this terrible sound."

"It must have frightened you and your brothers something awful," Meredith said, feeling heartsick for his entire family.

"I was the eldest. I knew I should *do* something...should try to help in some way," he said, shifting his far off gaze back to meet Meredith's. "So I ran down to the boat and put a hand on my mother's shoulder."

Sebastian stopped speaking abruptly, and Meredith saw a strong wave of emotion bring moisture to his eyes.

"What happened? What did she do when you tried to comfort her?"

Sebastian struggled for control. "What did she do?" he

asked in a tone so bitter, Meredith felt her own sharp intake of breath. "She jerked her shoulder away and screamed at me, 'Gemma's dead, don't you understand? *Dead!* Why couldn't it have been one of you *boys?*'"

Meredith gasped as if someone had punched them both in the stomach.

"Oh, God, *no!* She couldn't have said something so cruel! How horrible for you...and how devastating for your little brothers if they heard."

"They heard, all right. And if you ask either one of them what was their single memory of growing up in our family, they'll tell you this story, just as I have, though why I did, just now, I—"

Meredith had seen her share of grown men cry when their children were sick or dying, but Sebastian's show of emotion touched her deeply. She pulled him to her in a fierce, almost angry embrace and held him while his shoulders heaved in silent, long suppressed sadness.

"I don't care how grief-stricken your mother was," she whispered against his dark hair with a fury she felt equally for Christopher Stowe and anyone else she had ever known in the children's intensive care ward who so selfishly put their own feelings ahead of an innocent child. "That was a horrible, self-centered, *inhuman* thing to have said! She made her daughter's death about *her,* not about your poor, little sister or her family! Did she ever say she was sorry, or that she'd blurted out such wounding words because she was out of her mind with anguish?"

Sebastian shook his head against her shoulder. "No. She never did," came his low reply. "We all knew Gemma was her favorite. She was a sweet, pretty little girl..."

"So you don't think that in the intervening years your mom had any change of heart or regrets that she said such a horrible thing?"

He pulled away and met her gaze. "My youngest brother confronted her once at a rare family gathering when my uncle died and she denied it ever even happened."

"That must have made you boys crazy…"

"It made the three of us walk away and never want to see her again—or each other, for that matter."

"So when you saw her that night when we were in St. Austell…"

"My reaction is always rather visceral. I just want to escape." A look of embarrassment came over his features. "It's my very own brand of PTSD."

"Doesn't she try to contact you? You know, at Christmas, or your birthday?"

"Oh, she tries, all right, but all she wants to do is tell me what a bastard my father was for leaving her…what a poor, innocent woman she's been with sons who've deserted her in her hour of need, and, oh…would I please bring by a bottle of Old Grouse."

"Whiskey?"

Sebastian nodded. He shrugged. "I have one delivered every so often."

"God Almighty, families can be wretched to each other sometimes!" she declared ferociously, thinking of the way Ellie and Christopher Stowe's illicit affair had blown the Barton family to smithereens.

"For years I think my mother was actually out of her mind about Gemma's death," Sebastian mused, brushing away the remaining moisture from his eyes. "In the aftermath, Father didn't really comprehend her total neglect of us boys while he was away with the railroad."

"Didn't he protest when your Mother farmed you out to various relatives?"

"A few weeks after Gemma died, he went back on his regular travel schedule. Had to 'bring home the bacon,' he said. Taking care of children was Mother's role, in his view, and when she couldn't manage, sending us to relatives solved a problem for both of them."

"Good Lord, Sebastian..." Meredith murmured.

He shrugged again. "I think I mentioned that I was the luckiest of the three of us to have ended up with my father's brother at the dairy farm. He and his wife were kind to me, and my cousin was a good sort as we were growing up together. Best of all, I discovered how much I loved animals. It could have been worse."

"It *also* could have been better," Meredith declared. "Your mother could have fought to keep you together as a family. She could have been thankful she had three sons left to love!"

"Ah...but that was the role she allowed *me* to take on," he mused, his glance sliding away once again. "Fighting to keep us together as a family I mean. I was always looking for ways to get her to bring us back home."

Meredith sat up straighter and took his hand. "You know, Sebastian, that's pretty interesting that you say that, because isn't that what you're still doing? Trying to bring people home?"

His eyes widened as her words seemed to sink in.

"I never thought of it that way...but perhaps you're right."

"That's not all bad, you know," she said with a faint smile. "I do the same thing, really. I realized one day, long after my mother had died, that my goal as a nurse had been a driving desire to help make children well so the youngsters in my care could *return* to their moms, the way I never could. Maybe we should both pat ourselves on the back for making lemonade out of lemons?"

Sebastian reached out and skimmed one finger along her jawline in a gesture of such gentleness, her heart melted.

"Well," he said quietly, "it's nice to know I'm not the only Rescue Ranger around…"

"Oh, no…you've got plenty of company right here in this bed," she said, patting the mattress. Then, to lighten their somber mood she added with a grin, "Let's shake on that, pardner."

Sebastian took her hand, pulled her close, hugging her tightly against his chest.

"Fair warning, Meredith," he said with a tenderness that brought tears to her eyes. "I want to do more than just shake hands with you tonight."

⚬⟡⟡⚬

One afternoon a week after Sebastian's revelations about his fractured family life, Beven Glynn, his fellow volunteer on the Cornwall Search and Rescue Team, arrived with a newly acquired, one-year-old chocolate brown and white Springer Spaniel that he proposed enrolling in the beginning agility course Meredith taught on Wednesdays.

"Lilly, here, appears to be very bright and already quite obedient," Meredith said, having asked the dog to perform a few basics like sit, stand, and stay. "Why wouldn't you want her in Sebastian's preliminary search and rescue course? All she'll learn with me in agility class is how to jump through hoops, walk along balance beams, and dash through cloth tunnels. I'm sure you know that Springer Spaniels were used by your army in Afghanistan to ferret out bombs. They're excellent air-sniffing dogs. Frankly, I'd recommend her for the other class, especially given your work with the local team."

"I think I'd like to start out with agility training," he replied with a stubborn tilt to his chin. "Then, I'll see where it leads."

With a shrug, she accepted his money for August's four-week course and checked him into the class. In the hour-long session with five other dogs and their companions, Lilly seemed eager to learn, but Beven was an inattentive student.

Toward the end of the class hour, Meredith said, "No, no, Beven! You're not letting poor Lilly know what you expect of her." She asked for the lead and demonstrated how to guide the dog in a figure eight around the upright posts buried in the ground. "Here, you try. Start at the beginning and run the course again."

While she was demonstrating the proper technique to another class member, Beven started chatting with an attractive woman with a high-strung Irish Setter waiting her turn at the first post. Irritated by his lack of attention, Meredith glanced at her watch and noted with some relief that it was four o'clock.

"Time's up, everyone. Thank you for coming. See you next Wednesday!"

Annoyed by her new student's lackadaisical attitude, she retreated into Painter's Cottage and watched through the window as Beven walked off the field with the woman and her dog.

*I like the dog...but that guy is a total jerk.*

She filed Beven's non-refundable check into an envelope slated for deposit into Blythe's business account. With any luck at all, Mr. Glynn would be pleased he'd so easily acquired a lady friend that he wouldn't bother to come back for class the following week.

⚮

One early afternoon in mid-August, preparations were

in full swing for the final Barton Hall Farm-to-Table supper of the season. Claire Gillis and Richard were up to their elbows in late summer tomatoes slated for a starter course of stacked *caprese* salad consisting of the thickly sliced, plump, red San Marzanos, alternating with matching slabs of mozzarella cheese, fresh basil, and a drizzle of balsamic glaze.

All three children were dutifully setting the tables placed in a long row, end to end, between the rows of vegetable varieties in the garden. As Meredith passed by, she was heartened to hear Janet's laughter as the trio of cousins took turns placing the cutlery in the proper order, as shown them by Richard for previous dinners.

"Knife!" shouted Matthew.

"Spoon!" chimed in Lucy.

"Ta-da...*fork*!" squealed Janet, adding, "Next place!"

They had made a game of running around each other in order to position their respective pieces of flatware at the fifty place settings being prepared to serve their patrons that night.

"Wow!" said Meredith, pausing to admire their handiwork. "I am impressed! You three are doing a great job. Good going, cousins!"

Janet looked up and actually cast a proud smile in Meredith's direction before she placed a final fork at the last place setting.

"Are we having puppy class today?" she asked.

Meredith shook her head. "No, I bumped it 'til tomorrow, same time, though," she explained. "There's just too much we have to do getting ready for the dinner tonight."

"I know," Janet nodded in agreement, "we've had a lot of chores today." She turned toward Matthew and Lucy, appearing to be the leader of the band of helpers. "We have to go get the napkins, now." She looked at Meredith quizzically. "What do they call those here?"

"Serviettes?" Meredith answered.

"Right!" Janet exclaimed. "Let's go get the serviettes and put them under the forks. I'll race you to the pantry!"

And three children scampered off, with Meredith noticing that Janet appeared to have lost at least eight or nine pounds over the summer thanks to eating fresh vegetables and fruits instead of sweets, as well as playing rigorous games outside on the estate, in lieu of watching TV or staring at the Webkinz online game for hours at a time.

The summer in Cornwall had done the child a world of good, Meredith mused. That knowledge, along with the wonder of her deepening relationship with Sebastian brought her up short.

It was already August fifteenth. Soon the earth would tilt ever-so-slightly on its axis and autumn would be fast approaching. She had agreed to a four-month leave from her hospital in Jackson Hole, and now she mightily wished she'd requested six months.

But *then* what, she thought? What did the future really hold for her…and for Janet?

Sobered by such unsettling notions she'd been pushing to the back of her mind for weeks, now, she headed for the door at the rear of the kitchen. By this time, the children had been to fetch the napkins and were carrying a large basket between the three of them, filled to overflowing with freshly pressed, folded linen squares that would be placed under the forks.

"You guys are total stars," she complimented the threesome as they approached, heading back to the tables to complete the final, finishing touches.

Lucy smiled broadly and said, "Janet says *I* get to go

first, this time!"

"That's nice," Meredith said, nodding. "You each are taking turns?"

"Yes!" piped up Matthew. "Janet goes first next when we put the salt and peppers out since she let me go first, doing the knives."

Meredith gave Janet a hug, and for once, she didn't stiffen in her arms. "You are a clever girl to have worked out such a good system for setting the table. Richard and Claire are mighty lucky to have you all helping them like this." She released Janet and waved. "See ya!"

They proceeded happily to their tasks while Meredith reached the back step and paused to remove her Wellingtons. Carrying them into the mudroom, she donned the pair of comfortable shoes she kept there for walking onto the Persian carpets that filled the long hallways in Barton Hall.

She heard the murmur of voices in the kitchen and came around the corner just as Richard and Claire were embracing each other with a ferocious hunger that had little to do with the food they had been preparing. Apparently they, too, had taken note that the summer was speeding by.

"Oh...Claire," Richard said between fevered kisses to the base of her neck and the tops of her breasts beneath her shirt and apron, "I can't leave you in September..."

Claire's response was to begin a frenzied tugging at the front of Richard's shirt tucked into his trousers, insinuating her right hand beneath his belt.

On the long kitchen table, mounds of tomatoes and heaps of mozzarella medallions lay neglected, awaiting assembly on huge platters that would eventually be passed to tonight's guests, along with fire-roasted leg of lamb, a side dish that Claire had invented called "Duffy's Spuds," and blackberry *galettes*, rustic, free-form pies with a nutty, whole wheat crust. However, these culinary marvels were forgotten as the couple continued to kiss passionately, oblivious to the fact that Meredith stood frozen with surprise at the doorway, some twenty feet away.

"Oh, Claire...oh, God..." Richard said on a low moan.

"Here...let me," she urged, working impatiently to unbuckle his belt.

By this time, the eighteen-year-old had untied Claire's chef's apron at the back of her waist and seemingly had no plans to stop there. Meredith, embarrassed to be an unseen witness to such rampant desire, stealthily retreated into the mudroom, deeply troubled that Blythe's handsome stepson was clearly being skillfully seduced—however willingly—by an ambitious woman, nine years his senior, and technically, his employee.

Swiftly, she reached for her Wellingtons, doing her level best to ignore the groans and heavy breathing that continued to waft from the kitchen, through the back pantry, into the mudroom where Meredith fumbled to pull on first one boot, and then the other. Were they making love on top of the tomatoes strewn across the kitchen table, she wondered? How could they be so reckless, given the fact both Blythe and Lucas were in the house this afternoon?

She soundlessly opened the back door, sprinted across the courtyard, and rounded the corner toward the front of the castle as if pursued by banshees. Impulsively, she pulled out her cell phone to send an abbreviated text to Sebastian:

*Need to talk to U ASAP...*

Just as she pushed the 'send' button, she heard the crunch of wheels on the gravel drive near the front portico. She raised her gaze from the tiny screen just as a large, midnight blue Rolls Royce cruised to a halt. Much to her astonishment, out stepped a tall, good-looking man, in a past-his-prime sort of way, clad in an impeccably tailored pin-stripe suit. The arriving guest sported a dark blond ponytail favored by creative types living and working in Hollywood.

"Oh...my...God..."

*I don't believe it!*

It was Janet's father, fresh from the wilds of Alaska, via his Savile Row tailors.

And behind him emerged a stunning, honey blond beauty that Meredith calculated to be a woman half his age.

*As a cradle snatcher, Claire Gillis has nothing on Christopher Stowe!*

Less than five minutes later, the atmosphere within the crenelated walls of Barton Hall was charged like a summer storm crackling over the crags of Dodman Point. Fortunately, both Blythe and Lucas had, indeed, been inside the castle when Meredith, in a state of shock, escorted the film director, along with an actress he introduced as Avery L'Angella, through the massive oak door and into the portrait-laden front hall.

"Please just wait here a minute so I can inform Lord and Lady Barton-Teague that you're here?" Meredith asked.

"*Lady*? " Christopher said derisively. "Do *not* tell me my former wife has taken to styling herself an aristo here at their cunning B&B?"

"No," Meredith replied sweetly. "Queen Elizabeth did. Last year, Lucas was knighted for all his—and Blythe's— good works in the county. Now if you'll just wait here a sec..." she said, gesturing they should proceed to the library and have a seat.

Once Blythe and Lucas appeared in the book-lined room, the next few minutes were excruciatingly tense as the unlikely visitors were offered afternoon tea. Blythe swiftly disappeared to arrange its preparation, leaving Lucas and

Meredith to make small talk. Mercifully, the lady of the house soon returned and appeared to have matters well in hand, leaving Meredith to assume that Claire and Richard had ceased their heated embraces by the time Blythe had sought out their help in the kitchen and had pulled together a full-on repast of hot pots of tea, freshly-baked scones, homemade raspberry jam, and the requisite clotted cream.

Within minutes of Blythe's reappearance, Claire wheeled a tea trolley groaning with a beautiful culinary display into the chamber that also featured Lucas' impressive, multi-branched family tree hanging on one wall. Meredith studiously avoided Claire's questioning gaze and instead, stole successive glances at her cell phone's small screen to see if Sebastian had responded to her spontaneous SOS about Richard being embroiled in an affair with Claire that might well persuade the young man to abandon Oxford.

*What can of worms am I opening if I actually tell him about what I saw and heard in the kitchen? And now with Christopher's sudden arrival…*

Despite the growing closeness Meredith felt had deepened her relationship with Sebastian, he had steadfastly avoided telling her the reasons he'd ended his live-in arrangement with Claire.

But w*hy?*

Would a breakup so disastrous that it had prompted him to sign up for one of the most hazardous duties in the Afghan War not be relevant to whether Richard was in some jeopardy as summer drew to a close and he was due back at his university?

Suddenly, a message from Sebastian appeared with a soft "ping" on her cell phone's screen:

*I'll be at BH by 5.*

*Oh, great,* she groaned silently, wishing she hadn't

pushed the send button, given the scene that was currently unfolding in the library.

*Two crises for the price of one!*

Meanwhile, Blythe was busily pouring out cups of tea. "So, when's the wedding to be?" she asked, nodding in Avery L'Angella's direction.

"Wedding?" echoed Blythe's former husband.

"That's some engagement ring," she said, pointing to the sparkler on Avery's left hand. "Very impressive."

Christopher looked mildly discomforted at the directness of his ex-wife's comments, but Avery smiled brightly and held up her ring finger to showcase her diamond glittering in the light pouring through the tall casement windows behind her.

"Oh, I think we're just going to hit Vegas on our way back to LA, right, babe?" she said. "Something simple, ya know? No stress, no strain. It's the third time for Christopher, of course..." she added with a little giggle.

"Yes, actually, I *do* know that," Blythe replied, pouring hot, amber liquid into all the cups on the tea trolley. "Milk or lemon?"

"Oh, I dunno which..." Avery said, flustered, and looking to Christopher for guidance.

"A little milk in both," he said brusquely.

Lucas sat forward in his velvet upholstered, wing-backed chair.

"So, Ms. L'Angella," he said with the politeness honed from generations of being to-the-manor-born, "I understand you starred in Christopher's latest film?"

The actress smiled coquettishly at her handsome host and looked once again at her fiancé. "It's our second project together, though I played a teeny-weeny part in the last one, didn't I, babe?" she said, gazing at the director with what seemed to Meredith practiced adoration. "This time, when he cast me in *On High,* I had to tell him I had never, ever—not even *once*—worn a pair of hiking boots, let alone knew the first thing about mountain climbing! But he picked me anyway."

*I'll just bet he did!* thought Meredith grimly.

She would place even money that they'd had an affair on the first picture—when Ellie was still alive—to seal the deal. She glanced at Blythe and could almost sense that they both were having, perhaps, their first sympathetic thoughts in a decade for Ellie Barton Stowe.

"So, Christopher," Blythe said, all business. "Tell us what brings you here. I'm afraid we can't offer much hospitality as we're expecting fifty people to a seated dinner in about two hours."

"Oh!" interrupted Avery, "We saw the big sign at the entrance!" She turned to Christopher and said, "I'd just *love* to go to one of those eat-on-a-farm dinners...do you think we could stay for it tonight?" She glanced at her hosts. "I'm sure you wouldn't mind putting us up in this big old place. We'll *pay,* of course."

"We won't have time," Christopher said, dismissing her suggestion by setting his cup down and appearing to gird himself for the coming discussion. "I came because I wanted to know how Janet was getting along."

Blythe and Meredith exchanged glances, but Meredith spoke up first.

"Well, considering her mother died suddenly and she hasn't heard from you in nearly ten weeks' time, I think she's adjusted to being here in Cornwall with the rest of us remarkably well. It was very rough in the beginning but—"

Blythe interjected smoothly, "Meredith has been an absolute saint, Christopher, and frankly, I urged her to come over to Cornwall for the summer because having the care of an eleven-year-old suddenly thrust upon her without warning had placed too big a burden on her shoulders—to say nothing of my seventy-five-year-old uncle."

As if Meredith weren't in the room he retorted, "I paid their fares over here—business class!" He gestured in the direction of the mammoth genealogy chart hanging on the wall above Blythe's head. "And lounging around your castle, here, can't have been too great a hardship."

Meredith felt like flinging her cup of hot tea right at Christopher's head. Blythe, too, seemed highly incensed by his cutting remarks.

"I need to remind you, Christopher, that Meredith is a single woman with a full time job as a nurse, and her widowed father to care for, and to have a grieving child suddenly be *her* responsibility, with *you* making yourself virtually unreachable, it has been...well...it's been a bit much for *all* of us, but we've managed."

Christopher shifted in his chair and stared at the floor. "Well, after all it was Ellie's wish that Meredith—"

"That I become the child's *only* parental figure, Christopher?" Meredith interrupted as her ire soared in response to the man's unbelievable selfishness. "I don't think that's what Ellie intended at all! I was named *co*-guardian, with *you,* as you may remember, but as my 'co,' you've been completely missing-in-action!"

"Look, Meredith," he said testily, "I do appreciate how you've pitched right in, given the difficulties I had after...after Ellie died in the crash...and all the issues concerning the FAA investigation about the plane and getting the film finished on time. In fact, that's one of the reasons I came here today to thank you, personally, for stepping in."

"Well then, if you were so grateful for my help, why didn't you answer any of my calls or emails back in May that Janet wasn't doing well at all those first, few weeks?"

Meredith demanded, sensing that her Nurse Manager combativeness had suddenly taken hold. She absolutely *hated* when parents off-loaded their responsibilities for a sick child on someone else, and in many ways, poor Janet's abandonment by her father was as serious a malady as the kinds of illnesses some of the kids on her ward had faced.

Christopher was looking at her as if he couldn't believe anyone would question the behavior of a man who had a seventy million dollar film riding on his shoulders.

"If my secretary was lax in getting back to you promptly, I apologize, Meredith. She did send you my itinerary, didn't she? Got the tickets to Heathrow lined up, yes?"

"It's not the money, Christopher, that is in question here," Blythe intervened, and Meredith could see she, too, was barely keeping her temper in check. "It's the question of your daughter's welfare. Since you went A.W.O.L., she's been essentially orphaned." She abruptly turned to Avery and asked, "Will you be moving into the house on Bristol Drive, Miss L'Angella? I sincerely hope so, as it's the only home Janet has known her entire life."

Avery glanced nervously at her intended. "Well…ah…"

"That's one of the reasons we came here—"

"Unannounced," Blythe interjected.

"Ah…yes," Christopher said, staring at the floor once again. "Well, sorry I didn't follow *protocol*," he said with a nasty edge to his voice, "but I only have a limited amount of time in the UK this trip and thought it best to speed down here while I could. You know how impossible the cell phone service is here and—"

"It's much improved and we still have a landline, Christopher, reachable from the Dorset Hotel where I expect you slept soundly last night," Blythe replied.

"Well…whatever. I wanted to propose an idea about

the next...ah...phase of my daughter's education and care."

"Which is?" Meredith asked sharply.

Christopher looked first at her and then over to Blythe. "With Avery and I embarking on a...new chapter of our lives," he said, groping for words, "I thought...well, we thought that it might make sense to seek a slightly modified arrangement regarding Janet."

"Which is?" Meredith repeated as her stomach twisted in a knot around the scone she wished she hadn't eaten a few minutes earlier. She felt a deep rush of sympathy should Janet actually be bidden to return to Beverly Hills under the care of these two narcissists...yet Christopher *was* her father.

*Oh, God...this is horrible!*

"Well," he said with a practice smile he probably bestowed on his bankers, "believe it or not, Blythe, I *do* realize that Meredith, here, is a young woman with her own life to lead, and that Ellie was rather impulsive to bestow co-guardianship on her, given they weren't particularly close."

"Ellie wasn't close with anyone in her family after she married you," Blythe pointed out bluntly.

Christopher paused and Meredith sensed he had an acerbic remark of his own on the tip of his tongue, thought better of it, and focused on the campaign he had come to Barton Hall to wage.

"Well, that being the case, and since Janet has spent the summer here and, as you say," he shifted to address Meredith, "has adjusted rather well...perhaps...it makes sense that we make Janet's Aunt Blythe a *co*-guardian *with* you, Meredith. That way, the burden will be...ah...much less...burdensome."

"Less burdensome on *you*, you mean?" Meredith retorted, thinking *I can fling flaming arrows with the best of them!*

The Academy Award-winning director glanced over at his recently affianced as if seeking a "Bravo" for bearing the indignities he'd endured since arriving at Barton Hall.

"I think it's a plan that would benefit everyone," he answered stiffly.

"You'd make *me* her co-guardian?" Blythe asked, incredulous.

"Why, yes," Christopher said, as if nothing would be more natural in the world than to have his ex-wife take on permanent responsibility for the child whose entry into the world had so brutally caused the end of her first marriage.

Undeterred by Blythe's open-mouthed expression, he continued, "She can spend the time she's not here with you at Barton Hall—and with her little English cousins, of course—attending a good, British boarding school."

He waited for a response from the assembled and when he received nothing except stunned silence, he added brazenly, "I'd be most pleased to know she was being raised here in the UK, rather than in the…ah…rather materialistic culture that you, Blythe, of all people, know exists in Southern California, and have so totally rejected yourself, and—"

"Stop right there!" Blythe said, pushing the tea trolley away from her lap with a clatter and abruptly standing up. "Christopher Stowe, you have the most, absolute, bloody *gall* of anyone I have ever encountered in my entire life, *but*—" she emphasized, pausing with her forefinger in the air and her sweeping glance taking in Meredith and Lucas, "for all the *wrong* reasons, you may have come up with the very solution that we, at Barton Hall, have needed to find as the summer draws to a close." She beckoned to Lucas and Meredith. "Shall we retire to another room to discuss Christopher's proposal?"

# CHAPTER 14

Dumbfounded by everything that had happened since the moment Christopher Stowe's Rolls Royce had cruised up the drive, Meredith could only nod her assent to Blythe's suggestion and prepare to exit the library. Lucas, too, rose from his chair with an unreadable expression.

"I have to pee something awful," Avery complained. "Could someone tell me where I can find the little girl's room while you all have your pow-wow, or what*ever*?"

"Certainly," Blythe said, ignoring the Valley Girl intonations of her visitor. "Follow me and I'll show you where the nearest lavatory is on this floor.

Less than twenty minutes later, Blythe, Lucas, and Meredith re-entered the library single-file as late afternoon shadows sliced across the burgundy and royal blue carpets and warmed the brown leather sofas and club chairs that encircled the baronial fireplace.

Christopher and his fiancée were seated in the same spots as before. Claire had been sent in to clear the tea things and the pair looked as if they'd suffered almost unendurable boredom waiting for their hosts.

"Ah...the Committee returns," Christopher pronounced as Meredith and Lucas resumed their former seats.

Blythe, who had remained standing in front of the hearth flanked by massive brass andirons on one side and a priceless, waist-high Chinese vase on the other, announced to the visitors, "I've been selected as spokesperson for our response to your proposal. Meredith, Lucas and I are in complete agreement as to the following."

"Good heavens," Christopher Stowe replied in his clipped British accent. "Quite a united front. Should I have a solicitor in attendance?"

"You *will* need an attorney before we all sign off on this, " Blythe responded with a grim smile. "First of all, I will agree officially to become co-guardian with Meredith *if* you will put in writing the following items."

She glanced down at a piece of lined paper with the notes from their meeting held in the former housekeeper's small office off the kitchen.

"One: you will agree to fly to Britain to visit your daughter at least once every four months, regardless of where you might be. Two: you will immediately put two hundred thousand dollars in an escrowed educational account to pay for Janet's higher education, with an additional sum to be determined, should she decide to go on to a graduate school. Three—"

"What about boarding school in the UK? Surely you want *that* on your laundry list of demands?"

"We'll get to that later," Blythe assured him.

Christopher's lips settled into a straight line. "There's more?"

"Oh yes," Blythe replied, continuing, "Proviso Number Three...you will legally vest in Meredith and me *all* decisions about primary and grammar school—in consultation with you, of course—but with the two of us having the ultimate say."

"Which means I could be outvoted," Christopher pointed out peevishly.

"That is correct," Blythe answered. "We imagine that

Janet will want to determine, herself, where she'd like to go to college or university when she gets older."

"I see," was all that Christopher responded.

"Provisos Four and Five," Blythe continued, "you will immediately establish a second generous fund in Janet's name, with Meredith and me as co-administrators, to be distributed at fifty-five thousand a year, to pay her grammar school fees, plus yearly expenses related to her welfare while she is under our care, *and* another large sum each fiscal year that is equal to fifteen percent of your yearly future income, to be granted to her in a lump sum when she attains the age of thirty."

"Of course, I'd do all that," Christopher said with a dismissive wave of his hand, although Meredith noticed Avery giving her intended a poke in the thigh. "She also inherits the portion of Ellie's estate she's due when she reaches twenty-one."

"Yes, Meredith and I are aware of that, having reviewed Ellie's will just now. I'm almost finished," Blythe added with a thin smile. "And finally, Proviso Six: you will also rewrite your present will to give Janet an equal share in your estate with any others you so designate, including your future wife, Avery, and any children that may be a product of that and any other subsequent union. And in that proviso it will state that anyone who *challenges* your will receives a dollar. Period."

"Chris-to-pher!" Avery L'Angella was actually whining in response to Blythe's last condition. "That puts our baby and me *way* second…"

Meredith was caught completely off-guard by what she'd just heard Avery say.

*So the jerk got another woman pregnant out of wedlock, just like he did Ellie!*

Meredith glanced over at Blythe who appeared totally

unconcerned by Avery's admission she was presumably carrying Chris's child. Without the slightest hesitation, she continued reading her list of demands.

"Items One through Six have to be in *writing*, Christopher, and signed by all parties to this agreement, including Avery, here—as well as notarized," she said, "or I will not agree to be co-guardian."

"And I also will resign my role as guardian as well," Meredith chimed in on cue, though this statement was pure bluff, as she would never, now, leave poor Janet to the sole care of the child's father and soon-to-be-stepmother.

"I don't much appreciate being manipulated and hen-pecked by you two like this, I can tell you that," Christopher said, eyes narrowing. "Sounds like you want to make a pretty farthing on the deal."

Meredith could see that Christopher's last remark cut Blythe to the quick, and her cousin's reply had ice dripping from every syllable.

"So you actually think I would try to profit from a child who would have been my own, had you not had an affair with my *sister*? A child whose mother was tragically killed in a plane *you* owned and paid to maintain—poorly, as I understand from the FAA report investigating the crash— and who is a Barton by *blood*?"

Dead silence filled the room and echoed off the Barton family portraits that stared down at the tense group assembled in the circle of burnished leather chairs.

Then Lucas broke in.

"Why don't we just make this simple, Christopher?" he said pleasantly. "And as a matter of fact, you don't actually have much choice." All heads swiveled to stare at the Master of Barton Hall who had spoken very little thus far. "Of course, if you and your future bride want *full-time* responsibility for Janet as you begin your new…'chapter'…as you so euphemistically put it…we can ask Claire to pack Janet's things so she can leave with you today." He allowed his sentence to dangle, and then declared, "As for us, we're all willing to sign the agreement as just outlined by Blythe. So do let us know if it is acceptable to you before you depart," he added, glancing meaningfully at his watch.

Another bluff they had all agreed upon.

"And may I say," Meredith added, hoping she wasn't playing her hand too blatantly with these appalling creatures, "Christopher, you two and I know quite well that young Janet can be quite a…*handful* when she's an unhappy camper."

Stowe rose from his chair and his fiancée hastened to do likewise.

"So, tell me," he said acidly, "If I agree to all this, do you envision Janet living here in the UK in *this* commercial enterprise, or in the wilds of Wyoming, since that decision would now, under this agreement, be up to you two?"

Meredith looked over at Blythe. They hadn't had time to discuss what would happen, come September, but Blythe spoke first in even, clipped tones.

"We will want to talk that over with Janet, naturally. After all, she should have some say in how her life will be, henceforth, now that her mother is dead."

Christopher nodded, as if admitting defeat. "I'll have my solicitor draw up the necessary papers," he said.

"Actually," Lucas intervened swiftly, "we have kept all the notes from this discussion. *Our* solicitor will codify all the arrangements we've just stated here today, and then your representative can have a look at the paperwork and we can make any adjustments. That is, of course, *before* you leave Britain this trip. Shall we say two days from now?"

Christopher cast an appraising glance at his hosts and

Meredith who stood, now, in a united front on the carpet flanking the massive stone fireplace.

"Yes," he snapped. He turned to Avery. "Well, that's it, then. We'd best be off."

"Oh, babe…what about that lovely dinner we saw being set up as we drove in? I'm hungry! It'll take hours to get back to our hotel." She bestowed her thousand-watt smile on Blythe. "We could rent a room from you and stay the night in this big, old castle. Please, Christopher, please! I'm really pooped! And remember how the doctor said I shouldn't get over tired?"

"No, Avery. We're going."

"Don't you even want to see your daughter?" demanded Meredith, appalled that Janet's father could come all the way from Alaska and across the Atlantic Ocean and then blithely leave without even speaking to the girl, let alone spending some time with her.

"Oh c'mon, Christopher, that'll take us for*ever*!" Avery exclaimed, her botoxed lips in an even more pronounced pout than before. "You wanna go to London tonight so bad? Then, let's go!"

Christopher heaved an undisguised sigh of frustration. Meredith was at a loss to discern whether it was aimed at his fiancée or at the massively uncomfortable situation he'd found himself in.

"We'll motor straight up to London tonight and stay at the Dorset," he repeated firmly. "I'll ring Sir Anthony, my solicitor, en route and tell him to be prepared to receive an electronic draft document from you, Lucas, sometime tomorrow—that is if you have decent Internet service down here."

"We do," Lucas replied, and then smiled, "most of the time."

Christopher fished a business card out of his pocket.

"Here's Sir Anthony's contact information. Once the language of the agreement is settled, I'll visit Janet when Avery and I come back down to Barton Hall to have our little signing ceremony."

Meredith was about to protest, but Blythe quickly spoke up.

"That's fine. Let me show you the way out."

The group of five that had been conferencing in the library silently trod down the carpeted hallway, through the arched front entrance, and into the portico where Christopher's chauffeur stood at the ready next to the Rolls Royce, it's door to the plush back seat open and waiting.

The tall larch trees cast long shadows across the manicured grass. A hundred yards away, Sebastian's green Mini Cooper was visible speeding up the drive.

Just then, Matthew and Janet dashed around the tower that anchored the north face of the castle, with Lucy trotting along behind trying to keep up.

"I was right!" Matthew shouted over his shoulder to his cousin. "I said it was someone arriving in a Rolls Royce! I—" He stopped, shifted his attention, and pointed excitedly. "Look, it's Sebastian coming, too! Hooray!"

Matthew and Lucy forgot about the Rolls Royce and ran to the section of grass bordering the gravel circle that fronted the castle's entrance. Janet, however, remained where she was, staring at the unexpected sight of her father standing next to his sleek, midnight blue car.

"Hello, hello!" Lucy called excitedly to Sebastian who was unfolding his tall frame from the Mini. "Are you helping us again with the farm supper tonight? May I sit next to you when *we* eat, Sebastian?"

Janet, however, remained rooted to the spot, gazing at her father who now had his back to her while handing Avery into the back seat.

"Daddy? *Daddy*! You came!"

She ran straight for Christopher's legs and flung her arms around his waist.

"Good heavens, Janet!" he exclaimed, trying to extricate himself from her frantic embrace. "Really! Isn't this a bit excessive? How are you, my dear?" Without waiting for a reply, he took her by her upper arm and leaned toward the open door of the back seat. "I'd like you to meet a great friend of mine, Ms. Avery L'Angella. Avery, this is my daughter, Janet."

Before Avery could respond from the awkward angle in which she was being introduced, Janet scowled and said, "I already met her, remember? She came to the party you had that time when Mommy got so mad at you." She looked Avery squarely in the eye. "My mommy didn't like you," she said accusingly. "She said you were nothing but a tramp, and a horrible actress and that you were after my Daddy."

"That will be *enough*, young lady!" He glared at Meredith and said pointedly to Blythe, "I think it's fortunate, indeed, that you will soon exert stronger guidance in disciplining Janet. Anyone can see she's sorely in need of a lesson in manners."

By this time, Sebastian was standing some thirty feet from the strained circle surrounding the Rolls Royce. Meredith felt as if Christopher's words had virtually punched her in the chest, but before she could summon a retort, Blythe addressed her former husband coldly.

"Goodbye, Christopher. You'll receive the papers via an email attachment tomorrow morning. You have until three o'clock to reply by return email and until five o'clock the following day to arrive back here for the signing."

"We could accomplish that electronically, as well," he said curtly.

"No, indeed," Blythe retorted. "I want to see you put your fresh signature and/or initials on every single paragraph of this agreement." She turned to the assembled group and said, "C'mon everyone. Inside! Fifty dinner guests are about to arrive, but first, I think what's called for here is a great, big group hug," and then they marched briskly toward the castle's imposing door.

Meredith could not take her eyes off Janet who stood with a stricken expression as her father climbed into the car and shut his door without a backward glance. Christopher Stowe leaned forward in his seat with a scowl on his face and said something to the driver. Immediately the chauffeur put the vehicle in gear and in seconds, the luxury automobile sped forward, spitting gravel as it entered the long entrance drive. In its wake, a few pebbles stung Janet's ankles, causing her to cry out.

"Oh, sweetie, come here," Meredith cried and ran over to her ward. "Are you hurt?"

Janet's eyes were filled with tears that soon were spilling over and down her cheeks. Sebastian, too, strode over to the eleven-year-old.

"She made him leave," Janet sobbed. "He would have stayed with me, but she made him *leave!*"

Meredith exchanged a look of consternation with Sebastian.

*How do we explain what kind of a bastard her father really is?* her eyes pleaded to Sebastian, who had seen enough of the exchange to comprehend what was going on.

*Bugger all, Meredith, I have no idea...*he conveyed to her wordlessly.

Janet looked up at Meredith. "Is he really coming back tomorrow?" she said, hiccupping as tears continued to cascade down her cheeks.

"He has to go to London, tonight, sweetie, but he said

he'd be back the day *after* tomorrow."

"I hope he comes alone!" she said vehemently. "I hope he doesn't come with *her!*"

By this time, Blythe had noticed that part of their group remained outside and had turned around from the front door and retraced her steps to the drive. She cast a questioning glance at Meredith, and said, "The children are eating an early dinner so they can help later."

Meredith bent down to speak to Janet. "Do you want to have supper now, and be a helper to Richard and Claire, or would you rather have a tray tonight and...maybe read a Nancy Drew?"

Janet looked up and put her hand in Meredith's. "If I have a tray, would you and Sebastian come up to see me? I'm...I'm..."

"Tired, sweetie?" Meredith supplied the word sympathetically. "You worked so hard helping to set the tables. I'm sure everyone would understand if you just want to take it easy tonight."

"Thanks," she said in a small voice.

Meredith pulled Janet close to her and gave her a hug.

"Good plan," agreed Blythe quietly. "I have to change for tonight, so let me take you upstairs, Janet, and get you settled and we'll send up a tray."

"Does that sound okay, Janet?" Meredith asked. "Then I promise, Sebastian and I will look in on you once supper is over and the guests leave, all right?"

Janet gave a small nod of assent. Over her head, the three adults exchanged glances as if to say, "Can you *believe* what happened just now?" and then Blythe took Janet's hand and lead her inside the Hall and up the grand staircase.

⌒⌒

Sebastian and Meredith had no time to talk before the Farm-to-Table Supper guests began to arrive. He joined Lucas serving drinks from a make-shift bar while Meredith supervised a few of the young women hired from the village to help with the serving, and kept the big platters filled to overflowing with succulent pink slices of rosemary and garlic glazed lamb, the bubbling casseroles of potatoes, cream, fresh thyme, and shredded sharp cheddar cheese, and a mélange of al dente steamed garden vegetables for the guests.

"What did you text me about?" Sebastian whispered when Meredith brought a tray of clean glasses to the bar where Lucas and he had been serving wine all evening.

"The subject of that message may be the least of my troubles, now, but I'll tell you what it was about after we get through here," she said under her breath, picking up a tray of dirty discards.

"Painter's Cottage later?" he whispered with a mildly suggestive leer.

Meredith summoned a smile, though she dreaded initiating any subject that involved Claire Gillis, given Sebastian's stony silence whenever the two were within range of each other. "Painter's Cottage sounds like an excellent idea. Lots to talk about. But don't forget we promised we'd look in on Janet."

By eleven-thirty, feeling utterly drained by the day's events and the hard work everyone had contributed to another successful event, Meredith threw her dirty dishrag on top of the washing machine in the laundry room and stumbled outside toward the bar where Sebastian was helping Lucas put away the newly-washed glasses.

"I'll deal with the rest of all this tomorrow," Lucas said wearily. "We'll store them in the stone barn until next season, if it turns out these dinners earned us enough profit to do them again." He clasped Sebastian on the shoulder. "You were a brick, old boy. Can't thank you enough for *all* your help this summer. I don't think you drank enough wine in recompense."

"I enjoyed it," Sebastian said. He turned and put an arm around Meredith. "In fact, I've enjoyed every minute I've been at Barton Hall this summer."

Lucas offered a tired smile and bid them farewell, mentioning he had at least an hour writing up the co-guardianship agreement that his legal representative would look at before they sent it on to Christopher Stowe's solicitor.

Meredith had noted that all evening long, Sebastian managed to avoid any contact with Claire who, along with Richard, was constantly coming in and out of the kitchen with large trays of food that their helpers passed down the tables, family style. Now, as Meredith and Sebastian approached the rear of the Hall, he almost appeared to wince at the sound of laughter and teasing that could be heard through the pantry door as Richard and Claire finished washing the last of the large platters in the kitchen.

Sebastian seized Meredith's hand and said, "Let's run up to look on Janet...then we'll drive the Mini down to the cottage, all right? You must be exhausted, given the piece of the drama I witnessed as I arrived this afternoon."

"You don't know the half of it," Meredith said, and leaned against Sebastian for support. "But, yes, let's go up the back stairs," she proposed. "It's much quicker than through the front entrance and leads straight up to the corridor where Janet's room is." She led the way through the mudroom to the pantry that opened into the kitchen.

When they entered the large room piled high with dishes on the drain, Richard was seated at the kitchen table, skewering a piece of grilled lamb that he playfully popped into Claire's open mouth. She held his wrist and guided the morsel into her mouth, followed by a sensuous moan of pleasure as she began to chew, her eyes gazing intently into her *sous chef's.*

It was an intimate gesture, one that spoke of a familiarity that went far beyond two cooks sampling their wares. Both were startled when they realized Meredith and Sebastian were staring at them from the doorway.

Claire recovered first and set down her fork.

"Well, hello there, you two," she said, her other hand still resting on Richard's shoulder. "Wasn't our final supper of the season smashing, even if we do say so ourselves?" She gazed at her fellow chef and added, "Richard, here, made that amazing *caprese* salad that everyone raved about."

Meredith had seen *both* of them slicing endless piles of tomatoes and wheels of mozzarella in preparation for the evening meal. Her nonsense detector was loudly going off in her head as she realized that Claire was playing up to the man with a woman's most potent weapon—flattery. As for Sebastian, Meredith could almost feel him bristling with indignation at Claire's proprietary manner toward Richard, but rather than making any reply or even acknowledging Claire had spoken, he walked straight through the kitchen and mounted the old servants' stairs without a word.

Richard, his fair skin slightly flushed, smiled somewhat sheepishly in Meredith's direction and said, "Thank you both for being such huge help tonight. I doubt Claire and I could have gotten through this thing without you and Sebastian and the rest."

"You're welcome," she replied, adding a brisk, "Goodnight," hurrying toward the stairs to catch up with Sebastian who had disappeared into the darkness above. "We're just going up to look in on Janet."

Sebastian was still walking swiftly down the corridor

when Meredith spotted him at the other end of the upstairs hallway.

"Wait up!" she whispered loudly. "Sebastian!" she called, *sotto voce*, pointing to a door he'd just stormed past. "*This* is Janet's room."

As he retraced his steps, she carefully opened the heavy oaken entrance to one of the many guest rooms in the manor house. Janet was curled up in a fetal position on a large bed with a gold silk canopy and matching draperies soaring overhead. A brass reading lamp glowed rich amber beside her bed where she lay with a Nancy Drew mystery unopened on the silk brocade coverlet. She was sound asleep, along with Holly, curled up at her feet. A tissue was balled into her fist and she obviously had cried herself to sleep.

"Oh, the poor thing," Meredith murmured, her heart aching for the child.

"Let her be," Sebastian said softly.

"I'll just cover her so she'll know we came up to see her, as we promised," she whispered.

Meredith lifted a soft mohair throw tossed on a nearby chair and placed it gently over Janet's small form. Holly stirred and Meredith held up her hand, a signal to the dog to remain where she was "on duty." Meredith and Sebastian quietly backed out of her room, exited Barton Hall down the main staircase and out the front door, and then climbed into the Mini for the short drive to Painter's Cottage. Rex roused himself in the back seat and wagged his tail as Sebastian asked for a second time why she'd sent him a text.

"Did you want some backup support, given the arrival of that Rolls Royce?" he wondered.

"No, Janet's father and girlfriend arrived right *after* I sent you the text." She paused, and then plunged ahead.

"You know the scene you just witnessed with Richard and Claire in the kitchen? Well, earlier today, I was treated to something similar, only with more hand-to-hand combat," she added, raising an eyebrow. "They were basically ripping off each other's clothes in the kitchen."

"Meredith we've already been over this. It's really none of—"

"Richard's supposed to leave for Oxford in two weeks!" she cut in. "What if Claire is doing everything she can to—well, you know! Don't you think the time has finally come to warn his parents there may be some seriously nasty surprises heading their way?"

Sebastian appeared to draw into himself. "Well," he said, finally, "I'll leave that up to you to decide."

He parked by the side of the road flanking the field that sloped down to Painter's Cottage. He opened the wooden gate and released his dog to roam nearby for a bit. Then the three trudged across the pasture where the sheep huddled in a moist, loamy corner for the night.

"I don't know about you," Sebastian said as they switched on the bronze-colored lamp that stood in the windowsill just inside the cottage door, "but I am bone tired."

"Are those code words for 'let's just get some sleep?'" Meredith translated, trying to keep her tone light.

Sebastian sought her hand. "Yes, but just you wait until morning." He turned toward Rex and pointed to the fireplace hearth. "Go on, boy. Lie down." His dog soon found a spot on an area rug in front of the cold hearth and immediately closed his eyes.

"Well…" Meredith said slowly, her gaze lingering on Rex while she considered how best to restart a conversation about the touchy subject of Claire and Richard, "I would like to…ask you something else about tonight."

"What is that?" he responded warily.

"If you're so vehement that the heating up of Richard and Claire's relationship is none of your business," she said carefully, "then why did you angrily march through the kitchen just now and practically take the servant's steps two-at-a-time?"

She turned to face the large bank of windows overlooking the Channel, barely visible in the starlit night, and folded her arms across her chest. An unhappy silence bloomed between them once again. Finally, Sebastian spoke.

"Come on, Meredith, let's don't make a drama again out of this thing."

Stung, she strove to keep her emotions in check.

"It's not *my* drama, remember? It involves you and Claire and predates my appearance on the scene, by a long shot, though it seems to be impacting you and me."

Meredith had not forgotten her vow to allow Sebastian to tell her about the dark corners of his past in his own time, but summer's end was fast approaching, and the relationship between Claire and Richard appeared to be reaching a fevered pitch—with a possible impact the could spread far and wide.

She took a step closer to him and rested her hand on his sleeve. "Sebastian, why don't you just *tell* me what actually happened between you two? Did Claire do something awful? Something she could do to Richard as well?"

"Claire and Richard's current lust-fest has absolutely *nothing* to do with me, so I'd appreciate if you'd just leave it," he repeated evenly.

"I would, except that I'm beginning to wonder if Claire hasn't mounted some giant payback scheme here—and we're *all* going to suffer for it?"

"My guess is that Claire is going to do what Claire's going to do—for Richard's benefit or ruin—I have no idea, nor will I become involved."

Meredith's instinct was to pace back and forth in front of the big windows, but forced herself to remain where she was.

"So you don't think we should warn Blythe and Lucas that their new employee may be plotting the ultimate corporate takeover that would affect every aspect of life here at Barton Hall?" she asked.

"Count me out on *that* mission," Sebastian declared. She noted he surreptitiously glanced at his watch, as if timing how long he thought he could take this continuing conversation.

"So now I've got *three* problems!" Meredith said, her temper beginning to fray. "One: What's going to happen with Janet after today if her father won't sign the agreement that we outlined? Two: What's going to happen between our Heir to Barton Hall and our Fancy Food Wench and life here on the estate?" She halted and tried her best to keep her voice even. "And...three: why do you always avoid telling me why you ended it so precipitously with Claire—and why throw up a wall between us every single time the subject comes up?" She held up four fingers. "And now that I think of it, Number Three brings me to another problem: Four. I'm supposed to return to my life in Wyoming when September rolls around in two weeks' time and the fact that you're...you're shutting down like this again makes me think I should move up my departure date."

Sebastian scowled. A shock of his dark hair falling on his forehead added to her sense that just beneath the surface he was boiling with anger.

"Why are you using Claire to create some sort of crisis

between you and me?" he demanded. "I've told you: the past is the past and there's no point in raking it up—except you seem bound and determined to," he retorted, raising his voice.

"That's not it, and you know it!" Meredith said with exasperation. "After all that's happened between us this summer, I thought we had built some genuine trust in each other. That slowly but surely, there weren't going to be *any* areas that were 'off limits' between us anymore."

"This is not about my trusting you. And it's certainly not about *you*. At all!"

"Well, I'll tell you one thing it's about," she said, cut to the quick by his harsh words. "It's about a little thing called intimacy. Being straight with each other. Telling the truth about who we are and how we got to this point of making mad love to each other and sharing essentially everything else in our lives this summer. It's about *our* intimacy," she cried, fighting the catch in her throat.

"So you don't think we've been intimate *enough*?" he shot back.

Meredith felt a wave of absolute desolation over the way he was deliberately misinterpreting her words.

"Sorry if I sound naïve," she replied, fighting tears, "but I actually thought our closeness extended beyond that big, wide bed up there!" She pointed to the loft overhead and cast an exaggerated glance at her watch. "Hey, Sebastian, time's running out to come clean about what really happened to you in the last five or ten years. Tick-tock…the summer's almost over, you know. It's pretty close to the witching hour when I have to decide whether to buy a ticket to leave Cornwall in fourteen days or—or hang around here a while longer! What's *your* advice?"

"I must tell you, Meredith, I find your jealousy regarding this business with Claire very unattractive," he said in a clipped tone of voice.

Meredith simply stared at him, astonished.

"Don't you dare pull that Oh-So-British crap on me! You think this argument we're having is just about *my* jealousy?"

"Yes, I do."

"Well, it's not!" she retorted, incensed by his accusation. "I'm not jealous. I'm *worried!* I'm worried that Richard is going to either get sucked into something that will wreck his entire life and affect everyone here at Barton Hall, or he's going to get his heart handed to him by the savvy Ms. Claire Gillis."

She turned her back and said over her shoulder, "And now I'm worried about you and me. Since you won't tell *me* what she did to you years ago—or what you may have done to *her* for all I know—then the least you can do is to take Richard aside and make sure the guy has bought a box of condoms."

"Christ, Meredith—"

She whirled to face him.

"What?" she demanded. "That I'm a dog with a bone about this? Well, you bet I am! This is my *family*! And something you're not telling me is totally screwing up my life right now…and probably Richard's, too!"

She was startled when Sebastian abruptly turned his back, strode across the wooden floor, and opened the door to Painter's Cottage. Before she could say another word, he slammed it shut so hard behind him, one of the seascapes by Ennis Trevelyan crashed to the floor.

Meredith remained frozen where she stood, barely conscious of the bleating of sheep echoing across the fields in concert with the faint slap of the waves on the rocks below the cliff. Then, suddenly, she heard the roar of Sebastian's car driving at top speed along the road to

Dodman Point.

Rex raised his head and then pulled himself upright. Meredith was astounded to realize that his master had completely forgotten to take his dog.

She sank into the desk chair, stunned by Sebastian's furious exit. Suddenly, a warm muzzle nudged her thigh. She reached down to scratch Rex under the ear as a terrible feeling of loss and regret took hold. Surely Sebastian would cool off and come back, if only to return for his dog?

Five, then ten minutes elapsed while she remained seated with Rex's head in her lap. Finally, she murmured to her furry companion, "Well, boy...I guess it's just you and me here, tonight." She carefully guided him up the steep stairs that led to the loft. "Hop on the bed, 'cause I sure as hell do not intend to sleep alone!"

# CHAPTER 15

Meredith was too upset by Sebastian's angry and abrupt departure to do anything but throw herself onto the bed in the loft and stare at the ancient, beamed ceiling most of the night. Rex had soon padded downstairs and lay on the wooden floor in front of the front door, emitting heart-rending whimpers every so often, sounds that only echoed the misery she felt in her own solar plexus. She half-expected Sebastian to stealthily return in the middle of the night to fetch his dog, but by dawn's light, she was wondering if the man she'd fallen in love with were simply a guy—like Shep O'Brien—with too many wounds and too complicated a past to create the sort of life that she had begun to fantasize might be possible here in Cornwall.

*You sure can pick 'em, cowgirl...*

She glanced outside the small window nestled under the eaves in the wall opposite her bed. Fog the color of slate was somberly rolling off the English Channel enveloping the cliffs and the cottage itself in a misty shroud. The earth had definitely shifted on its axis and soon autumn and then winter would arrive with its persistent, cold winds off Dodman Point and a fire in the hearth every night. Summer was, indeed, nearly over. Her leave of absence at her hospital would officially end in mid-September. Decisions must be made.

She sat bolt upright in bed and pounded the mattress

on either side of her with both fists.

*No!* she thought with sudden fierceness. Sebastian Pryce was *not* Shep O'Brien!

Sebastian was one of the dearest people she'd ever know and invariably reliable, honest, kind—and the truest indicator of his character was that he loved animals as much as she did. *Something else was going on,* and she was sure their latest crisis had primarily to do with Sebastian's breakup with Claire long ago—and not with Sebastian and the Lady from Wyoming. But what in the world could it be? Claire had given her every indication she had put their unhappiness behind her and moved on.

*Why hadn't Sebastian?*

Meredith threw aside the feather duvet and jumped into the pair of jeans she'd worn the previous evening, pulling her sweater over her head. Even though it was only just after seven in the morning, she was going to pay a call to Limekiln Cottage. Surely, if Richard had spent the night with her, he had stolen back to his room in Barton Hall by now. If Sebastian wouldn't tell her what had happened between them, maybe Claire Gillis *would.*

"C'mon, Rex," Meredith called downstairs. "Let's go get her!"

ﾟＣﾉＯﾟ

The deep-set windows in the small, squat cottage constructed of local granite with a slate roof were dark and shuttered. Claire's dented Vauxhall remained parked nearby. Meredith's cheeks were cold from the brisk walk from her cottage to Claire's and she longed for a cup of good, strong coffee before embarking on her mission. However, she'd made no detour to Barton Hall's kitchen en route and now commanded Rex to sit while she tied him to a nearby tree with one of the extra leashes she'd always kept for her students in a basket at Painter's Cottage when they forgot to bring their own—an irritating but common occurrence.

"Stay, boy!" she repeated, and headed in the direction of Claire's front door. There had been a light rain during the night and Meredith noticed another set of tire tracks embedded in the soft earth near the cottage. She halted abruptly and stared at the ground. Near where the tire impressions ended was a dog leash she instantly recognized as belonging to Rex. It was damp and tangled and had obviously fallen out of Sebastian's Mini sometime during the night.

Meredith's heart was pounding as she considered the evidence that Sebastian had made a visit to Limekiln Cottage a few hours before she had. Since the Mini wasn't there any longer, he'd apparently been there and gone before dawn's light, which was just now breaking in the East.

A part of Meredith's brain ordered her to turn around and head straight back to Barton Hall and start packing. Whatever had transpired between Sebastian and his former ladylove didn't really matter, as far as Meredith was concerned. The salient factor was that the man she'd fallen in love with had come directly here to see Claire Gillis after storming out of her door. She didn't need anything else to tell her that her own relationship with Sebastian appeared as tangled as the leash that lay at her feet.

*Don't push against the river...go where the current takes you.*

Her tortuous ending with Shep had taught her to accept what was right in front of her eyes and not try to explain away disconcerting facts as something more hopeful than they appeared—or were.

The plain truth was, regardless of how she felt about

Sebastian, he had not truly finished with Claire, despite his declarations early on that she was not a factor in his life anymore. For good or ill, the woman mattered to him. Whether he'd been to see her to have it out verbally with his former lover—or something else—he had felt compelled to visit her cottage the previous night and had never returned to Meredith's to explain what was going on.

*And he didn't even come back for his dog.*

Even more disturbing, he was apparently unable to trust her with the truth of the unhappy past that he'd shared with Claire. He'd repeatedly shut out his current love whenever she reached out to him about the conflicts in his life that obviously still festered.

*I am crazy about the guy, but I'm through being a masochist over any man. I want someone who lets me in...like Dad did with Mom...*

For the second time that summer, a sudden, intense homesickness took hold of her and she longed to be sitting at the kitchen table with her father at the Crooked C Ranch, talking over the day's events.

*Ancestors or not, I guess I don't belong in Cornwall, after all...*

Struggling against a powerful sense of disappointment and regret, she forced herself to consider what a wonderful summer it had been in so many ways. Janet was truly changing into a sweet little girl with behaviors much more appropriate to her age and stage. Blythe had become far more than an amiable cousin, but a true friend and champion.

*Almost a sister*, Meredith thought, tears seeping into the corners of her eyes. Together, they would continue to help Janet grow into a decent human being. And best of all, she had loved getting to know the land of her forebears and would always find a welcome here...

*But without Sebastian in my life...?*

She wouldn't think about that now, she decided, picking up Rex's leash off the damp ground. She *couldn't* think about what the future would be like back in Wyoming. She would simply concentrate on figuring out what she needed to do to wrap up her obedience classes before she left England in September. And *then* she could decide what she'd do with the rest of her life…and how she would forget the rugged man in the red and black parka— to say nothing of the wonderful Rex.

But if there were no obedience school, she reminded herself with a start, a very important income stream would be denied Barton Hall. Would Sebastian want to carry it on without her, she wondered, as another layer of sadness and recrimination assaulted her.

*How had it come to this…and so quickly?*

She stared at Claire's silent cottage for a moment longer and then turned abruptly on her heel. In one sense, Sebastian was right. Claire's life and actions were none of her affair. It was all too much. She couldn't try to fix everything that had so rapidly gone awry. Richard would have to learn which people liked him for himself and which ones might merely want something from the youthful heir to Barton Hall.

And she would have to decide what was in her own, best interest. She fished in her pocket for her mobile phone and sent a text to Sebastian.

*Rex & leash R @ Barton Hall.*

She'd consign the dog's care to whoever was home and then head back to Painter's Cottage to prepare for a full series of classes scheduled for later in the day.

"C'mon, boy," she whispered softly to Rex. "Let me fasten your proper leash on your collar."

Despite her best resolve, she found herself fighting tears once more as she trudged down the gravel path in the dark, gloomy morning, barely able to make out in the mist the crenelated towers of Barton Hall some two hundred yards away.

*I miss Sebastian already...but am I the one to blame for this?*

The ache in her heart only became more acute as she grew painfully aware that Rex was happily trotting beside her—as if he considered her part of his family.

❦

Meredith dropped Rex off at Barton Hall, taught her morning class in the open field beside Painter's Cottage, and then walked back to the castle and entered through the rear door, finding Blythe an especially welcome sight as her cousin pointed toward a pot of coffee resting on the kitchen table.

"You just missed Sebastian," she said, indicating Meredith should take a seat while she poured her a cup of the fresh brew. "He picked up Rex about an hour ago. He apologized profusely for not staying to wait for you, but apparently he's got a very sick bovine."

"He apologized?" she asked doubtfully.

Meredith felt her cousin's searching gaze, but kept her own glued to the rim of her cup.

"He asked where you were," Blythe said in a questioning tone.

"He knows where I was," she replied, and then glanced at Blythe apologetically. "I can't actually diagnose what has suddenly gone wrong between the two of us since yesterday...just that it has, on a colossal scale."

"I am so sorry," Blythe replied softly. "He did seem rather subdued when he was here. Is there is anything I can do?"

"You are such a sweetheart," Meredith replied, shaking

her head. "But this is one of those things over which I have absolutely no control." She paused, and then added quietly, "Blythe, I think I ought to make my plane reservation to go back to Wyoming, probably leaving in a week or so. When should we discuss in detail the plans for Janet?"

"Right now is probably as good a time as any," Blythe said soberly. "Of course, we need to wait to see if Christopher will do what he says, and get the new guardianship papers signed, but barring some other-worldly overhaul of his personality, it's likely Janet will remain in our care as co-guardians, just as we outlined to him yesterday. Do you agree it probably makes the most sense for her to stay here, start at the village school with Matthew and Lucy, and see how she fares?"

Meredith nodded. "Yes, it offers her the most stability, especially since she made a genuine bond with your kids and after the way she's finally found her footing here, as you predicted she would. But are you and Lucas willing to take on the lion's share of her care?"

Blythe reached across the kitchen table for her hand. "I meant it when I said to Christopher that Janet was supposed to have been *my* daughter. My darling husband said last night he was behind our assuming the major responsibility for her, one hundred percent."

Meredith gazed at Blythe, attempting to keep the envy out of her expression. "I am so awed by the way you and Lucas have kept your love alive all these years."

"We're a good match, he and I," Blythe agreed, "and I thank my lucky stars every day that we two found each other. Plus I still think he's a pretty dishy guy," she joked.

Despite Meredith's best efforts, a tear slipped out of her eye and ran down her cheek. "I'm going to miss everyone so much," she whispered.

Blythe took her hand, her own eyes moist. "You know,

don't you, Meredith, that you always have a home with us? We'd love you to stay on, permanently."

"Don't think I haven't thought about that seriously," she replied, "but now that Sebastian and I...have encountered a pretty bumpy road..."

"Oh, sweetie, I am really so sorry," Blythe said, handing her a napkin to dab her eyes.

Meredith pounded the table lightly with one fist. "And I feel absolutely wretched that the obedience school can't run a while longer to keep more money coming in—"

"Oh, darling Meredith," Blythe hastened to assure her, "once that winter weather rolls in, even holding classes in the barn wouldn't appeal to many people around here. They huddle next to their fireplaces, waiting for spring." She laughed. "Even the dogs!"

"Well, that's a blessing. I don't feel quite so terrible that my set-to with Sebastian might have—"

"Caused us to go bankrupt? No!" Blythe interrupted with an encouraging smile as she reached across the kitchen table to squeeze her hand. "Your efforts and the other projects we did this summer have tided us over nicely, and we will be forever grateful." She sought Meredith's gaze as if willing her to absorb her next words into the marrow of her bones. "I learned when I first came to Cornwall that everyone has their own path, you know? If you feel you need to return to Wyoming, then that's what you must do. Just please promise that you'll come over at Christmastime? Janet's new Trust can pay for your expenses."

Meredith hesitated, fending off a sudden, sharp feeling of impending loss that she knew would only get worse if she returned to Cornwall so soon after her departure.

*Everyone has their own path...*

She heaved a sigh and replied, "Of course I'll come for Christmas. Janet needs to know we're all looking out for her, and besides, I bet by November, I'll be begging you to celebrate a good, old-fashioned American Thanksgiving and let me come back early with a turkey or two in tow."

Despite her joking words, for a second, Meredith feared she would put her head in her arms and give way to uncontrollable sobs.

Blythe said, "We're going to miss you hugely, dear Cuz," sounding as if she'd already accepted that Meredith would, indeed, be heading back to America. "And, by the way, I have nothing to base this on, " she confessed, "but I have every confidence things will eventually work out between you and Sebastian."

Meredith quickly took another sip of her coffee to avoid blurting out to Blythe the link between Sebastian and Claire. She also remained silent about her fears that Richard, too, might get his heart handed to him by summer's end—as she just had—due to some mysterious history shared by Claire and the man she now realized she loved beyond sense or reason.

*Stay on your own path…stay on your own path…*

Meredith clung to her new mantra, only confiding to Blythe sadly, "I really doubt Sebastian and I can work through this, whatever this *is,*" she replied. Mustering a wry smile to fight back the continuing impulse to cry her eyes out, she added, "But—hey—I like your concept of keeping the faith."

ে৩০৯

For the rest of the day, Meredith did her utmost to concentrate on avoiding any interchange with Claire and keeping her own focus on the final classes she had remaining. The next morning, her mobile phone pinged with a one-line text from Sebastian that he'd been called out by SAR in the morning and still had a sick animal to attend to at Cow Hollow Farm. An hour later another text from him stated that he couldn't teach his next-to-last Search and Rescue class in the mid-afternoon, ending with

*Can U sub today? Wainwright OK re: certificates 2-morrow if cow ill.*

Nothing else. No apology, no "what can I do to make it up to you for the inconvenience of having to teach my class." And certainly no explanation about his midnight visit to Claire's cottage or anything having to do with the two of *them*.

Meredith stared at her mobile's tiny screen and immediately went online, thanks to the Wi-Fi system Lucas had set up at Painter's Cottage earlier in the summer. She searched the available flights from Heathrow to New York the first week in September, and from there, back to Jackson Hole, Wyoming.

*Face it, cowgirl, it's way past time to head back to the barn.*

Then another thought popped into her mind.

*But what about keeping the faith?*

Blythe was the one who had faith that she and Sebastian could work things through. However, these latest, impersonal text messages felt too raw to discuss with anyone, including Blythe. And besides, with Christopher Stowe's scheduled return later in the day—hopefully with the legal documents in good order so that all parties would sign and Janet's future would be settled—everyone's attention was focused on the hope of Janet's father keeping his word.

Meredith somehow got through serving as Sebastian's substitute in his advanced training class. Then, at the start of the agility session, Beven Glynn surprised her by showing up. Afterward, he sauntered over, his dog on a leash held loosely in his hand. Janet, Lucy, and Matthew, who'd been faithful observers for weeks, now, scampered off toward the castle and their afternoon ritual of cookies-and-milk in Barton Hall's kitchen.

"I'm amazed you made it to class today," Meredith said to Beven. "Weren't you called out this morning on a SAR incident?" she asked, nodding goodbye as her students bid her friendly farewells. She called to them "See you next at your graduation!"

Beven paused and then replied, "I didn't go on any call this morning." He nodded in the direction of his dog. "That's why I could come to class."

Meredith felt as if someone had slapped her. She was dismayed to consider that Sebastian may have told her an out-and-out lie as an excuse to avoid seeing her—to say nothing of dumping his search-and-rescue class on her earlier in the day. She thought about the airplane ticket she'd purchased online and felt a stab of righteous satisfaction that her instincts had been right—and that it was, indeed, time to leave Cornwall.

Beven regarded her closely and offered a smile. "I say, Meredith, you look as if you've had a very long day. How about I treat you to a beer at The Fountain Inn in Mevagissey? They have a lovely little outside area and—"

"That's very kind of you Beven, but—"

"Look..." he countered quickly, "why don't I admit that I can pretty much tell you and Sebastian have...well...had a misunderstanding of some sort. Let me cheer you up."

Meredith looked at him narrowly. "And how would you surmise that?"

"You should have seen him lately. Scowling, touchy...like the old Sebo before he met you."

For some inane reason, Beven's description of Sebastian cheered her a bit, but she said nothing in reply.

Beven shrugged. "Just thought I'd offer a friendly shoulder, you know? I figured classes were winding down and just want to thank you for letting me enroll with my dog, right Lilly?"

Meredith patted Lilly's head, beset by a pang of guilt for always having such a jaundiced view of Beven just because that was Sebastian's negative attitude toward him. She glanced at her watch. She could do with a change of scene before Christopher Stowe was scheduled to arrive. A nice, cold been might take her mind off her troubles.

"Sure, Beven. A drink at a seaside pub sounds like a nice idea, but I have to be back by five-thirty. May I bring Holly with us? And then can you drop me off at the Hall before you head on home? Where do you live, by the way?"

"Mevagissey."

"Oh! Then I don't want you having to drive all the way there and back."

"No problem."

"Are you sure?"

"Absolutely. My car's parked across the field on the road."

"Then, let's blow this pop stand!"

"W-what?" Beven asked with a blank expression.

"Lead on, MacDuff," Meredith offered.

He wrinkled his forehead, still puzzled by her attempt to be amusing.

Beven Glynn obviously did not possess an ounce of humor when it came to the notion of "two nations, separated by a common language."

Not like Sebastian Pryce.

ↄ℧℧ↄ

The ale Beven chose for her when they sat down on the

outside terrace of The Fountain Inn was excellent, a local brew called St. Austell's. Afterward, he suggested that they take the dogs for a short walk along the cliffs overlooking the small harbor and its spectacular view as the sun was lowering in the sky above the broad expanse of a sapphire blue English Channel.

"And then, I must get back to the Hall. We're expecting visitors down from London," insisted Meredith, exhausted from attempts to make small talk with this tightly-wound, self-important member of the volunteer SAR team who doubled as single practitioner chartered accountant, his "day-job," as she'd discovered that afternoon. "Lady Barton-Teague also mentioned we also have a raft of travel agents arriving this evening," she added, "and so I need to be on hand to help prep the breakfasts they'll be wanting tomorrow morning."

"Doesn't Claire Gillis take charge of all that, now?" Beven asked, leading the way down a well-trod path along the cliff.

"Do you know Claire?" Meredith asked in as causal a tone of voice as she could muster.

"Only by reputation."

Meredith stared at the back of Beven's red and black parka, a twin of the type Sebastian wore often. "Yes, she's known as a very competent cook. More than competent, in fact. Barton Hall is lucky to have her."

"Like so many *others* have, I understand…"

Beven had not turned around, but Meredith was able to detect a mildly vicious double entendre in his words.

*What was the man actually saying?*

They continued to walk along in silence, drawing closer to a round, white, deserted cement hut that had once served as some sort of coastline lookout post, long abandoned. As they drew near the small structure, a tall, dark-haired man clad in a familiar, distinctive red and black parka suddenly appeared from around the corner of the squat building. Following him was another figure, wearing bright yellow foul-weather gear with H.M. COAST GUARD printed in black on his back.

"Well, what do you know?" Beven exclaimed, turning around to address Meredith. "Look who's here!" He turned back and called out to the two men up ahead. "Greetings, Sebastian! Hello, sir," he said to the Coast Guard officer. To Sebastian he added cheerfully, "Can't believe Meredith and I ran into you like this." He swiveled his head. "Meredith, I had no idea—"

"Yes you did," Sebastian cut in. "Wainwright set up a meeting for late this afternoon following our morning's debriefing to talk about our SAR team taking over the lookout. You were probably eavesdropping in the next room, as usual."

Beven smiled pleasantly as if Sebastian had offered them a warm greeting.

"Oh, that's right! I guess I vaguely overheard you were looking into our manning this lookout and putting kennels in the back for the new SAR dogs. I totally forgot about that when Meredith asked if she could join me for a beer after class. We've just had a lovely time over at the Fountain Inn and I wanted to show her the view from—"

"Wait!" Meredith interrupted. "Wait a minute, will you?" She looked directly at Beven and declared, "*You* invited *me* for a beer, Beven, just so we have that straight." Then she addressed Sebastian. "And let me understand something. Were you two called out on a search-and-rescue this morning, or not?"

"Yes," Sebastian replied, "we responded to a call—"

Swiveling her head toward Beven she said, "You told me the Cornwall SAR Team didn't *have* a call this morning."

"I only said I didn't go *out* on a call," Beven responded defensively. "It got cancelled when the missing bloke turned up, drunk behind a pub." He shrugged. "Certainly you must know by now, it happens a lot."

"Why didn't you just say that?" she demanded.

She took a step closer to Sebastian and nodded a perfunctory greeting to the Coast Guard officer who appeared mildly confused by the obvious tension radiating among his three visitors.

"You know, Sebastian, I believed you when you sent me a text that you were out on a call and couldn't teach your class—— so I *did* sub for you, though I hardly knew what in hell I was doing."

"Thank you," he replied. "The call got cancelled just as I got to headquarters, but by then, there was no time to drive to Painter's Cottage to teach the class. I picked up Rex at the Hall and immediately went back to Cow Hollow to deal with the sick cow we've been tending until it was time to come here to meet with the Coast Guard, as Colonel Wainwright requested."

"Well, are you still on for Friday's class, or is Wainwright taking it over?"

"I'll do my best to be there. The Colonel will hand out the certificates and see if he can recruit any of them for our SAR Team."

"I see…" she murmured.

She wondered why Sebastian didn't say anything more, now that they both realized Beven Glynn apparently took great pleasure in adding to the troubles between them.

"You noticed, I suppose, that Rex's leash was returned to you?" she said, looking him directly in the eye. "I found it outside…on the ground…near Limekiln Cottage."

Sebastian reacted with a startled expression. "*You* were the one who found the leash?"

"Yes."

"I didn't know where I'd lost it."

"Well, now you do. And so do I. You probably dropped it when you got out of your car in a hurry that night."

She grew increasingly uncomfortable to realize Beven was hanging on their every word. Then another thing dawned on her.

*I admit it...I am now, officially, a jealous fool, but I just can't help it!*

Adding to her misery, she suddenly realized that Sebastian now knew that *she* knew that he had paid a visit to Claire Gillis's place on the heels of their heated words at Painter's Cottage. Worse yet, he'd made no effort, to date, to explain any extenuating circumstances, or ask her if she'd actually spoken with Claire herself.

"Shouldn't you and I talk?" she asked quietly.

"Now?" he responded, and she had the sinking feeling that speaking with her was the last thing he felt like doing.

"No..." she murmured, "you're right. Not now."

Sebastian threaded his fingers through his dark hair and gave a harried glance at his watch.

"I'm sorry everyone," he said, "but I have a very sick animal at my farm and I need to get back there." He turned to the Coast Guard officer. "Thanks, James. I'll tell the Colonel that I think this facility will work well for SAR. I appreciate the tour."

For Meredith's part, she was desperate to depart from the lookout hut before anyone else could make an exit. What more did she need to know regarding where she stood with Sebastian, she thought, as a dull ache in her solar plexus nearly choked off her breath.

She turned to Beven. "I've got to go as well. No need for you to drive me back. I prefer to walk."

*Beven Glynn is the last person in the world I want to be with right now. What a complete* jerk!

She tightened her grip on Holly's leash, abruptly turned away from the group, and swiftly marched back along the cliff path, not waiting to see if Beven or Sebastian were following in her wake. Within minutes, she caught sight of Beven's parked car in the lot next to the inn, as well as the green Mini tucked behind a delivery truck where she hadn't noticed it earlier. Then, like an angel of mercy, she suddenly spotted Lucas Teague emerging from the back of the Fountain Inn's pub. He was carrying a huge, heavy carton marked "St. Austell Ale" in the direction of his battered Land Rover.

"Oh, thank goodness you're *here!*" she cried, rushing to open the car's rear door. "Here, let me help…and can I *please* hitch a ride back home with you?"

Startled, Lucas nodded as he heaved the box into the back. "Of course. Hop in."

"Great. And could we please step on it?"

Out of the corner of her eye she could see first, Sebastian, walking briskly along the cliff path with Beven strolling behind, both apparently unaware she'd run into Lucas Teague so fortuitously.

*Look at how pleased Beven is with himself!*

Her mind a whirl with dark thoughts relating to both Beven and Sebastian, she shooed Holly into the car and jumped into the passenger seat. Meredith would bet anything that the little creep of an accountant had engineered the entire fiasco of "running into" Sebastian, just for his own amusement, or as a put-down of his fellow teammate. Before Beven even set foot in the car park, the Land Rover was lumbering in the opposite direction, down the village road.

Lucas looked questioningly in Meredith's direction.

"Lovely meeting up like this, but what in the world was *that* all about?"

"I stupidly accepted an invitation for a beer from a guy enrolled in one of my classes who turned out to be a colossal jerk," she said, glancing into the rear view mirror as both Beven and Sebastian receded into the distance.

"Well, otherwise, how was your day?" he inquired, a droll smile playing across his lips.

"Funny you should ask that," she replied glumly. "I'll tell you about it later. Have we heard from Christopher Stowe yet? Any word if he's actually going to show up with the documents for us all to sign?"

"I had a call from Blythe just now when I was waiting to get the invoice for the beer. He should be at Barton Hall by the time you and I get there."

"Oh boy," she groaned. "The end of a perfect day."

# CHAPTER 16

Just as Lucas predicted, by the time they arrived by the back road and parked in the courtyard near the entrance to the mudroom, the sleek, midnight blue Rolls Royce was sitting in the gravel drive in front of Barton Hall. Blythe greeted Lucas and Meredith as they came through the kitchen, interrupting her instructions to Richard and Claire about preparing a light supper for a VIP group of travel agents who were scheduled to arrive momentarily.

"If their van comes down the drive while we're in the library, do let me know," Blythe urged, "and thanks for taking in the tea trolley just now. It bought us some time until everyone could get here."

Meredith could tell Blythe was feeling harried and out of sorts by the presence of her ex-husband and his latest fiancée who were waiting for them down the hall.

"Don't worry," Richard hastened to assure them with a crooked grin, "Claire and I are ready to offer our next raft of visitors the warmest of Cornish welcomes and get them settled in their rooms."

"You are the best!" Blythe declared, and patted Richard's arm. "Where are the children, do you know?"

Claire spoke up. "I thought I could organize a game of hide-and-seek inside the barn to give you time to conclude your meeting?" she suggested diplomatically. "I was just about to go up to the playroom and take them down the servants' stairs here, and out the rear entrance and through the back courtyard," she added with a knowing look cast in Blythe's direction

"Excellent idea, Claire," she replied with a wan smile of appreciation. "It's best we keep Janet out of the picture until all the documents are signed in the library—if they ever are," she added grimly. "With my former spouse, one never knows what will happen. But if all goes as it's supposed to, afterward, Christopher can perhaps take his daughter to dinner in Mevagissey or somewhere nearby."

Meredith suppressed a sigh. Claire Gillis had been the soul of politeness toward her, personally, and the pair truly had been a huge help all summer, witness their immediate sensitivity to the family crisis at hand. Telling Blythe and Lucas about her concerns regarding Claire and Richard would just have to wait, she thought. Or maybe she'd say nothing at all before she left for Wyoming. Again she reminded herself about Blythe's wise observation that each person has his or her own path.

*And besides…I have my own problems without meddling in theirs.*

Another wave of sadness and regret about the way things had ended with Sebastian filled her chest, but she stoically put it aside as Blythe, Lucas, and she walked down the carpeted hallway and prepared to deal with Christopher Stowe.

Suddenly, on the landing above their heads, the sound of pounding footsteps announced the headlong trajectory of young Janet taking the steps on the grand staircase, two at a time.

"I *told* Lucy and Matthew that blue car was Daddy's!" Janet cried triumphantly, skittering to a stop at the bottom landing. "He's here! He's *here!*"

Blythe and Meredith exchanged worried looks as the

youngster dashed past the adults and burst into the library.

Framed by the open, oaken doorway, Christopher looked up from his cup of tea that Claire had provided earlier, startled to see his daughter.

"Daddy! You *came!*"

Meredith's heart ached to see the little girl, looking slim and healthier, by far, than when she'd arrived in Cornwall three-and-a half months earlier, throw her arms around her seated father's neck and receive little in the way of affection in return.

"Janet! Please! You're acting like a little hoyden!"

He grasped her hands and forced them to her sides.

"But I'm so glad to see you," she said with a wounded expression. "It's been all summer," she added reproachfully. "And when you were here before, you didn't even stay for dinner."

Christopher rose from the settee and gestured to the blond actress who had been sitting beside him. "Can't you say a proper hello to Avery, Janet?"

Janet regarded her father's fiancée for a long moment and finally said in a low, but reasonably polite voice, "Hello."

Meredith crossed to stand next to her ward and gave her shoulders a squeeze, as if to say, "Good for you…" for her valiant attempts at civility in such a trying situation. Janet had come a long way, reflected Meredith, from the rude, unhappy little soul who had arrived in the Land Rover a few months earlier. Why couldn't Christopher reward her, at least, with a welcoming smile or a hug?

*Because he's a self-centered bastard…*

Blythe had said as much during their first transatlantic phone conversation when they discussed how to handle the question of Janet's care. Every interaction Meredith had had with the man only further confirmed Blythe's original assessment. As far as she could determine, Meredith thought darkly, the only men on the planet she admired currently were her father, Lucas, and Richard.

"So, Christopher," she declared, deciding she couldn't stand the suspense another moment. "Don't you have papers for us to sign?"

The film director shrugged and pointed to the Gucci briefcase next to his matching Gucci loafers.

"Right here. I've signed and notarized them, as dictated by Blythe and Lucas' solicitor, and so has Avery, so *you* all might as well too. Let's get this over with." He glanced at his daughter who was standing close to him and clasping his hand as if it were a life raft. "Janet, *please*," he said. "Sit over there, if you will. Daddy has some important business to conduct."

Janet sank onto the settee beside Avery L'Angella whose sullen expression indicated that the film starlet wasn't at all happy with having to agree to a legal arrangement that guaranteed Janet's status as a full heir to her father's fortune. Meanwhile, Janet herself watched warily as her father reached into his briefcase and pulled out a sheaf of legal-sized papers, handing them to Blythe.

"Let's just have a quick look," Blythe murmured, taking the documents from her ex-husband and walking toward the big desk near the secret bookcase where Janet had once been trapped in the tunnel hidden behind the shelves.

"Always careful with a contract, aren't you, darling?" Christopher said, and Meredith felt a *frisson* of discomfort at his sarcastic endearment in front of Janet, to say nothing of Lucas, who sat quietly under one of the family portraits. "Reminds me of our old partnership." He looked slyly at Blythe's second husband. "The woman's hyper-vigilance saved me a few dollars, I can vouch for that." His voice hardened. "I know you too well, though, Blythe, so don't try to pull anything dodgy at this stage."

"That's usually *your* approach," Blythe said mildly while continuing to read the document, word for word, as disquieting silence filled the book-lined room.

While Blythe continued to turn the pages, Christopher fidgeted in his seat. Janet stood up and edged closer to the arm of his chair, but her father utterly ignored her presence.

Finally he burst out, "Look here, Blythe…Avery and I signed what your man faxed us. Let's not *you* change anything, last minute, all right?"

"Signed what?"

Janet's young voice cut through the already electric atmosphere. Blythe looked up from the desk and reached for the tapestry bell pull that, in days of yore, could summon an army of servants. Meredith imagined that her cousin prayed Richard or Claire would hear the bell ring in the kitchen and come to escort Janet away from this tension-fraught meeting. Before she could speak, however, Christopher turned and sternly addressed his daughter.

"You should appreciate, Janet, what's being done for you here. Since you've apparently enjoyed your time in Cornwall, your aunt—with your uncle's agreement—is willing to be named legal guardian, along with your cousin Meredith and me, so you can remain here for the school year. We're just putting this in legal form," he added, casting a nod in Blythe's direction.

"But Daddy…I have *you* and so why—"

Christopher cut her short. "As you know, Janet, since your mother's death, I have been traveling to Alaska and back to Los Angeles numerous times with crushing responsibilities so that I can finish my film. Now I'll have to be in New York a few months to edit it. You can't really expect me to be your nanny, can you now, during this busy period? Which is why I thought it best for your cousin

Meredith and your Aunt Blythe to look after you this
summer in my stead. Now, they will do the same thing
during the school term. The papers we're all signing just
make it official."

"Auntie Blythe and Meredith have been great, but now
your movie's finished, right?" Janet said, a touching
eagerness creeping into her tone. "You have time, now, to
be with me, right? That's why you've come here again, isn't
it? I can go to school in New York and live with you, okay?
I promise, I won't be *any* trouble."

Christopher shot a pleading look at Blythe, and when
she ignored him to continue reading the documents, he
shifted his imploring gaze in Meredith's direction.

"Daddy?" Janet said, her voice rising up a notch.

"Now, let's not have any theatrics, my dear. We three
will decide what's best for everyone concerned, moving
forward."

At least, thought Meredith grimly, the jerk had the grace
not merely to describe what was best—and most
convenient—for *him*.

"But I thought I'd be going home with you after the
summer and—"

Again, her father cut her short and in the smooth tones
of an experienced negotiator, he continued as if she hadn't
spoken. "Now that Avery and I are together, we feel—"

Just then the door opened and both Richard and Claire
appeared at the threshold. When Claire saw that Janet was
in the room, she blanched.

"Oh! *There* you are. I went upstairs but I couldn't
find—"

"It's all right," Meredith interrupted. "But, maybe you
should—"

"I'm so sorry to disturb you," broke in Richard
urgently, "but the van with your travel agents is just coming

up the drive."

Blythe looked up from the documents. "Richard, could you and Claire please greet them and get them settled? Please tell them Lucas and I will be along shortly to welcome them officially."

"Of course," Richard nodded, casting a questioning glance at Claire.

"Absolutely," Claire agreed, darting a look in Janet's direction. "Is there anything else we can help you with?"

"Well, yes," Lucas replied quickly. He turned to Janet, whose injured expression was enough to make her guardians weep. "Janet, dear, could you go with Richard and Claire right now and help greet the guests? These are very important visitors, and I think they would like it if Richard *and* you could represent the family, along with Claire, to make them feel right at home until we all can join them."

Janet looked uncertainly around the room. "But, Daddy—"

Meredith jumped in, unable to bear the idea of Christopher rejecting his only child's desire to spend time with him. "You'll see your father in just a few minutes, okay? We'll be done in here shortly." She smiled encouragingly. "Richard would really appreciate your help, wouldn't you Richard?"

"I certainly would. We can wave the family standard together, shall we, Janet?"

Janet nodded reluctantly and followed Claire and Richard out of the library.

Blythe swiftly seized a pen off the desk and initialed each page and then signed her name on the bottom of the document that officially made Meredith and her co-legal guardians, along with her father, of Janet Barton Stowe, with co-custody and joint decision-making powers until the girl turned twenty-one years old. Her older cousin handed the pen to Meredith, who quickly wrote her full name on the line below Blythe's.

"Lucas, darling," Blythe said pleasantly. "As our local magistrate in Central Cornwall, would you please sign, too, in your official capacity?" She smiled knowingly at her husband. "Your waxed seal should suffice to serve as *our* Notary, making this document legal and binding on all parties as of…well…this *minute*!"

Lucas obligingly crossed to his desk, withdrew from a drawer a small brass crest with his family coat of arms, and patiently melted a dab of red wax on the last page of the document, pressing the round crest affixed to a small wooden handle into the warm, viscous wax to create the seal.

"How quaint," Christopher murmured sarcastically, as Lucas went about formalizing the document.

"There we are," Sir Lucas Barton-Teague said, signing his name with a flourish and then looking up at his wife with a faint expression of triumph.

Blythe capped the pen they all had used and said, "Well, then. *Done*." She looked directly at Christopher and asked, "Now, let's discuss where we all think it best for Janet to be in school in the coming year…and the kindest way to let her know whatever plans we jointly decided upon."

Avery spoke for the first time, but only addressed Stowe.

"Well, you still have to finish editing the film, Christopher, and after that, we'll have a lot of traveling and promotion to do. And what about planning the wedding?" she demanded. "If we're not getting married in Vegas on our way home on *this* trip, I just don't see how we can be expected to—"

Christopher interrupted sharply. "I'll handle this,

Avery." He addressed his former wife and Meredith with a disdainful wave of his well-manicured hand. "As I've said before, isn't Janet's schooling obvious? I'm just not equipped to have her with us presently. It wouldn't be fair to her and—"

"And it wouldn't be fair to *me!*" Avery interrupted, looking around the room as if to challenge the others to dispute established fact.

Blythe said, "Yes, I think we all agree that Janet's being based here in Cornwall undoubtedly provides her the most stability."

Ignoring his fiancée, Christopher asked both women, "Have you determined upon any boarding schools you think might suit?"

Meredith looked to Blythe for guidance. Her cousin's expression was cool and collected, as if she'd been prepared to answer this question for a long time.

"If you feel you aren't able to...have your daughter with you for the school year, then Meredith and I will discuss what *we* think best regarding Janet's education here in the UK, and let you know what we decided." She smiled faintly. "You needn't worry about vetting any of the institutions. She'll likely go to the same school as Lucy."

"Oh. Well, all right," Christopher said, not bothering to ask where those schools were, or why Blythe would send her four-year-old away to boarding school, which, of course she never would.

Meredith nearly chuckled out loud. Lucy and Matthew went to the same village school, less than a mile away. In this scenario, Janet would have a secure home, with two cousins to guide her path. With the various Trusts that Christopher had just agreed in writing to establish, Meredith could afford to fly over for Christmas, various holidays, and perhaps even get a month off every summer to come to Cornwall.

Once again, her heart gave a lurch as familiar thoughts brought her low: Sebastian would always be nearby, always a reminder of this summer in Cornwall.

*Well, you'll just have to deal with it!*

She wanted to do the best for Janet and if it meant coming to Cornwall to visit often, so be it. She gazed at the Barton-Teagues and felt a wave of gratitude for the many wonderful things that they had done for her over the summer—including supporting Janet in every way possible after Ellie's sudden death. They even had eagerly embraced the idea of creating a dog obedience school on their estate. Perhaps, thought Meredith, this summer had shown *her* a new path, should she decide not to return to nursing.

Best of all, she and Blythe had grown as close as sisters. Lucas, Richard—and yes, even Claire—had functioned as a tight unit in all the projects they'd launched in the time she'd been in Cornwall, including the wonderful Barton Hall Farm-to-Table Suppers. She was proud, too, that in establishing her dog obedience classes, she had been able to do her part during the estate's on-going economic struggle to survive.

And Janet, the angry, grief-stricken little girl of four months ago, had made tremendous progress toward accepting her mother's passing and had become "a decent human being," as Meredith had emailed her father just the other day. True enough, the child had inherited a very untypical family in Cornwall, but one that loved her and would take care of her, no matter how often her father disappointed her.

Interrupting her meandering thoughts, Christopher announced crisply, "Well, I guess that concludes what we came here to do." He shut his briefcase with a determined snap. "By noon, Friday, funds for the various Trusts will drop into the specified accounts at the Bank of England with Meredith and your name, Blythe, as Trustees," he added. To Lucas he said, "Please send copies of this signed agreement to my office in Los Angeles and to Sir Anthony in London, will you? That is if you can figure out how make them with that bloody seal of yours!"

"Certainly," Lucas agreed amiably. "No problem at all. I'll send them express."

"Avery, are you ready?" Christopher asked, sounding irritated and anxious to be gone.

Meredith quickly protested, "But I thought you might take Janet out to dinner and visit with her before you left. There are a number of restaurants in Mevagissey we can recommend. Or perhaps you'd prefer our cook to prepare you something here?"

Avery shot Christopher a pointed look and placed a vermillion fingernail on the crystal face of her gold, Piaget watch.

Nodding agreement, he said smoothly, "I'm afraid we can't stay any longer than we have already. We have a flight out of Heathrow early tomorrow morning."

"So you can't spend one hour with your daughter? You're heading from here straight to Heathrow?" Meredith asked skeptically.

"I'm afraid we must go," Christopher repeated stubbornly. "As you well know, it's four hours to the airport."

"I expect you'll have a miserable night at one of those awful places near Heathrow," Blythe said pointedly to the man everyone in the room knew would only frequent the Dorset or the Ritz when anywhere near London.

"Exactly so," he said stiffly, sounding like a James Bond character. "Thus I'm afraid we must say goodbye. And besides," he added, as if Janet's guardians were insensitive and obtuse, "as you've observed, it will only upset my daughter if we leave while in her presence. Better to just quietly slip away, don't you think?" Not waiting for any reply he picked up his briefcase and prepared to depart. "Tell her I'll be in touch," he added, as if referring to an actress who had just tried out for a part.

And without further discussion or farewells, the couple from Tinseltown marched out of the library and down the paneled hallway hung with portraits of Teague and Barton ancestors staring down at them.

The visitors swiftly disappeared through the front entrance to Barton Hall. Flabbergasted by the pair's hasty departure, the Barton-Teagues and Meredith retreated back into the library. Lucas strode to the drinks cart positioned against a window with tall, navy blue velvet draperies puddling on the floor and began to pour each of them a much-needed glass of sherry. Suddenly, Janet dashed past the open door, careening down the front hallway from the direction of the kitchen.

"Daddy! Daddy!" she shouted. "Wait! Don't go...*wait!*"

As Janet's piercing cries shattered the evening air, Meredith, Blythe and Lucas bolted from the library, down the hallway, and through the open front door in her wake. The three stood, frozen on the stone steps, watching Janet collapse in a heap where her father's car had been parked. The Rolls Royce's taillights were mere glowing, red pinpricks at the end of the drive.

"He left...he left without...*without*..." she shrieked. She turned to stare accusingly at Meredith. "You said...you *promised* I'd see Daddy if I helped Richard! You *promised!*" she cried, and put her face, soaked with tears, in her hands.

"Oh, Janet," Meredith cried, hastening toward the sobbing child. "I'm *so* sorry! He left here so quickly, and I—"

As one, Blythe and Lucas rushed to join her in trying to comfort the near-hysterical youngster. Lucas scooped her up in his arms while Blythe and Meredith swiftly encircled them, the adults a mass of shoulders and arms, all the while murmuring endearments, but providing no solace to a little girl whose father had so easily bequeathed his only child to them.

"Janet, sweetheart, I am *so* sorry!" Meredith repeated, near tears herself. "I thought he had planned to take you to dinner and—"

"Dearest, darling girl, we're here, Janet," Blythe soothed. "We're all here. We won't leave you."

Lucas carried Janet upstairs to her room, with Meredith and Blythe following close behind, silent, now, in the in the wake of the child's wails that echoed through the Hall.

"He gave me away...didn't he?" she cried against Lucas' shoulder. "He just signed those papers...and gave me *away!*"

◦↶↷◦

Later that night, Meredith woke with a start and peered at her bedside clock. It was two a.m. Her thoughts immediately flew to Janet and the hour it had taken, holding her as they lay together on the little girl's canopy bed, to get her to go to sleep.

Something had awakened her, Meredith realized, worried, now. She donned her dressing gown and slipped out her bedroom door, her feet silent on the jewel-toned Persian runner that stretched the length of the seventy-five-foot hallway. She heard muffled sounds down the corridor and sped to Janet's door. She cracked it open and realized immediately that Janet was awake and sobbing into her pillow.

"Oh, sweetie...it's me, Meredith," she said, swiftly crossing over to Janet's side and sitting on the bed. "Come here, come here, little one," she said, climbing into bed, gathering her in her arms, and leaning against the mahogany headboard for support. "It's all right...I feel like crying, too."

"Why? W-why did Daddy leave me here?" she cried. "Why didn't he want me to be *with* him?"

"I can't answer that, sweetie," Meredith said sorrowfully. "All I can say is your Auntie Blythe and I and everyone here are so very sorry you feel so sad. We love you, sweetheart..."

"But Daddy *doesn't!*" she cried, another wave of sobs overtaking her.

The door opened and Meredith saw Blythe outlined in the gloom. Janet's aunt climbed in on the other side of the bed, and together, the two cousins cradled the little girl until she finally fell asleep.

⚬꙰꙰ꙮ

The following morning, a hush had fallen over the entire downstairs at Barton Hall, despite a gaggle of travel writers in residence to whom Richard and Claire had fed a robust Cornish breakfast of fresh farm berries, homemade sausage, grilled field mushrooms, coddled eggs, and wildflower honey on Claire's freshly baked bread. All was quiet upstairs, as well, when Blythe set out from the Hall to conduct a tour of the grounds in hopes the visiting journalists would produce glowing articles about the charms of Barton Hall—magazine and online stories that would, hopefully, stimulate a flood of reservation requests next season.

As for Meredith, she'd tiptoed out of Janet's room at

dawn and sat in the kitchen drinking numerous cups of coffee, trying to keep her mind focused on her plans for each of the final classes she was due to teach this day.

Given her gloomy disposition in the wake of the previous day and night's tumultuous events, she wasn't even surprised when her cell phone beeped and a text from Sebastian announced that the ailing prize cow at Cow Hollow Farm was now deathly ill and that if matters continued as they were, Graham Wainwright definitely would have to do the honors distributing the Certificates of Achievement to members of the search and rescue class later that afternoon.

Meredith caught up with Blythe in the kitchen soon after the travel writers had made their departure.

"How'd it go with the scribes?"

"Swimmingly, I believe," Blythe answered, "but I'm totally drained, aren't you?"

"Totally." She told her about Sebastian's latest communication.

"So you have to do the honors at the SAR graduation class?" Blythe queried sympathetically.

"Apparently Colonel Wainwright will hand out the gold-edged certificates."

"Well, that's something, at least," Blythe said. Then she added, "I'm sure you, of all people, Meredith, know that losing a prize member of your herd is an awful thing for small farmers like the Jenners. Sebastian and Dr. Dobell must be frantic, to say nothing of William and Susanna. With the Mad Cow scares we've had…"

Blythe's words drifted off and her brow furrowed with concern both for Meredith and for her friends at Cow Hollow. Then she said, "I'll have to ring them later today and find out…how everything is going."

"Speaking of which," Meredith asked, stuffing a

rucksack with cheese and bread to tide her over while she
taught her final puppy obedience and agility training classes,
"Do you think I should look in on Janet before I head
down to Painter's Cottage? I thought maybe she'd like to
go with me."

Blythe shook her head. "I just ran upstairs after the
journalists left and peeked in on her. I think she's utterly
wiped out and I thought we'd just let her sleep."

Meredith nodded her agreement. "She must have cried
a river..."

"Frankly, I don't blame her," Blythe said somberly. "I
felt like doing exactly that, myself, after what we witnessed
yesterday. Sometimes I can't believe I was ever married to
Christopher Stowe. What was I thinking?"

Meredith shrugged. "You were young and he probably
hadn't gotten quite the swelled head he has now from all
the movie successes."

"And everyone around him treating him as if he were
God." Blythe smiled and held up her hand with the
beautiful family ring Lucas had given her when they were
engaged. "The right man came into my life and that made
all the difference." She reached for Meredith and gave her a
hug. "It will for you, too." And then added, "And who
knows? Maybe it already has?"

"I dunno, Blythe," Meredith said bleakly. "It's looking
less and less likely."

"Keep the faith, remember?"

Meredith barely nodded, picked up her supplies, and
bid farewell.

"Tell Lucy and Matthew they're welcome to attend the
puppy graduation at eleven and stay for the SAR festivities,
even if Janet doesn't feel up to it." She halted mid-way to
the door and turned back to Blythe. "How do you feel
about finding a puppy to give to Janet and your kids before

I go next week? I'm sure I could locate a good breeder if I asked people in my class."

"Good idea," Blythe said, sinking into a chair.

Meredith could see how exhausted her cousin was. "Hey, listen…we'll deal with the puppy issue in a day or two," she assured her. "I'll just put out feelers in class today. You take it easy for a bit, will you?"

"Thanks, I'm going to. In fact, I shall make myself another cup of coffee and then let Claire and Richard handle the prep for the tea room. I must say, they certainly have proven to be a dynamic duo, bless them. Thanks to their efforts today, I might even be able to steal a morning nap."

Since Blythe had brought up the subject of her two chefs, Meredith was tempted once again to raise the issue of Richard's increasing infatuation with Claire—and the *chef de cuisine's* obvious encouragement, despite the nine years' difference in their ages. How this might impact Richard's returning to Oxford this fall, or even affect the future stewardship of Barton Hall, itself, were serious issues.

*But they're not* your *issues, Meredith…*

Perhaps she should thank Shep as well as Blythe, she thought suddenly, for teaching her important lessons: stick to your own knitting! And don't volunteer advice unless asked. With a quick glance at the kitchen clock, she decided that given the time, she'd better be on her way.

# CHAPTER 17

A few hours later, Meredith felt nothing but relief when Beven Glynn failed to show up for "Graduation" at the conclusion of the final agility class. Next, she taught the last puppy obedience session and was happy to see Lucy and Matthew arrive in time to help her pass out the home-made "Canine Good Citizen Certificates" she'd created earlier on Blythe's computer.

All in all, she thought that the morning had gone well. She'd also remembered to make up three special "Perfect Attendance" certificates that she handed to the children, adding, "Take Janet's to her, will you please? You three came to every single class this session, so I thought you deserved to win an award, too."

"Oh, super!" said Matthew.

"These are so pretty!" Lucy squealed, pointing to the round seal that featured the profile of a Golden Retriever outlined in black.

Meredith didn't have the heart—nor did she want Matthew and Lucy to hear the news so precipitously—to announce her impending departure for Wyoming to the class members prepared to disperse with their wiggling four-footed charges. She fought the lump in her throat hearing their earnest petitions for her to continue the training course for their pets for an additional month in the autumn.

"My plans are not quite settled," she told them, offering her thanks. "I'll be in touch," she added, and immediately felt chagrined she had quoted Christopher Stowe.

Well, she thought, she had everyone's email address, so she would simply contact them the next day to announce her departure and to ask for breeder recommendations for Corgis, Cairn and West Highland terriers—small dogs that the three children could love and take care of after she and Holly returned to Wyoming.

"Didn't Janet feel like coming with you today?" she asked causally of Matthew and Lucy once her class had dispersed.

"Mummy said not to disturb her," Matthew said. He gazed at Meredith and asked solemnly, "Is Janet still terribly upset about yesterday, do you think? I wanted to go say 'hello,' but Mummy thought best to let her sleep."

Lucy piped up. "I could *never* sleep as long as Janet has, could you, Matthew? Even if my Daddy had been so mean, which mine isn't, *ever.*"

Matthew nodded. "I told Mummy that we'll be glad to share Daddy with Janet if she stays with us to go to school in the village."

Meredith's eyes stung with sudden moisture. She knelt on the grass and gathered Blythe's two youngsters in the circle of her arms.

"You two are just the dearest children in the world," she murmured. "I am *so* proud to be your cousin. And you have the best parents of all time, don't you?"

"*Yes!*" they chorused and turned to head back to the Hall for lunch.

"Here...wait," Meredith called, waving their certificates. "Don't forget Janet's!" The children returned to her side, hands outstretched. "And be sure to take this to her right away. I think it might help cheer her up a bit, okay?"

"And we can show it to Mummy and Daddy to prove we're ready for a new dog!" Matthew exclaimed triumphantly.

Just then, Meredith spotted Graham Wainwright coming through the gate across the field, shoulders back in his customary military posture, and striding toward Painter's Cottage.

"Hello, Colonel!" she shouted and waved as her visitor scattered a cluster of sheep while making his way in her direction.

"Sorry you had to wait!" he shouted in return.

"Oh, not at all," she said, waving back. "You're early, in fact. Class doesn't start for fifteen minutes." She turned to the children and indicated that they should wait to be introduced.

"Excellent!" the silver-haired ex-Army officer declared. "It's a good excuse to escape from headquarters and enjoy this brisk Channel air!"

Meredith smiled when she shook his hand. "Brisk it is, sir, with autumn soon upon us. I'm so grateful you could come hand out the certificates to the search and rescue class. May I introduce you to Lord and Lady Barton-Teague's children...this is Lucy, and this is Matthew."

"Hello," they chorused. Both children extended their hands as they'd been taught to do.

"Well, hello, there!" said the Colonel, shaking hands. "Delighted to meet you both. Do you help Meredith, here, give her obedience classes?"

"We watch!" Matthew said proudly, "and fill the dog bowls with water so we can prove to our parents that my cousin Janet and Lucy and I are ready for a new dog."

"Good show!" Wainwright said with approval.

Meredith turned to the children and urged, "Why don't you go up to the Hall and see if Janet feels like coming down to watch Sebastian's class go through its paces and the handlers receive their certificates?"

Both nodded and scampered off across the field and up the shaded path to the castle.

Graham Wainwright patted an envelope he held in one hand and braced it against his chest. "Got the official paperwork right here. Sebastian said you would be able to tell me if they all passed muster during their final examination last class."

Meredith kept to herself her gloomy thoughts on that subject. She'd already decided that she'd pass everyone in attendance, given Sebastian's excellent teaching and her own lack of knowledge on the finer points of canine SAR obedience standards.

But all she said to Wainwright was, "From what I observed taking over Mr. Pryce's last class, everyone in the course and their dogs appear to have been very dedicated."

The retired colonel cast a speculative glance in her direction. "Sebastian is a very excellent instructor from what I've seen within our own group of dog handlers."

When Meredith merely nodded, he paused, and then said quietly. "It is absolutely none of my business, but am I correct in surmising that you and Pryce have had some sort of misunderstanding? Frankly, I've never seen him so...so...down-hearted."

Meredith reacted to Sebastian's superior with utter surprise that he should be so candid about a subject she couldn't imagine the Colonel even alluding to.

"I...well...it's complicated in a way even I don't understand," she admitted finally.

Wainwright nodded sympathetically. "I can see you're a bit taken aback to have me raise such a...well...private subject. But I've seen certain, shall we say, 'adjustment' problems in those who've served in the Middle East.

Sebastian Pryce was evidently one of the best soldiers we had in the canine bomb squad, but no one comes home from Afghanistan unchanged, my dear. I do hope you'll...well...that you might allow him some time to sort out whatever has been bothering him. You both seem so...so well-suited, if I may say so."

Meredith was at a complete loss for words and ducked her head with embarrassment. And then a sudden thought struck her: Sebastian's refusal to reveal the devils he wrestled was utterly beyond her control—and perhaps his own. At least for now. She had done nothing wrong. Sebastian was simply a troubled man who had not worked through whatever events in his past still had power over him. Meredith had ultimately come to see that very same thing in her relationship with Shep.

If Sebastian erroneously suspected she was accepting Beven Glynn's attentions, or if *he* had been drawn back, if only for one night, into the arms of Claire Gillis, then *that* was the current reality and there was absolutely nothing she could do about it, other than to accept it, honestly acknowledge to herself she still loved him, and move forward.

She gazed at Colonel Wainwright and smiled warmly. "Thank you for your wise words and good wishes," she said. "It's true, I had really hoped things would have turned out differently between Sebastian and myself, but that just doesn't appear possible at the moment. I've had a wonderful summer, though, and learned an enormous amount about...myself, mostly. And I'll miss Cornwall terribly," she confessed, "but, I'm heading back to Wyoming in about ten days."

Wainwright shook his head. "Well, I couldn't be sorrier to hear that, Meredith. Apart from your friendship with Sebastian, I was hoping to persuade you to volunteer as

part of our team at Cornwall Search and Rescue. We
certainly could use someone with both your knowledge of
working dogs and your nursing skills, as you plainly saw
during the rescue of that boy up near the abandoned mine
shafts."

Meredith glanced down at the ground once more,
deeply touched. "That is so dear of you to say, Colonel,"
she murmured, "and if things were different, I'd take you
up on that offer in a flash." She summoned her most
cheerful tone, and added, "But I'll be back for Christmas
and I plan to spend as much of my summers over here with
my ward as my employers will allow. I'm sure we'll meet
again."

"Jolly good!" he declared.

Gazing at this kindest of gentlemen, another thought
came to mind. She fully realized, now, she couldn't *make*
Sebastian reveal events in his past that clearly presented
obstacles to his happiness.

*I can only be ready to listen if he ever decides to confide in me.*

An addiction counselor at her hospital once said to her
in the depths of her despair about Shep's inability to stay
sober, "Remember, Meredith, we never rule out miracles,
but it's best to live in the reality of today."

To her amazement, she found she was reasonably at
peace with this understanding. She smiled again at
Wainwright.

"Cornwall has acquired at least *one* new ex-patriot from
America, though, Colonel. My young ward, Janet, is going
to remain with her co-guardians at Barton Hall indefinitely
and go to the village school with her cousins."

"That's capital!" he said, "Sebastian told me about her
mother's tragic death and how you and Lady Barton-
Teague stepped right in."

"He did?"

"Why yes. He said how fond of the little girl he's become. And how much he admires you and Lady Barton-Teague for taking on such a huge responsibility."

Suddenly, the sound of barking interrupted their conversation and penetrated the constant wash of waves a hundred feet below the cliff. She looked over her shoulder at the first canine arrivals and their handlers who were advancing across the field.

"Ah! Brace yourself, Colonel Wainwright!"

Wainwright followed her glance. "Well, so I see. Here come the hordes!"

❧

Ninety minutes later, Meredith and Colonel Wainwright were handing out the last of the completion certificates to the proud handlers of the novice search and rescue dogs when the moss green Land Rover appeared suddenly on the far side of the field and screeched to a halt. Alarmed, Meredith watched as Blythe, Lucas, and Richard bounded from the vehicle, let themselves into the field, and swiftly headed in their direction while the final recipient shook hands with Wainwright and the class milled together in happy confusion.

"Thank you! Thank you, all!" Meredith shouted over the din, and then half-ran across the field to meet Blythe, Lucas, and Richard who were speeding toward her.

"Has Janet come down here?" Blythe shouted, even before she shooed away a cluster of sheep grazing peacefully a few yards away.

"No," replied Meredith, running a few yards more to meet the trio. "I thought she was still asleep—or with you."

Panting to catch her breath, Blythe said, "She wasn't in her bed when the children went to give her the puppy class attendance certificate. One of her suitcases is missing...some of her clothes...*all* of the Nancy Drew mysteries I gave her to read!"

"Oh...God," Meredith exclaimed, her heart turning over. "Look, Colonel Wainwright is over there," she added quickly, explaining to Richard and Lucas, "he was here to hand out the SAR certificates to Sebastian's class. Come on...let's tell him what's happened."

By this time, the handlers were proudly streaming across the field in the opposite direction with their dogs, heading toward their cars parked near the road. Lucas swiftly brought Wainwright up to date on events at Barton Hall.

"When did you discover the youngster wasn't anywhere in the house?" the Colonel asked.

Blythe spoke up. "About twenty minutes ago. I let our children run upstairs after they'd come back from puppy class to see if Janet was awake and felt like having some cookies and milk with Lucy and Matthew. Her bed was made and she was nowhere to be found. We made a quick search of the house and the outbuildings. Nothing."

*The child had made her bed!*

What a difference a few months had made, thought Meredith, but then the reality hit that Janet may well have run away in the wake of her father's virtual abandonment the previous day.

"Well, the fact she took some of her possessions is actually a good sign," Wainwright said reassuringly following Lucas' swift recitation of the previous day's events involving Janet's father. "If she were morbidly despondent, she would just wander off and possibly do herself harm. It appears as if she had some sort of plan in mind."

"She knows about Heathrow Airport," Meredith

murmured. "You don't suppose she'd attempt to make her way all the way up there to try to find her father? He said he was flying out of there for the States today."

"Wait a minute!" Richard exclaimed. "I saw her standing in the library sometime after I had lunch with Claire in the kitchen. I had a glimpse of her through the open door as I walked down the hall, but I didn't think anything about it. She was over at Blythe's desk...hunched over a book or something."

"A book?" Lucas responded. "What was on your desk, Blythe, do you remember? Another Nancy Drew mystery, perhaps?"

"No...but I keep my calendar and...my address book there," Blythe murmured her thoughts aloud. "That's about all that's ever on it...next to the telephone. Everything else is kept in the drawers unless I'm working on the ledgers or something."

"Shall we drive up to the Hall," Wainwright suggested, "and see if we can determine if Janet left either your daily diary or address book open to a particular page? Perhaps we can garner more clues as to where she might be headed? I've got my car parked near your Land Rover across the field. Shall you lead the way, Sir Lucas?"

"Right...let's do that, Colonel. And please do call me Lucas."

"And I'm Graham...no more 'sirs' directed at any of us, agreed? If we can't make head nor tail of this up at the Hall, I'll put a call into the St. Austell constable and if he gives the go-ahead, I'll alert the SAR Team to mobilize."

And in the midst of the worried group hastening back to Barton Hall, it suddenly struck Meredith that she might very soon be seeing none other than Sebastian Pryce and the amazing T-Rex.

ᏈᎸᏉ

Blythe's address book remained open on her desk in the library.

"It's on the tab designated 'P'," Lucas announced, peering over his wife's shoulder.

"Oh, good Lord!" Blythe exclaimed. "Half the Cornish names in the lexicon begin with that initial: Penpraise, Penhollow, Pettigrew…"

The rest of them gathered in a circle around the huge oak desk and watched as she ran a slender finger down the list of their acquaintances whose names began with the letter P.

Meredith hesitated while a half-formed idea swirled in her brain. Then she asked softly, "Do you have Sebastian's contact information in your address book, Blythe?"

Her cousin looked up and their glances held across the desk. "Pryce? Wait…I think so. I'm sure I put it in here when you and he—" She halted mid-sentence, but continued to search her list of addresses on the two pages that had been left open. "Yes! Here it is…the second from the last listing on the right hand page! You don't suppose…? But good heavens, Meredith, Cow Hollow Farm is eight *miles* from here," Blythe protested.

"Surely, Janet wouldn't have set out on her own to travel such a long distance?" Lucas declared.

"Perhaps she called Sebastian first?" suggested Colonel Wainwright, adding, "though I doubt the chap would have come and fetched her without your permission."

A few moments before hearing Wainwright suggest that perhaps Janet had placed a call to Sebastian before she disappeared, Claire Gillis entered the library and walked over to stand beside Richard.

"You know…" she said, and then she hesitated.

"What?" they all chorused.

"Janet was quite a fan of Sebastian, don't you think?" she ventured. She turned to Richard, "Remember how she was always pestering him to show her the dairy farm? She wanted to see how cows were milked, what Sebastian did as a large animal vet...that sort of thing. Right hero-worshipped him, she did."

Meredith certainly remembered Janet's near adoration of Sebastian when he taught his dog obedience classes and recalled the night when the child persuaded him to take her to the farm, interrupting the intimate dinner Meredith and Sebastian had planned.

"She's been to his place once before," Meredith said quietly. "She pestered him endlessly to show her Cow Hollow Farm, and not too long ago, he kindly took her on a tour. He even allowed her to visit Susanna Jenner's weaving studio."

Blythe pursed her lips in thought and then said, "Even if Janet couldn't reach Sebastian by phone today, she can be a very determined kid. I could very well imagine her setting out to find him, can't you, Meredith?"

Meredith nodded and looked at Colonel Wainwright. "I don't know if Sebastian ever told you, Colonel, but when he was a boy, his mother placed him with an uncle to raise. He had a genuine empathy for Janet's...situation. She sensed it, I think. I agree with Blythe. It seems perfectly possible to me that she just set out on foot..."

"Dragging her suitcase with her?" Lucas asked doubtfully.

"Well, why don't we ring the farm immediately?" Wainwright suggested. "See if she's turned up there?"

Within seconds, Blythe had pressed the phone expectantly to her ear. They all held their collective breaths while she waited for someone at Cow Hollow Farm to answer.

"Hello?" she said suddenly. "Yes, Susanna. It's Blythe Barton-Teague. Yes…we've so much to catch up on and I've been meaning to call you to see how your prize cow is doing. Oh, *no*! I am so sorry. When?" Blythe exclaimed, deep concern etched in her expression. "So William and Sebastian aren't there now? They've been gone all *day*?"

Meredith's heart sank. There'd be no Sebastian and no Rex to help with the search. She waited on tenterhooks while Blythe explained Janet's disappearance.

"So, you haven't seen anything at your farm? We thought she might have set out to see Sebastian. Yes, he's a great favorite of hers. Well, please do have Sebastian get in touch the moment they get back. Yes, if you reach either Sebastian or William on their mobiles, tell Sebastian just to text Meredith or Colonel Wainwright. I think we'll be calling out his SAR team and the constable, of course. Yes, you, too. And I'm so sorry about your cow."

Blythe hung up the phone. "Susanna has been in her studio most of the day, but she'll keep an eye out for Janet. Their prize cow died this morning. William and Sebastian have carted it over to a veterinary lab in Devon for tests. They want to confirm there is nothing about her illness that could be contagious and apparently there's even to be an autopsy. They're due back later in the afternoon, so Susanna will call on their mobile and see if they'll answer."

"Well, barring any news on that front," Colonel Wainwright responded, "I fear I'd better alert the St. Austell constabulary and get authorized to mobilize the SAR team."

❧❧❧

The next few hours were a blur in Meredith's mind. Just

as on the day of her arrival at Barton Hall, the circular drive facing the castle was littered with police and search and rescue vehicles forming a command post. A Coast Guard unit scoured the nearby beaches and cliffs, while Wainwright's team combed the estate's adjacent fields and higher elevations. Within a half hour of the group's fanning out, one member returned with a small suitcase in hand, at the same moment Sebastian sped up the drive in the green Mini-Cooper and walked directly toward Colonel Wainwright to report for duty, Rex scampering at his side. The two conferred for several minutes in private.

Unable to look at either dog or man, Meredith ran to the SAR volunteer holding the small, pink wheeled bag, a Disney character embossed in painted plastic on its side.

"That's hers! That's Janet's little bag!" she exclaimed.

"We found it behind a tree, not far from where the driveway ends," said the searcher. "It was pushed against the trunk with the handle tucked down, as if someone had carefully stored it there, intending to return to fetch it. All that's in it are some children's clothes and several books."

"Old Nancy Drew mysteries?" Blythe asked.

"Yes…that's right."

Blythe looked hopefully at Meredith. "By the time she reached the end of the drive, she probably got tired of hauling those heavy books behind herself and stashed the suitcase there to come collect later."

"But where has she *gone!*" Meredith said, fighting a mild sense of hysteria. Seeing Sebastian and Rex so suddenly had nearly pushed her over the edge.

"Well," broke in Colonel Wainwright, "I think we just keep pushing on. She can't have gotten far."

Sebastian strode to Meredith's side with his Border Collie galloping next to him.

"'I came as soon as Susanna called my mobile. We had

to drive the lorry back to the farm where I immediately jumped into my car and came directly here."

Despite the breach between them that had somehow grown as wide as a chasm in the Rockies, Meredith realized that she had never been so happy to see anyone in her life.

"Janet's father was here again," she explained swiftly. "He made Blythe as well as me official co-guardians of Janet so she could live here in Cornwall and go to school. After we signed all the legal documents, the bastard simply left without taking any time with his daughter at all. It was *cruel* beyond anything you can imagine!"

"Oh, trust me, I can imagine perfectly well," he replied with a grim expression.

"Janet cried and cried…all night, in fact. Blythe and I ended up staying in her bed with her till she calmed down. We thought it best to let her sleep, and I went down to Painter's Cottage to teach my classes, but we should have…" She paused and fought a wave of emotion that threatened to overtake her. "Oh, God, Sebastian!" she whispered. "She was absolutely heart-broken that her father had 'given her away,' as she said."

He reached for her hand. "Look, I know how frightened you feel, but we'll find her. Like Wainwright says, we just have to fan out methodically in all the directions she could have taken."

"But now they've found her suitcase and—"

"Blythe's probably right. She might well have simply abandoned it."

"Last night she sobbed as if someone had *died*, and then fell into an exhausted sleep. In fact, when I left to teach my final classes and to meet Colonel Wainwright at mid-day, I thought she was *still* asleep!"

Sebastian put his hand on her shoulder and Meredith sensed that he was resisting pulling her close only because the others surrounded them.

"What a terrible twenty-four hours you must have had. I was very sorry I couldn't be there today at my final class, but—"

Meredith felt a rush of anger she'd been trying to ignore in the days since Sebastian had stormed out of Painter's Cottage and texted her to take over his class. She knew she was being unreasonable, but she couldn't help it.

Fighting to keep tears at bay she said, "Oh, your class isn't important now. What matters is that Richard saw her looking at Blythe's address book after lunch. We think she was searching for *your* number." Meredith paused for a moment and then asked abruptly. "What calls did you get on your mobile today? Can you check?"

Sebastian fished his phone from the pocket of his red anorak and pushed a button. "I had it turned off while we were dealing with the autopsy. Funnily enough, my phone rang as soon as I turned it on, and it was Susanna, calling to tell me Janet had disappeared."

Meredith could see that his shoulders were slumped and he had the look of a man who hadn't slept in days. At the sight of him standing so close to her, all her resentment and disappointment over the developments of the past week suddenly seemed to melt away. Perhaps their relationship as a couple wasn't possible, now, she thought, but she felt a deep connection to Sebastian based on friendship that she hoped would endure beyond her summer's stay in Cornwall.

"Oh, Sebastian!" she blurted. "I am so sad for you all that the Jenners' prize cow died."

"We tried everything possible these last few days to save her," he revealed, with a look of thanks for her expression of sympathy. "Her stomach somehow got twisted and everything in her body eventually shut down. It happens occasionally—but we'll know, exactly, when all the lab reports come in. It's been a pretty ghastly few days, that's certain," he said, and she knew instinctively he was genuinely relieved that they were speaking to each other normally, at last.

"Ghastly," she agreed softly. "On about a thousand fronts."

Sebastian was now staring at the readout on his mobile phone. "I actually think there was another message when I answered Susanna's call, but in the rush to get here, I forgot to go back and check to see what or who it was." Then he exclaimed, "Good Christ! There's a voice message from Barton Hall on this. Did you or Blythe call me earlier?"

"No!" Meredith said excitedly. "But I bet I know who did!"

❧✵☙

As soon as Sebastian listened to the solitary message on his phone with Janet's distraught voice saying she was coming to see him, Colonel Wainwright notified the Coast Guard to stand down.

"We'll keep up the search within a three mile radius of here while Sebastian and Meredith drive slowly along the road to Cow Hollow Farm to see if Janet's actually walking there," he said to the assembled group huddled around the front of the SAR vehicle, a large survey map spread out on the hood.

Lucas asked Sebastian, "But wouldn't you have spotted her on your way here, or Susanna Jenner would have seen the girl if she'd made it as far as there?"

"Janet may have left Barton Hall up to five hours ago. Sad to say, I wasn't paying a bit of attention to anything but merely getting here when I drove from the farm," Sebastian admitted, "and Susanna said she hadn't *seen* anyone at the farm. However, she did mention that she had been busy inside her weaving studio today."

"Yes, she told me that too," Blythe said, nodding.

"Janet is a Barton," Meredith said with a grim smile. "She can be a very single-minded when she wants something. Especially when it comes to her fondness for Sebastian, here. I'm betting we'll find her en route."

Sebastian answered Meredith's pointed statement with an embarrassed chuckle, "Shall we go and see how devoted a hiker she might be?" He turned to Wainwright. "We'll call you right away if we spot her along the road to the farm."

"And we'll ring you if any of us locate her around here," Lucas said, nodding. "Meanwhile, we should probably offer some sustenance to all these searchers."

Blythe chimed in, addressing her stepson. "Richard, do you suppose that you and Claire could rustle up something simple for these fine people and set up a tea bar while you're at it? You can serve it all under the portico. And someone needs to be tending to the B&B guests coming in later this afternoon."

Richard said, "Claire's already got that covered. She just texted me from the kitchen that a party of five without reservations rolled up by the back entrance ten minutes ago. They had gotten completely turned around, but are delighted to have found us. 'Ka-ching! Ka-ching,' she wrote," he announced, pointing to his cell phone.

Meanwhile, Sebastian directed Meredith to find an article of clothing. When she returned with the familiar blue sweater, he took Meredith's arm and guided her toward the green Mini, with Rex following along behind. She called to Richard, "Can you be sure Holly gets her dinner while I'm gone?"

"Claire's got that covered, too," he said, and turned

toward the castle to lend his ladylove a hand.

*Well, isn't she a clever puss!*

And then Meredith chided herself roundly, for the truth was, all summer, Claire's help had inevitably supplied just what was needed at any given moment. She tossed Janet's sweater in the back seat near Rex who gave it a good sniff on his own volition.

A million thoughts and questions raced through Meredith's head as she and Sebastian drove at reduced speed toward Cow Hollow Farm. She forced herself to put them aside, however, intent on watching from her side of the road for Janet's small figure. And besides, she thought, there was so much she and Sebastian needed to discuss—if he were at all willing—and so little time, given the short drive to the farm.

"I missed you, you know," he said quietly, his eyes never leaving the roadside and fields on the right side of the car.

Meredith felt her heart give a startled, little flip, but she tamped down the hope that instantly welled inside and merely nodded.

Silence hummed in tandem with the cars engine. Finally Sebastian said, "I was going to come over this evening so we could talk."

"After we last saw each other at the lookout hut and when you didn't call, I thought…" she murmured. "But of course, I didn't realize how seriously ill your livestock was."

"I should have called anyway," he replied, "just to let you know what was going on, but given how put out with me I assumed you probably were—and I deserved it, by the way," he added wryly, "my mission today was just going to be to surprise you so you'd have to hear me out."

"I'd have wanted to see you, if for no other reason than to say goodbye," she said, focusing intently on the shoulder of the road and seeing no sign of Janet. She assumed the announcement of her imminent departure would take Sebastian by surprise, but it didn't.

"Graham told me just now that you've booked your flight home." He cast her a quick glance and then resumed gazing steadily on his side of the road. "I think he was politely attempting to point out to me what a complete arse I've been."

"That would be a 'complete ass,' yes?"

"A perfect translation."

She turned briefly to look at him and then shifted her gaze back to the left side of the road, continuing to search for the child's figure in the dusk fast enveloping them.

"Well, I'm heading back to Wyoming a week from Wednesday. At least, that was my plan until Janet...until *this* happened today.

"No, you're not flying back to the States!" he declared, banging a gloved hand on his steering wheel. "At least, not until we find Janet and you and I have about ten hours to sort out things between us."

"My ticket is in my purse, Sebastian, but I'll be willing to listen to whatever you want to tell me," she said quietly. Then, pointing out the window she exclaimed, "Oh, Lord, Sebastian! There's your farm. We've driven the entire route—and no sight of Janet!"

# CHAPTER 18

Sebastian wheeled the car into the Jenners' yard in near darkness and pulled up next to the Dutch door to his flat perched above the old livery stable. A door at the back of the farmhouse flew open, the light from Susanna's kitchen spilling out onto the stone stoop.

"Did you find her?" she called anxiously, walking swiftly toward the car as she wiped her hands on her apron.

"No, I'm afraid not," Sebastian answered, getting out of the driver's side door, holding Janet's blue sweater in one hand and his medical bag he'd taken to Plymouth in the other. "We're going to use Rex to do a search around the farm. I gather you haven't seen anything?"

"Well, I was in my weaving room all afternoon, oblivious to all until I got the call from you. I gave a good look around the grounds and in the cow barns you'd shown Janet on her visit here, but no...nothing I was aware of. William's in the sitting room just now, having a large glass of whiskey. What a day."

By this time, Meredith had emerged from the Mini and was enveloped by a hug of sympathy from Susanna while Rex wagged his tail beside them.

Meredith hugged her back, saying, "I am so terribly sorry you lost your prize cow. Did the stars decide to pee on all our heads today, I wonder?" she said, smiling weakly, adding for their benefit, "That's an old Champlin family saying my father made up when we lost a ewe on our ranch."

"Well," said Susanna gamely, "we'll just have to hold each other tight until the heavens shift and the stars go pee on someone *else's* head! Oh, it is *so* good to see you!" Susanna said, giving Meredith another embrace. She cocked a disapproving eyebrow in Sebastian's direction. "But we'll talk about all *that* later. William and I have been so worried since Sebastian called us earlier. There's absolutely no trace of the little girl around Barton Hall? It's an awfully big estate."

"The SAR team is still fanning out on the search," Meredith disclosed, hearing the fear that again crept into her voice. "She might have tried to walk along one of the paths across the fields, instead of the road, and got lost. We found her small suitcase abandoned beside a tree at the end of the drive."

Sebastian said quickly, "Let me just take my medical bag upstairs and then we'll set out combing this area."

"Can William and I help?"

"That's awfully good of you, Susanna, but Meredith and I are going to let Rex have a go, first. No point in exhausting everyone all at once. Come, Rex!"

The Border Collie took off like a shot, barking excitedly near Sebastian's front door.

"Well, that pup's certainly happy to be home," Susanna chortled. "Must be dinner time."

"Way past," Sebastian agreed. "I'll feed him and then we'll be off."

Meredith gave Susanna another hug, saying, "We'll call you and William right away if we find anything."

Susanna turned back toward the kitchen door and said over her shoulder, "We'll be in the house. And do let us know if we can feed *you* two, or anything."

Sebastian signaled for Meredith to follow him to the entrance to his flat. She felt her stomach clutch at the memory of the first time Sebastian had allowed her into his private realm. Flashes of their wondrous night together...the bubble bath...their picnic on his tartan blanket, and the wild, wonderful love they'd shared within these ancient walls brought tears to her eyes that she quickly brushed away with her sleeve.

Sebastian, too, seemed to be thinking of that visit, for he seized her hand halfway up the steps that were cast in shadow as the sun disappeared across the rural landscape behind them. Rex was already at the top of the stairs, prancing excitedly, and emitting little barks.

"Steady boy," Sebastian called. "Dinner's on its way. Let me just get the switch," he said as they arrived on the top landing. Light flooded the stone walled room. He set his veterinary medical bag on the floor near the stairs. "I can also quickly brew us—" He halted mid-sentence, pointing to his bed under the eaves and calling *sotto voce* to Rex, 'Sit! *Stay!* so the dog wouldn't leap on the coverlet or bark.

There, sprawled on his tartan blanket lay a small form, curled into a tight ball, arms clasped around a pillow as if holding on to a life preserver.

"Oh...thank...God!" Meredith whispered. "She *did* set out from Barton Hall to find you."

"I think Rex knew she was here the minute we got out of the car," he murmured, indicating the child's sweater he still held in his hand. "He wasn't barking for his dinner. He was barking to indicate a 'find!'"

Meredith shook her head in wonder. Still whispering she said, "She walked eight miles, all on her own, because somehow...she knew you'd understand."

"Understand?" he echoed softly as they both

approached the bed.

Meredith felt the tears that had already surfaced as she walked up the stairs now slide down her cheeks.

"Some part of her sensed that you'd know what it feels like to be shunned by a parent...to be cast off, as she was last night. She doesn't know your story, but I could always tell that she has felt a sort of kinship with you."

"And I with her," he said softly.

Meredith felt an even stronger wave of emotion fill her chest. She turned toward Sebastian and put her arms around him, seeking comfort and simultaneously yearning with every fiber to offer it as well...to him...to Janet...to every child she'd ever known who felt abandoned and betrayed when parents failed their offspring as Sebastian's mother and Janet's father had failed them. She tucked her head under his chin and they stood silently, locked in a fierce embrace.

Hoping she wouldn't wake the eleven-year-old asleep on Sebastian's bed, she said in a low, angry tone, "I can't *bear* to think what you and Janet have suffered from your god-damned rotten parents! I'd like to hog-tie them all and haul them behind a big, old raging bull!"

"Shhhh...shhhh...it's all right. Truly it is," he said softly against her ear.

"But it's *not!*" Meredith protested.

"Yes it is," he insisted, "because Janet and I have one thing in common."

Meredith pulled away and looked at him questioningly. "A bunch of deadbeat parents who should be horsewhipped?" she repeated, trying to keep her voice down. A rush of highly charged anger coursed through her when she recalled several adults she'd dealt with in the children's intensive care ward in Wyoming who had made the suffering of their youngsters a drama about themselves.

"You know how to tie up a hog?" he echoed, trying to coax a smile from her. "And besides, is that any way for a healthcare professional to talk?" he teased. "No...what we both have in common is *you.*"

A pain so piercing it nearly took her breath away shot through her. She loved this man, and in an instant, she clearly understood the meaning of the words he'd just spoken. He loved her as well. And he'd missed her in the same way she'd missed him. But he'd allowed them both to suffer for days without a word of apology for storming out of Painter's Cottage, or an explanation as to why he'd paid a visit to Claire that same night—and more significantly, what that rendezvous had meant to him.

She knew in a place where she never lied to herself that after the struggles they'd experienced all summer, she couldn't join her life to his if she always had to wonder what he was thinking, what he was feeling...and whether or not, *this* time, he would share at least some of the secret wounds that often drove him to pull away and shut down from the very ones who cared the most about his welfare. And as much as she adored Sebastian Pryce in a way she'd never felt with anyone before, including Shep O'Brien, she couldn't live in that dark place, ever again. That much she'd learned from Shep. She gazed down at Janet as an almost intolerable wave of grief for what would be denied her took hold.

Just then, Janet stirred on top of the tartan blanket, caught sight of them, and pulled herself to a sitting position on the bed.

"You weren't here!" she said accusingly to Sebastian, ignoring Meredith completely.

"I am very, *very* sorry that I wasn't," Sebastian replied, striding toward the bed. "I didn't know you were coming to see me, you see, and—"

"I walked all this way, but you weren't *here!*" she wailed with the perfect logic of a child.

And then Janet's cries became deep wracking sobs that tore at Meredith's heart. She ran to the bedside and gathered the youngster in her arms.

"Oh...you poor sweetheart!" she crooned. "Sebastian didn't know you were coming to see him," she repeated. "He was taking care of a sick cow that finally died and—"

"But I *c-called* him from Barton Hall and l-left a m-message...on his c-cell phone!" she cried. "And he n-never called me back!"

By this time Sebastian had sat down on the other side of the bed and cast his long arms around the two of them, pulling them both gently against his chest. "I didn't realize you'd called until just a little while ago, Janet, and look! Meredith and I came right over! We are *so* happy you're all right. Even Rex is happy...see?"

The black and white dog had stuck his muzzle on the side of the bed and was furiously wagging his tale.

Janet merely clung to them and cried all the harder.

"How in the world did you walk all the way from Barton Hall?" Meredith marveled. "You knew the way?"

"It was h-hard..." she stuttered. "I sort of remembered the way here from the time he showed me the dairy farm and I asked people. Some lady knew Susanna and drove me to the farm, the last part, and let me off at the gate." She brushed her hand across her eyes and sniffed loudly "I j-just wanted to see Sebastian."

Sebastian sat back and said, smiling, "Well, I *am* impressed—and very flattered. We could enlist you as a junior member of the Cornwall Search and Rescue Team, couldn't we Rex?" he said, glancing at his dog that, by this time, was curled up on the rug beside the bed.

"L-Look at him! He likes to be near us, doesn't he?"

she hiccupped, her sobs abating.

"He was searching everywhere for you," Meredith said. She glanced over at Sebastian with a start. "Oh my gosh! We should call Blythe and Susanna and everyone right away to tell them we've found Janet and that she's safe and sound."

Without reply, Sebastian pulled out his mobile and dialed, rising from the bed to speak first to Wainwright, next to Susanna next door, and then to whoever answered at Barton Hall.

Janet looked at her guardian with a frown furrowing her brow. "I thought you'd be mad," she said. "That I ran away."

"I was terribly, terribly worried about you going off on your own," Meredith replied, "and you did break Auntie Blythe's rule about letting people know where you are…but we all realize that you had a very bad day yesterday. We did, too. Everyone was so upset for you when your father left so abruptly."

"He likes *her* more than he does *me*," Janet said, and she began to weep once more.

"Oh, sweetie, I don't understand what your Dad was thinking or why he did what he did, but you need to know that the rest of your family loves you very much! And we all have some idea of how sad you were since your father came—and went—yesterday." She leaned forward and cupped Janet's tear-stained face between her hands. "You are so precious to us, Janet…and we are very proud of everything you've accomplished this summer."

"Really?" Janet asked in a small voice.

"Really, truly," Meredith said with a smile, brushing away Janet's tears with the backs of her fingers. "You may not have an ordinary-looking family any longer, but you must always remember, deep, deep down, that you've got a *different* sort of family that loves you very much. And it's made up of me, Auntie Blythe, Lucas, Richard, Lucy and Matthew...and your Dad, too, who promised he's going to see you on a regular basis."

"He won't keep his promise," she said, tears welling in her eyes again. "I just know he won't!"

Meredith was silent, wondering how to reassure the little girl without making guarantees she couldn't necessarily deliver.

Finally, she said, "Listen, Janet...even if your Dad disappoints you sometimes, you can count on the rest of us. Maybe your family in Cornwall might look to other people like a motley crew, but we are all people who care for you beyond anything, and will keep you safe, always." She stared deeply into the child's eyes, willing her to hear and understand her deeper message.

"And Sebastian?" she asked in a small voice. "And Claire and Mrs. Q? Can they be part of our family? I mean, since we're not such a regular sort of family?"

A deep voice interrupted their intimate *tete-a-tete*.

"You can certainly add 'Sebastian' to that list. But you'll have to ask Claire and Mrs. Q yourself."

Meredith looked over the top of Janet's head to lock glances with him, wondering in a hollow place in her heart if she would ever understand his complicated past. Then she gave Janet's shoulders a soft squeeze.

"Now that Sebastian's told everyone you're safe, let's get you home, shall we?"

Without even pausing to speak to the Jenners, the quartet quickly went downstairs.

"Janet, is it all right if you ride in the back of Sebastian's car with Rex to keep him company?" Meredith asked, wishing the eleven-year-old would have been small enough to cuddle in her lap on the return trip to Barton Hall. She could sense Janet's fragility and wanted to keep her close.

"Okay," Janet replied wanly, waiting for Sebastian to push back the driver's seat so the youngster and Rex could climb into the rear of the car.

Once all four of them were in the Mini, Sebastian asked, "Everybody buckled in?" and flashed a warm smile at Meredith as he put the car in gear. She smiled back, but her inner thoughts were swirling around the unanswered questions that had so exhausted her these last days.

Fifteen minutes later they were all sitting around the long, wooden table in the kitchen at Barton Hall having bowls of barley soup and soft, crusty bread that Claire had just pulled out of the Aga.

Following their meal, Claire and Meredith spent a subdued half hour washing the dishes in the double sink from the simple supper that had celebrated Janet's homecoming. Meanwhile, Blythe took all three children upstairs to tuck them in bed while Lucas, Richard, and Sebastian went to a lower field to see about a broken fence and to capture a few sheep reported to have been seen strolling along the cliff road. Complete darkness blacked out the view beyond the casement windows and the men were due back momentarily.

"Meredith, before you go, do you have a minute?" asked Claire, wiping her hands on her chef's apron.

Meredith hung her dishtowel in the drying cupboard, taking her time while she inhaled a long, sustained breath to calm her nerves in response to Claire's unusual request.

Barton Hall's permanent *chef de cuisine* motioned for them both to sit at the cleaned-off kitchen table where the antique cast-iron fixture above their heads cast a warm circle of light.

"So? What's on your mind?" Meredith asked.

For a long moment, the younger woman stared down at

her hands that were resting in her lap below the table.

"There are a couple of subjects that I...well, I think we should discuss in case your decision to go back to the States next week has anything to do with...with my past relationship with Sebo." She looked up and sought Meredith's gaze. "I figured from his—shall we call it 'coolness' when he's around me—that you might have surmised that it didn't end well between us. Well, you would be right. It didn't end well at all."

"Actually, I did gather that, though Sebastian hasn't given any details."

A mild grimace flashed across Claire's feature. "That sounds about right." Then she continued, "Well, just so you know, all that's over—*long* over—between us. My life, now, is very different than it was when he and I were together."

Meredith saw in her mind's eye Rex's leash lying in the tufted grass a few paces from Limekiln Cottage in the early morning hours after Sebastian and she had their blistering argument.

"How 'over' can it be," Meredith asked quietly, "when he visited you at your place...very late at night, I might add...less than a week ago?"

Claire blinked and returned Meredith's probing gaze with a puzzled expression.

"Sebo? At *my* cottage?" She gave a short laugh. "Not bloody likely!"

"Are you sure? It would have been last Saturday, or just after midnight Sunday morning to be exact," Meredith said, despising the waspish tone creeping into her voice.

Claire's calm, measured approach quickly dissolved and she slapped her palm angrily on the table. "That's not true, Meredith! Sebo has never set foot in my place here on the estate! As a matter of fact, last Saturday night after the farm supper, *Richard* was there. All night. In my *bed*!"

Incensed by the woman's cheek to speak so blatantly about her sexual affair with Lucas and Blythe's eighteen-year-old son, Meredith stared across the pool of light that separated them. "I think you may have gotten your nights mixed up," she said, tight-lipped. "Or maybe you just can't keep your visitors straight?"

"Cut it out, Meredith," Claire snapped. "Jealousy doesn't become you! That was a nasty crack, and I don't deserve it. I'm trying to tell you that you have no reason to doubt that Sebastian's in love with you...and you would be well advised to accept the truth that there's certainly *no* love lost between Sebastian and *me!* If you want me to tell you from *my* perspective the whole, sordid tale of why that is, I'd be more than happy to!"

*If I'm going to endure a sordid tale from anyone, it'd had better be from Sebastian!*

Rather than voice that thought, she replied curtly, "No, thank you, but I really have to ask you Claire...why have you raised with me the subject of your past history with Sebastian *now?*"

Claire paused, a look of genuine vulnerability reflected in her gaze.

"Because I realize that you two...well, you seem to be having difficulties and also because I actually wish Sebastian well. Now," she added pointedly. "Or at least I'm bloody sick of the polite but stony silences we exchange every time we meet. It's taken more than half a decade, but I understand much more about him...*and* about myself, now, and why things didn't work between us. I was barely twenty when I first met him, and the way it all happened in the end was...well, pretty gruesome. But it's long in the past and I just want—" Claire seemed at a loss how to finish her sentence.

"To be done with the misery?" Meredith interjected,

thinking suddenly of how she'd wished she could have closed the book a lot more gently with Shep O'Brien.

The younger woman met Meredith's gaze with a startled expression. "Yes, that's it, exactly! To have done with the misery. It was a shock to see Sebo again this summer after all that time, and to realize you two were...well...getting together."

"Well, we're not together, now, and part of the reason *does* have to do with you. How or why that should be, I still don't have a clue—and Sebastian won't tell me."

"Would you like me to?" Claire offered for a second time.

"No! Either he tells me himself, of his own volition, or I'm on a plane back to the States next week. If he doesn't think I'm trustworthy, we don't belong together."

Claire took another deep breath. "Well, I wish you luck, Meredith, truly I do. We'll all miss you. Frankly, between our Farm-to-Table suppers and your dog obedience school, our working together probably kept this place afloat."

Meredith felt another wave of guilt come over her with this latest reminder that her leaving Cornwall would deprive Blythe and Lucas of a modest, but significant income stream if the school didn't started up again in the spring.

*Why does everything in life have to be so complicated?*

Meanwhile, Claire's eyes were glued to her lap once again and she appeared to be marshaling her courage to say something else. For Meredith's part, she was glad to shift her thoughts.

"And what about Richard?" she asked, guessing the next subject Claire wished to bring up. "He's due to leave Barton Hall soon as well."

"Let's just put our cards on the table, shall we?" Claire said with a look of dogged determination. "As 'unsuitable' as it may seem to you, and probably everyone else on this estate—except Richard, of course—I'm in love with Richard. And he...well, I think it's fair to say he cares for me, too. I guess I'm asking for you to—" She halted mid-sentence, and then continued carefully, "I'm not really asking you to support us, but I'm asking for your understanding because I know how much Richard likes and admires you. And likes Sebo, too."

Meredith regarded Richard's lover with a narrowing stare.

"I can understand why you would seek for some sign of approval from the people Richard respects, but it has also occurred to me, Claire, how much you would enjoy taking on the role of Lady of the Manor, should you manage to marry the heir to Barton Hall—despite the serious differences in your ages and backgrounds."

There! She'd said it! She knew Claire would consider her statements merely more evidence of jealousy, but Meredith was truly concerned about the repercussions for Richard if Claire's affection wasn't all she said it was.

Claire put both hands on the kitchen table and looked as if she were about to lose her temper. In fact, she almost appeared to be counting to ten before she responded in a low voice.

"I'm not surprised you think that, given that I have no idea what Sebastian has or hasn't told you about us—even if he never gave the gory details to you about why we split up."

*Us.* That one word took Meredith's breath away, but she remained silent, awaiting whatever revelations Claire would choose to disclose.

"I can even see how circumstances might lead you to the conclusion that I am heartless, ambitious little tart, only out to advance myself, but—" Claire's voice broke and Meredith was startled to see that the woman was near tears.

"But strange as it seems, I love Richard in a way that even astonishes *me*. You don't think a former serving wench from St. Austell doesn't realize how 'unbefitting' it is for me to be completely daft over the young Master of the Manor?" she demanded.

"Claire, listen, I—"

"And it's not a ludicrous situation only because I'm older than Richard," she continued as if Meredith hadn't spoken, "but because of who *he* is...and who *I* am...and our very different 'backgrounds' as you oh, so politely put it. But I love him because of the kind of person he is!" she said vehemently. "I've never been with anyone like him! He's the sweetest, most considerate, most hardworking, most—"

Interrupting, Meredith surprised even herself with her next words.

"And it's perfectly obvious to me that Richard is crazy about you," she said. "But he's still a *very* young man who is only just moving out from the confines of his father's shadow. How much have you told him about your previous relationship with Sebastian?"

Claire gazed at her blankly as if she were shocked to be asked such a question. "I've told Richard everything there is to know about me, including what happened with Sebastian."

*Well, that's a damn sight more than Sebastian has ever told me!*

"You mean all this time Richard has known...and he still 'admires' Sebastian, you say?"

"Richard is wise, despite how young in years everyone judges him," Claire replied. "I confessed to him that much of what happened between Sebo and me *was* my fault, and he understood. He's like an old soul, who's been around this life more than once. He understood how *all sides* could have felt wounded by those events. And he loves me anyway, despite the whole, sorry tale, and admires Sebastian in so many ways."

"Well, look, Claire," Meredith said, a mortal weariness invading her bones, "if you're hoping for my blessing or something, I have to say that there is no getting around the fact that you're nearly a decade older than he is. I'd be lying if I didn't tell you I find that pretty worrisome in the long run and I pray that the affection you say you feel for him is all you claim it is. Richard may be an 'old soul,' as you say...and I agree with that in many ways...but he hasn't had the actual life experience you have, so I hope he'll keep his head and return to his university." She shrugged her shoulders, adding, "But that's up to him. You two have created a wonderful enterprise together with your Farm-to-Table suppers and you've been a tremendous help to everyone all summer, including *me*. You are really, really good at what you do, but—"

"But what?" Claire swiped the moisture from her cheeks.

"Here's where I am with all this," Meredith said as another wave of fatigue overtook her. "After Richard finishes Oxford, and if you two still feel the same way about each other, who am I to say you shouldn't be together? Frankly, I'm not doing so well in my own life, so I think I'll just take a pass on rendering a judgment about anyone else."

"Have you discussed any of this with Blythe? Your uneasy feelings about Richard and me, I mean?"

"I noted early on the obvious attraction you two had for each other, and since then, I've been tempted to voice my concerns to Lucas and her, because, as I say, I've been worried about this. But as you've observed, I've had my own problems...with Janet and...with other things. So no, I haven't spoken frankly about this subject with either

Blythe or Lucas—nor has Sebastian, as far as I know."

"Well, that's rather decent of you two, I must say," Claire murmured.

"And it's decent of you to try to clear the air between you and me."

It had taken courage for Claire to broach these touchy subjects with her, a member of Richard's family, and especially given their mutual connection with Sebastian. But the young chef had had the courage to plunge ahead and had spoken her mind. In a strange way, Meredith was grateful to her.

"Listen, Claire…thanks for bringing up the elephant in the living room that's been lurking all these weeks—or should I say the 'elephant in the castle,'" she said with rueful smile. "What it really comes down to is that Sebastian and I have our own problems to deal with that have less to do with you than I realized, and certainly *nothing* to do with Richard and you." She rose from the kitchen table. "Thanks for a delicious supper, tonight. It was such a nice meal to come home to after the day we had."

"You're welcome," Claire replied uncertainly. "Thanks for hearing me out. And I'm really happy that Janet was found, safe and sound."

Meredith headed for the servant's back stairs that would lead her to her bedroom in the North Wing. "Thanks. You know, I'm about to drop in my tracks. Will you say goodnight to everyone when they get back?"

She suddenly longed for bed. And besides, tonight she was in no condition to have the most important conversation of her life with Sebastian Pryce.

 ⚜

Less than five minutes after Meredith had retreated

upstairs, the door to the mudroom swung open and the sounds of Lucas, Richard, and Sebastian shedding their boots presaged the trio padding into the kitchen in their stocking feet. Claire had busied herself hanging up the last, cleaned copper cooking pot on the rack above the double-sized Aga cooker that had served meals for generations of inhabitants at Barton Hall.

"Got any more coffee?" Lucas asked, sitting down in the spot at the kitchen table where just minutes before Meredith had been. "It got quite cold out there in the fields. There's already a feel of autumn in the air."

Richard walked toward the stove and took down a tray, setting it on the counter nearby. "Here, let me get the cups." He looked around at the empty kitchen. "Where's everybody gone?"

"Mostly to bed, I think...or about to," Claire replied. "The B&B guests are drinking brandy in the drawing room. The children have been asleep for ages. Blythe never came downstairs after story time, and Meredith's just gone up." She glanced briefly at Sebastian. "She seemed totally worn out—and who wouldn't be after Janet's disappearance?"

Immediately, Sebastian said, "It's getting rather late. I'd best be on my way." He looked directly at Claire. "Will you be sure to tell Meredith I'll call her first thing tomorrow?"

Claire hesitated and then reached out and patted his sleeve.

"Absolutely. First thing. Or Richard will, if he sees her first, won't you?"

Richard nodded.

"Goodnight, Sebastian," she said. "Safe journey home."

Sebastian gazed at Claire, surprise clearly etched on his features that it should be his discarded lover bidding him a friendly farewell, but he only said, "Goodnight." He nodded at Lucas and Richard. "Goodnight, you two."

"'Night," they chorused, with Lucas adding, "And my gratitude for all your help corralling those sheep—not to mention joining the search for our human run-away."

"All in the line of duty," he said soberly, turning to retrace his steps through the pantry, the mudroom, and out the back door.

As he walked slowly toward his Mini parked in the inner courtyard, Sebastian gazed up at the glowing rectangle recessed into the thick, stone walls above his head. He could hear the soft clucking of ducks floating among the reeds on the ornamental pond at the bottom of the gentle slope where once there had been a moat. The sounds of sheep bleating in the cold night air alternated with the crack of waves off Portluney Beach. Overhead, lights on the second floor told him she wasn't asleep, yet she hadn't waited downstairs for him to return.

*You've done it again, Pryce old boy. You left the lady hanging...*

After he'd climbed behind the wheel, Sebastian sat in the driver's seat for a long time, not turning on the car's ignition.

*Meredith was leaving soon...*

She actually owned a plane ticket back to Wyoming. She was departing Cornwall on account of *him*. And why not? She had been patient with him. She had tried to understand and accept that he was wrestling with a number of devils, and she'd even revealed some devils of her own. And she had certainly waited a long time for him to come clean about what had happened between Claire and him, events so tumultuous that he'd nearly committed suicide by signing up for the army's bomb squad where he could have gotten himself and Max killed any number of times.

And what had he done *this* time around? Walked out on the woman he loved and slammed the door. Worse yet, he had taken his own sweet time about trying to sort it out and explain his feelings and his fear that he would always create situations where he shut out the ones he loved.

Sebastian leaned his head against the back of the driver's seat and shut his eyes, overcome by a sense of utter bleakness he hadn't felt since Afghanistan.

With a sudden movement, he banged his fist hard against the steering wheel.

"Bloody hell, Lieutenant!" he exclaimed aloud. "Take *off* your full-body armor, you idiot—or you deserve to lose!"

# CHAPTER 19

A swath of bright sunlight filtering through a pair of windows that faced Portluney Cove stretched across the Persian rugs carpeting Meredith's room. The sound of waves hitting the beach and the golden shafts from the sun warmed the burgundy silk coverlet on her massive, four-poster bed and forced her to open sleep-laden eyes. The warmth and colors suffusing her room felt as if she were lying inside the facets of a ruby.

For a moment, she reclined against the starched linen pillow case completely disoriented, wisps of disturbing dreams still swirling in her head, dreams that she was unable to find her departure gate at Heathrow Airport while a big clock with Roman numerals, rather like one Susanna had attached to the granite wall in Sebastian's flat, ticked away the minutes overhead, heralding the time her plane was due to leave for America.

As she swam to full consciousness, an oppressive sense of gloom descended that belied the sunny weather beckoning outside the stone walls of Barton Hall. She pulled herself upright, swung her legs over the side of the mattress, and eased her bare feet to the floor, grabbing her dressing gown from the bottom of the bed. Padding over to the window casement, she gazed beyond the rolling downs at the pristine sands of Portluney Beach and thought of her eighteenth century Cornish ancestors who most probably assisted smugglers coming ashore on that stretch of low-lying sand with their bounty of untaxed wines, lace, and other luxuries prized by Britons throughout the countryside.

She was soon to leave all this, she thought, her spirits sinking even lower at the memory of going down the hall twice in the night to check on Janet who finally seemed cried out by about four o'clock in the morning.

Meredith's thoughts drifted back to the end of supper last evening. She'd groaned inwardly when Sebastian predictably volunteered to accompany Lucas and Richard on their emergency mission to capture the sheep that had escaped and were wandering down the road dividing the bulk of the estate lands from the narrow fields that bordered the English Channel.

For her part, she was physically and emotionally incapable of joining the rescuing party or even remaining awake long enough to await his return. She'd retired upstairs and fell instantly to sleep on her bed, fully clothed, only to stir at the sound of a car's ignition below her window. She had scrambled to look out the leaded square panes in time to watch Sebastian's Mini come round the building from the courtyard and head down the drive, recalling with some annoyance how quickly he'd volunteered to tramp outside with Lucas and Richard in search of a few wandering sheep. Hadn't he said in the car earlier that they were long past due to have a serious talk?

*The Rescue Ranger grasps every opportunity to avoid confrontation...*

Sebastian had managed to pull his escape artist routine yet again. And once again, he had conveniently sidestepped a golden opportunity immediately following supper to retire to the library and hash through the unhappy events of these last days. It was just one more lost opportunity to sort out exactly why he had paid a visit to Claire's cottage, even if he didn't go inside.

The sane part of her brain protested that she was being judgmental and unfair about the previous night's events. Lucas had *asked* for Sebastian's help to corral the sheep, she reminded herself. The guest had just eaten his host's food. Everyone was as tired and wrung out as she had been, but lost sheep were lost sheep and each one was an investment in Barton Hall's bottom line that they couldn't afford to lose. Meredith, herself, could have joined in the search, given Holly's talent for herding lost sheep, but instead, she succumbed to her exhaustion—and disappointment. Sebastian wasn't trying to escape, a voice in her head chastised...he was just being polite.

You *were the one that didn't offer to help Lucas and went straight to bed without saying goodnight—or even leaving Sebastian a note.*

An unhappy thought struck her. Was it part of *her* pattern to play the escape artist *herself* to avoid disappointment and getting her feelings hurt if things didn't go precisely as she envisioned they should? That was certainly how she'd behaved with Shep, ducking several opportunities to put him on notice that if he didn't stop his excessive drinking binges, she would end their relationship. Instead, without any warning that she was moving out of their apartment in Jackson Hole, she'd just left.

Oh yes, she'd complained in an oblique fashion sometime, or gave him the silent treatment, staying over at the ranch until she figured he had sobered up and his remorse would keep his intermittent drinking bouts at bay for a while. But she'd never really called the question when he was *sober*. Did she sit down and look him in the eye and say that she couldn't live with not knowing when he would go off on another bender despite a string of remorseful promises that he'd seek help and get off the booze? Did she tell him she expected him to pay her back the ten grand she'd spent on his rehab when he finally *did* admit he knew he needed help? No, she'd played the martyr and the victim and Janet's arrival in her life had given her the perfect opportunity to get out of Dodge without ever offering a word of apology for having left so abruptly.

Not that she could have cured his alcoholism by letting him know she was leaving him, or secured a guarantee that he repay what he'd borrowed, but at least she would have been what she claimed she so admired: a straight-shooter. She could have let him know that she would always care about the alcoholic...wish him well, as Claire said she did Sebastian...but tell him she was moving out of their shared apartment in town because she couldn't live with his alcoholism. Their parting would have been clean...*honest*...and she wouldn't have to duck in a doorway, shamefaced at her cowardly behavior, whenever she saw Shep coming down the street in Jackson Hole.

The truth was, she'd allowed their situation to get so bad without laying her cards on the table that she ultimately packed her belongings while he was performing in a rodeo in Montana and fled back to the Crooked C Ranch, refusing to answer his emails or take his calls when he returned to the quarters they'd shared for two years. Even to this day, she had never told him face-to-face the cold, honest truth that his drinking—not him—had driven her away. When sober, Shep had been a considerate, lovely man. She never told him that, either.

*A real Dr. Jekyll and Mr. Hyde, that cowboy...*

True enough, but her sins of omission were the same ones she'd branded Sebastian with.

Shaken by such uncomfortable self-reflection, Meredith wandered into the bathroom, turned on the noisy taps, and decided she would first have a long, hot soak in order to greet the day. She watched the steaming water fill the tub and thought of the claw-and-ball bath in Sebastian's one-room loft above the former livery stable. She suddenly imagined herself driving to Cow Hollow Farm, today, to pay a call on Susanna Jenner at her weaving studio to see if there might be some items that were suitable to sell in the Barton Hall Gift Shop.

Her second mission, she decided suddenly, would be to have a private, serious heart-to-heart with Sebastian Pryce, win or lose.

*And if she lost?* challenged a voice in her head.

Well, she already had her airline ticket and would make certain that she made the flight out of Heathrow on time.

⁂

Just as Meredith was stepping into her bath, Sebastian wheeled his car into the rear courtyard and sprinted toward the door to Barton Hall's mudroom and pantry. He was unsettled to see both Richard and Claire sitting across from each other having coffee—along with Blythe—at the kitchen table. Several trays of scones were lined up beside them, the biscuits waiting their turn in the oven. Clearly, the trio had been up early, ticking off the chores of that morning as required when owners of a big estate like Barton Hall had few staff upon whom to delegate such menial chores. He marveled at how hard everyone worked to keep the mammoth operation going in the wake of tough economic times that had faced most of Britain of late. What a shame, he thought, suddenly, the Barton-Teagues wouldn't have the extra income from the obedience school he and Meredith had established over the summer. Classes could have continued at least until

October, he figured glumly.

"Why, Sebastian!" Blythe said, rising to welcome him. "Hello, again. Really, we should have offered you a guest room last evening after all you did for us yesterday. Come in, come in! Have some coffee and a nice, fresh scone."

"Good morning all," he said, with a brief nod to Richard and Claire. "I apologize for not calling first. Has Meredith come down yet?"

"Soon, I think," Blythe said. "I heard bath water running when I walked down the upstairs hall, not ten minutes ago. We've all slept in a bit this morning, except for Richard and Claire, here. What a day we had yesterday," she added, shaking her head. "I can't thank you and Rex enough for all you did to help us find Janet, to say nothing of those sheep."

"How *is* Janet this morning?" he asked, concern etched on his features.

"Meredith and I had a pretty rough night with her but I checked her again before I came down to breakfast and she's still asleep, poor dear. You just missed Lucas who took Lucy and Matthew to meet their teachers for the coming year. I thought I'd do the same for Janet later this afternoon." She smiled in Richard's direction and shook her head. "Summer's truly winding to a close, isn't it? Richard will be heading back to Oxford in a week, won't you sweetheart?"

Richard glanced briefly at Claire.

"Yes...but I'll be down to Cornwall whenever I can."

Blythe nodded. "We are going to miss you madly, but still, it makes sense for you to complete University, even if you decide later that you want to go to the Cordon Bleu."

"I didn't quite see that at first," Richard said with a sheepish smile cast in Claire's direction, "but now I do, too." Claire and Richard exchanged fond glances while

Sebastian regarded his former lover closely.

To his surprise, she smiled at *him* from across the table and said, "Blythe and I will hold the fort in the culinary department over the next few months. Things are already slowing down as the tourist season draws to a close," she continued, adding with a wink at Richard, "but Christmastime is something else entirely, Mr. Teague!" She gave Blythe's stepson a playful tap on his sleeve. "With the hordes of day-trippers demanding their fancy, holiday teas, you are going to need some serious tutelage in mastering Barton Hall's famous *Buche de Noel*."

Blythe laughed. "We're famous for *that?* Well, it's news to me, Claire, but if you two want to put us on the map for producing fancy chocolate confections this year, it's fine with us."

"We're going to play every culinary angle we can conjure, including our new Facebook page we're designing for the Barton Hall Tea Room, touting all our homemade holiday delicacies, right Richard? I'll make you a full-fledged baker, yet!"

"Absolutely right," he agreed with a wide grin. "Long live our *Buche de Noel*—which I've only recently learned from Claire is a miniature Yule log one can *eat,* made out of dark chocolate cake and rich cream. It's a brilliant concept!"

Just then, a voice from the servant's stairwell broke in quietly, "Well, good morning everyone. Planning Christmas already?"

With Holly at Meredith's feet, she and Sebastian stared at each other across the space of slate flooring that separated them. For his part, the presence of three others in the kitchen dissolved and he only was aware of a beautiful, slender figure in tight-fitting jeans and a cable-knit sweater standing before him with slightly damp, caramel-colored hair grazing her shoulders.

"Meredith..." he began.

"I can't believe you're here. I was just going to grab a cup of coffee and come see you today."

"You were? How splendid!"

His uncertainty about how she would receive this unscheduled visit abated slightly. He closed the distance between them, acutely aware, however, of the audience listening to their every word.

"I...I need to talk to you..."

"Yes, I suppose we need to tie up some loose ends about the obedience classes before next week," she replied, and he wondered if her casually mentioning her departure plans in front of Blythe and Richard signaled things had gone too far to be mended between them.

"Well, here's the thing," he said, feeling an awkwardness he hadn't experienced since the female gender first came into his consciousness as a teenager. He glanced with increasing embarrassment at the trio gazing raptly at Meredith and him with expressions that ranged from amusement to concern. "I think we should...should—"

"Look, you two," interrupted Claire, reaching for a biscuit tin and putting several freshly baked scones into it. "Why don't you take these down to Painter's Cottage and have a nice, long natter?" Next, she addressed Sebastian directly. "Will you please just tell her you're crazy about her and don't want her to leave?"

"I already have, but really, Claire!" Sebastian said, with an embarrassed glance at the lady of the house, "I doubt *you're* exactly the person who should be advising me."

Totally ignoring him, Claire pointed a finger at Meredith while Blythe and Richard looked on with bemused expressions. "And *you*, Ms. Meredith," Claire continued, "you had better see if this chap can tell you what's on his mind—and in his heart—any better than he could several years ago." Her glance included everyone, now. "And will all of you please remove yourselves from this kitchen?" She stepped away from the table, pointed to the trays of uncooked scones and rolls, and then swiveled her head, saying to Richard, "Except *you*, of course. Here, come help me get these heavy, bloody things into the oven, will you?"

Claire's audience, mouths agape, watched while she opened the Aga's lower cast iron door. Despite her commands, everyone remained frozen in place, astonished by Barton Hall's chef so suddenly having taken control in such a charged atmosphere. She smiled crookedly. "Well, for goodness sakes, if we want world peace around here by Christmas, we're just going to have to forgive and forget! Right, Sebastian?"

All eyes shifted to the tall figure clad in the red and black anorak with "Cornwall Search and Rescue Team" emblazoned on the back.

"As a matter of fact, Claire," he said, "you couldn't be more correct." He turned to Meredith. "Painter's Cottage?"

She hesitated for the briefest moment and then nodded. "Sure. Why not? I'll carry the scones."

The two turned toward the pantry, walked through to the mudroom and donned their boots in silence.

"Shall we take the dogs?" Sebastian asked finally. Rex raised his head from where he'd been lounging outside the door. Holly had followed Meredith and was furiously wagging her stubby tail at the sight of her canine visitor.

Meredith considered the suggestion for a moment and then couldn't suppress a faint smile at the sight of her dog's enthusiasm at seeing Rex through the mudroom's screen door.

"Well...sure. They can have a good run in the field down there."

Both dogs hopped into the back of Sebastian's car and their happy sounds filled the continued silence between Sebastian and Meredith as they made the short drive from Barton Hall to the cliffs overlooking the English Channel whose waters had turned aquamarine in the morning sun.

Within minutes, the green Mini drew up to the side of the road and Sebastian swiftly exited the driver's side to open the gate. The biscuit tin in hand, Meredith filed past the herringbone stonewall that bisected the field where Painter's Cottage sat perched on the cliff. To the left of its moss-covered slate roof, sweet-faced sheep grazed peacefully on a larger expanse of land overlooking a sea sparkling under clear skies.

Both dogs looked at their companions questioningly until Sebastian motioned to them and said, "It's okay...go on...have a good gambol in the fields, you two."

"But mind, Holly, *no* sheep!" Meredith called after her sternly.

In unison, the dogs turned their backs and Rex took off across the grass that sloped down to the cliff with Holly running behind him as fast as her short legs would carry her. Their happy barks faded as they raced across the field toward the cottage and not, Meredith was relieved to note, toward a small break in one of the stone walls where Holly had been known to sneak through to circle the sheep.

Meredith followed in Sebastian's booted footsteps across the expanse of damp, ankle-high grass, grateful she had worn her Wellingtons, and arrived at the oak door just as the dogs ran around the cottage to greet them.

"Sit! Stay!" Sebastian commanded as Meredith pulled the large, iron key from her back jeans pocket and opened the lock.

The sunlight that had filled her bedroom earlier upstairs at the Hall sought out even the darkest corners of the solitary room and the loft above. Ennis Trevelyan's two-hundred-year-old seascapes seem to glow in the shafts of golden light illuminating the cottage. At Sebastian's directive, Rex and Holly immediately trotted over to the cold hearth and settled down beside one another on the hand-hooked area rug carpeting the wooden floor nearby.

'It's the first of September. I guess summer is giving it one last push," she commented, setting the tin full of scones on the narrow counter in the galley kitchen.

She heard Sebastian walk up behind her, standing close while he put a hand on each sweater-clad shoulder.

"I wanted to have this conversation last night," he began, "but I think, this time, you were the one who ducked it."

"I think you're right," she replied, turning to face him and finding herself within the circle of his arms. "I got tired of waiting for days for you to say something—anything—about why you stomped out of here and went directly to Claire's place. Last night I didn't wait for you to return because I was drained and tired."

"It's taken me a while to come to you, I admit it," he said with an expression that seemed to imply he was asking for her forbearance, "When Wainwright dropped the bombshell that you were leaving, I decided I could no longer avoid finally having a sane discussion with you about what happened years ago between Claire and me."

"And the reason you went to Claire's cottage last Saturday night was…?" Meredith asked, attempting to keep a neutral tone of voice.

"To have a not-so-sane conversation with *her*, only I realized she already had company."

"But in the days that followed your leaving here, why not have that discussion with *me*?" she demanded, turning away to busy herself with opening the tin of scones to keep from throwing it at him in frustration. "I asked you to often enough, didn't I? But you just left me hanging…again."

"You were persistent, no doubt about that," he agreed. He moved to the side and she could feel him studying her profile. "Look, Meredith, I realized as soon as I'd gotten to the car that night I stormed out of here that I'd behaved like a complete numbskull, but I was pretty hot under the collar and I guess a lot of pent up anger propelled me to drive over to Claire's to have it out with her, once and for all."

"And?" Meredith asked over her shoulder.

"As soon as I got to Limekiln Cottage and I realized Richard was in there with her, I just stood at her front door for a bit and then I left," he said turning to gaze out the window at the bright morning sun that had turned the water rushing onto the beach a deep sapphire. "I suppose Rex's leash fell from the car when I got out in a hurry."

"You didn't even come back here for him."

"I was embarrassed, and I figured we could sort things out in the morning when we both weren't so upset."

"But you never offered to do that—and it's been over a week."

"Since I never had the conversation with Claire, I wasn't ready to talk to anyone about the past, especially you."

"I know," she said quietly. "Claire told me she'd never seen you that night when I asked her."

"You asked her about us the day you found the leash?"

"No, we talked last night, actually, when you went with Lucas and Richard to fix the fence and bring back the sheep."

Sebastian walked over to the desk and stared out the window at the sweep of coastline arching toward Doman Point.

"When I knew you'd found the leash in front of Claire's, I was even more at a loss where to begin to unravel this shameful tale."

"So you said nothing. You did nothing. You just left me hanging," she repeated.

He turned and said, "I did, and that was shameful, too. And I hope you'll forgive me for that. I did a lot of *thinking*, though, since I saw you and Beven that day. I wanted to find an opportunity to hash it out with Claire first, before I came to you, but in my typical fashion, I took my bloody time about it, and then three days ago our prize cow got sick..."

"Maybe it just wasn't a priority," Meredith said quietly. "Sorting out *our* misunderstandings, I mean. Or even just making a phone call. You figured I'd just wait around."

Sebastian grimaced. "No, that wasn't it at all. Anyone who's been around me these last days can testify to my miserable state of mind. But I'm such a typical, boring Brit, Meredith," he said, shaking his head in disgust, "and like so many of us idiotic blokes, I am an expert at avoiding confrontation. You know...the "Keep Calm and Carry On" philosophy we've talked about before? As you can see, that approach to life is absolute rubbish in certain situations and has continued to make my life a total cock-up."

"Well, as you know, I did speak to Claire, but not because I brought it up," Meredith disclosed, "but because she did."

Sebastian appeared startled. "What did she say?"

"That she's pretty much succeeded putting whatever happened between you behind her. She eventually offered to tell me what happened if I wanted her to."

"Did you ask her, then?"

Meredith shook her head. "No. I figured if you weren't going to tell me yourself, we shouldn't be together because you don't trust me, really, and—"

"Oh, I *do* trust you, Meredith. It's myself I haven't trusted."

"Well, whatever has been holding you back from dealing with your past, I've come to see that I don't want to spend my life with someone who won't let me in. Who makes me wait and wait when my heart is…so sore. All week, I've been telling myself to make peace with that decision and go home."

"And have you?" he asked, taking a step toward her. "Made peace with not being with me?"

Meredith felt her eyes grow moist. "I thought I had," she said, her voice breaking.

She quickly turned and focused her eyes on the open tin of scones so he wouldn't see she was about to burst into tears.

"You said that Claire initiated the conversation. What was on her mind?"

"She wanted me to know that as far as she was concerned, it was long over between the two of you," Meredith replied. "Mostly, she wanted to talk about Richard. She said she's truly in love with him—and I must say, I believe her. I think she genuinely cares for him and supports his returning to Oxford this autumn while she remains at Barton Hall working for the Barton-Teagues. Who knows how that will all turn out?"

"Bloody amazing," Sebastian said, almost to himself. "But to be quite honest, as this summer unfolded, I could see she's changed. Quite a lot, actually."

"Maybe that's why you went to Limekiln Cottage?" Meredith asked, making a show of putting the teakettle on to boil. "For old times' sake? To see if there was anything salvageable so you two might patch things up."

Sebastian took two steps toward her, seized her arm,

and spun her around.

"You are deliberately misunderstanding me!"

"No I'm not!" she cried. "I just want to know the *answer*."

Meredith turned back toward the kitchen counter so he wouldn't see the tears that had once again begun to edge into the corner of her eyes.

Sebastian reached for her, gently turned her to face him once more, and folded her in his arms, their bodies touching head-to-toe. She was instantly conscious of the way her head fit neatly under his chin. Worse yet, the comforting warmth of his flannel shirt against her cheek made her want to forget fighting any battles for truth or honesty in their relationship.

"Please don't do this," she said weakly. "Please let me leave with some shred of myself intact."

"Dear, kind, sweet, open-hearted Meredith," he said softly, kissing the top of her head. "I've made you play a terrible guessing game since that night I left here, haven't I? Can you forgive me for that?"

"No," she whispered.

The tears that pricked her eyes were now spilling down her cheeks. She used both palms against his chest to escape from his grasp.

"You've kept me guessing since the day I *met* you, do you realize that?" she exclaimed. "And, given all the other drama in my life this summer—coping with Janet and leaving Shep behind, and worrying about how my Dad is doing on the ranch—I know when I've reached my limit. I just want to be where there's some serenity in my life!"

She was fighting desperately to get a hold of her emotions. But instead of regaining her equilibrium as she took several deep breaths, a sudden wave of anger and frustration took hold.

She looked up at him full in the face and declared, "Sebastian Pryce, I've told you practically everything there is to know about myself—and except for your blurting out the terrible thing your mother said to you and your poor brothers when your sister drowned—you've explained virtually nothing about the course of critical events that have basically governed your entire adult life! And you know what? " she demanded rhetorically. "I'm tired of trying to read your mind all the time! I want a man in my life who occasionally lets me into his thoughts...and his *heart*!"

"That's why I'm here, now—"

Meredith abruptly walked past him and began pacing in front of the floor-to-ceiling artist windows that overlooked the sea.

"And when it comes to Claire and why you broke up...and your crazy, suicidal choice of enlisting in the Afghan bomb squad...and then coming back to Cornwall after Vet school and becoming a virtual recluse and signing up to be some holy Rescue Ranger to people who have fallen down mine shafts, and systematically shutting out those who really *care* about you—I'm *sick to death* of attempting to figure you out!"

Meredith buried her face in her hands, and fought against the sobs that had now moved from her throat to her chest.

"Come here, come here, darling," he soothed, stepping forward as he put one arm around her, holding her close to him and pressed her head against his shoulder with his other hand. "Those are a lot of questions buried in that one, long, declarative sentence, and if you'll just allow me a chance, I'll—"

Once again, she struggled to escape from his embrace, but his superior strength kept her trapped within the circle of his arms.

"I don't care what your answers are any longer!" she cried, her words muffled by his chest.

"Oh, yes you do," he crooned softly, "so you're not going anywhere yet, because I intend to volunteer answers to every single query about me and my past, whether you want to hear my responses or not. We can remain here all night, if we have to."

Just then, the teakettle began whistling, a piercing sound that cut off all conversation. Sebastian reluctantly loosened his grip, following Meredith to the stove and watching while she jerked the kettle off the hob.

She set the pot down on the countertop with a thud. "Why *now*, she demanded. "Why wait so long? Why didn't you—"

"Because I'm a slow learner," he said, removing her hand from the kettle. "And because a prize cow got sick three days ago. And because I've never met a woman like you…a woman I've come to see I can trust so completely." He popped a few PG Tips teabags into the brown ceramic pot and poured the water into it himself. "I don't think I've had a decent night's sleep in a week—and all because of *you*."

"And your cow," she said with a sniff, reaching for a piece of paper toweling to blow her nose.

Sebastian nodded. "Yes, our prize cow can be blamed for part of my silence, but I truly couldn't bear it another minute feeling the way I did ever since I slammed out of here. And when Colonel Wainwright announced you'd bought your ticket to the States, the thought of your leaving Cornwall…perhaps for good… *finally* made me see what a total wassack I've been—"

"Wassack? Sounds like a jerk?"

"An arse…ass…and I've been one regarding certain

subjects for quite a long time, I'm embarrassed to admit."

"For three months, at least," she declared, folding her arms across her chest.

"I'd call it more like three years, at least," he countered, "and probably longer, according to Claire, who had much the same complaints you do: that I'm secretive, elusive, damnably moody sometimes, and never say what's on my mind. And it only got worse after the blow up with her when we were living together in St. Austell."

Meredith took her seat at the small table and folded her hands in her lap, not saying a word. Sebastian carried the teapot and the tin of scones and placed them in front of her and then went back to retrieve two mugs and a small jug of milk.

"Looking back, I was definitely tough to live with in those days," he offered hesitantly, as he poured the amber liquid into both mugs. "I had so many unsettled issues with my mum. Claire and I were young and with wildly different temperaments. She loved a good party…loved to cook, even back then, and I hated having a lot of people in our place with whom I'd have to make small talk. We were chalk and cheese really, but—"

Meredith laughed, breaking the intensity that had been steadily filling all corners of the cottage. "But the sex was good, am I right?"

Sebastian took a seat across the table from her with a decidedly embarrassed expression. Meredith poured milk into their tea and looked at him over the brim.

"I only say that, mind you, based on rather circumstantial, but definitely first-hand evidence," she continued with a glance both encouraging and mildly flirtatious as she continued to sip from her mug.

Sebastian nodded, a small grin tugging at the corners of his mouth. "Well, when one is in one's mid-twenties and male, sex is definitely on the mind, and one tends to be attracted to certain...ah...physical, exterior attributes and puts up with a lot of things that aren't so appealing..."

"What sort of things?" she interrupted cautiously, sensing they were approaching the crux of the tale.

"At first, I ignored Claire's own mercurial moods when she couldn't persuade me to be the same sort of person she was. Then, I realized that a couple of nights a week she was starting to come back to our flat quite late and having drunk a great deal more than was good for her. She'd taken a job as a waitress in a first-rate restaurant, and then became a salad maker and eventually apprenticed herself to the pastry chef. Within a month or so after that, she said she had to work late and would stay at a girlfriend's once or twice a week so she wouldn't wake me up coming home. The truth was—"

"She was having an affair," Meredith guessed.

Sebastian nodded. "With an owner-chef at the restaurant by the name of Charles. Can't blame her, really. I was flailing around, not knowing what I should do beyond working for my uncle at his dairy farm—which I hated because it was being run as if we were in the last century."

"But what prompted the...big explosion with Claire?" she asked carefully. "Sounds pretty run-of-the-mill stuff to me. I'd call it garden-variety incompatibility."

"I wish *we'd* called it that and put ourselves out of our misery. But instead, we just muddled on, neither of us saying what was really bothering us about our life together."

"Big mistake," Meredith said, wagging a finger at him. "We should know."

"Definitely," Sebastian agreed. "The problem was, it turned out that Claire was having regular, sexual relations a couple of times each week with both the chef as well as with yours truly. When I found out, and confronted her—

fairly cruelly, I must confess—she sobbed that she really wanted to be with *me*, but that I had been so cold and uncommunicative towards her and that Charles saw they could be a team at the restaurant. He'd told her she was his dream girl, and so on. For her part, Claire found him a friendlier port in the storm, which, of course, was understandable, given what an absolute blighter I was being, mostly due to my on-going war with my mother about how she was neglecting my two younger brothers."

"Wow…" Meredith said on a breath. "That's a tangle, all right."

"Oh but it got worse," Sebastian said, pausing to take a deep draught of his tea.

"Worse?" echoed Meredith, a myriad of possible unhappy scenarios skittering through her brain. "Worse, how?"

# CHAPTER 20

Sebastian's gaze was glued to the top of the teapot and Meredith wondered briefly if he would continue the story of his tumultuous parting of the ways with Claire.

After a long pause he said, "Claire begged for us not to break up. To prove she wanted a fresh start, she quit her job and swore off her restaurant bloke and started a computer course. The problem was, we were both still miserable, as you can well imagine, because she'd loved learning the food business and hated being cooped up in an office, and I remained unhappy working for my uncle. And then, a month later..."

Sebastian brought his hand to his face and pinched the bridge of his nose as if he'd suddenly been assaulted by a splitting headache.

Meredith said, "Let me guess again: she discovered she was pregnant."

Sebastian looked up and met her gaze across the table. "Pregnant...with *twins*, the doctor had said, and completely mystified as to who was the father."

"Oh, no," Meredith groaned.

"One day soon after this confession, she came home from her medical appointment in a hysterical state. It seems the babies were two distinctly different weights, with one significantly smaller."

"I don't understand. Was one failing to thrive?"

"Tests were done and both fetuses were developing normally."

Meredith looked at him questioningly. "I don't understand?"

"Few people realize that a woman can be impregnated by two different male donors, so to speak, when two ovum are present in the same menstrual cycle."

Meredith's eyes widened as the impact of Sebastian's explanation began to dawn on her. "So you're say that, technically these were 'fraternal twins,' but the two eggs were fertilized by sperm from two *different* males?" she murmured. "I think I heard about this phenomenon when I was in nursing school."

"The difference in body weights could have been attributed to the fact I am over six feet tall and Charles is a very slender five-feet-ten. It was at this point that Claire spilled her concerns to the doctor and he informed her that, yes, it was possible that she had two different fathers for her two babies."

Meredith gazed across the small kitchen table in Painter's Cottage, unable to disguise the shock that Sebastian's revelations was having on her. Was Sebastian about to tell her that Claire and he had a child—or two— tucked away somewhere in the hills of Cornwall?

Rather than voicing her fears, she said, "A very obscure paragraph in one of my nursing texts is starting to come back to me. You probably know this, now…that a set of fraternal twins with different fathers is called 'heteropaternal superfecundation.'"

"Quite a mouthful," he agreed, "and yes, I found that out when I immediately did an Internet search and discovered that multiple sires are a common occurrence in animals such as dogs and cats. Stray dogs, for instance, often produce litters in which every puppy has a different father."

"But it's pretty darn rare in humans," Meredith said, the import of the situation starting to sink in.

"Very. A doctor friend looked it up in the literature and actually congratulated me for how rarely twins with two different fathers occurred—two point four percent—among human twins that originate as two separate ovum in a single menstrual cycle. However, multiple births run on *both* sides of Claire's family, so the odds of her being a 'double yolker,' as the good doctor so elegantly put it to me, were obviously higher."

Meredith took a long sip from her mug of tea to steady her nerves. "You know," she mused, "I remember reading in one of those supermarket tabloids about a custody suit over a set of fraternal twins, one baby Caucasian and the other definitely African American." She looked across the table, adding, "A definite 'Oops' for the mother after she delivered the babies."

"But when all parties are the same race—"

"There is no way of knowing with certainty without a DNA test of both fetuses if the embryos were fertilized by the same sperm donor, or by two different men," Meredith concluded glumly, wondering if the babies had, perhaps, been put up for adoption?

"Correct. There was no way of knowing parentage, especially given the fact that Claire was sleeping regularly with both Charles and myself around the time of conception of each."

"This is unbelievable…that this actually happened to you two."

"To us five." Sebastian shook his head. "It was pretty horrific. Charles wanted to claim parentage of both babies. I felt righteously betrayed by everyone involved and stormed out, demanding a paternity test and threatening to hire a solicitor, which I didn't have the funds to do, anyway. It was a royal donnybrook. So without telling either of us, Claire cracked under the pressure and simply disappeared for a week, saying she'd gone to visit her sister."

"And?" Meredith murmured, and realized she was holding her breath.

"She had an abortion." He paused. "Actually, make that two abortions."

"Oh God," Meredith said on a low moan. She could only imagine the torture Claire must have gone through to have taken such action, and then been faced with two raging bulls in the aftermath of her decision.

Sebastian nodded. "She was scared, shamed by me, and hounded by Charles. I, of course, was duly enraged by her betrayal. Charles, who was a Catholic, was heartbroken, furious, and afraid we'd go to hell. He tracked me down to tell me what she'd done, what a bastard I'd been, and that it was my fault Claire had made that decision."

"Did you believe that?"

Sebastian paused and then replied, "All three of us obviously played a part in the debacle, but at the time, I did, in fact, feel responsible for everybody's pain, including my own." He shook his head. "Who knows? Perhaps if we'd acted like the adults that we were far from being back then and sat down and talked it over, there might have been different choices made—or *together*, we might have decided Claire's course of action was, in fact, for the best...or at least Claire and I might have reached whatever decisions were ultimately made by deciding them together. As it was, it just remained a large, painful wound—for all three of us, I suspect."

"When you're in the middle of a tragedy like that, you just want to hide...or at least I do," she said softly.

"Well, speaking only for myself, mind you, I think I

went a little crazy. I was nearly thirty, but I suddenly felt like that helpless ten-year-old, unable to save my sister from the crashing waves, or sooth my grief-stricken mum. I started morbidly obsessing about how my sister had her life snuffed out at such an early age and how my mother 'wished it had been one of her boys'—and I couldn't stop imagining those two innocent, unborn children that perhaps I had created. Or *one* of whom might have been my child..."

"Oh, Sebastian..." Meredith murmured when he raised his hands to cover his face. She longed to throw her arms around him and offer comfort, but instead, she remained in her chair with the table between them, waiting for him to complete this unhappy saga.

Finally, his hands fell to his sides and he said, "One night, I went storming into the restaurant where I punched Charles in the face and then sped back to our old flat to tell Claire what a murderess I considered her to be." Moisture gathered in the corner of his eyes and his voice broke. "I just *lost* it that day when she came to the door. I went into an absolutely bloody, awful *rage* that had as much—or even more—to do with all the problems embedded in my own youth than with the choices she'd made. After a rather long rant, I marched out of the flat, filled with righteous anger, and never looked back."

"Instead, you headed for the Army recruiting office."

"In Plymouth," he agreed with a nod. "I wouldn't sign the papers until I was guaranteed a post with the bomb squad, hoping, I truly think, that I'd get blown to smithereens the first week."

"But you didn't, thank God," she whispered. *How much pain we subject ourselves to*, she thought, recalling the costs both to Shep and to her for her not having the courage to look him in the eye and compassionately tell him the truth:

that she cared for him but couldn't tolerate his drinking and for her own sanity's sake, she had to say goodbye. She wiped her eye on a napkin and then handed it to Sebastian for the same purpose. "It's kind of a miracle you're still here, don't you think?"

Sebastian gave a depreciating shrug.

"My wonderful dog, Max, kept me out of trouble scores of times. He was my good angel, that's for certain. That amazing nose of his kept me safe."

"And you never again spoke to Claire until the afternoon you saw her come out of the back door of Barton Hall with a chef's apron on?"

"I never did," he admitted. "I've let her be the wicked one and me the martyr until only very recently. I'd heard through William she'd gotten a job at Moorlands, but I didn't set a boot in that creamery until the day I met you and Blythe in the car park, and fortunately, I'd not seen her then, either."

"And how bizarre that Claire should be hired to work at Barton Hall."

"Well, seeing her again, I was forced to notice how different she seemed."

"How so?"

"Well, when I noticed the way she and Richard were together. How they labored side-by-side for a common purpose and were kind and thoughtful toward each other and shared laughter as well as the hard work of the meals they put on all summer. How could I ignore the fact that they had forged a much healthier relationship than the way she and I had been?"

"I can understand why now you might have some have regrets, Sebastian."

He reached across the table and covered the hands she'd wrapped around her tea mug with his own two.

Forcing her to look at him, he said, "Claire and I would never have been able to sustain the spark that had fanned up between us back then, Meredith, even if we'd been open and honest about every thought in our heads." With the first hint of amusement she'd seen in days, he added, "Chalk and cheese, I tell you…we were chalk and cheese. I had realized that about Claire and me long before you arrived that day when Rex, over there, behaved like such a lothario. And then, there *you* were," he continued with a tenderness that caught her off-guard. "My dream dog-lover…gorgeous and kind and funny and ultimately accepting of me, despite my dark side," he said with the grin that could always transform his entire expression.

"Dark is right," she said, mildly. "But I need to say something to you before you hand out any more compliments."

"What do you mean?"

"I realized—fairly recently myself, by the way—that I brought a few things to the table here that weren't so great…some of which came with me from across the Atlantic."

"Like what?" he asked curiously. He seized a spoon to swirl the teabags around in the big, brown pot a few times.

Meredith reached for the tin of scones and began putting them on a plate with a container of clotted cream and a small jar of raspberry jam.

"Like with Shep."

"Ah…the past complicating the present once again," he said, nodding.

"Like I never told him *why* I left. At the time, I thought it was obvious—his drinking—and that there was no point even discussing anything. But there would have been a point telling him *how* his drinking affected my life. Instead, I just moved out all my things when he was off riding in a rodeo, and I split."

"Split?"

"Left. Departed. I took the chicken way out and just wrote a note saying 'Don't call me, don't write me, don't attempt to get in touch with me by any means whatsoever.' And I virtually hid out at the ranch and told Security at my hospital not to let him get past the elevators—drunk or sober."

"A nice girl like you did all that?"

"And I let my Dad drive into town and yell the same thing to his face! "

Sebastian let out a low whistle. "That does sound pretty severe."

Meredith nodded. "So you see, I'm guilty of some of the same avoidance tricks you are," she said. "I turned tail and ran."

"Well, perhaps you felt the chap was dangerous to be around?" he suggested.

"But I could still have found a time and a safe place, like at my hospital with a third party present, to tell him calmly and with some compassion why I was ending it...why I wanted to move back to the ranch. He had a *disease*. When he wasn't drinking, he was a very sweet, loving man—and he loved *me*. Very much, I think. I owed telling him I loved him, too. Instead, I ran away, just like you did."

"Loved?" Sebastian repeated, his brow furrowed.

Meredith nodded. "I still care what happens to him, Sebastian, but like you and Claire, we would never be right together and my running away was the only way I knew to save myself from the insanity."

"Well, you know something? I am good and sick of— what did you say? Being a person who 'turned tail and ran,' aren't you?"

"Yes. Wholeheartedly sick of it."

"And there *is* such a thing as some people simply being a better match, wouldn't you say?"

"Probably…" she agreed, then, thinking of the love match between Lucas and Blythe, amended, "Yes, definitely."

He pushed away from the table and stood to his full height, gazing at her with a glint in his eye. "Would you care to allow me to demonstrate?"

Sebastian unzipped his anorak and hung it on the back of the chair.

Meredith gestured at his parka with a chuckle, "I guess you *do* intend to stay for a second cup of tea?"

Sebastian grinned. "See what I mean? You make me laugh and you're one of those people who are surrounded by sunshine. You balance me in a way no other woman has in my entire life."

"My yin to your yang? Or is it the other way 'round?"

"I have no idea what you're talking about. Come here, will you please?"

Meredith stood up and he immediately came to her side, encasing each of her shoulders in his large hands. "You know, I've never have told a single soul the entire, reprehensible tale about Claire and me. Until you."

"So why now?" she asked. And then blurted out the first thing that popped into her head. "Because I'm leaving in few days, right? You can tell one person and then be done with this sad chapter and never to have to speak of it again. A one-stop shop catharsis."

Sebastian looked at her with an expression that at first registered confusion. Then he shook his head in frustration.

"No!" he declared, pulling her close so they stood nose-to-nose. "I'm telling you all this because I want you to know everything about me…everything that comes in the package you'll be getting if I can somehow, some way, convince you not to leave Cornwall. To stay here. With me."

"But I've booked my ticket, and—"

"Do you understand what I'm saying here, Meredith?" he demanded.

"I'm not sure," she replied slowly, aware that she almost felt light-headed in the heat of his unwavering stare. "You want me to postpone  my—"

"Not postpone! I'm saying don't go. *Be* with me."

"In Cornwall?"

"Yes, in Cornwall!" he exclaimed, exasperated.

"And then what?" she asked. "I have my job at the hospital...I can't live off my relatives forever."

"For a smart woman, you are being woefully clueless, my Meredith."

"I am not your Meredith," she said quietly.

"No?"

His dark brows knit together once again and worry reflected in his eyes. Her tone had wounded him, she was sure, but she was done with trying to *surmise* what he meant when his words remained fairly cryptic.

"You want to hear it straight?" she said, vexed in a way she could hardly explain, even to herself. "I've had an...interesting summer, but—"

"I want you to *stay* in Cornwall!" he interrupted her. "I want you to move in with me at Cow Hollow Farm, or I'll move in with you here at Painter's Cottage or Barton Hall, if your relatives will have me." He ran the fingers of one hand through his dark hair as worry and urgency combined to produce words in a rush. "I want us to continue to run a canine obedience school together here—again, if the Barton-Teagues will have us—and share the profits with them. I want you to be on the Cornwall Search and Rescue

Team with me. I'd like to be a large animal veterinarian with my own practice someday, and also open a rare breed farm animal station on some land we buy with a house on it—I don't know how—but near Barton Hall so people can learn about the nearly extinct species that today's farm animals descended from and why we mustn't *let* these creatures go extinct! " He paused and inhaled deeply, "But most of all, Meredith Champlin, I want you to be my *wife*. Can I *be* any more specific than that?"

Meredith could only look at him, speechless, a million thoughts whirling in her mind. When she didn't answer immediately, he crossed again to the floor-to-ceiling window and stared through the glass.

Over his shoulder he said, "Perhaps this grand confession I've made here today elaborating all my sins offends you as much as my previous silences?"

Meredith buried her face in her hands, then looked up. She quickly ran to where he was now looking sightlessly at the panorama of sea and sky and curving coastline.

"Oh, God, no!" she cried, throwing her arms around his waist and pressing the right side of her face between his shoulder blades. "Come on, Sebastian! That's a whole, big speech you just gave. It's a lot for me to take in all at once."

He removed her hands from his waist and turned around, searching her face for the answer he sought. Meredith smiled.

"You've just made the longest, most heartfelt *proposal* ever spoken by a man accustomed to talking mainly to *dogs!*" she marveled, amazed that she could have woken up this morning as blue as she'd ever felt in her life, and now she could be one of those birds outside the cottage's tall windows, darting and dancing on the wind just beyond the cliff. She held out her arms. "Come here, you big lug! "

He stared at her with a puzzled expression. "Lug?

What's that?"

She dropped her arms to her sides. "Oh, hell...do you think we'll be trying to explain the English language for the rest of our lives? A lug is a loveable, friendly bear of a guy...maybe a little clumsy, but a—"

"Oh!" he laughed. "I'd say that's a rather apt description!"

She cupped his face in her hands, standing on tiptoes to bestow a kiss with the sole intent of expressing how astonished and happy she was. Sebastian's response was immediate, as it always had been between them, and he pulled her close, his arousal swelling against her thigh.

"Okay...I feel better, now," she said in a deliberately husky, come-hither voice, "With a little good will, just look how well we finally figured things out."

Sebastian's dark eyes held her gaze. "So is that an unqualified 'yes?'"

She gazed at him soberly. "Will you accept a *qualified* 'yes'? You're asking me to leave my country, completely reorder my profession, and ask my Dad to cope with our ranch all on his own from here on out."

Sebastian glanced away as if mulling over her last words, but Meredith guessed it was to hide his disappointment.

Finally he replied, "You're right, Meredith. It's a lot to ask, based on a three-month's acquaintance. Perhaps I overstepped—"

"Look," she interrupted. "How does this sound? What if I cancel my flight for next week, see if I can get the hospital not to fire me outright, and agree to stay through Christmas, at least? We have *so* much still to learn about each other, my handsome ex-Lieutenant, but since I don't want to be anywhere *but* Cornwall—and with anyone but *you*—I say we just keep on keeping on...and see where it takes us. See if we can sustain telling each other the truth most of the time."

She held her breath as she sensed the wheels going around in his head. Sebastian had pushed himself way beyond any sort of comfort zone. Would he retreat to safety now? Tell himself, "Well, I gave it a go, but she won't agree to my terms" and withdraw to a realm where he could forever avoid the almost brutal kind of face-to-face, honest exchange they'd had today?

His brown eyes were riveted on hers and she prayed her heartfelt, loving expression conveyed the hope and confidence she had in him to get beyond some of his self-imposed hurdles. They both tended to shy away from risk in favor of self-preservation, she considered silently. But this time, it was Sebastian who must make the greater leap of faith.

"Well…" he said slowly, "A step at a time is how it will have to be, I suppose," he replied. "Perhaps I can manage a new sort of 'Keep Calm and Carry On' wherein I'll keep calm and remember to tell you what's on my mind. Would that work?"

Gratitude and relief flooding through her, Meredith nodded slowly and lifted her face to be kissed again. In response, he leaned down, pulled her even closer, brought his lips to hers, and enfolded her in an embrace that sent waves of electricity all the way to her Wellington boots. When they finally came up for air, both breathless and smiling, Meredith looked at him with a saucy smirk.

"Hey, big guy. You want to really put your money where your mouth is?"

"Yes…whatever that means," he murmured, leaning down to nuzzle the soft skin beneath her ear.

"See that bed in the loft upstairs?" she asked, indicating the steep stairs a few feet away. "I missed out on the fun of luring you up there the last time you were at Painter's Cottage, remember? "

"Arse that I was...yes, I remember."

Sebastian allowed her to take him by the hand and they slowly mounted the steps. Both Holly and Rex lifted their heads off the hearthrug inquiringly.

"Sorry, guys," Meredith said over her shoulder as she and Sebastian paused half way up the stairs. "Holly! Rex! You *stay!*" She tapped a finger on Sebastian's chest. "Sebastian! You...*find!*"

"I'm shocked, Meredith, truly shocked by your behavior," he teased, patting her gently on her shapely derriere as they continued up the stairs. "It's barely high noon. Surely, you want to talk some more?"

She cast him a startled look over her shoulder, then realized it was merely Sebastian's brand of dry British humor.

"I say no more of this idle chit-chat," she replied breezily, reaching the top stair. "I think we're finally ready to move on from all this blah, blah, blah."

They stood on the landing where Sebastian had to duck to avoid banging his head on one of the ancient beams that held up the roof.

"You'll never know how happy I am to hear you say that," he said, scooping her jeans-clad legs under one arm and clasping her shoulders with his other as if he were about to carry her over a threshold. "And besides, we have the rest of our lives to natter away."

"You think so, huh?" she murmured as he gently placed her on the bed's coverlet and settled the length of his body against hers.

"I'll have to prove it to you, won't I?" he said, gazing down at her.

"No more stony silences or storming out of cottages,

deal? As we say in the pediatric ward, 'Use your *words!*'"

"It's a bargain."

"And I vow never to go to bed without kissing you goodnight or telling you why I'm peeved—if I am—agreed?" she added, deliberately looking up at him with a steady stare. "Those few things, alone, will go a long way toward taking care of whatever might come up, don't you think?"

Sebastian's banter ceased and his expression grew solemn. "Nobody changes patterns of a lifetime in a wink of the eye, I'm afraid. And mine certainly pre-date my military service and even the time I lived with Claire..."

Meredith reached over and brushed a lock of his dark hair off his brow.

"We just have to retrain both our brains to be straight-shooters," she proposed, and then squeezed his hand in a show of understanding. "As you've seen for yourself, I can occasionally pull the same nonsense you can."

"Not nearly as severe." Sebastian cast her a wry smile. "Maybe we can have a signal or something when one of us—probably me—is ducking an issue or erecting a wall."

"How's this as a signal?" She rose up on one elbow and gently tapped his nose with her forefinger, then leaned forward and kissed each of his eyelids in succession.

"Or how about this?" He gently pushed her back against the pillows, smoothed his palm under her cable knit sweater and T-shirt, and gently cupped her right breast.

"That works for me," she answered faintly.

And then the teasing stopped as he slowly pulled her sweater over her head while she, in turn, did the same for his flannel shirt. Soon their clothes were in a careless pile at the side of the bed.

"Oh, my," she breathed as she took in the sight of a chest that still bore the signs of a highly disciplined military

man capable of repelling down a cliff or carrying an injured
six-footer across a craggy moor to safety.

"Oh, my, yourself," he whispered, drawing her body
against the length of him so she would feel his high state of
arousal nudging her abdomen. "Can you tell how much I've
missed you?"

"It was your own fault," she mumbled, "but I forgive
you, especially if you'll just let me..."

She insinuated one hand between their bodies and
heard Sebastian's breath catch. Then she felt him relax
under her gentle touch, rolling on his back and allowing her
freely to explore that most vulnerable part of him.

"Oh, my, my, *my*," she murmured, as a warm flow of
moisture between her thighs mirrored the pleasure she
could sense Sebastian was experiencing as a result of her
ministrations.

"You...are...amazing," he said on a long breath, his
fingers threading through her hair as she moved lower on
his torso, kissing and nuzzling him until she thought she
would die of pleasure. Unable to stand their separation an
instant longer, she eased her body along his upper chest
and showered it with kisses until she reached his chin. "May
I have my way with you, my good, sweet Sebastian?" she
whispered against the faint stubble grazing her skin. "I want
you so much..."

"Oh, God, Meredith...what in the world have I been
denying myself all this time?"

"A lot of lovely things, Rescue Ranger. And I am more
than happy to show you exactly what. May I—?"

Sebastian allowed his arms to fall by his side. "I think I
can hazard a guess where you intend to ..."

"Yes?" she said, smiling down at him.

"Oh, very much...yes."

Meredith bestowed feathery kisses in regions where she

imagined Sebastian may never had experienced such intimacy prior to this most momentous of days. Then, she placed her hands on either side of his chest and pulled herself along his body, high enough to be able to meet his languid gaze.

"Well, pardner..." she drawled in her best Wyoming twang, "I'll need a little assistance if I'm going to continue this Wild West show for you."

Their laughter mingled as he raised his hands to encircle her waist and lifted her hips high enough to allow her to position herself above the object of her intense desire. Their gazes locked as she slowly, and with the calculation of a courtesan, joined their bodies until she sat astride his muscular thighs. Sebastian closed his eyes, and Meredith remained silent, both her palms resting on his chest.

With small, silky movements, she gently rocked against him and smiled as his eyes opened wide and she noticed in their dark depths a dangerous spark.

"Well, now, Meredith, my love, do, please, reveal what happens next."

Meredith brushed a length of her hair behind one shoulder and said with growing confidence, "I say we open the gates and let the little filly show her stuff." And an instant later, she began to demonstrate to Sebastian the skill of the horsewoman she once had been, a continent away.

Finally, Sebastian clasped her ribs with both hands and pulled her down to his chest. In a lightening move, Meredith found herself on her back with Sebastian looming above.

"I am stunned by, and oh, so grateful for the equestrian skills of the lady from Wyoming," he said, "but don't you think turn-about is fair play?"

"Oh, yes," she whispered. "I thought you'd never move on to the next event..."

Before long, they both cried out their gratification and joy, and when their breathing slowed and their heartbeats found a steadier rhythm, Sebastian rolled them both onto their sides and pressed his forehead against hers, their eyes inches apart.

"Do you know the moment when I first started to fall in love with you?" he murmured.

"When I yelled at you that Rex was trying to have it on with poor Holly the first day we met?" she whispered, adding with mock seriousness, "*Do* remember, please, that he didn't succeed."

Sebastian leaned the back of his head into the pillow and laughed.

"That should have warned me that you and your dog might be quite a handful." Then his expression sobered. "No, it was when you slumped against the wall in the smuggler's cave and cried with relief when we found Janet that time. I thought to myself, 'This is a woman who genuinely cares about others...and is not afraid to show how she feels.' And then on the day you joined us on the search for the little boy we thought might have fallen down the mind shaft—"

"But he'd climbed up on the old smelting stack," she said, completing his thought. "God, remember how his leg was bent under him? That was a pretty horrendous break."

"You were quite amazing that day, Nurse Meredith," he said, wrapping a strand of her hair around his forefinger. "I could just imagine how brilliant you must have been in that children's intensive care ward—"

"Brilliant? Not brilliant."

"Great. Competent. Wonderful," he translated, "but also, how much it must have taken out of you to do that work. In an incredible flash, I could imagine you staying here, living in Cornwall employing those skills in a way that wouldn't drain your spirit quite as much. And then, in the next instant, I imagined myself with you permanently in my life. And despite all the misery I'd experienced with Claire's pregnancy and its aftermath, I could envision you as a mother...and I wanted that for you."

Touched beyond her ability to reply, Meredith just stared at him, love and gratitude for his heartfelt words flowing from her eyes.

Sebastian paused, a rueful, almost shy expression flitting across his face. "I know you'll think me daft for saying this, but that day on the moor, I could even see *myself* as your husband, building a life together based on all the things we both love."

Meredith found her voice and chided him gently. "All this passed through that intelligent brain of yours in the space of a few seconds up on the moor?"

"Now don't make fun." He kissed the space between her brows as if anointing her to the role he hoped she would one day accept.

"Well, I have to admit...I felt it too," she said softly, "when the medevac helicopter whisked the boy to the hospital and you and I stood side-by-side watching it fly off into the distance." She flashed him a quicksilver grin. "But, then of course, I cannot tell a lie. I *also* felt a certain, electric attraction when I caught sight of that tartan blanket on your bed...to say nothing of my first view of *you* when you fetched me from your bed to the bubble bath that you drew for me that night at Cow Hollow."

"We'll have to do that again sometime soon," he murmured into her ear.

Meredith struggled to sit up, pulling a coverlet over herself for modesty's sake. She cast him a sideways glance.

"Over the summer, there have been so *many* moments when I felt myself drawn to you, Sebastian, and I thought

'Oh boy…what's happening here?'"

He leaned on one elbow and declared. "What's happening now is that I think I've just had a splendid idea! If you've got any bath gel left over from our last time here in the cottage, do you suppose this time, *you* prepare the bubbles in that tub-with-a-view downstairs, and lead me to it blindfolded?"

"Could dish detergent serve as a substitute?" she proposed with a mischievous grin.

"What?" he asked with a puzzled frown. Then, as recognition dawned, he chuckled. "Oh…you mean washing-up liquid, don't you? Yes, I think that would work in a pinch." He seized one of her hands and encased it between his own, saying quietly, "It has recently occurred to me that I'm not just in love with you, Meredith Champlin. I *love* you and everything about you." Kissing each finger on her right hand in turn, he murmured, "And I love Janet, and I love Holly, and I think your various Cornish and American relatives are just…smashing! And I find it quite astonishing how easy it is to say it all."

Meredith, thinking any children they might have would definitely share their matching brown eyes, leaned forward and whispered, "Well…just for practice, *pardner*, why don't you say all that again?"

# EPILOGUE

## THE BRITISH-AMERICAN TRAVEL GUIDE TO CORNWALL'S HISTORIC HOUSES, CASTLES AND GARDENS

Falmouth & Mevagissey/ Truro & St. Mawes, including the South West Coast Path

## BARTON HALL: CASTLE, GARDENS, AND RARE BREED FARM

*Location:* off the Gorran Haven-Mevagissy Road (GPS code: PL26 6LY)

The **Barton Hall Estates**, with its splendid turreted castle, renowned gardens, tea room, gift shop, and commercial nursery, is situated on the coast of Mid-Cornwall between Mevagissey and the River Luney, which rises near Hewaswater. Sir Lucas and Lady Barton-Teague (both descendants of the original families that inhabited Barton Hall for centuries) opened the property to the public a number of years ago, along with a second location, the Barton Hall Nursery on the A390, St. Austell Road at the Charlestown crossroads. A limited number of overnight guests are by reservation only.

**Barton Hall Tea Room** and the **Castle Restaurant**, under the management and supervision of Chef Claire Gillis, are now open to Barton Hall guests as well as the general public. Reservations recommended on weekends and holidays.

**Heirloom Edibles: Home Farm-to-Table Summer Suppers** are held on the estate grounds during the summer months under the supervision of Chef Claire Gillis and Richard Teague, son and heir to Barton Hall. Mr. Teague, who supervises the cultivation of heirloom produce on the property, has completed his studies at Oxford and will enroll in the London branch of the Cordon Bleu to further his training in the culinary arts. (A schedule for upcoming seasons is posted on the Barton Hall website)

**The Barton Hall Canine Obedience Academy**, under the direction of Dr. and Mrs. Sebastian Pryce (Meredith Champlin Pryce is a first cousin of Barton Hall co-owner, Lady Blythe Barton-Teague), offers an on-going programme that ranges from preparation for search and rescue dog certification; agility training; pet therapy training; and "Canine Good Citizenship" obedience classes for dogs six months and older. The Pryces are both members of the volunteer Cornwall Search and Rescue Team. Dr. Pryce heads up the K9 unit; Mrs. Pryce is a Registered Nurse, certified as an SAR medical specialist.

**The Barton Hall Rare Breed Farm**, opened in the spring of last year in the fields adjacent to Painter's Cottage, along with ten acres deeded as a Grace-and-Favor property to the Pryces for their lifetimes, is under the direction of Dr. and Mrs. Pryce, and features a variety of rare farm animals native to the British Isles, though many are in serious danger of extinction.

School groups, as well as the general public, are urged to make reservations as space is limited and private docent tours must be arranged well in advance. Dr. Pryce's large animal veterinary practice is headquartered at Cow Hollow Farm near St. Austell in partnership with William Jenner.

Barton Hall Estates ~ Hours:

April – September: *10:00–18:00 Tuesday through Sunday*
October – March: *10:00–12:00 and 14:00–16:00 Wednesday through Sunday*
Tea Room and Gift Shop: *Hours posted on the Barton Hall website*
Closed: *December and selected Barton-Teague-Pryce family anniversaries*

Website: www.bartonhallestates.uk.co

༺✿༻

"Well, what do you think?" Meredith asked Blythe, pointing to the proof sheet that the publishers of the latest edition of *The British-American Travel Guide To Cornwall's Historic Houses, Castles And Gardens* had sent her for fact-checking before it was scheduled to go to press. "They're going to list the link to the Barton Hall website *and* a separate link to our reservations page at the bottom, there, of the print version," she added, indicating to Blythe the precise spot the important information was slated to go, "as well as include a hot link back to us on *their* site and in the e-book version."

Blythe briefly scanned the proof sheets one last time and set them carefully on her desk in the book-filled library. Resting comfortably on the leather couch nearby, Holly, and two smaller versions of her Corgi self that the children had named Basil and Dill, slumbered in complete contentment while their three human companions were at school.

"You want to know what I think of this, personally?" Blythe asked, looking up from her desk at her cousin.

"Yes," Meredith asked apprehensively. She had been the member of the family assigned to work with one of the travel writers who had visited Barton Hall two summers previously and she suddenly wondered if she'd gotten "too commercial" for her very British-American cousins.

"I think it's *bloomin'* fabulous!" exclaimed Blythe with delight. "And so will Lucas and Richard and Claire—and that gorgeous husband of yours!"

She jumped up from her chair, grabbed Meredith by her two hands and danced a little jig on the worn Persian carpet.

"Oh, thank goodness you like it!" Meredith said with relief.

"Are you kidding?" Blythe said, chuckling. "At this rate, we should attract enough visitors this coming year to pay the bloody bankers and the Inland Revenue their outrageous sums and still have money left over to build a new greenhouse for Richard and Claire, not to mention putting a slate roof on the old stone barn overlooking Portluney Cove. You and Sebastian can finally have Susanna Jenner work her magic converting the barn into the house of your dreams so we can move you and Sebastian into a proper home before the baby comes!"

"Who wouldn't adore living in your castle," Meredith teased, "but you'll need our rooms for all the B&B guests you'll be having when this guide is published. And I must admit," she added, "it will be wonderful to have a home of our own near the Rare Breed Farm."

Meredith involuntarily cupped her hand on the almost

imperceptible bulge that confirmed that in four more months, give or take, there would be another cousin to add to the threesome currently enrolled as day students in the Mevagissey village school.

"And speaking of Baby Pryce, I still haven't told Janet yet," Meredith said, a worried frown creasing her brow. "I think she's having enough trouble adjusting to the tragedy that she won't be marrying Sebastian one day."

A voice from just outside the library door commented in a familiar, wry tone, "Oh, to be so admired by two such fair damsels of the same tribe."

Meredith felt a happy surge of surprise as Sebastian and Rex walked into the room. The Border Collie immediately sought out Holly and her two Corgi pups who flopped from the couch to the floor and all settled nearby on the carpet in the corner of the library.

"What are you doing here?" she demanded before her husband enveloped her in an embrace and kissed the top of her head. "I thought you were due to deliver a calf today."

"Our new prize Mum was magnificent and popped her baby out with very little help from me."

Blythe laughed and said, "What a shame. Meredith thinks you could use the practice."

"Oh, no, no, no!" Sebastian replied. "We've opted for the talented Doctor Vickery in Gorran Haven, haven't we darling?"

"Lord, yes," Meredith said, giving Sebastian's waist an affectionate squeeze. "But you'll be a great back-up."

"Thank you for your confidence," he said, holding her close. "And just to show my appreciation, since I have an afternoon free, shall I teach your agility class this afternoon, little mother?"

Meredith looked briefly at Blythe and tried not to smile. To Sebastian she said, "That is so sweet, but honestly, I'm fine! Doctor Vickery agrees, the more moderate exercise I get, the better."

"But showers are due to roll in off the Channel later today, and—"

"Listen, handsome, how about we take a picnic down to Painter's Cottage before the class and the weather arrive? And if there's a downpour, we'll cancel the class."

Blythe chimed in, "Yes, you two need to pick up on your honeymoon where you so abruptly left off a year ago—if only for an afternoon! You both have been so preoccupied with getting married last spring, and then Meredith's father visiting for a month in the summer, and *then,* surprise, surprise, you're pregnant last November— suddenly it's the beginning of April and summer's just around the corner again!" She made a gesture as if she were shooing them out the door. "Go on, go on...take the leftover paté from the British Food Writers reception Claire put on last weekend, grab a bottle of wine—"

"No wine for *you,* Ms. Mom-to-be," Sebastian interjected for Meredith's benefit.

"Oops, you're right," Blythe apologized, "but there are plenty of good things in the larder, so take whatever you want."

Meredith remained rooted to the carpet. Blythe cocked her head questioningly.

"Were those not good ideas? Maybe the thought of food is nauseating and you just want a couple of saltines...?"

Meredith smiled. "No, no...not that," she reassured Blythe. "The only symptom these first four and a half months is that I can hardly hold my head up past eight o'clock each night. No," she continued, "it's just that I want to say something vaguely profound to you both."

With Blythe and Sebastian gazing at her with curiosity,

she suddenly felt almost shy to express the thoughts on her mind.

"All those wonderful things about Sebastian and my last year that you just recited? Well, they make me want to say how much I love you both, and everyone else in this crazy three-ring circus we've got going here." She gazed at her husband of nearly twelve months with a heart filled with happiness so new and ever expanding, she felt an overwhelming need to express her gratitude for everything that had happened to her since that first summer in Cornwall. "But I also have some news…"

Blythe and Sebastian exchanged expressions of concern. Meredith turned to her husband and suggested he sit down as Blythe, too, sank back into her desk chair.

"I saw Doctor Vickery this morning," she began.

"And? Is everything all right?" they chorused.

Meredith nodded calmly, "Yes, as I said, I'm perfectly fine. Eighteen weeks along, and starting to have a serious baby bump."

A guilty look clouded Sebastian's features. "I am so sorry that I couldn't go with you for this appointment, but William's cow—"

Meredith said quickly, "I'm rather glad *I* get to tell you what I found out today." She paused and then blurted, "We're having a *girl*, Sebastian! A little girl! We can call her Gemma, after your sister." She bit her lip. "If that feels right for you, of course."

Blythe and Meredith looked at Sebastian expectantly, waiting for his response, but he had assumed a familiar, thousand-mile stare and said nothing.

"Sebastian…? *Sebastian*…what's wrong?" Meredith seized his right hand in both of hers and brought it between them so she could lean back to gaze into his eyes. "There always was a fifty-fifty chance we'd have a girl, you know," she said gently, praying he wasn't having the typical, male reaction to not having a son.

Neither of them noticed that Blythe had quietly slipped from the room.

"You don't understand. Claire's twins," he murmured as if to himself. "Both were girls. Charles told me that, just before I flattened him when he blamed me for Claire's...for what Claire had done to end the pregnancies." He grew silent for a moment, then said, "I couldn't stop thinking for years afterward that both baby girls...dead, just like little Gemma. It haunted me, really. For some reason, I felt sure you and I would have a boy, which would have been wonderful, too...but a girl...a *girl!*" he marveled. He clasped her shoulders and searched her face as if seeking confirmation that she understood the depth of his joy. "I could not be happier that it's a girl. In a strange way, it feels like a reprieve..."

"I'm so happy, too," she whispered.

"It's a pardon—"

"No!" Meredith countered fiercely, breaking away from his embrace and pacing in a small circle. "There's no reason to ask for forgiveness anymore. You've paid your penance and made amends, and so has Claire! The gods or fate or whatever you want to call it has *not* decided this for us. Our DNA and the sheer luck of which swimmer got there first created this little girl. You're *free!* This is *our* daughter and we totally deserve to have her!"

"But sometimes I feel—"

"Hear me, now, Sebastian," she said in a low, intense voice, clasping both his hands in her own. "You and Claire were young...you were dealing with childhood traumas not of your own making...shadows of your past! You, especially, have earned the right to be liberated from all that, now. You're with me. We're together and blessed beyond belief that we found each other. It's what I was trying to say earlier. Gratitude is the answer, not recriminations or wondering if you deserve happiness! You *do!* And so does Claire…"

Sebastian drew her tightly against his broad chest and said in a voice full of wonder, "We're having a *girl*…"

"And even if we name her Gemma—or we don't—she won't be a reincarnation of your sister or the unborn twins," Meredith insisted gently. "She'll be the perfect blend of you and me…"

Sebastian nodded. "Oh, what a beautiful, wonderful, sensible, *wise* woman you turned out to be."

She made a show of pushing out her modest belly, neatly confined within her trim pair of jeans—though she'd unfastened the top button under her cable knit sweater.

"And sexy, too, wouldn't you say?" she joked. "Though I am forced to admit I've already put on a few pounds. But when all is said and done, I do rather like the name Gemma, don't you?"

"Oh, to be sure, Mrs. Pryce, I definitely *do*." He bent down and kissed her slowly, deliberately, and in a fashion that made her feel very sexy, indeed. Then he abruptly broke their embrace, exclaiming, "Oh! Wait! Where's Blythe got to? I totally forgot…" and began digging in the inside pocket of his tweed jacket.

"What?" she demanded, observing how excited her normally taciturn husband had become. "What is it?"

He opened a stiff, white envelope and from it, retrieved a sheet of even thicker, white vellum of the finest quality, embossed with a gold crest at the top.

"Actually, before anyone, I should read it to *you* first." He cleared his throat, but before he could begin, Meredith was hanging over his arm, staring with widening eyes at the neatly typed missive that read:

*Dear Dr. and Mrs. Sebastian Pryce:*

*His Royal Highness, Charles, Prince of Wales, along with various members of staff from the Duchy of Cornwall, would very much like to visit your remarkable Barton Hall Estates Rare Breed Farm that was featured recently in The Plymouth Herald.*

*As I am sure you are well aware, the Prince is much interested in conservation subjects and sustainability efforts undertaken in the United Kingdom, and wishes to acquaint himself with the work you are doing to preserve certain rare species of farm animals indigenous to the West Country.*

*The Prince would also be pleased if a demonstration could be arranged of classes offered by the Barton Hall Estates Canine Obedience Academy's pet therapy and K9 search and rescue training that we understand takes place on your premises.*

*The Prince's equerry will deliver this inquiry by hand and discuss matters, assuming a visit can be arranged on a date and time mutually agreeable to all parties,*

*With best regards to Sir Lucas and Lady Barton-Teague, I am*

*Yours sincerely,*
*Ian Botham,*
*Pvt. Sec'y to HRH Prince of Wales*

"Oh…my…God! I can't *believe* this!" Meredith threw her arms around Sebastian with glee. "This will put the Rare Breeds Farm on the map! After a Royal Visit, tourists will beat a path to our door. And we'll be able to repay Blythe and Lucas for all they've done to help us launch this crazy project of ours! We can get to work even sooner on converting the barn—"

She suddenly halted, mid-sentence and peered at Sebastian with a worried frown. "Please tell me you'll persuade them to visit us sooner, rather than later, so I won't be so pregnant that I can't waddle onto the field with the pet therapy dogs that Holly and I have trained!"

Sebastian shook his head with amusement and pulled her close. "This morning, the Duchy's advance equerry delivered the invitation in person, as it said in the letter," he replied soothingly. "We've already compared calendars and decided to schedule it six weeks *after* the baby is due."

Meredith did some quick calculations. "How perfect! They'll visit us in September...my favorite time in Cornwall!"

"Really? September is your favorite time?"

"Yes...it's the final days of summer. The weather's lovely...most of the day trippers have gone home and we can drive down these narrow lanes in peace. *And* it's the month you asked me to marry you and stay in Cornwall."

"And all that makes you happy?" Sebastian asked.

"Oh, yes, my darling Doctor Dog," she replied, reaching for his hand to rest on her belly and perhaps feel the baby kick. "All that makes me *very* happy.

# AUTHOR'S NOTE AND ACKNOWLEDGMENTS

Sequels to novels are inspired by any number of reasons. *That Summer in Cornwall,* a contemporary, stand-alone sequel to my time-slip novel, *A Cottage by the Sea,* published fifteen years earlier, came to life because of one question that had long lingered in this author's mind: whatever happened to the three-month-old girl born to the odious British film director, Christopher Stowe, and Ellie Barton—that husband-stealing sister of my wonderful heroine Blythe Barton who eventually became Lady Barton-Teague?

Out of such musings comes months of work, which to me have been pure joy. Given my former life as a broadcast and print reporter, this work of fiction required a significant amount of research and was helped and improved through the efforts of many people to whom I owe my most sincere gratitude.

As noted in the dedications at the front of the book, for help and information on topics related to this story, I am deeply indebted to novelist Cynthia Wright; registered nurse Alison Thayer Harris; the wonderful people involved globally in canine search and rescue work; and most especially Anthony Jordan, Dog Unit Manager of the Devon and Cornwall Police, along with my British cousins and friends in the UK whose warm hospitality and knowledge of their country contributes so much every time I have the temerity to set a story in their neck of the woods. Any errors or omissions, however, are my own.

*That Summer in Cornwall* also grew out of the notion that I longed to make another foray into the land of my Ware ancestors who hailed from Clyst Honiton close to the border of Devon and Cornwall. These stalwarts departed from Plymouth, Devon in 1642, arriving in Plymouth, Massachusetts twenty-two years after the *Mayflower* had pioneered a similar route.

Back in August of 1994, my writer pal of long-standing, Cynthia Wright, and I rented a stone cottage through the National Trust, an old lime kiln near Fowey, Cornwall, next to a creek and a half mile from where our mutual heroine Daphne du Maurier wrote her first novel, *The Loving Spirit*, in 1931. On that trip we explored the real "Hall Walk," a National Trust path that begins at Bodinnick across the river from Fowey, runs past the footbridge near our rented cottage at Pont Pill, and up a few miles along a sylvan path to the village of Polruan.

On our most recent trip in October of 2012, Cynthia and I retraced our steps of nearly two decades earlier so that I could refresh my memory of that region and learn more about the wonderful work of the volunteer K9 groups dedicated to search and rescue efforts all over Britain. The trip also allowed Cynthia to research her new series of novels that deal with eighteenth century smugglers that inhabited the region we both love to explore.

One of the great joys of that sojourn was our stay at Caerhays Castle near Gorran Haven, the model for "Barton Hall." It is now possible to let rooms at this wonderful estate with its world renowned rhododendron gardens, and both Cynthia and I extend our thanks to Linda Mooney and her staff, along with the reservationists at Niche Retreats

who made our days in Bottom Lodge across from
Portluney Beach so idyllic.

The more I learned about the links between Cornwall
and its emigrants to America (and especially to the
Wyoming mines and ranches), the more the story of *That
Summer in Cornwall* simply fell into place. Not only were
there the expected connections of mining and ranching, but
I even discovered the Yellowstone All Corgi Club whose
activities in that part of the world underscored how hard
the "Queen's Corgis" work as sheep herding dogs in
Wyoming.

A further example of serendipity was the exhibit
"Risking Their Lives to Save Yours: Search & Rescue" that
was featured at the National Maritime Museum in nearby
Falmouth during my most recent research trip. To all who
had a hand in creating that amazing display featuring
everything from photographs of rescue efforts a hundred
years ago to the presence of a full-sized Westland Sea King
helicopter, I offer my profound thanks. My wandering
through this major exhibit averted endless hours of
research into the details regarding the amazing volunteers
and professionals whose bravery and skill save lives every
year in Great Britain. At the Maritime Museum, it was all
there for me simply to observe and absorb.

I must also offer my deepest gratitude to my "Beta
Readers," who scanned early drafts of the novel: Cynthia
Wright, of course; another wonderful novelist, Lauren
Royal; my friend and reader-of-long-standing, Diane Barr;
bibliophile Pat Boddy; my sister with whom I share the
Ware writing legacy, Joy McCullough Ware; "Nurse Alison"
Harris, a cousin who is always an inspiration and the
mother of my wonderful and perfectly-behaved
Godchildren, Andrew and Gracie who clued me into
Webkinz.com. (Alison got the prize for catching the largest

number of time-sequence and other crucial "dropped stiches" as the book went through multiple drafts). Diana Taylor, Professor Emerita, University of California at San Francisco School of Nursing, and advocate for women's health gave the sections dealing with emergency medicine the once over. Crucial, too, was the thumbs up via email from Anthony Jordan, Dog Unit Manager with the Devon and Cornwall Police, who read an earlier draft and answered endless questions about police procedure and chain-of-command issues during our initial interview.

Novelist Diana Dempsey gets special recognition for lighting a fire under me to launch this particular project and who served as a "consultant" all along the way.

I also extend my warmest appreciation to my son, Jamie Ware Billett, who always responds to my cries for help when it's time to integrate a new operating system into my computer, learn a new device like my iPad Mini, or on those occasions when "something terrible has happened" electronically and he comes to my immediate rescue, "screen sharing" with me across three thousand miles.

As always, I give love and appreciation to my husband of nearly four decades, Tony Cook, a "recovering journalist" and former television producer like myself, and currently the CEO of Cook Media, his own Internet marketing company. Thanks to his grandmother, who was born in Britain, Tony opened the door to my own heritage in England and Scotland, thus changing all our lives. Without our pulling our oars in the same direction, this book would never have materialized.

I pay tribute to all the dog lovers in my life: the Tuesday-Thursday-Saturday Women Dog Walkers Group for being great friends and good listeners; to film director Betty Thomas, a stalwart pal, "straight-shooter," and adopter of challenging dogs that only *she* could manage; to restaurateur Larry Mindel who made the wonderful Poggio's "dog friendly" with water bowls and doggie tie-up hooks outside his trattoria in downtown Sausalito, along with waiters armed with dog biscuits in their aprons; to Suzanne LaCock Browning, dog advocate extraordinaire; to Doris Day's Cypress Inn in Carmel, California where dogs are honored guests; and to writer and friend Gail Sheehy and her adorable Cholly Knickerbocker, East.

And, finally, I wish to extend my love to the Cavalier King Charles Spaniels in my life: our own Ensign Aubrey and Charlock a.k.a Cholly Knickerbocker, West; and my dear friend Jola Anderson's gaggle of four—all of whom repeatedly earn their "Canine Good Citizen" awards by proving each day that dogs teach us our best lessons about noble behavior and unconditional love.


Ciji Ware ~ Sausalito, California

# ABOUT THE AUTHOR

CIJI WARE is a *New York Times* & *USA Today* bestselling novelist, an Emmy-award winning television producer, reporter, writer, lecturer, and radio host. She has won numerous awards for her seven works of fiction, including the Dorothy Parker Award of Excellence; the 'Golden Quill' award for Historical Fiction; *Romantic Times Magazine's* 'Best Fictionalized Biography' for *Island Of The Swans* and 'Best Historical Novel' nomination for *Wicked Company.* Her novel, *A Race To Splendor* debuted in April, 2011 on the 105th anniversary of the devastating 1906 San Francisco earthquake and firestorm and was short-listed for the WILLA (Cather) Literary Award in 2012 from Women Writing the West.

Her most recent nonfiction, *Rightsizing Your Life: Simplifying Your Surroundings While Keeping What Matters Most* was named by the *Wall Street Journal* as "One of the Top 5 Books on Retirement Issues." *Joint Custody After Divorce: Making Shared Parenting Work for Mothers, Fathers, and Kids* has been a classic in the field for decades and is now available as an e-book. For seventeen years, Ware was heard daily as a commentator on ABC Radio & TV in Los Angeles. During her noted career as a broadcaster, she worked for PBS/KCET and all three major network affiliates, covering a wide range of topics in the areas of health, consumer and lifestyle subjects. Ciji Ware is also a sought-after event speaker, print journalist, (*AARP Magazine, Travel & Leisure* and other national magazines) and has the distinction of being elected as the first woman graduate of Harvard

College to serve as President of the Harvard Alumni Association, Worldwide.

Visit:

Ciji's Facebook page: Ciji Ware, Novelist

http://www.facebook.com/pages/Ciji-Ware-novelist/102621349810555

Her Pinterest page at: http://pinterest.com/cijiware/

Her website where she welcomes readers' comments at: www.cijiware.com

# By CIJI WARE

Historical Novels
*Island of the Swans*
*Wicked Company*
*A Race to Splendor*

"Time-Slip" Historical Novels
*A Cottage by the Sea*
*Midnight on Julia Street*
*A Light on the Veranda*

Contemporary Novels
*That Summer in Cornwall*

Nonfiction
*Rightsizing Your Life*
*Joint Custody After Divorce*

Coming Soon:
*That Autumn in Edinburgh* ~ contemporary sequel to *Island of the Swans*
*That Winter in Venice* ~ contemporary sequel to *Midnight on Julia Street*
*That Spring in Paris* ~ contemporary sequel to *A Light on the Veranda*

# READING GROUP GUIDE

1. At the beginning of *That Summer in Cornwall* we learn that thirty-three-year-old Meredith Champlin had her life turn upside-down when her first cousin, Ellie, is killed in a private plane crash and has made Meredith a co-guardian of her eleven-year-old-daughter Janet without informing her first she'd put those arrangements in her will. Does reading about this make you consider what you would do in this regard if writing your will? How would you react if someone made you a legal guardian of a minor child without your knowledge? What would you do if they died?

2. Meredith swiftly recognizes that raising a child with whom she has no previous history and who is having emotional difficulties in the wake of her mother's death is beyond the newly minted guardian's ability to cope. She reaches out to her older cousin, the child's blood aunt, despite the complicated family history between Janet's mother and Janet's Aunt Blythe, a woman who was previously married to Janet's father, Christopher Stowe. Given these tangled circumstances, would you have made the same choice as Meredith to take Janet to Cornwall, England for the summer?

3. Given what is revealed about the tumultuous

relationship between the sisters Blythe and Ellie, and its impact on young Janet, who do you judge among Ellie, Blythe, and Meredith truly had the child's best interest at heart? Why or why not?

4. Meredith and Sebastian Pryce, the former Lieutenant in the bomb squad in the British Army, have an unfriendly but comical first meeting the day Meredith arrives at Barton Hall. Have you ever experienced any negative "first impressions" that turned out to be far different that you expected? How able are you to reassess your judgment of someone whom you don't like very well when you first meet?

5. Sebastian appears very unwilling in the beginning of the story to reveal much about his family nor about various significant experiences in his past that continue to affect his life in the present. What were your reactions to his reticence? Were you sympathetic or annoyed by his behavior? Do you think Americans and the British are different in their approach to self-revelation? How would you have reacted to Sebastian's behavior if you had been Meredith? Would you have ultimately been attracted to such a personality, as Meredith eventually became?

6. As with *A Cottage by the Sea*, several characters in *That Summer in Cornwall* are coping with grief—from Janet's sudden loss of her mother in the plane crash, to Sebastian's experiences serving in the Afghan War and the tragedy of his sister's death by drowning, to Meredith's loss of her own mother and her decision to end her relationship with Shep O'Brien prior to coming to Cornwall for the summer. How do grief and the reaction to great loss affect the characters' actions?

How do those sorts of reactions complicate interactions between people you've known? What do you think are the healthiest ways to deal with major loss?

7. Meredith arrives in Cornwall after spending nearly a decade as a pediatric nurse caring for very sick children at a hospital where she lived in Wyoming. In what ways do you think that profession and the lifestyle she'd experienced having grown up on a sheep ranch affected the way she reacted to—and ultimately embraced—her environment at Barton Hall? Have you ever experienced visiting a place new to you and yet feeling very "at home" in strange surroundings? Could you imagine yourself becoming an ex-patriot in a foreign country?

8. Janet is described by Meredith early in the story as "the least likeable child she'd ever met, which was saying something," given she'd worked in a hospitable children's ward. Then, as the summer continued, the eleven-year-old begins to change her behavior. What do you think accounts for this? What measures would you have taken if a child as unhappy and "acting out" as Janet had been placed in your care?

9. Over the summer, young Janet becomes very attached to Sebastian and "shadows him like a puppy." What accounts for the child's gravitating toward an introspective man like Sebastian? Why do you think he appeared to understand and empathize with the troubled little girl? How difficult would it be for you to see behind "the world of hurt," as Meredith describes the abandonment Janet suffered and connect that event to the negative behaviors of children who appear antisocial? What role does abandonment play in this

novel as it relates to the life experiences of Janet, and several of the adults in the story?

10. Meredith and Sebastian discover toward the end of the story that they have a similar manner of coping with the fear of confrontation when there is conflict. Can you describe why the idea of confronting another person could have been something they avoided at all costs? How do you respond when faced with having to speak up calmly about important issues, especially when you know it might make others uncomfortable or angry with you? What sorts of agreements did the couple make with each other to try to overcome their habit of going to their corners and growing silent and resentful instead of speaking their minds?

11. Barton Hall's new cook, Claire Gillis, undergoes a major change in attitude as the story unfolds. Did her behavior and ultimate honesty toward Meredith and Sebastian surprise you? Can you think of instances in your own experience when wounded parties managed to overcome a trauma from the past? What other factors were in play rendering Sebastian and Claire incompatible as "chalk and cheese," other than their tumultuous breakup? What were the far-reaching consequences of those factors originating in their youth? What role did forgiveness play in the ultimate resolution of their conflict, and why do you think Claire and Sebastian were able to achieve that in relation to each other?

12. Would Meredith's story have been vastly different if she had gone through with her original plan to fly home in mid-September? What do you think would have been the result if she hadn't been open to examining her own

behavior regarding Shep O'Brien and been willing to listen to Sebastian finally reveal what had happened between Claire Gillis and him in the past?

13. *That Summer in Cornwall* takes place over a three-and-a-half month period, and by its end, many key aspects of Meredith, Sebastian, and Janet's lives have changed. What important element, or "change agent," made the difference in the way things turned out for each of them? Have you ever experienced big changes that took place during such a compressed period? What were those changes and how did they impact your life for good or ill?

14. There is a saying "It takes a village." In this story, a very disparate group of people—some related by blood, others not—came together in a specific place during a specific period of time and found a way to solve mutual problems ranging from taking care of a grieving child to finding a way for a large estate to survive financially during tough economic times. In your view, who was the primary leader in the effort to have various personalities pull together to solve a variety of very difficult problems? What did you take away from the examples of how people can work together for the common good?

15. The relationship between humans and their domestic animals play a key role in the connections between the principle characters in *That Summer in Cornwall*. At one point, Meredith assures Sebastian that despite the differences between American and British English, the two of them "both speak Dog." What was the significance of this statement and how did having a love of animals in general, and dogs in particular,

impact the couple's ultimately finding common ground and a lasting love?

Ciji Ware can be contacted at **www.cijiware.com**

APR 2 4 2013

CPSIA information can be obtained at www.ICGtesting.com
Printed in the USA
BVOW031850180413

318541BV00001B/25/P